W9-CBQ-187

FLINT'S
TRUTH

RICHARD S. WHEELER

FLINT'S
TRUTH

A TOM DOHERTY ASSOCIATES BOOK / NEW YORK

FLINT'S TRUTH

Copyright © 1998 by Richard S. Wheeler

This book is printed on acid-free paper.

A Forge Book
Published by Tom Doherty Associates, Inc.
175 Fifth Avenue
New York, NY 10010

Forge® is a registered trademark of
Tom Doherty Associates, Inc.

Library of Congress Cataloging-in-Publication Data

Wheeler, Richard S.
    Flint's truth / Richard S. Wheeler. —1st ed.
        p.   cm.
    "A Tom Doherty Associates book."
    ISBN 0–312–86367–5 (acid-free paper)
    I. Title.
PS3573.H4345F6   1998
813'.54—dc21   98–11952

First Edition: May 1998

Printed in the United States of America

0   9   8   7   6   5   4   3   2   1

A journalist is a grumbler, a censurer, a giver of advice, a regent of sovereigns, a tutor of nations. Four hostile newspapers are more to be feared than a thousand bayonets.

—Napoléon Bonaparte

FLINT'S
TRUTH

1

Sam Flint could see the bonanza town, Oro Blanco, nestled in a hanging valley a mile or so ahead, but he reined in his impatience. Grant and Sherman were tired. The wagonload weighed more than two mules should have to tug, especially uphill.

Flint dropped to the ground and walked beside black Sherman, the off mule, knowing that the move would spare the team a hundred eighty pounds. The bulk of the load—a Washington flatbed press, several cases of Caslon type, page forms, newsprint, a cask of powdered ink, and his personal gear—weighed enough to have been hauled by four mules.

A half mile below the booming gold camp, he came upon the cemetery on an arid flat dotted by juniper and bristling with headstones and picket fences. Someone was being buried. A hundred or so mourners stood around a priest dressed in a white lace chasuble. The bare-headed swart men clutched their sombreros. The women had veiled themselves in black mantillas. The crowd made a defiant black hole in a sun-whitened, glaring land that made his eyes water.

Flint paused to let his mules rest. The distant mass of mourners paid him no heed. He wondered whether Oro Blanco would be largely Mexican—he could compose a story in Latin as easily as he could in English. But not Spanish. Maybe Oro Blanco wasn't the place to set up shop. His newspaper needed English-speaking readers and advertisers. He would write a generous obituary for the dead Mexican and hope some of the mourners could read it. The dead, as much as the living, deserved respect.

A good newspaper, he thought, should weigh death even more than life; each day the rolls of the quick and the dead changed. Nothing graced a public paper more than its esteem for those who had toiled, laughed, and wept before passing into the beyond. Flint remembered Seneca's thoughts about death: A punishment to some, to some a gift, and to many a favor.

He hawed his reluctant mules, and they toiled up the last slope to the fabled gold camp. It seemed preternaturally quiet, but it was midday and hot, the siesta hour. He supposed the boomtown would spring to life upon the evening breezes. Along the road he had been told that Oro Blanco would be his best bet. It had no paper, not even a job printer, and boasted a lusty population of three or four thousand. Its mines were fabulous and its future bright.

Well, he would see. The road leveled suddenly at the south edge of town, and ahead stood ramshackle buildings—some of framed canvas, some of adobe, but most of them plank—along a twisty main street running on both sides of a lively creek somewhere high in the Mogollons. The rows of buildings lining the street stood a vast distance apart, perhaps a hundred yards. Most had galleries, which shaded the earthen sidewalks in front. On this main street he spotted a tin-roofed mercantile, a dry-goods store, two blacksmiths, a few restaurants and saloons, a milliner, a hardware store, a cobbler, two tonsorial parlors, a land office, a tinsmith, a cabinetmaker and mortician, two butchers, a bakery, a dairy, a greengrocer, a harness shop, a mining-equipment dealer, a Butterfield stagecoach station and yard, three one-story hotels, and a dozen other rickety enterprises. Not one of the outfits bore a Spanish name.

Above the right side of town stood the mines, one crowding the next, with gallows frames poking the azure sky and heaps of yellow-and-white rock mounded below. Unlike the town, the mines looked busy. Smoke and steam billowed from the boiler rooms. The occasional distant rattle of an ore car reached Flint's ears. The mines of Oro Blanco ripped out gold even while the town slept.

Under the mines stood row after row of frame houses, looking like false teeth, most of them clapboard and all of them unmistakably the work of Yankees. Sprawled across a flat that rose gently into coppery foothills, on the other side of the main street and creek, slumbered low adobes amid a chaos of squash gardens, animal pens, and wash flapping softly on clotheslines. The creek cleaving Oro Blanco had more than divided it into east and west precincts.

Flint halted his mules again until their flanks stopped heaving and then let them water a bit at the tumbling creek. He wanted to talk to some of the town fathers. If Oro Blanco didn't fit the bill, he would rest his mules for a day or two and head somewhere else. A young editor needed plenty of scrappy advertisers, a few hundred readers, some job printing, a shop, and a booming burg with some promise.

He spotted some duffers whittling on a bench in the gallery shade of Strong's Hardware, but he would consult them only as a last resort. Bench sitters could be garrulous old fools. The nearest thing to a town father would probably be the marshal. Flint hawed his mules forward, looking for something that approximated a jailhouse, and was rewarded at last by the sight of a tiny board-and-batten crackerbox at the far edge of town, on the Anglo side. A gilded green plank affixed over the door said CITY MARSHAL.

Flint peered into a twilit cubicle that barely encompassed a battered desk in front. The town marshal was nowhere in sight, but a prisoner in the tiny cell to the rear snored softly. The prisoner stirred, affixed a black gaze upon the intruder, yawned, and sat up. He was fleshy and lacked a recent scrape of the jaw.

"I'd like to speak with the marshal," Flint said.

"What do ya want?"

"A few facts about Oro Blanco."

The man yawned and stood. Only then did Flint discover that the cell door was ajar.

"Who are you?" asked the man, shifting a holstered revolver around.

"Samuel Flint. I'm thinking about going into business here."

"What kind of business?"

"Weekly newspaper. Job printing."

"You an editor?"

"Editor, printer, businessman, reporter, newsboy. You don't have a paper in Oro Blanco, right?"

The man pushed open the creaking cell door and considered Flint. "Don't rightly need one," he said. "But a job printer'd be handy. I have the devil's own time getting posters and flyers and notices printed up in Silver City. But there's no call for a newspaper. Nothing ever happens here."

"Of course things happen. There's always news."

"There's no news."

"Am I right? Isn't this Oro Blanco, boom camp, site of half a dozen bonanza mines? Isn't this the camp that's growing by fifty people a week?"

"We do just fine without some reporter poking around, making trouble. We have no trouble, and we have no news." The marshal eyed Flint malevolently.

The young man took a new tack. "I'm looking for a shop and a place to live."

"There ain't none, at least on the right side of town. Every room's double-rented. They're putting up new places fast as they can, but it don't help none."

"What about the other side of town?"

The marshal stared. "You don't want to go there."

"Are there buildings available?"

"Few adobes with dirt roofs. Leak all over your shop, wet your paper every time it rains. Look, Flint, you stay on your side of town and leave the greasers to theirs. All you get is trouble over there."

"Well, I'll look around," said Flint. "What'd you say your name is?"

"I didn't. It's Crawford. Learn the ways of the town, Flint."

"I always do," Flint replied. "That's my business." He stepped into the white glare of the midday sun.

That was a story, Flint thought. There always were stories. This sleepy camp exuded them, and he would ferret them out and print them. This mining town fairly oozed with stories that no one wanted aired, least of all the public officials. He sighed happily. Publishing a rag in Oro Blanco was going to be fun.

He drove his refreshed mules up and down the streets and alleys, mapping the helter-skelter city. The Anglo side radiated energy, even during the siesta hour. Unfinished buildings stood everywhere. Bright, newly minted signs announced week-old businesses. Carriages and wagons and their dozing teams dotted the streets. He saw not a tree nor a lawn; not a garden nor a park. Those who lived in that precinct had no appetite for beauty or serenity—only for gold. They would snatch it one way or another; if not directly from the quartz veins, then from mercantiles, hurdy-gurdies, saloons, dance halls—all arrayed to mine the miners.

Sam Flint knowingly eyed the chaotic streets, a hard decision upon him, one with grave financial consequences. If he looked long and hard, he could probably find a saloonkeeper or shop owner who'd partition off the rear of his building and give Sam an editorial sanctum—for a fancy boomtown price.

Flint's purse was thin, but money wasn't the price he worried about. On this side of the main street, his paper would be a prisoner, his measured thoughts held captive. Perhaps he would have no choice, but before coming to any decision he would survey the other precinct.

He turned his mules, crossed the town's sole bridge, studied the merchants on the west side of the avenue—mostly Mexican but a few with Yank names—and headed onto a side street. There, just off the main artery, he beheld a small adobe building, once a cantina and *mercado* but now empty. It had a roof of patina-green sheet copper, an oddity in southern New Mexico Territory. He tried the door, finding it desiccated by the dry air and furnace heat. It shrieked open. Sunlight filtered through small windows onto a desolate roomful of dust and empty shelves. Flint decided it could become a newspaper office if the building could be rented or bought—provided he decided to stay.

2

At the Gold Star Livery Barn Sam Flint negotiated with a gimpy hostler for the care of his mules and storage for his outfit, and then he headed toward the main street, where half a dozen gaudy saloons occupied a single block. He intended to assuage two thirsts, one for drink and the other for information. He wanted to find out a lot more about the burg before he settled down to publish a weekly rag.

He pushed through bat-wing doors into the first likely joint, called the Stamp Mill. He found himself in a long, dark cavern of a place, with a bar along one side and some gambling layouts covered with cloth at the rear. Only one bartender and a pair of regulars occupied the place, but it was midday; Flint guessed that after the shift finished, the saloon would spring to life.

"Mug of beer," he said to the keep, a chunky man with a walrus mustache and an ax-blade part in his black hair.

"Haven't seen you before," said the keep, filling a battered mug from a keg.

"I'm fixing to go into business here. Thought you could tell me a thing or two."

The keep took Flint's two-bit piece and returned no change. "What kind of business?" he asked.

"Job printing and a weekly paper. Oro Blanco doesn't seem to have a printer."

"We could use one, all right."

"Tell me about the place."

The keep shrugged. "Little Mexican village, couple hundred greasers until last year. It got its name from some gold they dug out of a few ledges up above. But they missed the big stuff, right under their noses."

"How many people here?"

"Some say three thousand, some say four."

"How are the mines doing?"

"There's three big ones, Golconda, Gold Queen, and Pandora. All booming right along. Gold Queen's built a mill and smelter. Some placer claims and some smaller outfits, glory holes, too. Ore's getting better and better, and no one's saying the place'll blow away in a year or two."

"Where does a printer rent a shop?"

The barkeep grinned cynically. "You set up a tent. Same for a bunk. Forget boardinghouses or hotels; they're all double-rented. Most new men just put up a wall tent until they can do better. You can get fancy and frame one up with studs. Weather's mild; no one suffers."

"I saw an empty adobe with a copper roof across the way. I thought I might rent that if it's available."

"Mister, you don't want to rent that."

Flint sipped the lousy suds and pondered that puzzle. "Looks good to me," he said. "Solid building, rainproof—I've got paper to worry about—and empty."

"Look, stranger, that's greaser town."

"All right, so it is. It's the only place to set up. Who owns it?"

"You ain't hearing me."

Flint shoved his empty mug toward the keep, who filled it. Flint paid with a worn shinplaster this time.

"It looks to be an abandoned cantina and *mercado*," Flint said, not relenting. "Looked like living quarters behind, too. I'm surprised no one's fixed it up. Any building in Oro Blanco could be put to good use."

"Stranger, you ain't listening."

Flint grinned. "All right, tell me."

"That was the Escalante place. He was the mayor, the *alcalde* of the Mex village. Until last winter, anyway. He was just getting in the way of everyone."

"So?"

"So he's not in the way anymore."

"What happened?"

The barkeep frowned. "Let it go, stranger," he said.

"Who was being buried when I drove in?" Flint asked.

"The old woman. Mrs. Escalante."

"What'd she die of?"

The keep shrugged. "Who knows? Mex die from things you and me never heard of."

"A widow, I take it."

"You ask a lot of questions."

"I'm a newspaper man. If I publish a paper, I've got to know the history."

The keep smiled faintly. "That's what I hate about newspapers."

"Well, yes," Flint agreed. "These Escalantes, how old were they?"

"Oh, getting along."

"They had children?"

"Greasers all have children."

"Who can translate for me?"

"The priest, when he's around."

"Where will I find him?"

"How should I know? No one goes over there."

"Why not? They're people."

The barkeep rinsed a glass and stared at the two regulars, who were listening quietly. "What's you name, stranger?"

"Sam Flint, lately of Cincinnati."

"Back east. You don't know about things out here. We need a newspaper, but you're what we get. All right. I can't keep you from going across the street, but don't believe a word they say."

"What'll they tell me?"

"That's for you to find out, Flint." The bartender turned his back. "You can take your trade elsewhere."

Flint knew the interview had come to an end. He also knew he might have trouble rooting a paper in this town. He would have to sell ads and find subscribers, and he'd already made some sort of bad impression. It was as though the town harbored a guilty secret. The constable, Crawford, hadn't seemed happy about a paper, and this bartender hadn't either. Bartenders were usually among the most affable of men, full of fact and fiction and eager to share it, ready to give a newsman the scoop about almost anything. Flint wondered whether he had simply run into a pair of soreheads, but his instinct told him he hadn't; he would find the same reception elsewhere.

He drained his warm beer, wondering whether to stay. Plenty of towns ached for a newspaper. A new town gets a paper and business quickens, the news gets collected, the town can boom itself, and people don't feel so isolated. He wasn't sure he would make Oro Blanco his home, but he wasn't ready to quit. Not yet. Not when there was something that people didn't want discussed in public.

Maybe Oro Blanco would be a one-issue town. Maybe he would get his story, sell a few ads, bring out one issue of the new rag with the story in it, and get chased out. That had happened to him once. He laughed—people sometimes regarded newspapers as cocked pistols.

He stepped into hot sun again, and crossed the wide boulevard at the bridge. He walked easily into the Mexican quarter, along twisty streets that probably weren't streets at all, just trails between the crumbling adobes. He discovered ragged, laughing children everywhere, wheeling and swooping like flocks of crows. He passed women who eyed him neutrally, their faces impassive. He passed grandmothers dressed in black rebozos even in the heat, watching him from seamed faces. He didn't feel antagonism.

The church was obvious, its massive walls of crumbling adobe rising squat and low on a knoll. He didn't have to hunt for the priest, either. The padre stood waiting, as though Flint had an appointment. He wore a loose black cassock; the chasuble had been put away.

"The children tell me things. I am Juan de Córdoba," the man said.

"Children?"

"The little ones watched you walk around the *mercado*."

"Yes, I did. I'm Sam Flint. New here. That's a good building. Why's it empty?"

The priest smiled slightly but didn't respond.

"Is it for rent? I came to ask who owns it. If you'd translate for me—"

"It might be," the padre said. "Why do you wish to rent it?"

"I'm a printer and editor. I need a building so I can publish a weekly paper. And do some job printing."

"Ah, I see," said the priest. "*Un periodico*—a newspaper. It is a weapon placed in mortal hands for the good or bad, is it not?"

Flint felt he was being examined, but he didn't mind. "I like to print all the news, and I do it without regard to consequences. Which is why I rarely survive for long. Pretty soon I offend someone, and then the weekly newspaper's on the road again. I tend to favor the virtues."

"Ah, that I understand. Few men favor the vices. Who do you offend, Señor Flint?"

"Well, I pick on bullies, and I like to keep an eye on constables and judges and officials and the like."

"Ah, I see. But what if the bullies are your own kind, and what if the helpless are—greasers? Eh?"

Sam Flint caught the drift of all this. "Well, that's how come I get booted out so often. Put a type stick in my hand, and pretty soon there's people who're planning to tar-and-feather me and businessmen yanking out their advertising."

"A man who rubs the hair the wrong way, *por seguro*, Señor Flint."

"No, just a man who's got his feet dug in and likes justice."

"It does not make you much of the money. You are going to want the credit, *verdad*?"

"No, I can pay a little. I hoped maybe you'd help me negotiate some rent, if it's agreeable. Take me to the owners?"

"The church is the owner now. As of this very day. This morning we buried Señora Escalante."

"You? I'd rent from you?"

The priest nodded. "If I choose to rent to you. I am not persuaded."

"I heard that the Escalantes owned the place. What happened to them? Why was it closed?"

De Cordoba shook his head. "I could tell you the story, but you would believe those on the other side of the Avenida Virgen de Guadalupe—they call it Virgin Avenue." He smiled faintly.

"I'm open-minded."

"We are all bound by blood and tongue, señor. I will not discuss this further. As for the rent . . ." he shrugged. "I am at your mercy."

"I was hoping to start at twenty dollars a month, raise it to thirty when the paper prospers."

The priest remained silent.

"I suppose that's too little. It's all I can do. If I can't get this, I'll have to build a tent-frame place."

"Too little, Señor Flint? There are not thirty pesos among all my people. It is a fortune."

"Twenty dollars?" Sam was thunderstruck. "How do they live?"

"They do not live. They barter. They bring me a squash or some chiles. A few wash the clothes for the *oreros*—the gold seekers—for centavos. Some cut the firewood for them, for centavos. Some raise the *vegetales*—the vegetables—for them, for centavos. But mostly they barter."

"Would you let me try the place?"

"How can I not, for twenty dollars?" the priest replied. "Maybe you are sent from God."

3

Sam Flint moved swiftly into his new quarters. He wrestled his
composing equipment into the gritty cantina, where an ancient
cast-iron stove stood ready to melt type metal. He made the little
mercado his sanctum, or editorial offices. He found a two-room
apartment in the rear, with a beehive fireplace in each room.
Once the priest showed him into the building, Flint had no trouble recruiting boys to haul the stuff from the wagon. They
squinted up at his clean-shaven face and his six-foot-tall, lean
frame as though they were studying a mountain; nodding shyly,
they set to work with visions of centavos in their heads. The
heaviest item, the flatbed press, they ganged into place with as-
tonishing ease. It took only an hour, and when he surveyed the
result, he knew he could not ask for a better place.

In a few days, he would produce the first issue of *The Oro
Blanco Nugget*. He enjoyed naming his weeklies. By the time he
rolled into a town, he knew what he'd call the paper. He'd called
a cow-town weekly *The Trail Driver*, and a railhead paper *The
Freight*. Whatever the place, he fitted himself in, got to know the
merchants, looked into local troubles, and then began composing stories as he set them in his type stick, row upon row of let-

ters that he slid into galley trays and then into page forms, to be printed. It was his life, and it was an adventure. He never got rich, but he couldn't imagine doing anything else.

He had been lucky to get out of Colorado Territory with two hundred dollars. He laughed: It seemed it was his fate to make hasty exits from frontier towns that didn't appreciate his sublime intelligence, his lofty integrity, his spotless honor, his keen fairness, his vast erudition—or his barbed humor. His virtues were pretty much hidden, especially to himself, but his humor was always visible and was the real reason for his peripatetic life. In Ophir, a silver camp, he'd managed only seven mocking issues before they took after him with bullwhips and threats of jail. It was odd how little attention the minions of the law in the territories paid to the First Amendment—especially when they themselves were the cynosure of various news stories that hinted of fat wallets, milking the humble, roughing up the unwanted, or an excess of partisanship.

He usually lasted about a year. He couldn't remember a time when he'd left some western metropolis—a future London of the Plains or Paris of the Mountains—of his own volition. He never sought trouble; it somehow sought him. That was because of his way of infuriating people. He'd come to realize that he was born to suffer. He was afflicted with an insatiable curiosity, which always led to his asking embarrassing questions, which in turn led to exposés and indignant editorials—which led to mob violence. He'd pulled buckshot out of his hide once, been horsewhipped once, and had seen one of his little shops burned to the ground by a rich cattleman and his cowboys.

He couldn't help it. He was simply irreverent, and there seemed to be an endless supply of little frontier burgs pining for newspapers as long as the editors kept secrets. Judging from his original impression of Oro Blanco, he'd be on the road again in six months.

But that was the past. His business now was to start up a new rag. The next step, which he had perfected in several cow towns and mining camps, was to print up some flyers announcing the new weekly and then go out to sell ads and collect news. He wasn't worried about a lack of news. If news was skimpy, he would publish Plato or Aristotle or maybe Caesar's *Commentaries*. All these he had acquired in the academy. The son of a headmaster could only be a scholar, even if he didn't wish to be one.

As he whipped letters into the type stick, composing his flyer, he found himself intrigued by Oro Blanco, an old New Mexico village that had boomed into a wild gold camp, rending the social fabric of the villagers. Maybe he could do something about that, but not just yet. He had to meet a few dozen people first. He'd offer every merchant in town, from barber to saloon-keeper, a free card, or announcement, in that premiere issue. He'd found that technique a great way to garner future advertising and build a solid commercial base for his papers.

By the dinner hour he was getting mighty hungry—no one had an appetite like Sam Flint—but he persisted. He wanted his flyers printed and dry by dawn. At last he mixed up some powdered ink and water, ran a proof copy, corrected it, and then printed up fifty flyers. These would tell townspeople that the first issue of *The Nugget* would appear June 17, 1870: The weekly would report all the news fearlessly and impartially, put Oro Blanco on the map, report national and international events, and provide advertising space for all merchants wise enough to call attention to their products.

He didn't finish until sundown, well into the June evening, and by the time he scoured the ink off his fingers and pulled off his ink-stained printer's smock, he was ready to explore Oro Blanco. A steak first, and then some red-eye, or panther piss, or popskull, or whatever the local painkiller.

He stepped into a lavender hush and drew a few lungfuls of the dry, sweet air. This boomtown enjoyed an exquisite perch in the foothills of towering, piñon-timbered mountains. Piñon woodsmoke scented the air like incense. There, on the greaser side of town, a great peace embraced the humble adobes, but across Virgin Avenue, some wild vitality and a faint hum announced a dragon that never slept and never slowed and never looked back.

He hunted for a beanery and finally selected a likely-looking place called The Boston, upslope from all the Virgin Avenue saloons. He entered a solid building, which looked as though it had been designed to last centuries, and found himself gawking at an elegant restaurant with dark walnut wainscoting, snowy linen on the tables, severe ladder-backed chairs, waiters in black, two dazzling crystal chandeliers, and very few patrons, all wearing suits and cravats.

It was going to be too expensive, and Flint retreated, only to be waylaid by a handsome gray-haired woman with refined features. She was dressed head to toe in navy silk, relieved only by white lace at the collar and a brooch of pearls at her bosom.

"It's not too late to dine, but you're not properly attired," she announced in an accent that was unmistakably Back Bay. Flint knew at once how the establishment got its name.

"Well, I'll leave, then. I didn't quite realize—"

"Oh, fiddle. You go into the Gentlemen's Parlor and select an appropriate suitcoat, and I'll forgo the cravat this evening because it's late. But I do maintain standards, you know."

"Ah, I'm new and I'm just finding my way—"

"There are two plates, one a dollar and a half and the other two dollars. We don't have a menu. Decent food's hard to find here. Come along now."

Flint sighed. He could eat for two or three days for the price of a meal here. But he found a serviceable suitcoat and let himself be led to a lamplit table beside the far wall. Much to his astonishment, the lady seated herself opposite him.

"I like to get to know my customers," she said.

"Uh, I'm Samuel Flint. From, uh, Cincinnati."

"At least you're not from the far west," she said. "I'm Amelia Lowell."

"Lowell? The Boston Lowells?"

"By marriage. My late husband was one. I've been widowed seven years."

Suddenly the editor wanted to know a lot more about the proprietress of a strange enterprise in a wild mining camp.

"You're wondering, of course, why I am here in a boomtown instead of in the Athens of America, where I spent my earlier life. I came because I've a mission. Look around you. This is more than a restaurant, you know. At the rear are chambers where gentlemen may gather. That cage there is a private bank—I transact business for chosen customers. That dais over there is for lecturers: I turn this into a lyceum on occasion, although proper speakers are difficult to find.

"Now, to assuage your curiosity, I am here to uplift the West. These crude camps are scandals. They want civilization. They want culture. They want education. They want manners. I chose this because it's the worst possible place, a continent away from Boston. If I'm able to tame the awful impulses that draw people to places like this, I will establish Bostons throughout the west and save the Republic from ruin."

She gazed at him amiably, with gentle eyes and a well-bred smile. "Now what do you do, young man? You're not a miner."

"I'm going to start a weekly newspaper. Uh, I'm an editor."

"A weekly newspaper?" Astonishment and delight lit her face. "I shall write a column. I wish to scold this barbarous place on an installment basis, as regularly as mortgage payments."

"Uh—"

"Don't say 'uh' like some idiot. How were you born?"

"Uh, the usual way."

"No, no, into what sort of family?"

"My father's the headmaster of a boys' academy in Cincinnati. I was a compulsory scholar—antiquities, classics, Latin. I served in the war, corresponded for the *New York Herald*, and then escaped into the Wild West, where I'm an itinerant, regularly driven out of the burgs where I publish for the crime of truth-telling."

"Perfectly extraordinary. Are you attached? A family man?"

He wondered whether to go into all that. "No," he said, resolutely. "I'm afraid I broke a lady's heart."

"Ah, you rascal."

"I loved her dearly, but I couldn't settle down. The war did something to me, left me restless. If I'd married my beautiful Nancy Lee, I'd be a schoolmaster now, slowly dying in Ohio. We were engaged, the date was set. Breaking it was the worst thing I've ever done."

She studied him. "No, if that's how you felt, you did the right thing. Marriage for her would have been an ordeal."

"I guess you're right. Maybe someday . . ."

"Young man, someday will never come. I know your type. I don't suppose there've been others."

"I've never lasted in one town long enough—"

"Ah, excuses! Someday a fetching little thing will knock you silly."

"Uh, may I order now?"

"It's on its way, dear man. We permit wine in the dining room, and you may imbibe ardent spirits in the club. The clubroom fee is ten a month."

"Newspapers don't earn much, madam."

"You're half my age, but I will permit you to call me Amelia. How much will you pay me for my weekly column?"

"Mrs. Lowell, I may not accept it. I shall have to see whether you drive away advertisers and subscribers."

She laughed gaily. "I'm a caution. I do my stabbing with quills and nibs, my dear, not broadswords."

"A newspaper happens to exist to disseminate news. It also entertains. And the ads are a service to both customers and merchants. I'm afraid I can't turn it into a partisan—"

"Why, dear Mr. Flint, The Boston will purchase a handsome

ad in every issue. And we have our Lyceum Evenings to advertise. I happen to have a competence from a little knitting mill in
Lawrence. If you can't pay me, why, I'll pay you."

"Uh—"

A suave waiter rescued him and began dishing medallions of
beef, twice-baked potatoes, Parker House rolls, and a spinach
salad from pewter salvers onto Limoges china. The proprietress
watched sternly and finally nodded the waiter away.

"There you are," she said. "That's good port in the wineglass."

Flint, suddenly intimidated, dropped the snowy linen napkin to his lap, grasped his knife and fork with finesse—and
gratitude toward his mannered parents—and began a dainty
dinner in the town of Oro Blanco in the Gila Wilderness of New
Mexico Territory.

Mrs. Lowell smiled slightly and remained seated. She obviously had business to transact.

4

Like all frontier camps, Oro Blanco welcomed the new paper joyously. Sam Flint visited the merchants, saloons, and restaurants, sold fat advertisements, offered free cards to all, and in the space of two days garnered enough business to fill two of his four pages.

He toiled by lamplight deep into the evenings, building the ads and bordering them with ruler lines cast from type metal. Some merchants had asked him to compose the ads; others had lists of merchandise to sell, or slogans to print up, or even an occasional epigram. All these Flint studied closely; they gave him insight into Oro Blanco and its life.

At first, when Flint announced his locale, the merchants were taken aback. "Over there?" they would ask, eyeing him dourly. "The old *mercado*? Surely you'll move as soon as something opens up on the right side of town."

"No, I'm staying," Flint replied a dozen times.

"Flint, you'll move across the avenue—or fold up," some responded, an undertone of menace in their voices. Others eyed him long and hard and asked a soft question: "What are you for, Flint?"

Sam Flint always smiled, said he was independent, and simply dismissed the matter. The merchants would get used to him; they always did. But he knew he was on probation. If he didn't move to the gringo side of town and fly their colors soon, the ads and the support would tail off swiftly, and even worse things might follow. He was all too familiar with bricks flying through a window and threats pinned to his door.

But Flint had no intention of moving. He liked Father de Cordoba; he liked paying rent to the church; he liked not being beholden to the financial moguls of Oro Blanco.

In came the townspeople, wanting cards announcing their political candidacies, their homemade bread, their squash or zucchini, their sewing and laundering, and, in one case, a parlor house for gentlemen. Flint accepted them all. He took in some job printing too: flyers for the hardware store, restaurant menus, business stationery. In the space of a few days, Flint met an amazing number of the citizens of Oro Blanco, but never a Mexican. Not even the priest showed up. Most of those who entered his shop paused, looked about, and allowed that it was good to push the greasers back from Virgin Avenue. Flint never responded. He had quite the opposite intention: to lower the barriers and welcome Oro Blanco's original residents to the new side of town.

But of those plans he said nothing, not even to Amelia Lowell, who was fast becoming his confidante and certainly his primary source of information about Oro Blanco. He dined at The Boston each subsequent evening, even though he could scarcely afford the stiff tariff for a dinner, because the amazing Amelia devoted herself to informing him about everyone in town—the managers of the mines, the merchants, the saloon-keepers, right down to the drunk who spent more time in Crawford's iron cage than he did on the streets.

He learned that Oro Blanco brimmed with a transient, gold-fevered population that cared little about schools, an infirmary, city taxes, roads, garbage, the precarious water supply threatened with pollution, the shoats and roosters in the streets, and the wholly inadequate justice system which ignored the occasional violence in the saloons and picked on the greasers.

Flint sighed as he began writing his new paper's credo. Years before, he had fought with the Ohio Volunteers to free the Republic of slavery; he had been a Lincoln man then. He still was, even though times had changed. He had principles: freedom, justice, and charity; a bias toward the humble. His weeklies featured loud and bellicose opinion columns combined with impartial news coverage—no censorship. If Mr. Gold Company President got pinched for abusing his mutt, the news would duly appear in Flint's columns. It had always cost him subscribers, but that's the way he was. He would publish whatever he felt like publishing and deal with the threats later.

Which reminded him to build a subscription notice that would go right smack on page one, and to find a couple of newsboys. They had always been his principal means of circulation, hawking the ten-cent papers on the streets, keeping two cents for themselves and bringing him eight cents a copy. He had engaged nasal, squeaky boys and, once in a while, an old codger or wounded Civil War veteran to hawk his wares. Once he had even employed a desperate, hoarse woman who wanted respectable work. He gave it to her until he was kicked out of town. She never quit until she had sold a hundred of each issue, two dollars to live on for a day or two. He had never learned the other ways she eked out a living.

One afternoon Amelia Lowell dropped by. She peered about, missing nothing of the way he had set up shop in the old adobe building. "What's your rent?" she asked.

"I pay Father de Cordoba twenty a month."

"You should pay more," she said.

"I will when I can. He was grateful."

"I don't hold with the Papists. All those silly plaster saints and bowing and scraping. But I like the man. I'm going to write about him. Here's my column. I won't ask you what you think, because it doesn't matter."

Flint took the screed with trepidation. He could barely decipher her untrammeled hand.

"Do you always move your lips as you read?" she asked. "I thought you were a classics scholar."

"You write in a difficult hand," he said.

"Oh, that. Everyone always dithers. Shall I read it to you?"

"No, let me struggle."

She laughed, a faint edge on her pleasure.

For her debut, she had targeted Crawford. The constable needing replacing, she opined. He kicked innocent dogs, jailed the humble, extracted bribes from fallen women, toadied to the mine owners, fostered divisions, enriched himself, ignored due process, levied impromptu fines, used vagrancy charges to mulct perfectly upright newcomers, and on and on.

"I suppose you can prove all this beyond doubt," he said.

"It's common knowledge."

"That's not enough."

"I shall parade his victims before you. And I shall get Father de Cordoba to back me up."

A certain dread suffused Flint. He was used to combative journalism, but not this. "He'll harass us both," he said. "I'd like you to try some other topic. This is the first issue. If I publish this, true or not, there won't be a second, and I'll be staring at blue sky through bars."

"Mr. Flint, have you no backbone?" she retorted.

"On occasion, but never the first issue. I present myself to the world as a puppy with a wagging tail."

"Perhaps you don't wish to reform this vile place?"

He sighed. "This'll be a one-issue town," he said, ruefully. "Crawford'll see that there's not a second. They have ways, you know. Especially if they're in cahoots with the JP or the local moneybags. It's best to get a weekly established for a few issues before getting into trouble."

"Well, I have *my* ways," she said.

He didn't doubt that, but he did doubt that her ways would

have any effect against a mean and conscienceless constable and his minions. "How about delaying this for a few weeks? Write me something about vile western manners or something."

"Western manners don't exist, just as the English tongue ceases to exist west of the hundredth meridian. But, Mr. Flint, manners are nothing. I'll write about manners on an off day, when my brains rattle. We shall tackle the administration of justice first."

Sam Flint reminded himself that he had never been married and thus never in the past had experienced henpecking. "Well, how about toning it down a little?"

"I already have. I've reduced it to the blandest folderol my pen is capable of."

"Ah, I'd like to show you how to say things delicately."

"Discretion is a virtue. So is prudence. But gad, Mr. Flint, what a pair of miserable virtues. I think maybe you should start a paper with some whalebone in it."

Flint caved in. "All right. I'll run it."

"I'll hold you to it. I'll be watching," she said. "It's going to be on the front page in large type, or I won't contribute any more."

"You won't?"

She laughed. He hadn't expected that. He hadn't heard her laugh. She had a silvery, tinkly, Boston-lady laugh.

She vanished into the glaring June afternoon, a whirl of black silk, Brussels lace, iridescent pearls, and chalky hair. Flint read the column with trembling hands. It dismayed him. He needed to protect himself. The best he could manage was to put her byline at the top and a little disclaimer at the bottom: "The opinions of contributors are not necessarily the opinions of *The Oro Blanco Nugget.*"

He toiled steadily through the afternoon, completing a story about the paper, a feature with news items about citizens (which he had gleaned from Amelia), the past week's docket from the justice of the peace, some business news he'd gleaned from the merchants he had visited, and a resounding town-booming editorial. That was always popular. Whenever he arrived in a burg, he boomed it: Oro Blanco was the golden crown of New Mexico; its mines would last for generations; it was populated by intelligent, progressive gentlemen and ladies; its crime rate was minuscule and its wide streets were safe for women, children, dogs and garter snakes; it was an outpost of civilization. . . . He had boomed so many towns the words became rote.

He reminded himself as the dinner hour approached that he had yet to corral some newsboys. He hung up his printer's smock and headed across Virgin again, looking for adolescents with leather lungs and a will to earn. But boys turned out to be a rare commodity, at least at that quiet hour. What he found instead was a gaunt girl of thirteen or fourteen selling wildflower bouquets for two cents each.

"Miss—"

"Buy some flowers, buy a bouquet for your sweetheart. Just two cents."

"I don't have a sweetheart."

"Well, buy 'em for your horse." She turned to Flint. "Hey, mister, two lousy cents gets you a nosegay for your cabin."

Flint shook his head and tried to slide by.

"Hey! Two beat-up copper pennies!"

"I don't have anything to put it in."

"Wear 'em behind your ears, mister. You can sing in the opera."

He laughed, dug in his britches for a coin, and handed her a dime.

She squinted at it. "I suppose you want change," she said. "I guess I'll have to find some."

"Missy, I don't really need a bouquet."

"Sure you do. Give it to your bartender. He'll like it." She grinned.

Flint eyed her. She was so skinny she looked like a fence post. Her skirts were rags. Her grimy feet had no acquaintance with shoes. Beneath the feistiness lay a desperation that set her mouth hard and sometimes bled out of her eyes.

"You still hanging around? You'd better buy one for your dog."

"I'll take two," he said, handing her two bits.

She stared at the coin. "Don't you have a few pennies?"

"Take it."

On the brink of tears, her buoyancy gone, she stared at the coin he pressed into her palm.

"Miss, would you like to make more money than this?"

She glared at him. "My ma says I should kick pimps in the shin."

Flint howled, while she daggered him with a righteous, jut-jawed squint. "No, no, I mean selling my new paper. I'm an editor. Sam Flint. Tomorrow I'll have papers to sell, *The Oro Blanco Nugget*. I need newsboys—or newsgirls. You sell them for a dime and keep two cents. You'll sell lots. Everyone wants papers."

"You really want a boy. You're teasing me."

"No, I mean it. You're the best little saleslady I've ever seen. If you'll be here tomorrow morning, I'll bring you as many papers as you can sell. Maybe a hundred."

She gaped at him. "Two dollars?" she whispered.

"Maybe that, maybe more, maybe less. What's your name, miss?"

"Libby."

"Libby, how can I get in touch with you—if I need you to sell papers?"

"My ma says to whistle the cops when strange men ask stuff like that."

"She's wise. What does your father do?"

She seemed to fold into herself. "He died in the cave-in at the Goldbug. We came here to the dry air to help my ma. She's got consumption." She looked as if she would crumple. "She can't get up anymore."

"Where can I find you and your mother, Libby?"

"Mind your manners."

"All right. I understand. Here's a shinplaster. Buy some good food for you and your mother."

She gazed at him distrustfully but took the fifty-cent paper, fingering it doubtfully.

"I want you to be my newsgirl. Tomorrow morning at eight, right here. All right?"

She nodded, clutching the coin and the bill, unable to stem the wetness in her eyes

"Libby what?" he asked.

"Libby Madigan."

"Well, Miss Madigan, maybe this is the beginning of something good."

Sam Flint decided not to run Amelia Lowell's bombast on the front page. Instead, he put it on page three, which he called "The Agora." Then, just in case people didn't know the Greek word that originally meant marketplace but came to be understood as a political assembly or place to exchange views, he explained all that. "The Agora," he said, would be the place for many views.

He suspected it wouldn't do a bit of good. The formidable Mrs. Lowell would descend upon him and accuse him of cowardice. Crawford would come after him with whips. But it was his paper, and he would operate it his own way. The front page would feature his "Statement of Principles" and his town-booming piece, intended to give *The Nugget* a pleasing demeanor.

He snugged the last of the type into the chase, or page form, between ruler lines, added a wooden block known as furniture to fill space below, and then clamped the chase tight with the wing nuts at either side. With a mallet and a block of hardwood, he tapped down the type until it rested perfectly flat, providing an even printing surface. Using an ink-soaked chamois ball, he smeared ink over the type, laid a sheet of newsprint in the tympan, and slid it over the inked chase. Then he lowered the flat platen of the press, making an impression on the paper, and withdrew the printed page for proofreading.

When he had finished, he began the two-up print run. Producing a newspaper was a brutal task on his small handpress. He had to ink the type before each impression, feed each sheet of paper onto the tympan, and then lever down the platen. After he had printed two hundred copies of pages one and four, he pulled those chases from the bed onto his stone, or iron-topped table on coasters, and then slid the chases containing pages two and three onto the press bed. Then he printed the other side of the sheets.

By nine o'clock he had finished, and he turned to wash down the press. He was still young, but printing two hundred copies was enough to exhaust him. And he wasn't done with this issue, either. He still had to unlock the chases and break down all the type, returning the capitals to his upper case box and the lowercase letters to their nests in the lower case box. He wondered how the older printers managed.

In the morning he hand-folded the sheets. At last he had a first edition. He hefted as many as he could carry and toted them across Virgin Avenue, looking for Libby. She waited there, solemn-eyed, pale, ragged, and barefoot, selling her wildflower bouquets. She looked as though she could hardly believe he had come.

"Here you are, Miss Libby. These are *The Nugget*. You just wave them at people. Tell 'em it's the very first issue. They'll all want to buy. You charge a dime. Can you make change?"

"I can't even make spit."

"Well, you'll pick up change soon. Sometimes if you can't make change, folks'll buy anyway, give you a bit or two bits. Have you a safe pocket to put the money in? Most people are pretty decent, but when you get a little ahead, you might hide some of your profits somewhere."

"You think girls are dummies," she said, pulling an ancient leather sack from her pocket.

"Can you do it? Hawk the paper? Have you ever heard a newsboy yell the headlines? Hold up a paper to everyone who passes by? Want me to do it a while?"

"I'll sell every paper. I won't stop until I do. I could sell papers to burros. I could sell your sheet to the Queen of England."

He liked that. She peered at him from that pinched little face, her brown hair pulled back into a ponytail. She wasn't in much better health than her mother.

"How's your mother?"

"I fed her some potatoes last night. She didn't eat much, but she smiled. She doesn't smile anymore. She hasn't eaten for days. She's dying."

"If you'd let me, I'd like to come visit someday."

She eyed him solemnly, not quite certain about him. "I just want to sell lots of papers," she said. "When do I get my two cents?"

"Later on. Bring any papers you can't sell back to me, and we'll do the accounting."

She nodded and turned to see whether there might be likely prospects, but the street offered no buyers.

"I've got to deliver an issue to each advertiser, Libby. Then I'll check with you again."

He retreated to his press to collect another fifty papers and a list of advertisers. Few of them had paid. He would show them their ads—proof of publication—and try to collect on the spot. It would save billing and it would bring in cash. Then he would sell them a new ad.

That morning he hiked from merchant to merchant, giving each a paper. Most of them studied the little rag eagerly—the arrival of a newspaper in a frontier camp was news in itself—and greeted Flint with great cheer. John Strong, the hardware man, paid for his ad; so did Harry Nussbaum, the tonsorial artist, and Sorley Mulligan, who ran the Good Luck Saloon and

Arcade. The milliner, Mrs. Duffy, said she'd pay later; send her a statement. But the cobbler, Horchhoff, insisted on paying three issues ahead for exactly the same ad. Hastily, Flint penciled accounting into a little notepad he carried in his pocket.

Hesitantly he entered The Boston and handed a copy to his amused colleague. She withdrew a pince-nez from a tiny case and surveyed the front page, her eye cocked. Then she discovered her column on page three, under "The Agora" rubric, and laughed delicately. "You pulled the teeth of the lioness," she said.

"No, it's all there, as you wrote it."

"With a cordon sanitaire around it." She laughed. Then she studied her quarter-page ad on the back page. He had spent time on it, achieving a typographical grace rarely seen in his papers because it consumed time to produce.

"You misspelled *hors d'oeuvres*, dear Mr. Flint, making your education suspect. Perhaps I won't pay you until next week, when it's repaired."

He wondered suddenly if Mrs. Lowell was an ally after all. But then she slid into that silvery Boston laugh and motioned him toward her black-walnut accounting wicket. "Here's your twelve-fifty, my dear."

"Mrs. Lowell, you're running a private bank. How about—"

"I'll start an account," she interrupted. "Shall it be in your name or the paper's?"

"Mine," he said. "And I'll add this while I'm at it." He pulled greenbacks from his worn billfold, keeping back ten dollars.

"It'll be a nice little weekly someday, Mr. Flint," she said. "We'll get some whalebone around your middle one of these times."

He scarcely knew what to say to that, so he pleaded the press of business and retreated into the blast of the sun.

Oro Blanco wasn't a large town, and periodically he checked on Libby. She had taken to her task with gusto and was drawing people from across streets. "Read *The Nugget*," she bawled. "Get the news. Line your birdcage. Start up your stove with it. A lousy ten cents for all the gossip in town."

He enjoyed that. She was earning two cents every few seconds. Seeing she was running low, he hurried across Virgin to collect his last fifty papers. He could print more and sell them tomorrow if the demand kept up.

When Flint returned with his resupply, he discovered Constable Crawford roaring at Libby as he shredded the last of her papers and threw the remnants into the wind. Her leather coin sack poked from the pocket of his suitcoat.

"You big crook," she yelled. "Mind your manners, you big galoot."

Crawford spotted Flint approaching and redoubled his roaring. "By God, I'll teach you to print that garbage about me, Flint. You're under arrest. So's she."

"What law've we broken?"

"What law? It doesn't matter what law. *I'm* the law. You're going to the calaboose. So's this little vagrant. I'm gonna fine you every dime you got and kick your butt out of town."

Flint felt his rage building. "Give her back her money. She earned it. It's not yours. And state the law she's broken or let her go."

For an answer, the marshal raised his club. "Gimme those papers," he yelled.

Flint didn't. "There's no point in it. A hundred fifty've been distributed. You can't stop news."

"Gimme those rags or I'll pulverize you for resisting arrest."

Flint judged that the man meant it. He handed the offending papers to the constable. "Let her go," he said quietly. "Give her back her money. She has nothing to do with it. It's my paper."

"She's coming. I'll show the little snot what it's about. I'll fine her so much she'll rot in my little iron cell for a year."

"I didn't know constables levied fines."

"I do. Me and the JP. All right, move."

"What are you arresting us for?"

"Insulting public magistrates."

"Those aren't crimes in any lawbook I've read. I want to see the statute. There's the small matter of the Bill of Rights. Freedom of the press will not be abridged, right? Bring a libel suit if you don't like it. It's not a criminal matter."

"Flint, shut up."

"Who'll feed my mother? She's too weak to get up," Libby whispered.

"No one'll feed her. That's your tough luck, girl."

"I'll remember that, Crawford," said Flint. "A good quotation for the next issue. 'Who'll feed my mother?' "

Crawford booted Flint in the shin, shooting pain up his leg. Sam's anger flared up as he clenched his fists and then slowly wrestled back his wrath.

"All right," he muttered. "Come on, Libby. Constable, when the town reads those papers and hears about this, you'll regret it."

Crawford snarled but didn't say anything. Across the street a crowd was gathering. The constable addressed them. "If I hear one yap out of any of you, I'll come after you too."

"What's the charge?" asked one bold fellow. "Telling how it is in this camp?"

Crawford roared but checked himself. He was not only outnumbered but getting into trouble. Instead, he prodded Flint and Libby toward the tiny plank cubicle at the end of town, while the crowd eddied along behind, watching the whole show.

"Oow!" she bawled.

Flint realized that the crowd would be his salvation—in time. But not until Crawford did his share of blustering. The constable could not hold a child with a helpless, dying mother for long; nor could he do much to Flint without enraging all those miners who witnessed it. But he and Libby would probably lose that purseful of coins. It would be something to write about in the next issue. He intended to produce one, even if he composed and printed it in his wagon, a few miles out of town, beyond Crawford's jurisdiction. Not that that would stop the man.

The constable prodded his prisoners into the building and into the foul, iron-barred cell, where another prisoner waited in quiet dignity, sitting on the plank bench.

"Well, Mr. Flint, we got their attention," said Amelia Lowell unflappably. Then she reached for Libby and drew the weeping girl into her ample embrace.

6

Marshal Delbert Crawford wasn't a man to let emotions rule him, and now he regretted the public display of temper, watched by a growing crowd of townsmen, mostly tough miners. They had watched him rip papers from that snot of a girl and pocket her wretched little sack of coins. They had watched him collar the new editor and haul him off. The truth of it was that Flint's rag hadn't said anything everyone in town didn't know: Crawford ran Oro Blanco with an iron hand, for the people who paid him to do it. But he hated to see the fact in print, appearing official and indelible. It had triggered a murderous rage that had taken him to the brink of clubbing Flint. He could have handled it better.

Everyone in town knew him for what he was, and he made sure that no one could do a thing about it. It didn't matter what they thought. They all were sheep. It mattered that he would make enough boodle over the next year or two to be comfortable for life. He had all the right people in his pocket. He had been appointed by the territorial governor, along with the justice of the peace, Pete Peters (furtively known in Oro Blanco as Saint Peter) and Bulldog Malone, the mayor. The governor had intervened in a little dispute with the greasers about whose town it was.

Crawford smiled faintly. He had the whole lot in the jug, but that didn't resolve anything. Assorted miners had congregated outside, whispering and waiting through the early evening. He needed to consult with Peters and Malone, but first he needed to chase away the mob. He pulled his double-barreled scatter-gun from its wall rack, checked the loads, and stepped into the street.

"Get outa here," he yelled. "Go on, before I arrest you all."

He judged there to be about twenty. No one moved. He leveled the shotgun at a big miner. "You. Beat it."

The man stared insolently and stepped back a few paces.

Crawford cocked his piece, its snap audible in the silence. But the man had quit retreating. "Keep walking or you're dead. You're threatening the law, disturbing the peace."

The man reluctantly backed up. So did the rest. But the miners didn't leave. The marshal didn't like it. If he shot into that crowd, he'd buy more trouble than he wanted.

"Look, I got some prisoners here. They're gonna be charged with inciting to riot, sedition, and a few other items. I'm here to keep the peace, and it's gonna be kept. Now quit interfering with the law."

"Let 'em go, Crawford," said the big one. "They done nothing but tell the truth. The girl's done nothing but sell papers."

The constable contained his contempt. "You, come here. I'm locking you up. One step backward and I'll shoot—resisting arrest."

The miner weighed that and didn't move.

Crawford stepped forward from the jailhouse, his piece leveled until there was no chance of the man's surviving the double-ought buckshot in each barrel. "Come with me," he said.

The galoot did. Crawford worked around behind the man and pushed him into the jailhouse and then into the cell. They were all sheep—he could deal with a whole mob if he had to.

Bulldog Malone hurried in just as Crawford turned the key. He eyed Flint, the girl, the galoot, and that Lowell biddy and grimaced. "You weren't subtle, Delbert. You got to put some boot polish on everything."

"Grab that scattergun on the rack, Bulldog. We got a riot coming out there."

Malone didn't. "This stinks," he said. "Let that girl go. That's what's riling them. There's more collecting out there every minute. The saloons are emptying."

"So what?" Crawford said and wished he hadn't. Even a bunch of miners knew how to tie a noose. "All right. But the others stay."

"I'm not leaving until they leave," said Libby.

"You're lucky I'm not letting you rot in there," Crawford replied, swinging open the cell and yanking her out.

"Give her the money you stole," Flint said.

Crawford swallowed an urge to pound on that crack-brained printer. "That's her fine. Disturbing the peace."

"You're a naughty fellow," said Amelia Lowell. " 'God bears with the wicked, but not forever.' Miguel de Cervantes said that. When will God stop bearing with you, Marshal?"

"Shut up."

"The proper way to address me is to request that I remain silent. Lord Chesterfield said that a man's own good breeding is the best security against other people's ill manners. I am secure, Mr. Crawford."

Crawford shook the girl. "If I catch you selling papers on the street again, you'll get a whipping. If I catch you selling anything on the streets, flowers or whatever, I'll come after you. It don't matter to me who or what you are. It don't matter to me if your ma's the Queen of England. If you see me on the streets, get outa my sight. What's your name?"

"Libby."

"Libby what?"

"Elizabeth Grace Madigan."

He herded her to the door and pushed her out. "All right," he yelled. "She's free. Now go home, all of you, before you get into big trouble with me."

"You're a crook," she yelled.

"Let the others go, Crawford," someone yelled.

Bulldog Malone loomed in the jailhouse doorway. "The constable's got to process them, bring charges. That was a seditious piece in that rag. They'll be arraigned. Bail set. If they can post bail, they can go until they're tried."

"Let 'em go, Bulldog. There wasn't a thing in that piece that wasn't true."

Crawford made note of the man. He intended to knock some heads in the next few days. A good-size mob had collected, but he judged they were curiosity seekers. They didn't act like they were about to string up rope. Some of them carried beer mugs or saloon glasses in their hands. The girl started to leave, but someone caught her arm and whispered to her. She stayed.

Bulldog herded the marshal inside, and they locked the door behind them. "Delbert, thanks to you we got a mess. If we cave in, they'll get out of hand. If we don't cave in, it could be our necks."

"May I quote you, Your Honor?" asked Flint through the bars.

"You won't be printing any more rags," the marshal snapped.

"Maybe we can wait 'em out," Malone mused. "It ain't like a bunch of miners to stand in the street all night when the saloon rails beckon. Just settle back and wait."

His musings were interrupted by an imperious rap on the door. "It's Weed," came a muffled voice.

Mason Weed, sole owner of the Golconda, the biggest of the mines, was the original discoverer, the man who grabbed the turf from the greasers, the man who got the governor to appoint a white men's administration, including Crawford. The constable let him in and barred the massive door again.

"Good evening, Mason," said Mrs. Lowell. "I suppose you've come to wave your Merlin's wand."

"Good evening, Amelia," the man replied. "We'll settle this in a moment." He turned to the constable. His sheer presence always intimidated Crawford. Something in his burning-coal eyes beneath those massive shaggy gray eyebrows, or his glacial face surrounded by a mane of gray-shot black hair—his mere *presence* was as much as Crawford could endure. That and Weed's awesome wealth, connections, and power.

"Now you've done it, Delbert. This harebrained conduct will cost you your job if it happens again. I should get rid of you right now, but the timing would be bad. Throwing a desperate girl into jail for peddling papers. You're an idiot. You've taken leave of your senses."

"She was peddling that stuff. She's got a mouth."

Weed smiled thinly. "That stuff. As if she wrote it or had even read it. Thanks to that charitable act, you've got about three hundred miners out there waiting to put your neck in their noose. Unlock that cell."

Reluctantly, Crawford did, wondering why he obeyed like some boy. His prisoners stepped into the tiny front room.

"Amelia," Weed said gently. "You've had your fun. You won't be writing any more catty items like that. Things may not be quite right here, but this is a new mining camp; things are in transition. In time it'll become a settled, prosperous town."

"For you or the Mexicans?" she retorted.

"Amelia, we'll discuss that later. History is history; progress is progress. Life is always compromise between expedience and principle. You're going to compromise. Believe what you will, but if you write any more of these little bombasts, your gracious restaurant and lyceum won't have a single patron. And you'll be catching a stagecoach for the long trip back to Boston and codfish."

She didn't reply. They all knew he had the power to enforce his will. Weed turned to Flint. "I read your little newspaper, beginning to end. Most commendable. We need a paper. We need local news. The merchants need a place to advertise their wares.

"I know Amelia, and I know exactly what sort of pressure she put on you. Her very persuasive manner, and a quarter-page ad, did it. She simply won't take no. I'll wager she wanted it on the front page. I note that you ran the piece with a disclaimer, distancing yourself. That was wise. We need a positive paper here. We have a growing town, an opportunity to become a golden city. You caught the tone perfectly in your front-page credo. Of course you'll stay."

Crawford listened incredulously. Weed was caving in.

"Now, Mr. Flint," the mine operator continued, "I'm going to arrange matters in a certain fashion to remind you of your responsibilities. You'll find that your advertising will drop to almost nothing should you attempt to publish a rabble-rousing rag. But you'll be rewarded for publishing a progressive, forward-looking paper. I'll see to it."

Flint looked as if he was about to speak, but instead the young man simply smiled insolently. Crawford wanted to pulverize him.

Weed turned to the miner. "I know you. You're Jack Treat. You work at the Golconda. Your sense of justice involving that hapless girl was commendable. Now you hop out there and tell your fellows that it's over. I've arranged for everyone to be released. There'll be jobs tomorrow for everyone who goes on home now, but no jobs for those who hang on here making trouble. Am I clear?"

Treat nodded, and Weed ushered him out.

"All right, now. It's all over," Weed said. "Amelia, we're going to have a little private chat at your splendid emporium now."

"I'll take notes," she retorted.

Crawford wanted to pitch her back into the cell, but a swift and deadly piercing glare from Weed quieted him. They were caving in. He hated it. If that mob saw that it won tonight, his work would be a lot harder from then on. And it'd be a lot tougher to line his pockets. There were moments when he itched to shoot that mining mogul right between the shoulder blades.

Weed escorted the freed prisoners out and quietly closed the door behind him.

"You lost," said Bulldog Malone. "I think you should be grateful. You were backed into a tight corner. Delbert, you keep forgetting that we're up for reelection in November."

"We'll get in. I'm not worried about it."

"Well, start worrying."

"Bulldog, I want two more city policemen. I'll wring their salaries outa the sporting houses."

The mayor arched an eyebrow.

7

Set free, Libby Madigan fled the jailhouse, heading for Mr. Berghoff's butcher shop. Sometimes the butcher would give her a soup bone when she didn't have anything. The next day, after she had sold a bouquet, she would give him a penny for it.

But he had closed for the night. She had been detained too long at the jail. She and her mother wouldn't eat. She felt the pinch of her empty stomach and the craving for food again. It was all too familiar to her. She fought back despair. Life had become so desperate, and she hardly knew if she or her mother would survive another day.

It had been such a good dream, selling papers. How could she know that they said something awful about the marshal? She had only read the front page and didn't know what was inside. Mostly she had been busy hawking the papers. Everyone wanted one, and her stack of them had melted steadily. She was going to earn more than two dollars that day—enough to feed herself and her mother for several days. The hurt where the marshal's heavy hand clasped her thin shoulder lingered like some malign force, and she remembered how helpless she was to resist as he steered her to jail like some common criminal. She didn't know what she had done, and the anguish had lanced her.

She hurried to her little cabin with the bad news that they would starve again tonight. Her mother weakened each day as the consumption ate away her lungs like maggots at work on rotten meat. Her cough had worsened, sometimes doubling her up and causing her to spit blood. Mostly she stayed in bed. Libby knew that her mother would die soon—and then what? The thought terrified her.

The whole Madigan family, almost, was dead. Her two younger brothers, Christian and Patrick, had died of the lung disease, and now her mother could number her days. Her father had given up his profession as a stonecutter to bring them here, where the air was dry and it was said a lunger might recover. He had gotten a job mucking ore in a little mine called the Goldbug, where he was one of five men, and he had built their one-room cottage of adobe and rock. Things seemed better until he died, buried in a small cave-in. Gil Toole, the mine owner, bought a funeral and gave the widow a week's pay. A month later the little mine ran out of ore and shut down. Then Libby and her mother had nothing, and her mother had grown too weak to wash or cook. For a while her mother could sew, and that had brought some pennies. A woman who knew how to sew was a rarity in a mining camp. But then other women arrived who sewed better and faster. After that, Libby plucked wildflowers and sold little bouquets, and the pair starved.

She found her mother abed in the darkness. They couldn't afford a candle or lamp oil.

"I don't have anything," she whispered. She clutched her mother's cold hand while she told her about the harrowing day.

"Libby, for me it doesn't matter. For you it matters. Thank you for trying so hard, dear," Maureen Madigan said before convulsing into a racking cough.

Libby wept, but there was no time for weeping. She had to find firewood. They couldn't afford to buy any, so she scavenged, often finding bits and pieces at the mine, the leftovers from the timbering of the shafts. She felt so weary and hungry she scarcely knew where she'd find the energy to collect an armload. But if she got wood she could brew some of the precious tea she had hoarded, and her mother would be strengthened a little by that.

"I'll make tea in a bit, Mama," she said.

"Yes, that would be nice, Libby." Her mother's vocal chords had been affected by the consumption, and she spoke hoarsely. Libby remembered when her mother had had a beautiful voice like ringing bells. She loved to read poetry to her children, especially Wordsworth's sonnets and his "Tintern Abbey." She had been a schoolmistress then.

They had laughed in those days. Their little white cottage in upstate New York wasn't a mansion of the rich, but they had the special riches of a close-knit family and a small, steady income with a little left over for candy on Saturdays in Watkins Glen. But that was before the sickness stalked them like an avenging demon, making them pay for their happiness. First it withered her brothers into gaunt, pale skeletons and then murdered them; then it struck her mother. That's when Garth Madigan took his daughter and his stricken wife to the desert, where the dry, sweet air might heal Maureen. And it had started to help—before the quartz-bearing rock crushed the life from him one awful afternoon.

Libby hastened through a deepening twilight to the mine buildings and to a certain place beside the carpenter's shop where scraps of unusable wood—knotty or rotted lengths, cuttings, splintered ends—collected. If this supply ever vanished, she didn't know what she would do; she needed a bit of wood to cook. But tonight there was plenty, and she snatched up as much as she could carry in a big armload.

When she returned through the lavender dusk, she beheld the man—Mr. Flint—at her door.

"Ah, there you are, Miss Madigan. I had a time finding you," he said.

She didn't want company, especially the company of this newsman whose paper had gotten her into trouble and robbed her even of her few pennies.

"Please go away."

"Let me help you with that," he said. He set down a basket.

She dropped the wood into a heap beside the door. "Mr. Flint, I don't want to sell your papers. I don't want anything to do with you."

"I can understand that. I'm printing more, but without that column of Mrs. Lowell's. You'll have a hundred more to sell tomorrow if you wish, and no one will bother you at all."

She felt weary, and the knot of hunger in her stomach had become unbearable. "Please, sir," she said. "Leave us alone."

"Well, if I must. But I brought you something. It's a dinner from The Boston. Mrs. Lowell put it in this basket for you."

"Food?"

"Crawford took every penny you had. I thought—"

'Oh, Mr. Flint. It's—it's—we're so hungry!"

"Your mother's with you, I take it? May I meet her?"

She nodded numbly. She could smell the food now, its savory odors making her wild with hunger.

She unlatched the door and bid him enter the darkened room, eyeing her mother nervously. Maureen Madigan lay on her bed.

"Libby?" she asked, then coughed terribly again.

"This is Mr. Flint, Mama. He brought us food."

"Mr. Flint? Food?" Her mother seemed confused.

"A dinner from The Boston, ma'am."

Libby realized her mother could scarcely see the man.

"Here," he said, handing her the basket. "You two eat."

"Eat?" her mother asked, in wonder. "Have you thanked Mr. Flint?"

"I . . . haven't had time. It all just happened."

Her mother coughed and then sucked air, trying to get enough into her lungs to speak.

"We bless you, Mr. Flint. That's all we have to give—the blessings of God upon you for this kindness. Will you share this with us?"

"I've had a bite," he said. Flint seemed at a loss for words. He peered about in the gloom, registering the desperation of his newsgirl. "You eat. There's some fine sliced beef, some soufflé, carrots and broccoli in a cheese sauce, some rolls and butter. . . . You eat, and perhaps I can build a little fire so you can see with the stove door open."

He built a fire while Libby and her mother ate. Libby devoured everything; nothing had ever tasted better. Soft rolls radiating the smell of yeast, creamy butter, succulent beef dripping salty juices, steamed carrots and broccoli in a cheese sauce! She wolfed food so fast that a knot of pain built in her stomach. Her mother swallowed slowly, wearily, almost without caring. She had told Libby that the lesions that had started in her lungs were devouring her throat, and now every bite seared her esophagus. But she did eat, pushing back tears.

"Mr. Flint," Maureen said, "that was the most delicious meal we have ever had. Libby and I wish to thank you."

He turned to her, looking troubled but saying nothing. The fire behind the stove's open door cast orange bolts of light hither and yon. The poverty did not escape his eyes, and Libby felt embarrassed. He didn't have to inquire about their circumstances. It was all there for him to read. "Mrs. Madigan," he said, "is there no one in all Oro Blanco to help you? Is there no charity?"

"We've always gotten along. We don't want charity. Libby's strong. What we need most is a real job for her." It was all that Mama's vocal chords could handle. She broke into one of those racking, gasping coughs again.

"Sometimes a newspaper can do things," he said. "A newspaper is a voice crying in the wilderness. An editor is set on Earth to sound the trumpet and cast light upon darkness."

He stayed a while more, not asking questions. Libby was glad of that; she didn't want to talk about her family. But she knew he was absorbing information all the same, his eyes alighting on tintypes of her father and her brothers. Then he rose.

"I've some printing to do," he said. "Miss Libby, if you'll be at the corner at noon, I'll have some papers for you to sell, and they won't get you into trouble."

She nodded. The strange man and his promise of help brought her close to tears. She was tired and scared and didn't know what was going to happen when Mama died. She just wanted to be taken care of a little. Maybe laugh sometimes. She had been hungry so much she didn't even think about having good times or meeting other girls or anything like that. She thought only of keeping her mama alive and her little cottage a haven. Silently she saw the man to the door and impulsively clasped his rough hand. Then he vanished into the night.

"Libby," her mother whispered. "He's your only hope. When I'm gone, he'll help you. He seems a good person."

"You'll get well, Mama! With some good food now, you'll get well." Libby's eyes brimmed with tears.

Her mother smiled. "We'll dream of it, Libby. We'll dream hard. As long as we have dreams, we're alive. There's no sin in dreaming a dream."

8

Mason Weed admired Golconda from the window of the superintendent's office. He had created this mine. On three levels deep in the earth, one hundred twenty miners mucked and drilled the quartz and rhyolite veins that were yielding a small fortune in gold, at a profit of a thousand dollars a day. Next to the headframe, a boiler house powered by cordwood from the Mogollon Mountains generated the steam to run his hoist, drive the Cornish pumps that sucked seepage from the bowels of his mine, and push fresh air to the miners.

He watched mule-driven ore cars haul country rock to the slack pile and other cars, filled with good ore, to giant hoppers where it could be loaded onto freight wagons. Even though much of what happened at the mine occurred underground, he could still feel its pulse and see busy workers from his spotless window, which his man cleaned every morning.

This was a splendid mine, and he had an interest in several others in the Oro Blanco district. The future was incredibly bright—provided the town made progress. He lacked skilled help and wished he could attract a hundred Cornishmen, those elite kings of the pits. Worse was his transportation problem.

There wasn't a rail or a crosstie or boxcar within two hundred miles. He needed capital to develop the mine and the town, and capital was shy. It didn't flood into a place as remote as Oro Blanco. His several trips to the financial houses of New York and San Francisco hadn't pried loose a dime. So this mine, and the others, suffered from gross inefficiencies wrought by wagon transportation.

But now the town had a newspaper, and it just might be the ticket. A newspaper sailed information out to an uncaring world. A newspaper could put a city on the map. A newspaper in the right hands would trumpet the town's promise, its virtues, its opportunities. It could agitate for a railroad. In the right hands it could promote policies that would make businesses more profitable. It could be a sane voice against vice. There were all too many tinhorns and scarlet women, saloons and dance halls in Oro Blanco. It could publish weekly accounts of mine production, which would not, in the larger world, be missed by venture capitalists. And best of all, a newspaper could supply him with a voice on crucial issues, such as wages, town ordinances, taxes, and public safety. It would also provide advertising, which would help his multiple enterprises—a mercantile, a hardware, a small bank, and the Gold Star Hotel—to prosper.

Yes, it was time to pay young Flint a visit. Those vagabond printers tended to be an independent sort, and if Flint proved impossible, why, Mason Weed might just import another printer and start his own paper. He should have started a paper a year ago. But Flint looked like a reasonable young fellow, one who would bend under some gentle authority. Flint, after all, was indebted to Weed for bailing him out of the marshal's maw. And that would help.

Mason Weed knew he conveyed a certain impression but couldn't say just how he did it. Perhaps it was simply his age: At fifty, he was at the height of his powers, with attentive manners, immaculate dress, and an ease of command. He had always been a serious man. Not that he never laughed, but from adolescence onward he had conceived of life as a hard climb, requiring discipline and mastery, and somehow that had coalesced into a formidable power among men. They called him mister. He always felt it among others—the respect, the caution, the deference. His word usually sufficed.

That seriousness had not entirely blessed his life, for it had somehow alienated him from women. Beginning in his youth, the serious young Weed had been disappointed in love, not once but several times. Women flirted with him hopefully but then mysteriously distanced themselves, as if his politeness and solemnity were a plague, a curiosity. He could never understand why women often loved bounders and giddy fools with no future and passed by a serious man.

He was a good marriage prospect, courteous, reasonably regular of feature, and competent, and yet no women ever seriously considered him. Once he had come close to a union, only to be abandoned at the altar by the lady, Margaret, who rudely neglected to show up at her own wedding. She sent him a perfumed note afterward, regretting her lapse and telling him she just couldn't manage being married to a gentleman like him. He had felt grateful not to have tied the fatal knot with a woman like that.

It had been a turning point in Weed's life. After that, he regarded women as an alien race. He couldn't fathom them, and they certainly didn't fathom him. He had turned, more seriously than ever, to making a success of himself. Life was too serious to waste in women's parlors.

Weed had heaped up riches, but happiness seemed to lie just beyond the horizon, always tantalizing him. Once he had gotten so melancholy he thought of dosing himself with strichnine. He couldn't quite fathom why: He had everything, and he could get even more. His life was preoccupied with wealth, and he played out his moves like a chess master. But the more he succeeded, the less happy he was. It puzzled him. He had conquered the world, but he didn't like himself.

He kept telling himself that his parents, Frederick and Veronica Weed, would be proud of him had they lived. They believed in industry. He had been a more or less dutiful son. But the more he thought of these things, the more his misery clawed at him. Something in his nature was keeping him from enjoying the fruits of his genius. But he knew how to deal with that: His life was simply incomplete; he would conquer another world or two, and then he would find the peace that eluded him. Someday, when he was the richest man in the Territory, he would have what he yearned for.

He abandoned his gilded office and set off on foot—exercise was healthy—to an encounter with young Flint. That meant, of course, crossing the Avenida Virgen de Guadalupe to a quarter where he was despised and feared, but it didn't matter. The peasants, inertly blocking progress, would eventually be ground away by the tides of life. It really wasn't his doing. Progress was impersonal. If he hadn't developed the Golconda and the new town, someone else would have. The results would have been the same.

He stepped into the decaying adobe building and found everything exactly as it had been. Flint had done nothing but scatter his sparse equipment around, making not the slightest effort to beautify the earthen place. Weed discovered the young man breaking down pages, swiftly tossing each letter into its pocket in the case boxes. Flint looked to be in his thirties, tall and clean-limbed, with a certain dignity that Weed admired. He spotted a friendliness of eye, and a mouth that could break into a husky laugh. This editor was a man, not a boy, and he took life earnestly, as did Weed himself.

Flint nodded but didn't pause. This interview, Weed deduced, would be conducted while the editor labored.

"Mr. Flint, I just dropped by to pay my compliments," Weed began easily. "Don't stop just for me. I know how busy printers are—setting type, breaking it down. Why, it's a task that staggers the mind."

"That's all dumbwork, Mr. Weed. The hard work's thinking up what to say. And finding the courage to say something that needs public airing when it might cost me subscribers or advertisers. If I lived only for my purse, I'd be in another business."

"You could use some help, though, I can see that. You're stretched pretty thin here."

Flint paused, as if anticipating what was to come. "I like my independence," he said. "I'm not in this because I like printing. Setting type is grubby, mindless work. Printing is even worse. I end up exhausted and ink-stained. I'm in it because I can say a few things in public and better the human condition."

This one showed signs of intelligence, but Weed didn't mind. "Well, I just want you to know I'm behind you, and if that fool of a marshal pesters you again, come to me. I'll settle his hash in a hurry."

That did stop the editor's hands. Flint eyed Weed skeptically. Then he started pitching type into pigeonholes again.

"The town needs a good paper, one people can trust," Weed said. "Everyone needs it—merchants, the mines, bankers. We need a solid paper to put Oro Blanco on the map. We're a going city. You're a little isolated over here, but eventually you'll meet all our good people across the avenue. That's where the progress is, in New Town. I imagine you could find space to rent over there if you want. I'll make some inquiries. I think some merchant'd wall off a rear room for your paper and put in a side door for you. It'd be more convenient. For you every minute counts, getting news, reaching advertisers. If you'd like me to help—"

"I'm quite content right here, sir. The church owns the building. My rent goes into Father de Cordoba's pockets. Helps the poor, I imagine. At least the *campesinos* don't have to support him when they can hardly feed themselves. They don't have a dime over here, you know. This place is fine. Good, watertight roof, which I need, low rent, fewer visitors."

"Well, it looks odd, Flint. A paper should look progressive

as well as be progressive. Public appearances are important, you know."

"Well, that's about right, Mr. Weed. Appearances count. As long as I'm over here, everyone'll know I'm my own man. Lots of people, including your marshal, told me not to rent here, but that just whetted my appetite. I'm letting your side of town know something. I write according to my lights. I'm not beholden to any faction. They won't always like what I say over there, and that's the mark of a good paper. If they liked every word, then I'd be producing propaganda, not news, not truth, not a vision of civic virtue."

This man would not be very tractable, which was a pity. But Weed couldn't help respecting an independent-minded man like Flint. "Well, Mr. Flint, marketing's important. If you want ads, you've got to have connections. You need to sit down with the merchants and lift a drink with 'em. They'll be sources of news. Once you call them by their first names, you'll hardly have to ask for ads. They'll all run standing ads in issue after issue, and they'll keep up with the payments too. That's how business is. It's a lot of intimate connections, mutual help, so we all can prosper." He paused. "Of course, if you just want to be ignored, or see your business go to any rival that sets up shop here, why then you can ignore your contacts and friends and struggle alone."

Flint grinned. "I'm my own man, sir. If people buy my rag, I make a profit. If not, I pack up and head for another burg."

"Well, I admire an independent spirit. I never could work for anyone else. But it requires common sense. Setting up shop over here in greaser town isn't common sense."

"It says exactly what I mean it to say, Mr. Weed. Marshal Crawford got my message fast enough. I made an enemy there. You saw my credo on the front page. I mean every word of it. If you want a paper in your back pocket, start your own. I'm peculiar that way."

Weed sighed. "What's your background, Flint?"

"Son of a Cincinnati schoolmaster; I'm fluent in Latin. My field was ancient history. Once you've read Cicero and Cato, Mr. Weed, you're never the same. Once you've followed Plato or studied Aristotle, your mind focuses on larger, grander visions than grubbing for money. Once you've tackled Caesar, you know about public affairs, courage, and diplomacy.

"I was headed toward being a chalk-dusted teacher myself, until the war came along. After that, the Union Army—a foot soldier with the Ohio Volunteers, in the trenches. They made me a corporal because I could read and write. I was also a correspondent for the *New York Herald*, wrote dispatches for James Gordon Bennett. That taught me my trade. Got out without a scratch. Dumb luck. I wasn't in the path of a minié ball. After that, I got restless. I could never be a teacher after being shot at by half the Confederacy. So I scraped up an outfit and headed west. I set up whenever I see a likely town."

"You don't stay long, it seems."

Flint smiled. "I do some good before they drive me out. I've lasted a year or two in some places. I'll tell you something: There aren't many places that want an editor to have a little fun with certain topics."

"What sort of topics?"

"Skullduggery. Injustice. Crime. Suffering. Theft. The arrogance of people in power. The plight of the poor. The injustice we visit upon colored folks. The basic ideals that bind us together. The things that separate an honorable man from a crook."

"I've never heard of a paper that delved into that. I thought your task was to gather the news."

"That's it exactly," Flint said. "The news. The real news. You'd be amazed the amount of news that people don't wish to see in print."

"I see," said Weed, swarming with reservations. He knew better than to argue with a young man with a skull full of ideals. *The Oro Blanco Nugget* might not be bad, but it'd take watching and a certain amount of careful string-pulling. With an editor like this, one had to feed certain facts and conceal certain others—and pull the alligator's teeth. On the whole, he concluded, it would be better to wrestle with Flint than to start up his own paper.

"I always admire young idealists," he said. "You're better than the young fellow who thinks only of himself. I'm going to be sending you a lot of news. Weekly production from all the mines. I'm privy to all the figures, not just my mines. Employment figures. News of new developments. Assay reports. Known reserves. Geology. I'm glad the camp has a paper to make these public. You come see me anytime. I'll always have time for a visit, and maybe I'll be able to explain things that may elude you. Just tell my man you'd like to see me. And of course we'll have some dinners at The Boston. Great old gal, Amelia Lowell. She's putting a nice veneer on a rough mining camp. She's a little dotty, and I wouldn't recommend publishing her again. You might lose advertisers."

Sam Flint grinned and nodded but never stopped breaking down the last issue.

Mason Weed stepped into the harsh sun and hurried across the Avenida, feeling confident that Flint could be managed with the carrot and the stick.

9

Amelia Lowell no longer saw Sam Flint walk through the doors of The Boston. She understood why. Her frank column had gotten him into grave trouble. And, of course, the price of a meal at The Boston would deter him as well.

She regretted his absence. He could well become her most valuable ally. She would try to act with more discretion next time, but that was always a struggle. She had always been blunt and plain-spoken, a trait that made civilized and urbane Boston too confining. She had reached the point where she couldn't bear Boston, with all its politeness, cultivation, manners, and temperance.

She had within her a furnace of passion that would not brook civilized restraints. In the end, she had become virtually an outcast in her native city. Ralph Waldo Emerson had once chided her, saying all mortals had the means to govern their souls and she should take hold of herself and reach a truce with her appetites. That only made her feel worse. She had ungovernable feelings, and if they were bottled up, they hurt.

The roots of her pain lay in an imperfect world, in the suffering and anguish she witnessed everywhere, among the privileged and the destitute. If everyone was so miserable, why not change things? It was folly even to think it, she knew that. In the end she had fled west, driven from civilization by both the pain in herself and the pain she had witnessed. In Oro Blanco, people knew her as a cultivated woman who brought graces to frontier society. They didn't know that within her private person lay a driving need to live in a place without rules or tradition, and a terrible sensitivity to the cruelties life inflicted on the helpless, including the humble Mexicans, impoverished widows and orphans, and all the butterflies broken on the rack of life.

She well understood that these two qualities formed a paradox. Her soul was divided between civilization and utter freedom. The woman who was bestowing manners and cultivation on Oro Blanco was a woman who couldn't live with constraint and who would leave for another raw place the moment she triumphed. She could not explain her contradictions and kept sane only by ignoring them. But she could laugh, and in her vast amusement with her mad nature she dissolved her anguish.

She settled at her escritoire and scratched an invitation on a card: "My dear Mr. Flint, I shall expect you for dinner this evening at six." It was less an invitation than an imperious demand, but he would come. She slid the card into an envelope and handed it to her man.

"Take it to Mr. Flint at once," she said.

She would have to decide what to ask of him and what to reveal of herself. Much of herself—and certain of her activities and causes—she never revealed, especially her payments to the Santa Fe lawyer. If anyone in town knew she was financing Baca's suit, they'd kill her, woman or not. She smiled, enjoying that little escapade above all else.

Flint arrived promptly at six, looking big and bookish in a tweed coat. He might suppose he had left his father's academy behind, she mused, but he hadn't. He reminded her of a prematurely crotchety young professor. She ordered for them both, playing the hostess but secretly enjoying turning the tables on a man.

"Now then," she began brightly, the hospitality done with, "I suppose I should apologize for getting you into hot water with Marshal Crawford. It wasn't bright of me."

She expected agreement, but he didn't respond.

"I don't suppose," she said coyly, "you wish to continue with my column."

"No, I'm afraid not, Mrs. Lowell."

"Well, that's what I imagined." She laughed. "I have better ways, you know. I'm going to instruct you about this town. We're going to pull skeletons out of closets, rattle bones, unbury the dead. It all comes to my ear in The Boston, you know. I know more little secrets than anyone else, and I'm going to feed them to you one by one."

"That sounds like fun, but a weekly paper's a business. I report the news. I stir up the town. I set tongues wagging."

She waited while her man placed a glass of port before them both. She hadn't asked Flint if he liked port; it wasn't necessary. If he didn't, he should learn to, like any proper man.

"Here's to a wicked little weekly," she said.

He considered that, grinned, and touched his glass to hers.

"Now then, my dear Flint, if I know certain parties in Oro Blanco, you've already been invited to become a part of, shall we say, the business community?"

He looked startled.

"I thought so," she said, enjoying this. "Mason Weed has pined for a paper for a long time. He's got the most to hide and the most to gain, and he needs one. I suppose he offered to uproot you from the Escalante cantina and deposit you on these friendlier shores."

"I turned him down."

"And he pretended that was acceptable to him. Of course, my dear Flint, you made a terrible enemy. Tell me, isn't it strange to you that you've scarcely arrived, scarcely learned a thing about Oro Blanco, and yet people like him—and me—are maneuvering just as hard as we can to corner you?"

He sipped his port. "I noticed," he said. "In Weed's case, he added a few veiled threats too—such as his own competing paper."

"He'd do it, of course. He's entirely capable of moving in his own little propaganda sheet and a bought-and-kept editor."

"I think I'm enjoying this," Flint said. "So far, you haven't threatened me with competition or with pressure on my advertisers."

"Oh, I just might," she said. "I don't suppose you've ever met such strange pressures when you've brought your little paper to a new town."

"I haven't been to many towns," he said. "But you're right. Usually they leave me alone—until I begin publishing things they don't like. But that usually takes a few weeks or months. That's what's different about this. I suspect you were exaggerating in that column and Marshal Crawford is a better man than you think."

She eyed him patiently. "That wasn't ten percent of it, Mr. Flint. The man ought to be in his own calaboose."

"Well, then, Mrs. Lowell, tell me what you know—and more to the point, how you know it. Your accusations weren't exactly grounded in fact, were they?"

She demurred. These things had to be explained in proper order. "Later," she said. "When you understand certain things."

She could sense that the young man was becoming skeptical as well as impatient with all the cat-and-mousing. "You're going to be my guest for dinner every night for a few weeks," she said.

"I can't do that. I won't be in anyone's hip pocket."

"I don't have hip pockets, Mr. Flint. Whalebone stays, yes, but not hip pockets." She smiled brightly. "But I like a man of principle. It means you're doomed to a life of poverty, like a monk. But also to a life of interior joy. I should imagine you don't mind looking in the mirror when you apply your straight-edge every morning. It's an honorable young face."

She was being amusing—to herself—and wished she wouldn't. It was one of her nasty habits.

He gazed at some vague place beyond her. "I'm not much for repartee," he said, "and I'm no good at small talk."

She liked that too. "Very well, I'll start by telling you the town's most terrible secret, the main reason why powerful men—from Weed and the mine owners down to the town marshal—are plenty concerned about keeping a leash on you.

"The truth of it is, Mr. Flint, that no one on this side of Virgin Avenue owns the land under his feet. That includes me. That includes the mines. If the land should ever be returned to its rightful owners, who have valid title to it, you can see what would happen. Every mine would go to the original Mexican landowners, every building, every house, every store. And the owners would be owed for every ounce of gold illegally taken from the mines."

Flint looked skeptical. "There are always land disputes when mines are involved," he said.

She waited until her man had served dinner, spooning it from silver salvers to her Limoges service. She nibbled at the mutton, but her appetite for telling the story was larger than her appetite for mere meat.

"The Escalantes, who ran the cantina and mercantile for generations in the very building you now rent," she said, dabbing her lips with white linen, "were the owners of all this land, many leagues in every direction. It's all private land, part of a grant given to the family by the kings of Spain in the 1750s. Both the treaty of Guadalupe Hidalgo, which ended the Mexican War, and the Gadsden Purchase agreement guaranteed that the real property of Mexican landholders would remain intact; the United States would recognize all private holdings. I suppose you can imagine the rest."

She certainly had his attention. He stopped chewing his mutton and waited.

"When some prospectors, grubstaked by Weed, found gold here almost four years ago, the Escalantes were doomed. They fought the thievery, of course, but our good, upright fellow Yankees soon took the land and its fabulous mines without a shred of legality. It wasn't hard, not when those in the way were Mexican peasants and a country priest. It went to the territorial court, whose Yankee judges—political appointees of the Grant Administration—found no merit in the Escalante land patent and permitted Weed and his men to file regular mining claims on it. Later they applied for a townsite patent."

"What happened to the Escalantes?"

"That's a story for another time, Mr. Flint. For now, all you need to know is that the matter is still pending. The Escalantes' attorney, Alonzo Baca, in Albuquerque, unable to get justice in the territorial courts or from the territorial governor, is preparing a case he will file in the Federal District Court. Weed and his friends won the first round simply by arguing that the Escalante grant is a fraud, and the territorial judge was all too happy to agree.

"Since then, Baca has been collecting evidence. He's employed an attorney in Seville—Spanish possessions in the New World were governed from Seville, you know—and when the fair copy arrives, the case will be simple enough. Baca's expecting it momentarily. There's no copy in the City of Mexico or Chihuahua—they seem to have disappeared. Meanwhile, Baca and Weed's attorneys wrestle over lesser matters, such as putting the profits from the mines into holding until the case is settled. And as you surmise, Mr. Flint, our dear Mason Weed is doing what he must to stop it. He will do absolutely anything to avoid losing his claim to the mine. Now you know why he wants no crusading little newspaper snooping around here."

Flint dabbed at his lips with his napkin. "You're on Baca's

side even though it might cost you title to the land beneath our feet?"

She smiled. "The Escalante estate, if it wins, would give this lot to me." She didn't say *for certain favors*.

"But the town—it'd be uprooted."

"No, not really. Juan de Cordoba isn't the sort, although the people here don't know that. He won't uproot white settlers. He's a more generous soul than his tormentors, who wish to uproot his whole parish. It's the mines, Flint, the mines. The gold. The parish would like royalties, the usual twenty-five percent. Weed and his dear honorable friends aren't inclined to pay it. All they want is to postpone the new trial until they've gutted the mines and fend off Baca's motions of *lis pendens*, which would tie up the assets until adjudication, and holding arrangements. The Golconda yields a profit of a thousand dollars a day—that's the net profit, Mr. Flint, not the gross. When the mines give out, the white men's side of Oro Blanco will die with them."

"And then they all turn it back to the Mexicans?"

"Oh no, my dear. They're out to win it all. They covet the grazing land. There's about ninety square miles involved. Maybe fabulous lodes still waiting to be discovered."

"And what happens to the Mexicans?"

"The strategy, Flint, is out of sight, out of mind. Now what do you intend to do about it?"

"Print the news. I'm not in the crusading business."

"Yes you are. I can tell." She eyed him knowingly. "What are your weaknesses?"

It startled him. "That's the first time anyone asked me that."

"I'm a Lowell. I ask what I will. You won't confess. Mason Weed'll find them out before I do. And turn them against you."

He surrendered. "The long list or the short one?"

"Whatever suits your fancy. If you were a Papist, this would be the confessional."

"A scholar's conceit."

"Rubbish. I want the real weaknesses. Are you a liar?"

"Madam—"

"Oh, tut-tut. Spill it out."

"I'm a man alone. I don't mix with others. I don't hoist the cup with my advertisers or smoke cigars with politicians. I keep to myself. I avoid matrimony; it'd pin me down."

"That's nothing. What is your real weakness? Temper?"

"I get mad, say things I regret. I mock others in print."

"We all do that. What's likely to bring you down?"

He pondered that. "Idealism. I have a vision of what men and social arrangements might be."

"Ah, my dear Flint," she said. "A Cicero. Or Cato the Elder."

"No, Francis of Assisi."

She pondered that. "You are a contradiction, Mr. Flint," she said at last.

10

Sam Flint was just about ready to put his next issue to bed. The news hole wasn't very large to begin with, because every merchant in town had jumped in with an ad—this issue would sell everything from corsets to coal. And then people had brought him their own news. He scarcely had to hunt for it. All week they had wandered into his sanctum to tell him of a business opening, a marriage or two, one death, some mine production figures (supplied by Mason Weed), a little boy's narrow escape from a rattlesnake, an Algernon Swinburne poetry program at The Boston Lyceum, a dogfight in front of the Stamp Mill Saloon, an announcement from Marshal Crawford that firecrackers were not to be ignited before six A.M. on the Fourth of July, and a combined story about three Fourth of July picnics, a doublejacking contest for miners, and a box social put on by the Baptists.

He had acquired more than two hundred subscribers and had scarcely found time to do his bookkeeping or make labels for the post office. He needed a clerk, at least part-time. With Libby's street sales, the second issue would sell twice as many copies as the first. He had been swamped, working deep into the quiet evenings to prepare the issue, grateful that so much advertising had diminished his news columns.

The Anglos had approached his lair in the old cantina warily at first, afraid of greasers carrying daggers and rare tropical diseases. But that traffic had given him some understanding of where he stood. Just about everyone over there on the bustling Yankee side of Oro Blanco had blamed Amelia Lowell, not *The Nugget*, for riling the authorities. Hadn't *The Nugget* put her column in a place for private opinions? Everyone knew the Boston woman was dotty anyway.

So that had passed, or at least the citizens of Oro Blanco thought it had. In Sam Flint's mind it had not passed at all. The marshal's abuse of office was a live issue and one that would soon be aired. They would find out that Flint wasn't quite the good fellow they thought, and didn't run with the lemmings.

Sliding the last of his type from the galley tray into the chase, he discovered he still had seven inches of column left over. He could stuff it with fillers, of which he had hundreds— jokes, aphorisms, bits of wisdom, puzzles, most anything to fill up a column in a hurry. He had put his classical education to use and had scores of them that were simply the thoughts of Socrates, Aristotle, Marcus Aurelius, Cicero, Plato, Plutarch, and other ancients. No one could accuse Sam Flint of failing to educate his rough readers.

Seven inches. Lots of filler material on hand. He considered Seneca: "The good things of prosperity are to be wished; but the good things that belong to adversity are to be admired." But his unruly independence got hold of his soul. He could spend two or three hours without throwing himself off schedule. He hung up his printing smock and clambered into his tweed suitcoat, which he knew was ridiculous and uncomfortable in late June in southern New Mexico Territory. He armed himself with a pair of pencils and his notepad and hiked through the greaser quarter to the Parish of San Juan church.

He discovered Father de Cordoba hoeing a squash garden

behind his small abode rectory. The padre worked barefoot, in a loose cassock, with sweat beading his brow.

"*Buenos dias*, Mr. Flint," he said, resting on his hoe. "You come to give me rest from chopping the weeds? They are *salvajes*—how is it said?—savages that steal the water and the sun from my plants. The bad weeds, eh?"

Flint could see that the padre had barely checked them. He had chipped into the hard caliche with that ancient hoe and had watered each plant with a bucket apparently toted clear from the tumbling creek in the middle of Virgin Street.

"You've got some squash coming along, Padre."

"Ah, yes, the *esquash*. Some food for me to eat for a few days. I do not like to trouble my flock with my little hungers. They do not have much food. So I do not molest them—how is it said?—with the bother. It is the temptation with all the *padres* to put the fat on their bellies from the sweat of the people. I do not do this. *Pero*, I do not like chopping the weeds and putting the water in the ground. It is like wearing the shirt of hair, does it not? But I make the penance, *que no*?" The gaunt padre smiled, a question in his eyes.

"I'm just looking for news, Padre. I'd like to cover what happens over here, even if your people can't read it. Maybe you can read it to them."

"News? You want some *noticías*, eh?" The sweating padre studied the newsman. "Why do you suppose there is the news on this side of Avenida Virgen de Guadalupe, eh? All that happens is on the other side. What do these people do here but make the work for food?"

Flint felt himself being gently rebuffed, or maybe accused. "There's always news—if nothing else, marriages, deaths, weddings, christenings. . . ."

"Ah, you want *noticías* like that. Are you sure you wish to print these little things? It will waste the space in your Yankee paper, yes? Perhaps you want only the words to fill the empty places."

Flint winced. "Filler material, yes. Balance too. Fairness."

"Ah, I see," the padre said. "You have the few *centimetros* of the blank paper, and you have the—principles. *Como? Pues,* maybe I will help you with news of the greasers. On the Saturday *proxima* we will celebrate the Holy Sacrament of Marriage at eleven hours of the morning. Manuelita Chavez will be given in marriage to Refugio Torres. Now, is that the news?"

Flint was swiftly recording that. He nodded. "Who are the parents? Tell me more."

"Ah, Manuelita's mother, she is called Adelita. She buried Manuelita's father last year after he trip the feet over a rusty plow and his jaw it is locked. Refugio's father is called Rafael, and his mother is called Maria. Rafael makes the adobes and sells the wood to make the fire. There, does that give you the— what does one say—*satisfecho*?"

"Satisfaction? Well, no Padre."

De Cordoba chuckled. "There will be the *baile* that night, a dance for the bride and groom, and Sylvestro Peralta he will come from Silver City to make the music. Now, *por seguro,* you have enough news of the greasers."

"No, Padre."

"No? *Pues asì,* I will give you some more of the news for the *yanquis*. We will have the christening at mass on Sunday. Margarita Consuelo Concepcion Alvarez, the daughter of Pancho and Delores Alvarez, will be baptized into the faith and the Holy Church. The infant will wear the christening gown made by her Great-grandmother Alvarez and used many times by the family. *Ahora,* does that suffice?"

"Well, I thought you might have more news than that, Padre."

"I do have some. But not for you, Mr. Flint."

Sam Flint wondered about that. "Try me out," he said.

"It is not the filler material from the Mexicans," the padre said.

Sam waited, his pencil poised, and finally the priest began.

"The creek that divides the Avenida, our people draw their water from it. Sometimes they are getting *enfermo*—sick. The water once was clear and bright, good water. Now, *de vez en cuando,* it is milky, or yellow, because of the mines above, and my people drink it and get very sick to the stomach.

"I have seen the assays from the mines. Gold, much gold. Silver, lead, copper, tellurium, and arsenic also. When it makes rain, the water from the waste that is made into piles up above runs into the sweetwater creek we once loved. Whenever they call me because Juan or Miguel has a sick stomach, I bring them water I carry from far above the mines and make them drink it until they do not get sick.

"I am going to dig a *pozo*—a well for the village. It is a difficulty to get my men together, and we do not have shovels and picks, but we will dig it. We will line the well with rock and build a stone parapet around it to keep the animals and the dirt out. Then the bad water from the *yanqui* mines will no longer poison us."

"I'll write it, Padre."

"Are you sure this is a thing you wish to do?"

"A well is news. Poisoned water is news. The world's full of good people. Put the news in a paper, and maybe some people will give you tools or come help."

The padre smiled wryly. "And who would help the greasers, eh?"

"I don't know the town. Maybe no one. But I'll do this: If you need a pick or a shovel, I'll get one at the hardware store."

"That would be an act of *caridad*, Señor Flint. Charity. The Lord would bless you, I think. Surely."

"When are you going to start digging?"

"To get ten husbands of Oro Blanco together to dig the wells is like driving a thousand of sheep with one dog, Mr. Flint."

"Where'll the well be?"

"You will see the place below the *iglesia*, on the plaza. We call that barren flat place the plaza, but it is a flight of Hispanic fancy. Where the stake is, there will be a well or they will get the long speech about *perezozidad*, the laziness, every Sunday and holy day." He laughed.

Flint took his leave and set to work composing his stories from that side of Oro Blanco. It took him longer than he had supposed, and when he was done he had twenty column-inches of type to wedge into his seven-inch hole.

From page two he extracted two business openings and a hay theft the marshal blamed on "outsiders," meaning greasers. Flint kept the type intact in the galley tray, for use next week. In the newly opened hole he placed the wedding, the *baile*, and the christening. In the seven-inch hole on page three, he inserted his story about the well, quoting Padre de Cordoba at length.

With many new subscribers and another two hundred for street sales, Flint knew he would be printing deep into the night. He ran off the sheets on one side, and while those dried he wolfed down a quick biscuit-and-gravy supper at a beanery called The Ritz that he frequented because meals cost two bits. He had declined Amelia's invitation, wanting to avoid obligation to her. He knew that luxurious dollar-fifty meals didn't really come free.

In the midsummer twilight he walked over to the Madigans to let Libby know she'd be hawking papers instead of bouquets the next morning. He knocked, but she didn't answer. From within he heard terrible spasms of coughing. Then, between the coughing, Maureen Madigan invited him in.

"I could tell your knock, Mr. Flint," she said, lying on her pallet. She looked pale and hollow-eyed and clutched a grimy rag stained with blood she had coughed up. "Libby's getting wood at the mine. Thank heaven they throw out the scraps."

"I wanted to let her know that the next issue'll be out in the morning, and I'm counting on her to sell it."

Maureen coughed. "She'll be there. She made two dollars and eight cents last time. You're kind. We've eaten all week, things I've hardly seen for months. I'm feeling a little better."

"I'm glad of that. You could use some sun."

"What I could use, Mr. Flint, is unimportant. I live for Libby now. She's all the future I have. Mr. Flint, after I'm gone, and if you would be so kind, look after her. She's too young to . . . know about evil."

"I'll do that, Mrs. Madigan," he said over her coughing.

"Will you?"

She had seen through him. He was too much a vagabond and loner to look after anyone for long.

"I'll do all I can for as long as I can."

"That's a better answer," she said.

11

Sam Flint suspected that *The Oro Blanco Nugget* wasn't going to last long. The paper was going to be on the wrong side, just as it was already housed on the wrong side. He knew it when Amelia Lowell told him her story. He knew it when the priest told him more. And he had a lot more to learn, such as the fate of the Escalantes—owners of the Mexican land patent, owners of the cantina, the mayor who was suddenly deposed by the incoming Yankees.

He didn't exactly trust his sources. Amelia was long on gossip and tended to exaggerate. The padre could be harboring bitterness or telling only some fraction of the story. He would need more, probably from the Albuquerque lawyer, Baca. And when he got his story, then what? Set it, run it, see every copy swiftly destroyed and himself run out of town? The ruling elite knew the story; the thousands of newcomers didn't and wouldn't unless he broke it. But what good would that do?

He could not answer the last. This was really a story to ignore, a fait accompli that could not be undone. There wasn't much justice in the world, especially with the clash of peoples.

White Europeans were simply overrunning the continent as a matter of Manifest Destiny, indifferent to the plight of those who had occupied it before. Flint doubted that any of the newcomers to Oro Blanco gave it much thought or even found injustice in it. He'd heard over and over that the continent was there for those who would use it and build a civilization upon it. What Indian had done that? Or what Mexican?

No, the reality was that he could publish the Escalantes' case down to its last naunce and never move the residents of one side of Oro Blanco to make amends or do a thing about it. He doubted that even the Federal District Court or the Supreme Court would overturn history. Baca, up there in Albuquerque, might achieve some sort of settlement, but *The Oro Blanco Nugget* would only exacerbate the trouble, and every issue would breed resistance among those whose land titles and mineral patents were clouded. He could scarcely imagine the merchants of Oro Blanco advertising in a paper that was challenging their ownership of the ground under them. Neither could he imagine producing a single issue without the town officials, Mayor Bulldog Malone, Justice of the Peace Pete Peters, and Marshal Delbert Crawford—who had added two new officers to the town constabulary—clamping him by the throat, literally or figuratively.

And yet the town was awash in guilt. He'd sensed it the day he rode in and talked with the surly marshal. That guilt ate like a cancer at its happiness. He'd been in various boomtowns, and if anything marked them, it was a sense of frantic fun and adventure. Not Oro Blanco. From the moment Crawford had scowled at him and scorned the prospect of a newspaper, Flint had known something was gravely wrong. Most of the people flooding into the new camp didn't know about its shaky foundations, and those who knew kept silent about it, hoping that the suit being pursued by that greaser lawyer would just vanish.

That evening Flint walked into The Boston bearing a

not-quite-dry copy of his second issue. Amelia swiftly joined him, balanced a gold-rimmed pince-nez on her formidable nose, and read the issue with amazing speed while Flint sipped his port.

"You must learn to spell better," she said. "You're wanting a good Boston Latin School education. You don't spell *accommodate* with one *m*."

Flint sighed. He was waiting for her to say something about the Mexican wedding or christening, the pollution of the creek, or Father de Cordoba's proposed new well over there.

She studied the inside pages. "You're going to be on probation," she announced. "They can't rightly jail you or boycott you or pester you for doing little stories about weddings and baptisms, can they?" She laughed that tinkly ladylike laugh of hers. "But they'll read something into it. You're on the wrong side, and this issue will set them against you."

"Well, I'm that, all right. I was born on the wrong side."

"You're going to do the Escalante grant story and end up like Joan of Arc, being toasted to death. Do you wish to be a martyr? I suppose so. I can see it in your luminous face. A shaft of light from God bathes you."

"Tell me the rest," he said, taken aback by her insight.

"Oh, the rest. That's right, I only began to tell you about the Escalantes. You've the same fatal weakness that I have. I can get away with it, but you can't. Let me say it, and they'll go around telling each other that Amelia's dotty. But if you say it, my dear young man, they'll find ways of stopping your heartbeat."

"I'm not so sure of that. I think the unjust are afraid and weak, always looking behind them to see who's following, always on the brink of making grave mistakes."

"Ah, to be young again," she said.

He quietly ate the medallions of beef. The Boston's meals were always a treat. Amelia Lowell was a perfectionist in every facet of her life.

"The Escalante family possessed this land for three generations," she said. "It's a grant from the Spanish crown, not a

Mexican grant, and it encompasses three leagues in each direction, a nine-mile square, or eighty-one square miles. The crown was encouraging settlement along the northern frontiers of Mexico by giving land to those who would come here. There was constant danger from Apaches.

"The settlers mostly raised sheep and cattle. But they found a little gold in ledges here, and this village became the heart of the holding. The Mexicans of Oro Blanco didn't really own the land under them, but the Escalantes never enforced their right to a rent. A village was a good thing. That's how it was, Mr. Flint, until some Yankees found rich gold deposits within sight of the village—deposits that eluded the Mexicans because they lay under some porphyry.

"Almost before he knew it, Ramon Escalante was dealing with a crowd of Yankees who'd staked out standard mining claims according to United States law and were camping in a crude town on this side of the creek. Ramon and his wife, Mercedes, operated the *mercado* and cantina; he was the mayor, or *alcalde*, and pretty much everything else here. Of course, all those Yankees bought their supplies at his *mercado* at first and ate at his cantina—and utterly ignored his right to his own property. As word spread, the Yankees flooded in, outnumbering the Mexicans.

"Ramon Escalante appealed to the priest, Padre de Cordoba, who's been here many years and could speak a little English. But every attempt they made to drive the gold-mad Yankees off Ramon's property was rebuffed, eventually at gunpoint. It was robbery, pure and simple, although the Yankees pointed out that they had found the gold and thus were entitled to it."

"But what about the courts? Didn't the Escalantes seek justice?" Flint asked incredulously.

She sniffed. "The territorial courts, my dear Flint, are entirely in the hands of the Sante Fe Ring—Catron and Elkins and that crowd. There's scarcely a Mexican man in the territorial government except for display, like a cottonwood *santo*. To answer your question, yes, Ramon Escalante and the padre traveled clear to Albuquerque, dodging Apaches, and engaged Alonzo Baca, an attorney there who practiced in the Third Judicial District. The Escalantes, for all their holdings, had little cash, really; they eked a living from the store and cantina, ran cattle and sheep, and lived mostly by barter.

"Baca took the case. He sought an injunction against all further development in the district, supplied the proofs of ownership, and cited the language of two treaties.

"Ah, Mr. Flint, the ingenuity of the political hacks on the bench knew no bounds. They couldn't really squirm out of an airtight case, but neither could they permit mere Mexicans to stop white men's progress." Amelia smiled wryly. "They found a way to wiggle out of it. The territorial court blandly announced that the Escalante grant was a forgery and the Escalantes never owned one hectare. Then that pig of a territorial governor declared that the mining claims were all valid and the whole holding was public land that could be claimed and settled."

"Well, what happened to Ramon Escalante?"

"Be patient. It's a long, nasty story. The Yankees running the Territory knew perfectly well that going to law was beyond the Escalantes' financial capacity. But Alonzo Baca continued. He's a quiet man, the size of a wren—with a heart the size of Paul Bunyan's. He switched from the territorial courts to the Federal District Court—which was not under the control of the Sante Fe Ring—and he filed his appeal. He wanted a *lis pendens* declaration to freeze the assets and an injunction prohibiting further mining or building on any town lot until ownership was established. Meanwhile, he was offering Mason Weed and Jasper Twigg—owner of the Gold Queen—and others the right to lease the mines for the standard twenty-five percent royalty, which they refused. They held the acts—they spoke English, and their allies ran the Territory. Januarius Campbell, the federal district judge, did grant the injunction, but it didn't do much good."

Flint listened pensively. The town had a guilty secret after all, just as he had intuited the day he arrived and found that the town marshal didn't really want a newspaper. He glanced around The Boston, wondering whether other ears were listening to Amelia. No one seemed to be paying any attention to her— or him.

"That writ was too much for our greedy countrymen," Amelia continued, obviously relishing the storytelling. "No one would enforce it, especially the federal marshal, a member of the Santa Fe Ring. And the territorial government declined to send its own peace officers to shut down the mines. Mason Weed's brutes chased away the padre and Ramon Escalante at gunpoint, threatening their lives. And just for spite, the Anglos appointed their own mayor and justice and constable and had them endorsed at Silver City, the seat of Grant County. It was theft, Flint. And there was little a poor brown Mexican could do about it.

"Still, Baca, that tiny tiger, persisted. Six months ago, he obtained a federal writ holding our Yankee friends in contempt of court and mandating the territorial government to enforce all federal writ. Naturally, the territorial officials managed to do nothing and declawed the two deputy federal marshals by means no one understands—the rumor was that the two marshals suddenly got rich. The marshals came to serve the writs and returned to Albuquerque the same day. Both resigned a few weeks later.

"Well, Mr. Flint, the white gentlemen who are extracting gold from those cliffs now felt genuinely threatened. Escalante's bulldog, Baca, had teeth. They reasoned that they had to destroy Escalante. A strange midnight raid by masked Yankees was the result. They stripped the *mercado* of its merchandise, wrecked the cantina, and bound and gagged the elderly Ramon and Mercedes. They warned him he had twenty-four hours to leave the country. When his neighbors came to the rescue, they found Ramon dead of a heart attack. And Mercedes had turned old overnight, half mad with terror and grief. She survived two months.

"As she was barren, the will gave the estate to the San Juan parish church, or rather to the bishop in Santa Fe in trust for the parish. But, my dear Flint, it's not over. Alonzo Baca continues, mysteriously financed by someone. And some say that the life of the padre is in mortal danger.

"Now what are you going to do about it?" Amelia asked, her gaze boring into him. Clearly, she had taken sides and wanted Flint on hers.

He didn't hesitate. "After I confirm the story with the padre, and meet Alonzo Baca, and look at the records, I'll print it," Flint said, with the sense that it would be the last thing he ever put into the paper. He wondered what drove him—this was not the decision of a prudent man.

"Have some port, my dear," she said. "It's red as the blood you'll be leaking."

12

Sam Flint thanked Amelia Lowell and escaped into the darkness. He was only the editor of a fledgling weekly, and the massive injustice she had described seemed a dangerous secret. Here he was publishing his weekly in the Escalantes' building. It dawned on him that even those innocuous stories about weddings and christenings on his side of town could be viewed—by those with guilty consciences, or no consciences at all—as inflammatory material. It was probably true that most of those Yanks who'd bought town lots and started businesses had never heard the story and that only the cabal who pushed the Escalantes off their ancient ground really understood the situation.

Yet who could say what one editor of one precarious weekly might achieve? Maybe all it would take would be the light of truth thrown into dark corners. He would need to document the story and then publish it all at once, not piecemeal. If he published any of it before he had completed his investigation, his sources would vanish, and he probably would be driven out of town. He wouldn't last in Oro Blanco in any case, but he hadn't lasted long in any of the other towns he'd settled in. He would publish an amiable, discreet paper while he marshaled his material.

In the morning he hooked his fractious mules to his wagon and drove his subscription papers to the post office, and then hauled a larger bundle to the corner of Virgin Avenue and New Mexico Street, where he found Libby Madigan waiting eagerly for him.

"I was afraid you wouldn't come," she said.

"Why, Libby?"

"Because of what happened before."

He laughed. "We both learned a lesson. There's not a word in this paper that criticizes anyone in Oro Blanco. You'll have no trouble."

She sighed. He thought she looked a little less pinch-faced. Her sales last week had at least given her food. "How is your mother, Libby?"

"Mr. Flint, she's in a bad way, coughing so much I can't stand it. But she's eating a little. I think she's better. She asked for greens, and I'm making salads. And I got some milk from the dairy too. I helped her sit in the sun yesterday. She hasn't sat in the sun for a long time. But she's . . . oh, Mr. Flint, I'm so scared."

"What does the doctor say?" He knew what she would say and regretted asking. But she surprised him.

"He says she needs good food, lots of rest, dry air, and time in the sunlight every day. He wants her to have vinegar and honey in a tea. He says that those drive away sickness. He says garlic helps too. Dr. Worth comes whenever I ask."

"He's a good doctor, then," he said, noting the name. He would do a story about Dr. Worth.

He settled the stack of papers at her feet. "I'm trying one hundred twenty-five this time. Think you can sell them?"

"I'll sell 'em to dogs and cats if I have to."

"Good, Libby. You'll be here a long time. But don't neglect your mother."

She eyed him reproachfully.

From his wagon he extracted some additional papers and began delivering them to his advertisers. With each visit he attempted to accomplish three things: supply proof of publication, collect for the ad, and sell more space in the next issue. The deliveries would take the rest of the morning. If he could afford a printer's devil, the boy would be breaking down the pages or composing ads or setting fillers. But he couldn't; such luxuries would have to wait.

By noon he had accomplished most of his business and had a sheaf of orders for new ads, as well as some negotiable paper. There wasn't much legal tender in Oro Blanco, but the merchants managed without it, mostly by writing drafts on their accounts. All this he would take to Amelia and let her sort it out. A few of his advertisers had joked about all the troubles besetting the previous issue, and most had blamed Amelia for it. Flint listened carefully. One thing was plain. None of these businessmen believed a word she wrote.

He found Libby at her corner, with Crawford towering over her reading a paper, along with a new constable, built like a boxer, with a droopy mustache. Libby looked subdued.

"Does it satisfy you, Marshal?" Flint asked. "Are we going to have a little censorship again?"

Crawford glared from ice-cold eyes and studied the sheet. When he had finished, he tucked the paper under his arm. "You're just itching for trouble, ain't you?" he said.

Flint shrugged cheerfully.

"Itching for trouble," Crawford reiterated. "And you'll get it."

"You owe me a dime, sir," Libby bellowed.

Crawford smiled. "City gets one free," he said.

"The city can pay, same as anyone else," Flint replied.

"Tough, ain't it?"

"A lawman's supposed to uphold the law, not violate it," Flint said. Petty graft irked him, especially when he was its victim.

Crawford laughed, and the new man smiled. Flint's hands had balled into fists, and the two were watching, amused and itching for the opportunity. But Sam Flint cooled himself down and turned away. There were better ways.

The fear slowly faded from Libby's face. She had sold a third of her copies and had several dollars on her.

The constables meandered away, and Libby began to tremble. "Maybe I shouldn't sell papers," she said.

"You have courage, Libby. They won't hurt you. You've got lots of friends in Oro Blanco. Remember how the miners came to the jail last week?"

But Libby had withdrawn somewhere into herself.

Flint considered it a matter that required attention. A paper under steady harassment from official bullies could neither prosper nor publish freely. He turned his mules toward the Golconda mine for a talk with Weed. This was going to stop, one way or another.

He learned from a clerk that Weed was lunching at The Boston, which suited Flint fine. He had deposits to make there, and it would help to have Amelia listening when he braced Weed about the town's marshal.

He saw Weed dining alone, and Flint plowed across the dining room, with Amelia clucking behind him.

"Weed, I want to talk to you," Flint said.

Amelia protested. "Mr. Flint, I require civility here," she said.

Flint glared at her and at Weed, who dabbed his lips with a napkin. "Your man Crawford just lifted a paper from my newsgirl without paying. It may be only a dime, but it's also theft."

Weed smiled. "I'm afraid that's scarcely my jurisdiction, Mr. Flint. I happen to be a private businessman."

"Make it your business. The matter, small as it is, will be in the next issue."

Weed shrugged. "I'd like to return to my lunch now, if you will," he said. "Good afternoon."

Flint felt like a fool. He retreated, while Amelia followed with lips pursed.

"Really, Mr. Flint—"

"Deposit this in my account," he said, slapping his receipts into her hand before storming out. He knew he had offended his one ally in Oro Blanco.

He had a temper. On the street once again, he admitted it. The small things galled him more than the large ones. He could understand someone who stole a fortune; he couldn't understand a constable who stole a dime paper and harassed a desperately poor girl. Well, he'd write up the episode and make a fool of himself again next week.

All of his life he'd wrestled with passion against the ordinary vices and follies of the human race. And it had always gotten him into a jam. His father, the headmaster, had told him to grow up. He'd heard that refrain fifty times since. Mature people ignored such minor injustices—that's what the message had been. He wasn't going to back down. A man with a badge, capable of stealing a newspaper, just might be capable of mulcting larger sums from his victims.

Back in his shop, he began breaking down the pages, working furiously, his mind hot with indignation.

Some while later—he had lost track of time—the man himself materialized in his shop. Mason Weed entered, studied Flint's shop and editorial sanctum with his glistening, intelligent black eyes, and approached Flint, who refused to acknowledge the mining magnate's presence.

"I like integrity in public and private life," Weed announced without preamble. "I tell you what, Flint. I'll order a subscription for the city of Oro Blanco. They're always pressed for funds, you know. They shouldn't be lifting your newsgirl's papers any more than they should be grabbing a doughnut from a restaurant. Public officials must be trusted. It breeds a certain unrest if they aren't."

"All right," said Flint. "It's fifty cents a month by mail."

"Very good, Flint. Now you won't print that item about the marshal, will you? It wouldn't benefit anyone."

Flint stopped sorting type and met Weed's placid gaze. "I'll print it. The only way to stop abuse is to throw light on it."

"I was afraid of that, Flint," said Weed. "Cancel my subscription, then. I had entertained hopes you'd help the town to progress."

13

Juan de Cordoba purchased a good pick, maul, and spade from John Strong, the gringo hardware merchant. The padre was spending the last of the rent money.

These would hasten the digging of the well. His people had few tools, and often poor ones. Never comfortable on this side of town, he headed toward Avenida Virgen de Guadalupe, but was waylaid by Marshal Crawford and a new policeman, a short and wide ape wearing a steel badge on his pigeon chest.

"Hey, Padre," the officer called. "You ain't buying that stuff to dig that well, are you?"

De Cordoba nodded.

"Well, Mayor Malone says no. That's a public park and he don't want a well in it."

"The land belongs to the church. It is not the mayor's privilege to say no. What, may I ask, is the reason?"

"He didn't give a reason. He just said, 'Don't let 'em do it,' so I'm not. You start digging, and I'll corral that bunch and fine 'em."

"Your excellency, the little plaza before the church is a *paseo*, a place where all the people may walk. It is owned by the church. The people need the public well. The well is a thing of dearness to all the people, and the water will always be there for those who have the thirst."

"Look, de Cordoba, I've got my orders. I don't know whose land it is, but it's not the church's. You're all squatters over there. Not a deed. Not a survey. Nothing ever conveyed to nobody. There's no Escalante patent, that's what the court said. There's no legal description. The way the greasers do it, one league from the yellow rock, to the old juniper that died two centuries ago, and thence two leagues to the plaster saint—you know how they did it. It's all *stupido*, your greaser ways, savvy? That church don't own the land under it. It's all public land, and since it's in the city, Malone's word is law. So you just vamoose over there and keep your nose clean." The small ape was grinning.

De Cordoba turned polite. He could be so to a degree that was magnificent. "Forgive a poor priest, but I thought the court had said it needed more evidence, such as a fair copy of the grant from the City of Mexico. Does this poor servant of the Lord make the mistake?"

"Don't get smart, Cordoba. No digging. That's the law."

De Cordoba knew better than to pursue the matter. He genuflected out of ancient habit: When you passed or approached the altar, you genuflected. This altar was a *diablo*, and the padre feared he had committed a small idolatry, which he would list among his failings for that day. He made his way across the Avenida, back to his own kind, feeling remorse that he could not bang the skulls of those two hombres until they rang like bells. But he was an emissary of the Holy Church and could not indulge his own feelings, even when they boiled up and over the lip of his seething soul.

It was all so plain. On the gringo side of the Avenida they had run out of space. Only three blocks separated the Avenida from the mining claims, and all those thousands of them had squeezed into every last corner. For months they had cast covetous eyes upon the generous flats where the true village of Oro Blanco had nestled for a century. Now they were going to take it away. The prohibition against digging the well was a harassment, like everything else. Let a *campesino* or a *poblano* propose to do something, and the gringos would say no. There were more and more torments, such as the curfew. Crawford would permit no Mexicano over in the gringo side of the Avenida at night. A Mexicano could come and buy from the merchants by day and make himself invisible at all other times.

When the marshal had announced that to the padre half a year earlier, the padre had asked whether it was law, and whether such law was in accord with the Yankee Constitution. And Crawford said it was his own rule, and its purpose was public safety. A curious argument, the padre had thought, since the sleepy village witnessed no crime to speak of on his side of the Avenida.

There were more troubles too, such as confiscating the wages of the Gomez brothers, woodcutters who sold burro loads to the gringos for their insatiable stoves. That had happened after some gringo woodcutters arrived in town. Suddenly it seemed that Eduardo and Tio Gomez needed a permit from the marshal to sell wood, although no one had ever told them. It was one of Crawford's surprise rules. After that, the Gomez *hermanos* and their *esposas* starved.

But Crawford was one of the conquerors, and that explained everything. When the Yankees took over long ago, the padre—then a seminarian—decided he must learn their tongue, the better to serve his own people. And along with it, a lot of the principal documents and ideas of the conquerors, including their excellent Constitution, an admirable document, and a lot more. It had been a wise move to learn English.

He did not consider himself an excellent priest, though not a bad one either—a humdrum one, he had decided long ago. He had never been one of the fat, cruel clerics who expected starving peons to feed him. But neither had he turned the whole twenty dollars over to charity. He bought beans and flour and lard so he didn't need to depend so much on his parishioners— at least that's what he told himself. He bought stationery, a pen and good steel nibs, a bottle of ink, and some stamps, all of it pure luxury. And a notepad to write in too, all for the sake of vanity. He wished to write letters, write ideas in his notebook, write stories, write a daily journal. This was indeed an indulgence, especially when so many of his flock barely had enough to eat. But that's how he was, neither very bad nor very good. He would have to do better.

In fact, his latest brush with gringo officials had started a small brushfire of anger in his soul, maybe even a sinful one. He intended to give his people a well before they all got sick from the polluted water. Yes, maybe it was in the hearts of the *diablos* on the other side of the Avenida that if the greasers got sick and could not find good water, they would all leave like sheep, and the gringos would have all those buildings and Oro Blanco would have a place to grow.

They had their law on their side. Like most such villages in Mexico, the little adobes of the peons lay on land that had never been deeded to them by the *hacendados* and *grandées*. Generations of Escalantes had simply nurtured the village, doling out sites for homes, for the church, for the few small businesses, without ever transferring titles or surveying lots. Yet in Mexico these holdings would always be secure; the peons possessed their homes by a sort of social contract. No such rules as the ones the Anglos had invented were necessary. But that made everything on his side of the Avenida even more vulnerable— even his church, which stood on ground some Escalante had measured and staked generations ago. These Yankees could sweep it all away with their brooms.

He had his well diggers, after virtually threatening them with excommunication if they refused, and in the cool of this evening, after vespers, they would begin. Now he would have to tell them that it might cost them some time in the iron cage if they did. But not for long. The town marshal could not keep ten greasers in jail for digging a well in their plaza. If he tried, the wrath of the *gobernador* and others would fall upon him.

All his *obreros* showed up at the appointed hour, along with their wives, children, the town's stray dogs, and a few roosters. Some had tools, and the priest added the ones he had bought. They would work in two shifts, as there weren't enough tools, and later, when they sank the shaft a ways, there would not be room for all of them in it. The water table was not far below, about ten feet. They would cut a twenty-foot shaft deep into the aquifer and line it with dressed rock. The rock wall would rise three feet above the ground, so no one would fall in and no manure or debris would sour the well.

"We are going to dig now. The gringo marshal does not want us to, and anyone who is afraid of him can leave now." The padre waited, satisfied by the courage he saw. Indeed, a certain defiant pride filled their calm faces. He didn't know how calm those faces would be when the marshal and his ape showed up. "Soon we will have sweet water, and our *viejos* and others won't get sick from it."

The padre blessed them, and then swung the pick into the earth as a symbolic act. It was important to him that he share the danger and the labor with his hombres. When Crawford came, the padre intended to number himself among the diggers.

The work went swiftly, and no gringo came. Some chopped the hard caliche with the picks while others shoveled, and two hauled the extracted clay away in ancient wheelbarrows. They laughed and sweated and sang, and in very little time they had cut a ten-foot-diameter hole two feet deep. And still no official came. The priest feared that the gringos might sabotage his well, but there were always things to fear. One needed faith. He had never stopped believing that across the Avenida were many friends, some of them powerful—and not the least of them Amelia Lowell.

By dusk his workers had driven the well six feet down, never flagging, while the whole village watched and joked and made the work light with their cheer. They had already reached damp, soft clay, which made the work easier and faster. But at eight feet they would strike stone, if this well was like the ones the gringos had dug on the other side, and then it would be hard and slow. The wives of the hardest workers were the proudest of all, for their men had won honor that evening. But it was time to quit. They would start again in the morning and work until siesta.

"*Bueno, bueno amigos,* we will meet in the morning," the padre said. "Take your tools and get a good rest. We will soon have sweet water."

That's when Marshal Crawford arrived, along with another constable that the padre had never seen, this one thick, slouchy, and mean-eyed. The marshal created a pool of silence around him. Everywhere pretty señoritas stopped talking, *niños* stopped running, and old men stopped joking.

"De Cordoba, I told you, but you weren't listening. Fill it up," he said.

"We will have a well, your excellency."

"You heard me."

"It is not your land and not for you to say, your excellency." The padre smiled gently, but he did not bow this time.

Crawford didn't say a word. He studied the sweat-streaked hombres and then nodded to his partner. "All right, Bugs, we've got a load of greasers for the tank." He turned to the padre. "We're taking them in, and we're confiscating their picks and shovels. That's what you get for defying the law."

The padre nodded. "Very well then. You will take me also, because I dug it myself."

"All right, you come too. Sounds like a confession, don't it, Bugs?"

The padre turned to his hombres and told them in their own tongue what was to come. "We will soon be free, and we will have our well," he said. "This is necessary and a part of what we must go through to protect ourselves, our homes, and our rights. Don't be afraid, and rejoice before God."

Some of the men smiled; some looked frightened. All of them worried about the loss of their precious tools, the very tools that sustained life when used in their gardens. The padre could not help that, nor did he know how he could replace the tools. And he wasn't feeling as brave as he sounded when the constables drew their sidearms and herded his parishioners toward the Avenida, their wives weeping beside them.

14

The women came to Flint with tears on their cheeks. He couldn't fathom what had happened, but he knew trouble when he saw it. He stuffed a notepad into his old tweed coat and some pencils in his pocket and let himself be led through the streets, past humble adobe houses with strings of chiles, the color of dried blood, hanging from their doors and *vigas*.

They took him through the twilight to the plaza and the diggings, but no one was digging and the padre wasn't present. With his fluent Latin Flint grasped a little of what they were saying to him in anguished tones: The police had come and taken the men away, and Father de Cordoba too. But for what? It baffled him. And why did these poor creatures think he could do anything about it? They took him for a friend. Probably de Cordoba had said some things to them about the paper and its editor.

He let them lead him across Virgin Avenue to the little jailhouse at the edge of town, and there the women waited silently, fear and anger in their faces. The barred window shed orange light. The door was closed.

He gathered his courage and walked in, beholding a crowd of Mexicans in the cell, along with the padre; a pile of picks and shovels lay in a corner, and Crawford and a new officer were enjoying the spectacle.

"What's this, Marshal?" he asked. "Why are these men here?"

"None of your business, Flint. Vamoose."

"We're here because we dug the well," said the padre. "Our good mayor has made it illegal to dig wells, apparently. Or at least for greasers to dig wells."

Flint eyed the crowded pen. Ten work-weary brown men stood quietly behind the bars, their expressions ranging from anger to disdain to fear. "That so?" he asked. He turned to Crawford. "It's illegal to dig a well in Oro Blanco?"

"None of your business, Flint."

"It's the newspaper's business, Marshal. I report the news. What law is this? Was it ever published? Doesn't the Territory require that a law be published before it's enforced?"

"Beat it or I'll throw you out."

"It wasn't published, Mr. Flint," said the priest. "No one but the mayor and his cronies knew of it."

"But why?" Flint asked.

The padre shrugged. "You can guess. The plaza is the church's land. The marshal has no right—"

"Shut up. You, Flint, get out or I'll toss you out."

"When'll they be released? What's the charge?"

"I'll release them when I feel like it."

The priest said, "He's taking the shovels and picks. These men will have nothing for their gardens."

"Why're you taking their tools, Crawford?"

The marshal surged up from his chair and swung menacingly around the desk. "Git!" he said.

"Well, I'll report that you declined to say what the charges were and all the rest," Flint said.

"You're not gonna report anything. You're not going to put one word in print. If you do, I'll come in there and bust up your place so bad you'll never print another paper."

Flint smiled though his stomach churned. "It'll be the lead story, Marshal. If you won't give me the facts, I'll talk to Bulldog Malone. When's the trial?"

"Out!" The marshal bulled his way toward Flint and bowled into him with a powerful shoulder. Flint staggered back and tumbled through the door, which slammed shut behind him. The women gasped.

"I'm sorry, I can't help. I'm just an editor," he said to their uncomprehending faces. He knew what this was about: Make it hard enough on the greasers and they'd get discouraged and leave. He sighed. He'd print it all, no matter what the consequences.

He left the women to their vigil and walked down Virgin Avenue to The Stamp Mill Saloon, the fanciest dive in town. He headed past the ornate mahogany bar and backbar to the gambling room at the rear, where miners and sports crowded around the green-baize faro, roulette, and poker tables. Two crystal chandeliers with eight oil lamps on each cast dazzling light over the scene. Bulldog Malone occupied his usual cage on a platform. There he could overlook his dealers and tables and make change.

Flint knew the man only by sight. Mayor Malone dressed elegantly in a black cutaway, a crisp white shirt with fresh-starched collar and cuffs, and a headlight diamond in his paisley cravat. He eyed Flint with intelligent blue eyes that missed nothing.

"You the editor," he said.

"I'm on a story, Mayor. The marshal's holding ten Mexicans and the padre in his jug. The crime was digging a well on the plaza. What's that about?"

Bulldog Malone's eyebrows rose into innocent peaks. "I hadn't heard of it," he said.

"Look, Mayor, Crawford said you made an ordinance against

digging wells. You mind telling me when that was done and when it was published? And why?"

"Ordinance? I don't recollect it."

"Then why are some Mexicans in the lockup?"

"Beats me," Malone said. He grinned cheerfully, enjoying the badinage.

"Maybe for the sake of justice you'd better go tell the constable that he should free the prisoners. And return their tools to them."

"Flint, what he does is his business. I wouldn't want to interfere with the processes of justice. It'd be unethical, you know." Malone shuffled a stack of poker chips.

Malone sure had a way about him, Flint thought. "I'll quote you," he said.

Malone smiled. "You do that. Now if you'll excuse me—"

"No, I'm not done yet. The padre told me they're digging that well in the plaza because the creek's polluted by the mines, and his people, especially the old ones, are getting sick. Now, digging a well's a good idea, isn't it, to protect the health of people here?"

"Oh, Flint, I can't comment on that. I think it's all tied up with the lawsuits. I have to be impartial. Public official, you know. Maybe the greasers don't have a right to dig there. Maybe it's not their land."

Flint scribbled that. "They've had it for a century, Malone. The priest tells me that the plaza's really on church land, given to it by the Escalantes long ago."

"Oh, I'd never heard that, Flint. It's all so confused."

"Can you give me one good reason why they shouldn't be allowed to dig their well, Malone?"

"I think land should be left alone until the courts decide whose it is. Maybe the new owners won't want a well just there."

Flint scribbled that down too. "Well, do you want to have sick people here? Maybe an epidemic of something?"

"It wouldn't reach our side. We've good wells here. And

anyway, they never come here except to buy a few things. They can always get water somewhere else. Above the mines, for example."

"How about here, Malone?"

"Mr. Flint, our water is our own here. As mayor, I'd discourage them from dipping their rather unsavory buckets into our clean water."

Flint scribbled it down. "It's simple, isn't it? They haven't got any way to defend themselves. Make it bad enough and they'll quietly leave, and you and your town-lot company—oh, I've poked around the records, Malone; you own a large chunk of the town-lot company—can grab it. Just drive away these humble, helpless people with some sharp lawyers and a little rough stuff by your constables, and you'll have it all.

"Your town marshal's even confiscating the tools they use for their gardens. Know why? In lieu of a fine that your alleged justice of the peace, Pete Peters, will impose on them. And there isn't a thing they can do. I expect the exodus to start tomorrow. You'll push them out of there in a few weeks—long before all those lawsuits are settled." Flint paused. "Would the mayor wish to call this organized theft?"

Malone smiled. "How you do fantasize, Mr. Flint. That's really rather libelous, you know. We've a criminal libel statute here in Oro Blanco. I just enacted it. You defame public officials, you're subject to a thousand-dollar fine and up to five years in our little jail."

"Fine, I'll quote you. I don't think anyone ever heard of it."

"Oh, we have lots of statutes. You're new in town, so you wouldn't know them."

"One thing I know, Malone, is that they haven't been published in my paper."

Malone eyed him amiably. "Take my advice, Mr. Flint. We've a fine, booming town here. You can support the progress or fight it. We need a paper, but not one that resists the future.

Now then, I'll have my man escort you to the door—unless you wish to game a little." He nodded to a nearby gent.

Flint felt a powerful hand grip his shoulder with the weight of an anvil. He turned and stared into the eyes of a smiling ox of a man, bulging out of his cutaway suit. He felt himself being propelled through the saloon and into the night.

Flint stood stock-still in the darkness, letting his pulse return to normal. He'd gotten fired up again. He stared toward the little jail up the street, thinking that Crawford would supply neither water nor food for his prisoners that night. Maybe that would go into the story too. The women still stood there, defying the curfew and waiting for the release of their men.

He sighed, knowing the suicidal impulse that was building in him. Crawford meant business. He'd wreck everything Flint possessed, throw him into that pokey, and toss away the key. But that didn't intimidate Sam Flint. There were ways, and he'd practiced them before. The white light of truth was its own strength. That was why the unjust preferred the dark.

A man could write letters. He'd start with one to Baca, and another to the federal district judge, Januarius Campbell. There were decent men in the Territory, and he would find them.

15

Maureen Madigan wrestled with death all of her waking hours. Consumption had scoured her lungs and was now attacking her throat so that she could scarcely breathe and could not easily swallow. She lived in a red haze of pain.

She felt helpless. She could not stop the disease that was devouring her lungs, infecting her esophagus and throat until every breath and bite of food wrought searing anguish. She could not help Libby much, except to love the child and say yes or no with the adult judgment the girl had not yet acquired. But even that was reason enough to live. Libby needed a mother for a while more.

Actually, things had become a tiny bit better these past few days. Libby was selling lots of copies of the new paper, and not a few miners, who had noted her pinched face and shoeless feet, had handed her two bits and told her to keep the change. Libby had brought home almost five dollars, more money than they had seen in months. And with this sudden precious hoard, she had bought good food and some elixirs.

Maureen had been dying as much from starvation as from consumption, and her still-young body—she was thirty-six—

leaped as she slowly swallowed bits of meat, some cow's milk, lots of greens and squash, and porridge. It made Maureen almost giddy to be fed after so many weeks of hunger.

She had even felt herself rallying, but she couldn't get out of bed for more than a few minutes without gasping for the air her lungs no longer pumped into her bloodstream. Dr. Worth had wanted her to sit in the sun, get as much of it as she could stand, and suck in the clean, dry desert air. He wanted her to sip a tablespoon of whiskey every four hours and drink a tea laced with honey and vinegar, which seemed strange. Libby had gotten these things for her, and she was trying them though she had no faith in them.

Yesterday and today, with Libby's help, Maureen had managed to reach the chair at the front of the cottage and sit for a while. The food had helped, though Maureen knew it only delayed the inevitable. If only Libby could earn enough to feed them both, Maureen might live long enough to help Libby find safe harbor.

Oh, but dying was hard. She didn't wonder whether she could endure it—she had no choice. But she no longer mattered; only Libby mattered. All that was left of the Madigan family now rested in the one slip of a girl. If it weren't for Libby, Maureen would gladly have drifted away long ago.

She wasn't certain what lay beyond. Some moments she thought there would be utter nothingness, a true end, without a consciousness to know anything. But at other moments she thought maybe, just maybe, God would be there in some sunny upland of the universe, a high, sweet plateau where she would find everyone, her parents and grandparents, aunts and uncles, her dear Garth, suddenly taken from her in the mine, and her two dear boys, Christian and Patrick. Oh, to gather them together and love them all again in an eternity of springtime!

She had mostly gotten past her anger at being murdered by disease in the bloom of her womanhood. It was a waste of energy to fight it. She had escaped her bitterness too, from all the blows that had landed on her: disease, the loss of the boys, the trip to desert air soon followed by Garth's death, and then desperation and hunger. It just didn't do any good to weep or rage.

Still, she wanted to be a mother and a model for Libby, so even when she didn't feel cheerful, she spoke cheerfully, and when she didn't feel hopeful, she made a point of expressing hope, and when she hurt to the point of tears, she smiled and hid the raw pain that deprived her of peace. She wondered how much Libby really knew—and sensed that the girl knew a lot of it. Some things couldn't be hidden. The thought filled her with helplessness again.

A week ago, before Libby had begun selling papers, Maureen had given herself no more than sixty days of life. Now, with food in her, she decided she would live—had to live—six months, even if she survived only by sheer will. One hundred eighty days. Maybe long enough to usher Libby into womanhood.

When Libby returned to the little miner's cottage that afternoon, Maureen felt the need to plumb the future with her daughter. She watched Libby unload the sack of scrap wood she had collected at the mine and build a fire in the old cookstove for a meal. There was enough rolled oats for some good oatmeal gruel tonight, and Libby still had some dried apples.

"Libby, dear, are the spring wildflowers dying out now?" she asked, ending abruptly with a cough.

"They're gone, Mama."

"Then we can't count on anything from them anymore. Have you given some thought"—she felt her chest convulse, and she coughed up a terrible glob of blood into the rag she kept at hand—"to selling other things?"

Libby shook her head, looking as though she didn't want to think about that and appearing too weak and broken for such a young child. The food of the past few days hadn't done much to reduce the peaked, pinched look upon her face. She had some of Garth's red hair, though softened into strawberry, and a few of Garth's freckles too. Garth was Irish; Maureen was Scots; they both were Catholic, although now Maureen wrestled with it all. Her bright, green-eyed Celtic child was coppery gold, yet worn and sunken on the brink of womanhood.

"I have an idea, Libby. I think maybe Mr. Flint might need some help, just a wee bit of help. He doesn't have a printer's devil, but I'm sure he'd hire one if he could. It's a mad drudgery making a paper and unmaking it."

Libby turned from her supper chores. "Me, a printer's devil? But they're boys."

Maureen coughed terribly and wiped blood from her lips. "Libby, you know how to sew a good stitch, small and even. I've watched printers pluck type; it's not so different. You're smart too. I've taught you your three *R*s. I want you to go to him, dear, and if he says no, then ask if you could work an hour or two a day for free, just to learn. When he sees what you can do, why, Libby, he'll spare you something. Maybe you can earn enough for some shoes before it gets cold."

Libby smiled dreamily. "Shoes? Can I have shoes?"

Maureen smiled. Dreams were the things that wrought miracles. "Yes, you could earn some shoes. And you could earn a pretty dress."

"I don't want them," Libby said.

"But, Libby—"

"Mama, all I want is for you to get well. You're getting better. You're eating now. You'll get better, Mama, and we'll be happy."

Maureen closed her eyes at the pain of soul and body that shivered through her. She suddenly felt so weak she could barely talk. A dream of health and happiness was something she had surrendered long ago, faced with the slow death of her body. And yet . . . no. She would not hope if she could help it. Hope was cruel.

"Libby," she whispered, "please try, first thing in the morning. I have a good feeling about that young man. He'll do what he can."

"Well, I know what he'll say."

"You don't know!" Maureen said sharply and tumbled into hacking pain again. When she had recovered, she wiped her eyes. "The flowers are gone, Libby. What will you do when you're not selling papers?"

She shrugged. "Maybe there won't be a paper for long. The policemen don't like him, and they glare at me. I don't know if I want to sell papers."

Maureen closed her eyes against the weariness. She felt that familiar helplessness again, weak, without sovereignty over her body or her surroundings. *My Lord and my God,* she said. She couldn't pray much anymore, so filled with doubts and disbelief. But she could manage that as a sort of plea, a few words that brimmed with her thousand desperate needs.

Libby helped her sit up in her grimy pallet and handed her a spoon and a bowl of the oatmeal. Eating was an ordeal. She had to gulp food between her desperate breaths and feel it slide through her ravaged throat, down her ruined esophagus. Maureen ate very slowly, dreading the pain but rejoicing in the rare feeling of being filled.

She wondered about life: Why did some die easy deaths while others died dreadful ones? Why had her happy family, with no true wickedness in it and only a few venial sins, been demolished, while vicious men enjoyed everything life offered? Were her troubles the price she had to pay for the years of joy and rollicking fun and love spent freely? Let some priest answer that if he could!

She stared furtively at her daughter, who was spooning down her gruel. She loved the child's beauty and her brightness and her courage in the face of devastation. Maureen Madigan quietly wept in the twilight.

16

Even before Sam Flint had finished scraping off his stubble he heard a tapping on the door. Muttering at the early intrusion, he answered it and found Father de Cordoba standing in the golden morning sun. The sight startled him.

"I thought you were in the pokey."

"The *juzgado*, yes—the pokey. That is a word I have not heard, Mr. Flint. No, they let us out at *medianoche*—midnight. *Buenos dias.*"

"Well, come in. I'll be with you in a moment."

"*Perdoname.* I come too soon," the padre said. "I have much of the worry."

Flint finished his shave, put on a shirt, and pulled up his suspenders. He needed his morning dose of coffee, but that could wait. He found de Cordoba slumped in the cantina, looking sleepless and worn.

"Forgive me," the padre said.

"I was up; planning on going to Pete Peter's court. I was going to take it all down, names, charges, fines, the whole works. Unless they barred me from court, and if they did I would have a story too. Star chamber and all that."

"No, they let us go. It was a thing to scare the greasers." He used the word with just the right inflection of contempt. "I was watching them with the eyes. They did not write down a name or make a record. And they did not put the matter before the court, where there would be a record made, *que no?* Now they can deny the whole thing and point to the blank pages."

"Did they keep the tools?"

"Yes. My people have very few of the shovels left for their gardens. At least, *gracias a Diòs*, they have the hoes for the squash and beans. But next year . . ."

"Well, Crawford has a nasty little habit of keeping other people's property."

"Mr. Flint, I hope you do not write this story in your *periodico*. My people would only suffer, and you would have much trouble, I think."

"I'm going to write it."

The padre sighed. "That is why I come to see you now. We need you to speak for us, but if you make the other *yanquis*— what is it you say?—*inojoso,* angry, I think the gringos will chase you out of the town."

"If I don't make a stand now, it'll only get worse. I'll take the risk, Father. There's one thing you should know: People who work in darkness hate the light."

The padre shook his head. "That is why I have the worry. You have the ideals—*un idealista*—an idealist? Or, *quizas,* just stubborn, like the burro."

"Both. There's evil in the world. A paper's a weapon against it. If I wanted to get rich I'd be a politician. Now, are you going to dig that well?"

The padre sighed wearily. "I do not think I can get my people to dig the well again. My friend, they were badly frightened, and they have had the six shovels and the four picks taken from them, and the church lost the new pick and the shovel too. I can not make them do that. They will have to drink the bad water or bring it from above the mines."

"Maybe you could get some boys to bring it—all you need is drinking water, you know."

"I'll ask the *poblanos*. But it is not their way. . . ." He eyed the newsman. "There is talk of leaving. That is what the marshal wants—to chase out the greasers. Then there will be no church in Oro Blanco, and no Mexicano to benefit from the Escalante will, *por seguro*? Who will fight for it? Will I stay? *Ay de mi!* They would like to drive me away first, like the mad dog. Then the Escalante inheritance would mean *nada*. They have their ways, *mi amigo*."

"I'm afraid you're right."

But the padre grinned, baring ruined teeth, a grin almost macabre. "But a priest must never fear the death. I know all about *muerto*."

"It won't come to that, de Cordoba."

The priest didn't reply. He stood, his black eyes dancing with a knowledge of some secret future, and smiled. "Señor Flint, it is time for me to recite my breviary and take a little siesta. That is what greasers do, take the siesta, *que no*?"

"I wish you wouldn't talk like that."

The priest laughed hoarsely and let himself into the sunlight. "I would make a good gringo," he said through the door.

The priest left, but the gravity of his person lingered behind, filling Flint with a sense of portent. He headed gloomily for the cantina kitchen, ground some coffee beans, and lit a fire in the stove, though his mind was on larger things. He fried some *huevos rancheros* and added a dollop of refried beans and ate without paying much attention to what was on his plate.

There was always the temptation. It made business sense to shut up. The threats had been plain: Crawford's threat to bust up the equipment and confiscate the papers; Bulldog Malone's threats of phony lawsuits and fines, to enforce nonexistent laws that would have no standing in New Mexico Territory. Flint would do what he had to, and he'd be wily about it. The galleys for that piece would stay hidden until the last moment. The issue would be delivered to merchants' doorsteps at night and stuffed into the post-office chute at an odd hour. Let them tamper with the U.S. mails if they would. He laughed at himself: He was impossible, maybe solid bone from ear to ear, but that's how God made him, and that's how he would play out his life—an educated idiot.

He wasn't ready to write the whole story of the Escalante grant and the great land robbery, but he was ready to tell about an incident in the plaza of the old part of town and what it entrained. Later, when he had the larger story together, he would surprise them, come at them from a quarter they least expected.

He liked that sardonic priest who spoke to him as if he were one of the Anglos overrunning Oro Blanco. The man was as superstitious as all the rest of them, of course, prophesying his death. Flint wanted to plumb the man's mind. He really hadn't talked with de Cordoba about larger beliefs and insights, about what the padre thought of the gold, or the bustling town built without permission of the landowners, or what the padre thought about Yankee democracy, or what system of stewardship and authority the priest might prefer. Ah, these were things to mull with an old friend, maybe over a chessboard—but that would come.

Flint composed his story placidly, confining himself to the starkest facts and writing without passion. One by one the lines formed in his type stick, and one by one he moved the completed and justified lines to the galley tray. He resisted the itch to tell more than the story, to imply more, to speculate about motive. He could report news, or he could write an accusation. He stuck to the former. It came to only ten column-inches. When he had finished, he proofed the story and then carried the heavy galley tray into the kitchen of the cantina and slid it into the ornate oven. It would stay hidden there until the hour he printed the next paper. "Ah, Mrs. Escalante, I hope you are proud of me," he muttered to the silent walls. "I'm going to cook a dish in your oven."

He did not lack for things to do. He needed to order paper, which would come from Denver by mule train or ox team. He examined his ink barrel and decided to wait. His money had run out in spite of the success of his first issues. He needed to dun some advertisers. Most paid slowly. A few crafty merchants would delay as long as they could and with as many sleazy excuses as possible. That was a universal reality familiar to every editor in the West. Some would profess to have lost the invoice; some would claim not to have seen the ad in print. Others would deny ever ordering the ad, which is why Flint always wrote out an order form and asked the merchant to sign it.

He was just about to tackle the unpleasant world when a vision of strawberry gold slid timidly into his sanctum.

"Libby! Fancy seeing you on a Tuesday!" He noticed how nervous she seemed. "Is something wrong? Is your mother—is she in worse trouble?"

She shook her head. "Could I work for you?" she blurted.

He wasn't surprised and wished he could say yes. She and her mother were still desperate and couldn't live on a newsboy's—or newsgirl's—income. "Libby, I . . . I don't earn enough to keep myself afloat. I don't know how—"

"I'll work for free," she said fiercely. "Until I learn. Then you'll have more time to sell ads."

"I can't let you work for free, Libby. You need money. Maybe you could help in a restaurant."

"Mama said you'd help us. You'd let me learn, and when I was worth it, you'd pay me. That's how everyone starts, she said. With an apprenticeship."

He studied the barefoot, ragged girl, reading the eagerness and courage in her face. A few days of eating enough hadn't wiped away the emaciated look. "Libby," he began gently. "Being a printer's hard work. I couldn't apprentice you without paying something, which I don't have."

She looked so crestfallen that he winced.

"The spring flowers are gone," she said. "I need something to sell. Maybe I can find something." She turned.

"Libby, can you read and write and do figures?"

"Mama's a schoolteacher. What do you think?"

"Can you spell?"

"Try me, Mr. Flint."

"How about an hour or two a day for a big lunch? I keep a pot of beans on. Not very tasty, but they'll fill you up."

She grinned suddenly, and sunlight radiated from that strawberry-framed face. They had come to an agreement.

He wondered how to start her, and finally decided to give her the hardest, most tedious task. He still had a page that needed to be broken down. "All right," he said. "I'll have you return all these letters to the case boxes. The capital letters go into the upper case, the other letters into the lower case. Like this." He pulled a line of type free and began tossing the letters swiftly into the myriad little pockets, never missing or making an error, explaining as he went along for a few minutes. "And mind your *p*s and *q*s. They look alike. See this *q*? It goes over here, not with the *p*s."

She nodded solemnly.

"Do you think you can do this? You have to be totally accurate. Each letter has its own place. If you put them into the wrong bins, you'll cost me hours of trouble."

He read the dread and determination in her eyes and wondered if she could do it. Then he stepped aside and let her try. She was slow but she was careful to avoid errors, and he didn't have to correct her. He preferred that to speed.

"All right, Libby," he said. "It's eleven. You work until noon, and I'll dish up a plate of beans. All you can eat and some for your mother."

He should have expected the tears in her eyes.

17

Flint quietly collected news during the next days, usually setting the stories as he composed them in his mind. A big Murphy freight wagon, owned by the Gilluly brothers, had overturned on the Oro Blanco grade five miles below town, spilling an assortment of dry goods, tinned food, and casks of pickles.

Fire had consumed the Modern Livery Barn, frying six horses and a mule and burning seven wagons and buggies. It had been started by a dozing hostler who was smoking a cigarillo. The fire had barely been contained by a bucket brigade drawing creek water. Had there been a breeze, the whole Yank side of town, with its plank buildings, would have turned to ash. The episode reminded Flint to editorialize on behalf of fire-control measures: water barrels at every corner and a volunteer fire company. Fire was the plague of frontier towns, eventually consuming most of them. Without serious fire control, Oro Blanco was doomed.

He had a funeral to report as well. Rollin Wool, the dry-goods man, had died of a tumor on the brain, leaving his surviving son, Rollin Junior, to run the store. Sam Flint paid attention to deaths and funerals and wrote respectful obituaries. There were some in his profession who argued that the press belonged to the living and that deaths should be briefly noted. Flint wasn't of that school. An obituary, in his estimation, was a summing up of a valued human life. He had discovered over the years that even the most obscure people had lived lives filled with courage, struggle, and determination. No one was insignificant.

Flint interviewed the son, Rollin Junior, in his apartment above the store and discovered in the story of Rollin Wool a life of bravery and conviction. The man had grown up on a frontier Wisconsin farm and became a farm-implement dealer in Ripon, selling one- and two-bottom plows, harness, scythes, grain bins, dump rakes, harrowers, chicken wire, and feed grains. He had been an early abolitionist and a founder of the Republican party. When war came, he found the courage of his convictions and enlisted as a volunteer in the Union Army in spite of his middle-age. He had been breveted to lieutenant following a courageous maneuver at Vicksburg. He had lost his wife, Polly, to the summer complaint in 1857, and a married daughter to childbirth in 1860, yet he carried on with courage in making a better world.

Flint attended the funeral as well. The family had belonged to the Congregational Church, but Wool was buried by a Methodist circuit rider and laid to rest in the Oro Blanco cemetery below town, which had been parceled into plots, as if Heaven had been platted into picket-wire pens for the various denominations. They all would approve, over there on that Yank side of town. They would not approve his plan to give the deaths and funerals of the Mexicans the same loving and respectful attention. But it was his paper, and as long as he had the freedom to say what needed saying, their disapproval wouldn't trouble him.

Flint gave the Wool funeral eighteen column-inches and a front-page position. He knew it would make Rollin Junior an ally and advertiser, but that wasn't his purpose. Flint was as obtuse about business angles to newspapering as anyone alive. His purpose was to celebrate a life lived with grace and passion.

It hadn't taken long for his shy, quiet assistant to make herself valuable. Libby came long before her appointed hour and performed tasks she saw fit to do, such as sweeping out the grubby shop. He started her proofreading and found she knew all the common words but not some of the fancier ones he loved to slide into his stories. He always let his erudition show, in part because the English tongue offered such delicious choices, and in part because of vanity. He had a vocabulary that was probably ten times larger than that of the average man. He watched her consult his old Webster's over and over, something the usual printer's devil wouldn't think to do. The girl would educate herself.

He ached to pay her more, but he was running the shakiest of enterprises, and the order for more newsprint put him in the hole. Still, what little he offered was worth something. At least the two women would have food, and he sensed that it was the one thing that might prolong Maureen Madigan's life. Not that death would be unwelcome in her case. From what Flint knew of consumption, its final torments—the pain, the gasping for air, the lesions that migrated to other parts of the body—could yield only the worst sort of suffering. But no mortal ought to die of hunger. Not her, not anyone.

He had begun to assume responsibility for the mother and daughter, and the thought worried him. He might be producing his last paper if Crawford drove him out of town or ruined his equipment. Flint wished he didn't have that reality inhibiting him, tempting him to pull his punches, to produce a paper pleasing to the unjust potentates who ran Oro Blanco. The women would be the first casualty. When Libby began selling the next issue, they would take her papers and her money and treat her even more roughly. It made him wish he had landed in a burg free from the usual vices and corruption. But when had he ever found a place like that in the American West?

He wondered if Amelia Lowell might help—and doubted it. The woman loved to do good, as long as goodness involved public policy, public attitudes, distribution of taxes, public justice. But not once in his many talks with her had she shown much interest in the suffering of private persons. She had philanthropy but not charity, and even her own staff received barely a living wage. Still, hadn't she sent the basket of food to Libby one night? Maybe Amelia would come around.

There might be one other who would help the women, in spite of his own desperate circumstances: Father de Cordoba. Flint decided to talk to the padre when he could.

As publication day approached, Flint agonized about the danger to Libby. He had to prepare her, but he didn't know how. He finally simply told her while she cleaned the press with an oily rag.

"Libby, there's something you should know. This next issue's carrying a story that Marshal Crawford doesn't want published. It's about harassing the Mexicans when they tried to dig their well."

She eyed him solemnly. "Will he take my money and put me in jail again?"

"He might. But I think we can outwit him for a while. You'll sell a lot of papers before he catches on and comes after you. Maybe you can hide the money, or most of it."

"Will he tear up the papers again?"

"Who knows? I think he will. He's warned me not to publish this or I'd get hurt."

"Then why are you publishing it?" She eyed him sharply, as if he were alien.

"Because I have to. A paper helps the world just by throwing light on things—especially wrong things, injustices, cruelties. He's trying to harass the Mexicans. They need a well. There's no laws against wells, but he invented one just so he could scare them. He took their tools too, just the way he took our money. That was their real punishment. I think he'll do that again, and worse."

"What's he got against Mexicans?"

"I can't answer that, Libby. Most of the people on your side of town don't like them. The Mexicans speak a different tongue, look darker. People think they're lazy and dumb and don't want to learn about their ways. But it's more than that. The Mexicans really own the land under us all, and it's being stolen from them."

"Own the land?"

"It's a big story I'm working on. I need a lot more evidence before I publish, but I'll share what I know with you."

"Will they close you down?" He read the fear in her face and understood it. Would they shut off her and her mother's only hope of surviving?

"They might," he said.

She stared at the floor. "It'd kill Mama," she whispered. "Do you have to print this?"

There it was, the thing that tore him to pieces. "Libby, I have to print it. It's a duty; it's something larger than me. I'd hate myself if I didn't. Good, innocent people have been trampled on. I have to do it."

He didn't expect the response she gave him. She smiled. The sun from the window caught her strawberry hair, lit her pale flesh, sparkled in her eyes and seemed to limn her bright spirit. "I'm glad," she said. "You publish it. Mama and I'll get along. If it's right, you have to do it."

"Oh, Libby," he said, swallowing hard.

"I'm tough," she said.

"Tough enough to face that jail again?"

"Mr. Flint, for months I've kept Mama alive all by myself. Maybe I'm not grown-up yet, but I can work somewhere. Maybe I can do dishes or sew. Maybe I can cook in a restaurant. I can scrub clothes."

He marveled at her will and courage. "Libby, we're in this together," he said. "We'll just keep on as long as we both have breath in us. Now, how would you like to learn about printing the paper?"

"Teach me," she said bravely, her eyes alight with joy.

He extracted the galley tray containing the fateful story from its hiding place and carefully slid it into its hole on the front page, adding some lead to tighten it up. Then he turned the wing nuts of the chase, clamping the type into the form. She watched as he loaded paper onto the tympan, inked the type, and levered the platen. She gasped when she saw two printed pages emerge before her eyes. After a little, when she had absorbed the rhythm, she helped him, and the work went fast.

They ran two hundred fifty copies.

"We'll let the ink dry," he said. "I'll deliver some of these at dawn. Before the town is stirring, Libby, I'll meet you on the corner, and you'll sell all you can."

She cocked her head at him. "It's like giving a gift to those poor Mexicans," she said. "I like giving gifts."

18

Mountain Jack Treat looked for Libby Madigan, but she wasn't at her usual place on the corner. He wanted a paper. It was Wednesday, the day of publication, but the barefoot newsgirl wasn't selling them. He didn't like that.

He already knew what was in the paper. The word had filtered from the top hands to the hoist men to the muckers and powder men throughout the day, and by the time Treat came off shift at six in the evening, he knew that *The Nugget* had run a story about how the marshal had stopped the greasers from digging their well and had locked them up, and the priest too. The paper offered no explanation for this strange business.

Treat wanted a mug of beer—ten hours in the pit always sweated him dry—but that could wait a minute. He hiked across Virgin to the Mexican quarter, peered into the windows of the darkened Escalante building, and found no sign of the editor. Treat surmised that Crawford and his bullyboys had collected Flint and that poor girl and thrown them into the pokey again.

It wasn't right. He tried the door, found it open, found a stack of *The Nugget* on a counter, and took two copies, leaving two bits on top of the stack. Out in the street he read the issue carefully. The matter-of-fact story about the incident occupied the lower front page, beside some funeral coverage. Mountain Jack Treat could find nothing inflammatory about the story. If these were the facts, then there was no cause to harass Flint or that child.

The man sighed gently. It was a hard world. It had been a harder world in Cornwall, with the tin stanneries failing, and it had been a hard passage to the New World in the bilge of a four-master. A Cornishman might bring his skills to the mines of the West and earn a living wage. But he didn't earn much here and wished he could do better than three dollars a day, if only to feed his seven-foot-high, ax-handle-wide carcass. The bleddy lords here were merchant princes rather than titled aristocrats, but they all had the same notions about a man's toil. Something would have to be done. A working stiff was just a little better off than the slaves that the Yanks' war had freed.

He stalked to the little jailhouse, intending to have a wee peek, and pushed inside. Sure enough, there was the barefoot girl, her cheeks wet, and the editor, Flint, behind the bars.

"What do you want?" asked the marshal.

"Just wondering why you've got that pair in the bleddy sty," Treat said.

"Inciting insurrection. Now vamoose before I throw you in too."

"Insurrection, is it? I don't read insurrection here." He waved the papers at the marshal.

"Gimme those," the marshal said with iron in his voice.

"You don't happen to own them," Treat said.

"I'm taking them anyway, you big galoot, and then you're gonna get out of here and mind your own business."

"What's the charges? Maybe I can post bail."

"I told you to mind your own business. What's your name, Cousin Jack?"

"They call me Mountain Jack Treat."

"I'll remember the name. You were here the other night disturbing the peace, and I made the mistake of letting you go."

Treat turned to Flint. "What've they got you for, eh?"

"Reporting the news. She's in for selling newspapers. A pair of felonies in the marshal's book. You might let the town know, Treat."

"I'll do that. And Miss, if he doesn't get you out of here fast, the lads and I'll pull this little woodpile down and stuff it into the marshal's drawers."

"Please don't! Just tell my mother so she doesn't worry!" she cried. "She's sick."

"Ah, Miss Madigan, if this sidewinder doesn't let you out fast, I'll just do that, and more."

"All right," said Crawford in a deadly dulcet tone. The marshal's hand rested on the grip of the revolver sheathed at his side. His eyes didn't blink, and something in the voice told Treat that the marshal ached to be disobeyed. The Cornishman shrugged, his pulse rising, and retreated into the blistering light, the papers still in hand.

Outside in the clean air, Treat cooled himself down. He wanted to pound on the marshal just for the jolly sport of it. Instead, he hiked over to the Escalante building and bought himself another couple of papers to hand out. In a way he was enjoying this. He loved trouble and he loved justice, just as much as he hated lords and ladies, whether the American or English variety.

He headed for the Stamp Mill, his thirst building almost as powerfully as his itch to talk with the bleddy mayor, Bulldog Malone, back in the gambling room. Treat ordered four mugs and emptied three before getting down to business. Amazing how the Golconda sucked the juices out of a man. Sipping the third mug, he wished he could have good English ale instead of this bitter brew, half cat piss and half soap water. But the suds settled him down and brightened his outlook. He carried the last mug into the gaming parlor.

"Ah, Bulldog, what've they got the poor newsman and that wee child locked up for this time, eh?"

Bulldog Malone shrugged. "None of my business what Delbert Crawford does."

"Could it be that little story about locking up the Mexicans? I can't see the harm in it. Nothing but facts."

"Look, Treat, this new editor, he's a troublemaker, and as long as he is, Crawford's gonna teach him manners. He's a slow learner."

"And what of the girl, your lordship? She's got a dying ma to care for. Is he gonna let the lunger woman die, locking up a twelve-year-old child, eh?"

Malone shrugged and dug dirt from under his thumbnail.

Treat sipped. "The marshal's just harassing those greasers, Malone. Wants to get rid of 'em, that's what. Same with that editor and that girl. Seems to me if there's no law broken, he shouldn't be locking them up and taking the girl's dimes from her, or the picks and shovels and hoes from the greasers. It's a bleddy outrage."

Malone squinted at Treat. "You mind your own damned business, Cousin Jack. This is city business."

"It's monkey business, dearie. There's nothing wrong with the story in this here paper. But maybe it shines a little light where you high-and-mighty folks don't want any."

Malone grinned. "Let me buy you a mug, Treat. Damned if you're not soretoothed tonight."

"No, Malone, no more beer. I'm asking you, as a decent, fairminded Irishman, to go over there and get them out. Get that girl out so she can go take care of her ma."

Malone shrugged. "Look, Cousin Jack, it ain't proper for a mayor to mix up with the justice system. Those two, they'll get arraigned for whatever they done and go before Pete Peters and get themselves fined. That's how she be here."

Mountain Jack Treat pushed forward slowly over the bar, until his face was only inches from Malone's. "It ain't justice, dearie. I've got a little bit of say with the miners, you know? Little bit of say. And what I'm gonna say is, don't never come into the bleddy Stamp Mill again. And they'll do it. Nary a bleddy man from the pit'll come in, and nary another either. It ain't much we have, but we can take our custom elsewhere. I'll be taking it around. We're your best customers, dearie. You might say we're your only customers. And there's six hundred of us."

"That's illegal, Treat."

Treat laughed easily, his voice booming through the place. "Another bleddy law thunk up by our mayor. Now, Malone, you were appointed this first term, but you've got to stand for the office in November. I'll be telling the lads how it goes with you, eh?"

Bulldog Malone eyed the miner malevolently. "I'll get you, Treat. By God, you may be twelve feet high, but it's no match for a marshal and a warrant."

The evening was getting better and better. Treat grinned, fisted his mug, and wandered over to the tables, where plenty of the lads still sucked a few suds. It didn't take long to tell the whole story and pass out the papers. At Treat's signal, forty-three miners set down their mugs and walked out, with a few hoots and whistles at Malone. Treat watched them go, watched the tinhorns running the games at the back gape at the exodus, watched Malone's white flesh redden and his black eyes burn like the coals of hell.

"The lads won't be back, Malone—not until I give the word," he said and walked into the night. Outside, he corralled his brothers from the pits—work-worn men, some suffering from miner's lung, but men filled with a certain zest for life in spite of the hard toil they engaged in. "Tim, Mike, Sanders, all of ye. Spread the word. Mountain Jack Treat says no mining stiff spends a nickel in the Stamp Mill until Malone comes around."

"Watch your back, Treat," said Jacobowsky. "He'll have his Irish up, and they'll find ways to hurt ye bad."

"There's a lot of me to hurt," Treat said. "And a lot of me to fight 'em."

"Just the same, Treat, use some sense. Oro Blanco's not run by Malone, but by Weed and Twigg and them. They'll lock us out until we cave in."

"Are ye afraid, lad?"

"I'm a mining stiff, Treat. I've a daughter to care for."

"Aye, lad, we've got our kin to care for. Maybe we should try to care for some more, eh? Like that poor Madigan child? Was it so long ago that good Garth Madigan was mucking ore in the Goldbug up the road? Have ye forgotten how the rock caved his head in, leaving a widow with consumption and a wee girl, eh?"

"No, I haven't forgotten," Jacobowsky said. "But we could raise a charity for her."

"It might keep them in bread, lad, but it won't help that editor Flint any. If we want progress in this town, I think the stiffs'd better stand beside the man. He's trying to make things better."

Treat led them down to the jailhouse again, to begin a vigil. Maybe there would be blood spilled this night, but one way or another the stiffs would spring the prisoners. They didn't have to wait long. Bulldog Malone showed up, disappeared into the jailhouse, and then appeared in the lamplit doorframe.

"We're not releasing this pair until this mob goes home," he said.

"And then you will?"

"We might."

"Without charges? And without stealing Libby Madigan's cash? Every penny back, or we won't budge."

Malone ducked in, consulted, and reappeared. "All right. If that's how you want it, they'll rot in there, Treat. We're not letting them go as long as this mob's here. The law don't bend to mobs. You try messing around with us, and we'll show you who's in charge. We know how to deal with troublemakers. We're fining Flint every cent he's got, and that's that. We're confiscating

Flint's type in the morning, and the Madigan cabin too. And you're going to watch it happen."

"We'll stay, Malone. And ye'll not see a mining stiff in the Stamp Mill ever again."

Malone laughed. "We'll see about that. If you try a boycott, Weed'll lock you out. You knotheads can be replaced, and you first of all. Besides, whoever heard of a stiff that wouldn't take a drink? That boycott won't last a day. Now if you don't want to get hurt, vamoose."

No one moved.

19

Mountain Jack Treat watched his brother stiffs drift away after a few minutes. They had come off a ten-hour shift, tired and hungry, mad with thirst, and had other things on their minds. He didn't try to stop them.

"Just steer clear of the Stamp Mill until I give the word," he said, and they nodded. They would do that much. They were good lads, and there were plenty of saloons in Oro Blanco. At least the pressure on Bulldog Malone wouldn't stop.

He had a self-imposed obligation, and he hurried through the night to the Madigan cottage, which lay dark in its little hollow near the mines. He knocked, and a woman responded with a hacking cough. He opened the door.

"Forgive me, Maureen Madigan. It's Jack Treat here, a miner with the Golconda."

She coughed in the darkness and finally asked him in. "We have no candle," she said. "You've come about Libby. They've taken her again."

"That's right, ma'am. They've got her and the editor, Flint, in the calaboose again, and for nothing. There wasn't a thing in the paper that wasn't as true as a plumb bob."

She sighed. "That's the problem with *The Nugget*," she whispered. "I had such hopes. For Libby, not for me."

"Don't give up the hope, Maureen Madigan. Flint's a good man, and he's got more friends than he knows—lots of the stiffs in the pits. We'll see he gets a fair shake or no gold gets mined in this town. Not a lad'll walk into Bulldog's sporting palace until it's over. I passed the place comin' over and had me a peek. Three tinhorns, two barkeeps, Malone, and two serving girls, just twiddling their thumbs."

"It frightens me."

"I have no help for it, ma'am. But I'm a fair man in a brawl, and I'll see what I can do. I can knock heads, gouge eyes, and bite ears good as the best."

Her laugh turned to coughs. "You frighten me," she whispered.

"Now, ma'am, ye need to be fed. Have ye some food about?"

She sucked in air and then spoke. "I fed myself. Ever since Libby's brought a little food, I make myself get up."

"What did ye have, ma'am?"

"Some gruel."

Treat eyed the cold stove. "Ye didn't cook it, ma'am."

"No, but I put the rolled oats into water and added some salt. It doesn't take cooking." She coughed. "I can't talk anymore."

"All right, ma'am. I'll be making sure you're fed. I'll talk to the stiffs. Is there anything you need? Have ye wood for a fire?"

"No." She coughed. "Just get Libby out. She's not yet thirteen, you know. It seems so cruel."

"I'll get her out if the stiffs have to tear that jail down," he said.

She was breathing hard, so he said good-bye and slid out. Even a short talk drained her. "I'll bring ye some firewood," he said.

"Thank you. God keep you, Mr. Treat," she whispered hoarsely as he closed the door.

He didn't know where Libby found wood, but he knew he had a little, so he headed for his own cabin, plucked up an armload he'd bought from the greaser woodcutters for a few cents, and carried it to the Madigan place. He heaped it beside the door and simply shouted to her that it was there.

He headed into a bleak night, weary from his own toil and oppressed by the world's cruelty. When he reached his cabin, which was dug into the hillside and covered over with plank and canvas, he felt reluctant to go in. From where he stood he could look down over Oro Blanco. The lanterns of the saloons along Virgin Street glowed brightly, but beyond, in greaser town, a vast blackness reigned. Just below, where merchants, tradesmen, mine owners, and the city's captains had built their houses cheek by jowl, many lamps filled windows with yellow light. Farther away, the red lamps of the parlor houses shimmied in the wind. All the life and energy of Oro Blanco had gathered on one side of Virgin Street, the fruit of gold and all those who served its goddess. It was all progress. That's what people said. And most everyone wanted to drive away the greasers so that progressive white people could settle where the valley ran wide and the land lay flat.

The lamplight wasn't enough to dim the stars, and he studied them operating in their orbits by eternal laws. Little changed in the universe: it was orderly. Everything changed where man had a hand. Man was disorderly—and lawless. Treat thought that none violated the laws of God and nature more than kings and dukes and barons on one side of the Atlantic and ruthless princes of business on this side. He felt a weight lift from him as he drew strength from the serenity of the skies.

He was unflaggingly cheerful, and this melancholia had been rare. Tomorrow he'd pick up the cudgel again. Word of the boycott would filter into the night shift, and nary a lad would fill the saloon at four in the morning, which was the other busy time in Oro Blanco. He never understood the mysterious ways the word traveled among the lads, but it always did. Bulldog Malone would cry uncle when the second shift failed to walk through his bat-wing doors.

The next morning Mountain Jack Treat awakened itching for a good brawl. He was always happy when he could employ his seven-foot-tall body, his yard-long arms, his meathook hands, and his ax-wide shoulders in a free-for-all. Maybe he could arrange one. He washed up, using the white-enameled pitcher and washbasin on the dry sink. He dressed in his usual dirty union suit, britches, collarless shirt, and jumper and headed down to the Widow Penrose's place to buy a pasty for his lunch-pail. After downing a mug of tea and a bowl of beans at the Argonaut Cafe, he headed up the hill for the Golconda, passing the empty Stamp Mill en route. Its silence swelled his delight in the new day.

At six, with the mine whistle still ringing in his ears, he boarded the cage, dropped past native rock to the three-hundred-foot level, and stepped out into the dark vestibule along with the rest of the stiffs. He carried his lantern and two spare candles. His shift would run almost three candles. At the face he and the lads eyed the rock, looking for signs of a charge that hadn't blown, but they didn't see anything out of the ordinary. A mound of rubble lay before them, waiting to be broken up into manageable pieces and mucked into the one-ton ore cars that a blind mine mule would drag to the lift.

"Well, lads," he said. "It's all gold, but nary a piece of it do we own." He plucked up a piece of ore and found a thin thread of whitish-yellow native gold, alloyed with silver, wandering through a smoky quartz. "It's a dollar in my hand, and they own me for three dollars a day," he said, enjoying the morning ritual. He began to pull off his jumper; he'd work up a sweat fast, despite the damp chill of the hole.

But the shifter they called The Stork arrived.

"Treat, come with me. And bring your lunch pail," the foreman said.

That didn't sound good. A man called away from the face usually left his lunch pail. The Stork took him up in the lift and then to the superintendent's office suite, where two clerks in green eyeshades bent over ledgers like acolytes before an altar. The Stork nodded Treat into the lush office of Mason Weed, where the great man sat behind a beeswaxed oak desk.

Weed surveyed Treat coldly. "You're discharged," he said. "Troublemaker."

"Troublemaker, Cap'n?"

"Troublemaker. I don't need any of your sort around the Golconda."

"You mind telling me what trouble I made, Cap'n?"

"That's not the way to address me, Treat. It's insolent. You lack manners."

"Well, Cap, I lack manners then. But I asked ye a fair question."

"You're interfering with the due process of law, Treat."

"I'm what? You mind spelling 'er out, Cap'n?"

Weed looked impatient, as though he wanted to dismiss Treat out of hand. But he explained, in a slow, weary matter, as if talking to an idiot. "Treat, Marshal Crawford tells me you've collected a mob again and have threatened the process of justice."

Treat grinned. "Yup, I got the stiffs together, Cap. But it wasn't justice we were threatening. The marshal's got that little girl, orphaned by a cave-in, in his jail again for the awful crime of selling papers. The stiffs, we don't like that a bleddy bit."

"Treat, you have no say in it. You're causing trouble and endangering the progress we've made here. You're out, and I'm making sure you'll be blackballed at every other mine here."

"Well, Cap, if that's how you pay hard work—I shoveled more'n my share, maybe because I can fit two average stiffs into my pocket—and if that's how you pay a man for honest labor, who's done ye no harm, then I'm mighty proud."

"Out." Weed flicked a hand toward the frosted-glass door.

Treat stepped toward the desk instead, until he loomed like

an alp over the immaculately groomed magnate. "Cap, it won't do ye any good. The mayor won't see any trade until his rat terrier lets Flint and the Madigan girlie loose. And he's not gonna see a stiff in his dive until the girl's money's returned, her house's safe, and Flint's paper is safe." Treat grinned and bent over Weed like a cloud blotting out sun. "You can discharge every stiff in Oro Blanco, Cap'n, and it won't get you any progress."

"Get out before I call for a constable, Treat."

"Tell you what, Cap. The stiffs are gonna dig the greasers a well. If that padre says his people need a well, he's gonna get one. If you don't like it, call in the army, because your marshal and his scatterguns won't be enough."

Treat watched the cap's pupils dilate and shrink and felt the tycoon's fear radiating upward. Treat grinned, pulled back, and ambled out, whistling a ditty. His pulse had barely lifted. Too bad Weed hadn't punched him. Then it would have been more fun. It'd be a good piece of work to pull apart that flimsy jail with his bare hands.

20

Bulldog Malone, rarely an unhappy man, was unhappy now. For three days his trade had scarcely paid for the lamp oil. He lowered the price of a mug to a nickel and attracted a few stiffs, but he hadn't broken Mountain Jack Treat's boycott. His tinhorns were threatening to quit the green baize, along with the buxom serving girls and the mixologists. The few merchants and tradesmen who drifted in peered around the silent emporium nervously, bought a mug of pilsner, sipped it as though it were rat poison, and fled to cheerier precincts.

As any saloon man knew, a classy joint in a gold-mining town was a gold mine in itself. Every day, the Stamp Mill had catered to three or four hundred miners and a couple hundred more tradesmen, peddling so much pilsner and red-eye that the Irish dandy with the meaty face and pomaded black hair had become a local legend, exciting whispers about three mistresses, solid-gold spittoons, and wine cellars groaning with Beaujolais. But now he could walk through his brightly lit emporium and hear his own footsteps on the planks. No ivory ball rattled around the roulette wheels. He heard no clink of glasses or jingle of coins. All this was costing him and his concessionaire gamblers an incredible thousand dollars a day. The Stamp Mill had been grossing close to thirty thousand a month.

The urge to kill Mountain Jack Treat bloomed in him. Weed had fired and blackballed the man, but yesterday Treat had opened up a new saloon, The Miner's Home, right across Virgin Street on the wrong side of town. He'd taken over an old iron-works there, had some barrels of Albuquerque beer and a barrel of Kentucky whiskey shipped up from Silver City, and was already in business. Yesterday, Treat's first, The Home had done a land-office business, and at this very moment a Silver City outfit was unloading a dozen more fat barrels for Treat's plain saloon.

He guessed the miners had put up the cash. It took only a little rent and eighty dollars' worth of booze to start up a saloon. Malone himself had started with a tent, a bar consisting of a plank sitting on two barrels, a few tin cups, a cask of sour beer, and a couple of bottles of red-eye that usually scorched the tonsils of astonished pilgrims. Saloonkeeping beat digging in mines and required little capital. And now Treat threatened to wipe out Malone's business—from the wrong side of Virgin Avenue too.

Malone wanted to shut the man down, but that would make more trouble with the stiffs. If he had Crawford simply shoot Treat for some infraction, the miners would tie some hemp nooses. Malone hated to bargain, but he figured he'd better. And Mason Weed wanted him to. Weed had breathed such scorn on Malone, Crawford, and Pete Peters that Hizzoner the Mayor had slunk out of the mining magnate's office yesterday like a whipped dog.

Malone, full of grievances, bulled past the teamsters toting beer barrels into The Miner's Home and corraled Treat behind his plank bar.

"Look, Treat, we can talk. This place for sale? I'll buy it. If it ain't for sale, maybe I'll shut it down."

Mountain Jack Treat grinned and said nothing.

"All right, what's your price, Treat?"

"You let Flint and Libby Madigan out of jail, and the lads

might wander into your place. I can't force them, you know. They like it here. No tinhorns to gouge them. No serving wenches poking their fingers into purses."

Malone didn't mind letting the prisoners go. Crawford and his deputy constables, Billy and Bugsy Bowler, had rolled up a wagon and hauled away Flint's case boxes full of type. And Pete Peters had already executed a document confiscating the Madigan cottage in lieu of a fine. "All right, I'll arrange it, Treat. But they're leaving Oro Blanco."

Treat grinned again. "Sorry, Malone. The lads bleddy well won't set foot in your place, not until Flint gets his type back, not until that poor wee girl and her sick mother are left alone, and not until ye pay the child every cent ye took from her. This time ye destroyed about a hundred papers and took about seven dollars from her, of which she earned two cents out of each dime. Ye'll pay it all back, dearie, to the last bleddy cent. Ye'll put every last bleddy piece of type back into Flint's plant and leave the newsman alone. Ye'll not pick on them ever again. He'll print what's the news. If ye pick on him, ye'll not win the election next November. Neither will Crawford or that bleddy hangman Pete Peters. Ye bleddy well listen: I don't have all the lads, but most of 'em agree. So it's up to ye, sweetheart. Stop this bleddy scandal and make good the theft from the wee girl, or Oro Blanco won't be good to ye."

Malone seethed but saw no choice. "All right, Treat. It'll be done. But watch your back."

In a black humor, Malone trooped to the jailhouse to consult with Marshal Crawford. He didn't find Crawford, but he did find one of the new men, Bugsy, a pink pug from the East. "Let 'em out," he roared, "and tell the marshal to take that printing stuff back to Flint's place."

The pug grinned insolently. "I take me orders from the marshal, sor."

The unshaven, weary Flint and the unwashed, pale girl watched from behind the iron bars.

Bulldog Malone growled, snatched the surprised constable's stick, and whacked him on the side of the head and a few times on the shins. The man tumbled to the floor. "You have bad manners. Coppers should have sweet manners," he said calmly to the writhing pug. "Now, jocko, where's the girl's stash?"

"I don't know. The marshal, he spent it maybe."

Malone booted the pug. "Well, jocko, the marshal's cost me three thousand skins. I'm going bankrupt. He's got nothing but bone in his skull. He's cost me trade that I won't get back. Now give me the cash."

The pug constable clambered up, dug in a bottom drawer, and came up with nothing. "He spent it," the pug said.

"That wasn't smart. I've got seven hundred miners waiting to see that coin in the girl's hand. Fork it over."

"Who says I got any?"

"Jocko, you've been shaking down the madams and collecting the city licenses for a week. The girl had seven dollars; you fork over the skins or taste the stick again."

Bugsy Bowler didn't argue. He pulled a bag out of his britches, dug in it, and handed Bulldog Malone the boodle.

"And some for the first time, jocko."

The constable didn't argue. He handed up more bills.

"All right. Tell Crawford to lay off before he gets the whole joint in a uproar. Now gimme those keys," Malone said, pointing to a ring of them.

Moments later the mayor released Flint and the girl, who eyed him questioningly. "You're free. There's no charges. Here's the girl's cash. Flint, your stuff'll be brought back. Girlie, your mother's all right, and your cottage is your little castle. Now, the two of you go across Virgin to The Miner's Home Saloon—it's new as a day-old puppy—and tell a big galoot called Treat that you're free."

"Why?" Flint asked irritably.

"Because I told ya to, and because I'll drive ya there with the stick if ya don't, boyo."

"I'm going home," the girl said.

"Ye'll spare a minute and do as I say. Tell Treat you got your money back. Treat's the one taking care of your ma."

She puzzled that a moment. "Then I will thank him," she said quietly. She looked and acted thirty years old, Malone thought.

"Who's Treat?" Flint asked.

"Ye'll find out and bless the day his mither bore him," Malone said.

He watched the bewildered pair trudge across the broad avenue and kept on watching until they found Mountain Jack Treat's place and entered.

He turned to the constable. "Jocko, tell Delbert I want to see him. I'm gonna go talk to Mason Weed. Send him up there."

The pug nodded.

A half hour later Bulldog Malone found himself in Weed's cushy office, along with that fat toad Pete Peters and Delbert Crawford, looking sullen and throwing darts of rage in all directions. Mason Weed listened carefully, his attention full on Malone, with occasional glances at the marshal.

At last Weed sighed and gazed out the window at his mine, a posture familiar to Mayor Malone. It meant Weed was formulating his words carefully. He was like that. At last the entrepreneur turned to them.

"We've been reckless," he said. "Or rather"—he fixed Crawford with his relentless gaze—"you've been reckless. That's the polite word for it. Putting an orphan girl in your jail. And worse, stealing her purse. And clamping down on Flint for a perfectly accurate and unemotional story about the well. There's four thousand people in this town, and over six hundred are miners—here in the Golconda and the other mines and a few glory holes. They vote, and all three of you are up for election in November. They spend money, as Bulldog has just found out. They outnumber a town marshal with a pair of deputies—"

Crawford was about to growl, but Weed cut him off. "No,

Delbert, they're not sheep, and yes, they'll face shotguns if they must. Especially with this Treat leading them. Delbert, don't underestimate them. Not now, not ever. They could tear that little plank jailhouse of yours to bits, and you along with it."

Malone felt a violent heat radiating from Crawford and wondered if the man would go berserk and shoot the cut-glass chandelier.

"They may be brutes, but brutes shouldn't be enraged," Weed continued relentlessly. "They can walk out. We could fire them all, and it'd cost us a month of production before we got new crews in. I don't want that. No mine manager wants it, for the obvious reason that Baca's suit could go against us in the federal courts. The faster we get the gold aboveground, the less the suit means. My attorneys are filing delaying motions constantly. If Baca finally wins and the greasers take it all back, there won't be anything left in the pits—unless the miners walk out." He glared at the marshal. "If they walk out, I'll wring your delicate neck." Then he turned to Pete Peters. "And if they walk out because you've mulcted them, I'll wring your neck too."

Weed stared out at his mine, readying his next barrage. He turned to address them again. "You've got the subtlety of sledgehammers on anvils," he said. "From now on, you're going to use what few brains you possess, or you'll be in trouble with Twigg and me and the rest of the mine managers."

They could make or break the Stamp Mill, Malone knew.

Weed smiled suddenly. "The miners made good use of simple economics," he said. "A boycott. They decided not to spend a nickel in your gambling emporium. Three days, three thousand dollars. Even a gambling monopoly can't stand much of that."

"That's over, I hope," Malone said.

"Not until you return Flint's type," Weed reminded him. "And even then you won't get your patronage back, thanks to your pal the marshal there, with his lead-pipe solutions. Malone, if you're hurting, you can blame yourself and this gyppo cop outfit you've hired."

Malone glowered, without an answer coming to mind.

Weed smiled again. "As it happens, we can wield the same weapons. We're going to have our own newspaper, our own trumpet. I'll start one. We'll publish biweekly. We'll throw a few doubts on Flint's assertions. We'll line up the merchants for ads—another way of applying some pressure. And we'll drive Flint out of business in a few weeks. It'll be called *The Progress*. We're going to support progress, and we're going to win the custom of every business in town."

He turned to Crawford. "And you, my friend, are going to curb your wolfish ways. If you rile up the miners one more time, I'll make sure you're turned into a soprano. Let the girl alone. Let Flint alone. We have better ways."

Malone knew he was listening to authority. He hadn't felt like this since he had been an altar boy.

21

Sam Flint blinked at the sun as though he had never seen it before. After three days in that miserable pen, he stank; his face was stubbled. He wanted to wash himself and shave and become a man again. But he had promised to present himself to the stranger named Treat who presided over a new saloon that had miraculously appeared while Flint endured the jailhouse. So he and Libby walked wearily across the vast width of Virgin Avenue and crossed the bridge from one world to another, each brimming with unspoken questions.

Libby had seemed less embarrassed than he by their enforced intimacy, perhaps because of her sheer innocence. He had given her the wooden bunk and himself tried to sleep on the grimy plank floor. But her not knowing whether her mother was being cared for had been a nightmare for the girl. They both thought her mother would be dead, and it came as a surprise that a man named Treat had cared for her.

The discomfort, filth, and thin gruel twice a day had been vile, but not so grim as the utter helplessness that had engulfed Flint. One of the few comforts to a man in a jail is that he has rights, guaranteed by law and by public scrutiny of public servants. But Flint knew that in Crawford's case, the law meant nothing. Statutes were something to ignore. The town marshal did whatever he felt like doing, without reference to the books and with even less heed to the laws of God. Crawford was one of those masterless men who were, at bottom, worse than wolves.

The marshal and his deputies had tormented Flint and Libby. "You'll never see daylight again, suckers," they'd said. "You'll hang for sedition. You'll dangle for anything else old Pete Peters comes up with. It's over, you boneheads. You're dead. The girl's ma's croaked. Ya ought to join a parlor house, kid, pretty little tart like you."

After Treat's visit, no citizen had been allowed in the jailhouse. Flint supposed no one knew he and Libby were in the cell, nor did anyone care. He had never felt so helpless. For hours Libby sat on the bench, quietly mumbling her prayers, fashioning a way to live with dignity through the degradation. Libby had been the stronger, always believing things would turn out well. Just outside was clean air and sunshine. Hardship had tempered her steel. Never did she accuse him of getting her into this mess or ask him to print less than the truth in the future. If anything, she became proud of being associated with *The Nugget*. The paper's integrity gave meaning to her imprisonment, and with each hour that meaning deepened in her.

"Here's what I owe," she said once they had crossed the avenue. "They gave me seven dollars. I get a dollar forty."

"Take two dollars. You had some tips too. You've suffered. You need money for your ma. We'll just talk to Treat a moment and you go on home, make sure she's all right. Let me know if there's trouble."

"All right, two dollars," she said. "I guess I earned it."

He took the rest of the bills reluctantly, wanting to give the whole sum to her, but his own finances were desperate. "Well, I'll pay you more for your apprentice work. You'll be earning it soon."

She followed him through the door into a dark, roughly

furnished saloon, its bar built from planks and its tables and chairs cobbled together from rough-sawn lumber. Half a dozen miners hugged their mugs at the tables. A few more leaned into the bar, all of them pit-wearied men.

"Ah, they let you out, lass," said the giant behind the bar. "It's high time." He surveyed the two, his gaze resting on Libby's small money pouch. "Did they treat you proper?" he asked.

"Who are you?" Flint asked. He had seen this miner in town but knew nothing about him.

"Jack Treat. Lately employed by Mason Weed. I organized a little boycott of the mayor's emporium. Says I, 'Malone me friend, you'll be letting those two poor souls out, and you'll pay them back, and you'll be putting back everything you took from Flint's plant immediately. And until you do, nary a stiff in the pits'll enter this place or sample your wares.' " He laughed dryly. "Well, Mr. Flint, Bulldog Malone isn't a believing man, and it took 'im three days to decide that Mountain Jack—that's how I'm called—was telling the honest-to-God cast-iron truth."

"You got us out? I'm grateful—to you and all the miners. I didn't know I had friends."

"Were you mistreated? Beaten?"

Flint sighed, remembering. "Not physically. But words can pound the hope out of a man, Treat. They told me I'd hang. Told us Libby's mother had died. Shamed Libby's womanhood."

Treat growled. "I'll bleddy well strangle that Crawford," he said. "Lass, your pa, Garth Madigan, mucked ore in the Gold-bug, and it's said he was a proud man and good. We've made sure you ma doesn't lack anything. We'll be remembering Garth Madigan now, and we haven't forgotten ye."

Flint saw tears welling in Libby's eyes. These were the first. She had endured the arrest, the insults, the theft of her coins, the torments and mockery of those barbarians with fortitude. But finding love in a hard and uncaring world brought those tears, and she suddenly clung to Flint's arm.

Treat went on. "Himself, Mason Weed, fired me for being a troublemaker, but the lads decided we needed a wee friendly place and put me into this business, over two hundred of 'em, each giving a wee bit. Now, Flint, we're seven hundred in the pits, and we've laid down a few rules. We'll not enter Malone's place ever again if he harasses you, your press, or Miss Madigan here. We won't stand for it. We'll tear his jailhouse into planks, or we'll walk out of the pits if it happens again, and old Weed can discharge us all.

"Go wash up, man, and scrape the jail out of your skin and your soul. Ye've a friend among ordinary working men. And you, Miss, ye've a friend among all who've broken rock and shoveled and timbered, just like your pa. If ye lack a thing now, ye come to any man up from the pits, and tell him what the need is, and we'll see to it. That's a promise for as long as a stiff gets a pay envelope."

"Thank you," she whispered. "But I can earn my keep, if Mr. Flint'll have me."

"Of course I will, Libby," Flint said. "You go home now and keep your mother from worrying. She must be desperate for news. We've done what the mayor wanted. You're free. Come to work early in the morning. We've a lot to do to catch up."

She peered earnestly up at him, embraced him suddenly with her slim arms, and then fled into the bright, aching sunlight.

Mountain Jack Treat watched her vanish into the sun. "We've been a wee bit slow," he said to Flint. "Not seeing her when she was selling wildflowers before our eyes, not thinking when she was selling your paper. Few of us knew Garth Madigan. He mucked for that little mine that failed. But the stiffs"—he waved at the quiet men who were blotting up all of this—"and me, we'll keep her safe." He fixed Flint with a bold glare. "Did they molest the child?"

"No. She scarcely understands any of that. They threatened her a little, made some bad jokes, but it sailed past her. I would've strangled anyone who touched her."

"Those new constables, Flint, I'd swear they have a jailhouse sheen to them. Crawford's pugs have long records somewhere."

"They do. I heard enough while I was in there. They're just waiting for me to say it in print too."

Treat drew a mug, let the foam settle, and handed it to Flint. "On The Miner's Home," he said.

Flint drank it greedily, nodding his thanks.

"You'll be wanting to rest, lad. Be off now if you wish, and come by soon. We've some talking to do. I'm of a mind that a decent paper can help this little town. I don't expect you to be agreeing with me all the time, but I expect a man who's a man'll put out a paper that's a terror to evil."

"I just report all the news, Mr. Treat," Flint replied. "Including the news some people don't like to see in print."

"That's it exactly, lad. Just print all the news and forget the rhetoric."

"Sometimes I'm in a mood for rhetoric, Mr. Treat."

"Ah! Let me tell you, Flint, sometimes I'm in a mood for fists, meself. Ye've got rhetoric; I've got knuckles." The giant laughed, and the whole adobe building seemed to reverberate with his joy.

Flint thanked his new ally and trudged back to his plant. The press, the forms, the type cases, the cask of ink, and all the rest had vanished. Maybe they wouldn't be returned, in spite of Treat's assurances. *The Nugget* was probably dead, and Flint was certainly broke. If he ever did get his equipment back, he could probably publish unhindered for a while—until he riled someone else. He was a stubborn cuss, and if he ever saw his press again he'd do a lot of riling, starting with a detailed story about this affair. Let them respond to *that*, he thought. He smiled, knowing he was a glutton for punishment. Who but a punch-drunk newsman would be concocting inflammatory stories the hour he escaped the pokey?

He built a fire, started some water heating, and then flopped on his pallet. Odd how tired he was, though he had done nothing physically exhausting for days. A jail could weary the spirit. When the kettle of water was warm he scrubbed the jail out of himself, starting with his hair and then the rest of him. He sharpened his straightedge on a strop, lathered up, and scraped days of stubble from his cheeks. It felt good. One of the ways jailers made their prisoners feel bad within their hearts was to keep them filthy.

He would clean himself and clean the town. Mountain Jack Treat's support had heartened him. He had a few allies now; he was no longer a man alone. But the support of a few hundred miners didn't mean he was solvent or that the merchants wouldn't shut him down or that the officials wouldn't harass him one way or another. He knew he had not seen the last of Marshal Crawford's miserable little jail.

After he had dressed himself in his only change of clothes, he emerged into a twilight. The dome of Heaven, with the first bright stars poking through, offered uncanny delight. There was no iron bar between his eyes and the stars.

He wanted to talk to Amelia Lowell, but not tonight. He resisted going to the Madigan cottage too. In the morning he would learn how things stood. Tonight he needed to celebrate being a free man in a free nation. First, some dinner, then he would walk out upon the innocent wilds where there were no prisons and no men trying to steal a land grant—and where he might consult with God.

22

Flint stuffed his famished body with beef and potatoes at the Elite Beanery on Virgin, thinking meat had rarely tasted so succulent. Then he headed into the Mexican quarter, toward the path he knew would take him up the valley where he never had been.

The Mexican side of town was dark but alive in the soft summer twilight. They couldn't afford candles and lamps, but that didn't stop them from gathering in front of their jacals to talk and smoke and laugh in the sweetest hours of the day. Around him he heard the soft staccato of Spanish and the yip of dogs as he passed the forlorn well in the plaza and the adobe church and continued through cultivated flats devoted to squash and beans and chile plants.

He felt free, and his body responded eagerly as he stretched his legs. His spirit floated in front of him, racing away from iron bars and doors and men wearing the steel emblems of authority. He walked for ten minutes, past cattle and burros, goats and sheep, as the plots surrendered to grassy foothills. The ancient village of Oro Blanco still produced much of its own food and fiber, and its humble citizens lived contentedly, without the restless ambition that bored like a worm through the souls of their Yankee neighbors. Flint knew he was not one of them; he had his own ambitions and was not by any means a placid man. But tonight the venerable village ways were the medicine he needed.

A figure loomed ahead in the dusky purple light, and Flint overtook Father de Cordoba, who was ambling along in no hurry at all. The padre seemed preoccupied for a moment, and Flint supposed the man was reciting his breviary.

"Ah, it is you, Señor Flint," he said at last. "It is a good evening for a walk."

"I didn't mean to bother you, Padre."

"You do not bother me. I welcome the *visita*—the visit. The *camino* takes us up to forests a league ahead, but I do not walk much so far. Maybe tonight we will. Tell me, Señor Flint, about the three days and nights in the *carcel*—the jail."

"I didn't know anyone knew."

"Everyone knew. The gringos all knew."

"How did you know?"

"You were not in your shop. The girl was not at her corner. How could anyone not know?"

"I thought we were forgotten."

"*Nunca olvidado*—never forgotten. The man Treat and the miners got you out. You should have seen Bulldog Malone's saloon. It was as if the Four Horsemen of the Apocalypse had run through it." De Cordoba laughed gently.

"They let no one into the jailhouse. Libby—the girl—suffered, but she was braver than I. She said her prayers and waited."

"And you?"

"It was hard. Crawford and his pugs obey no rule, no law. We have a Constitution that gives us rights, but they ignored it. They never brought charges. They never arraigned me. They laughed when I asked for a trial. They even threatened me with hanging, and by then I believed them."

"Hanging? For what?"

"Sedition."

De Cordoba laughed, and soon Flint did too. "But tell me, Señor, how did you face death?"

"I didn't. I would have done anything, said anything, betrayed anything to avoid it. I am a coward when it comes to pain and death."

"Ah, I often say that of myself. What would I do, I ask, if I were asked to betray Christ or die? Would I go to the wall shouting *'Cristo el Rey'* the way brave men do? Ah, but you do not have religious war in the United States. In some provinces of Mexico, they shoot the priests and close the churches, and some men betray God and other men shout the name of the Christ before a bullet finds their hearts. Some men who shout the name of the Lord deserve to be shot, because they stole from the *peones*, the peasants, and robbed the women of their virtue all their lives. But some men who shout the name of Jesus are martyrs and saints. Tell me, Flint, what is it that gives men the courage to face death like that?"

"Belief, I guess."

"More than belief, Señor Flint. Some men see *la luz brillante*, and after that they are burning brands, risking *mucho y todo* to bring the light to others. *Una luz tan precioso.* Do you have such a light?"

Flint pondered that. They walked up a steep stretch and paused, winded, at the top.

"I have a vision of a better world, or perhaps I should call it an illumination, Padre. That's why I have a little newspaper—or did have. I have some ideals, but I don't know if they're worth dying for. One needs something grand to die for. I'm not inclined to throw away my life on public ills. I didn't want to die just because I published a piece about the well that I was forbidden to publish. That wasn't enough to die for."

The padre chuckled softly. "You will have to slow up, Señor

Flint. My legs are half as long as yours, and I have twice the age." He paused in the dusty trail, breathing hard. "No, the well was nothing to die for. But you might sacrifice yourself for something *mas grande*—much larger. But what?"

Flint enjoyed the padre's probing. "I fought in the Union Army and risked death plenty of times. Mr. Lincoln said it was for the sake of the Union. Later he got around to saying it was for emancipation, which I take to be justice. It never seemed right to keep part of us in bondage. But I didn't want to die for that, even though it was a flame burning in us. We thought God was on our side, and we sang a song called 'The Battle Hymn of the Republic.' "

The priest pondered that for a moment. "Tell me, Señor, did they harm the señorita? I have the worry over such a thing."

"They threatened her. But she's an innocent girl and the threats sailed by her. She was very brave. I figured if they touched her, I'd kill one with my bare hands before the rest killed me."

"Ah, you would sacrifice your life for the honor of a girl. That is real, Señor; justice and union and freedom from bondage are abstract *cosas*. Now you are close to what I, if I am brave, might die for. I might die for *Jesucristo*."

Flint sensed that the padre's conversation was leading somewhere. Discussing the things one might be willing to die for was not ordinary talk. They walked quietly a while, enjoying the gentle evening.

"The señora, Amelia Lowell, has told you about how things are," the padre said.

Flint nodded.

"It is in the courts of law. Certain *yanquis* wish to steal everything. Alonzo Baca defends the church and the greasers."

"I wish you wouldn't call yourselves that."

"Ah! I will make the apology. All my life I have known that de Cordoba has an unruly tongue. Now you know the story,

Señor Flint. The theft of the Escalante grant, the corrupt officials and judges. The heroic efforts of Alonzo Baca, who scrapes up *dinero* somewhere and keeps on. The señora says you are going to write about this in your *periodico*, and this will expose the crime and rescue us. Is it so?"

"Yes, but not right away. A story like this, Padre, has to be anchored down. Amelia Lowell is a great lady. Also very opinionated."

The padre chuckled softly.

"I am checking everything. I need to talk to the attorney, Baca. See the court records. And I need to talk to you too."

"I am always ready to talk."

"All right. If I have questions, I'll come to you."

"I have many documents in the—*como se dice* house of the priest?"

"Rectory. I'd like to see them. You'll have to translate for me."

"The court documents are the *inglés*."

"Then expect me soon. When I have all the facts together, I'll do the story."

"Ah, Señor Flint. A moment ago, I make the question about what you would die for. Now I make it again. *Entende?*"

"It won't come to that, Padre. Weed and his plotters would only destroy themselves. Any attempt to harm me would come after I publish the exposé and point straight at them, so it would do them no good, destroy them."

"Ah, you think so, *sí*? When you have the officials and the courts, it does not matter how the finger points. They will want to make an example, and you will be the example."

Flint wanted to object but held his peace. It all seemed unreal to him. Truthful publishing always involved a certain risk, and in his day he'd encountered angry or demented people, but never a conspiracy to murder him.

"There is much at stake, Señor. A fortune in gold and land. A few Mexicanos and a country padre are in the way of progress.

So I make the question, What you are willing to die for? It is what you must think about before it is too late."

"It won't go that far." Flint eyed the little priest. "What if I don't publish that story? What if Weed and his cohorts take everything away from you and your church and the Mexicans who've been here for generations?"

"Then we will move away," the priest replied.

"That's not right."

"Have you a better way for us, Editor Flint?"

"Have you tried a compromise? What would happen if you offered to deed the mine properties to Weed and his colleagues? Yes, you'd lose the gold, but you'd save the Escalante grant. That might end the struggle in the courts. You know how long a mine lasts? Maybe a decade. Someday, perhaps in your lifetime, this'll be a dead town. We gringos'll all go away and the Escalante grant will be yours again, for the parish, for all your people down there."

"It is a temptation. But the church cannot condone theft. Shall Holy Mother Church be a party to stealing an estate that has been given to God? And if we compromise and give the thieves what they took, will the North Americans stop pressing for the rest—rich lands for the grazing, forests full of the timber, and maybe more of the gold? Now I must tell you about the Latin soul, Señor Flint. *No hay compromiso.* We do not compromise. *Aquel abogado*, the attorney Baca will not. I will not. It is not even possible. We are born with the fire in our souls. It is *todo o nada*—all or nothing, to the very death."

"Does Weed know that?"

Flint sensed more than saw the padre's smile. "You *norteamericanos* are beginning to understand us. We are quiet, we are simple, we are like the sheep, we are sleepy—and we are lions who will shed blood. That is why, Señor Flint, they will soon decide to kill Baca and then me."

The padre indicated that he wanted to turn back. Flint

paused, enjoying the velvet air, the last blue of the setting sun, the first stars, the occasional scent of piñon pine drifting down from the high country. The padre lumbered ahead a while and then let Flint catch up.

"There are no bars of the jail here, Señor Flint," he said. "I walk here in the evenings after vespers. A free land frees the spirit. A good companion is always welcome."

"I'll join you," Flint said.

23

Mason Weed surveyed the two gents who stood before his desk. The older one peered at Weed from watery blue eyes set in a ruined red face. The man had seen the cork end of many a bottle. The younger one looked like a stupid ferret. The pair had arrived that afternoon in Oro Blanco as the result of a swift, hard search for some journeymen printers and newspaper editors.

Weed had already purchased a plant, sight unseen, from a Denver broker he trusted, telling the man simply to supply everything he might need and send it by the fastest freight. Finding an editor who could be trusted proved a more difficult matter. Weed would own *The Oro Blanco Progress* and employ this pair on salary. The ownership, however, would remain secret. For public purposes, the new rag would be owned and managed by Phineas Clegg, the elder of this motley pair.

He surveyed Clegg again. He thought Clegg might last until his first stemwinding drunk—before wandering off, never to be seen in those precincts again. Meanwhile, Weed would keep on looking for an editor.

"Mr. Clegg," he said genially. "And you, sir? I didn't catch the name."

"I'm Printer's Devil."

"I understand that, but what's your name?"

"Printer's Devil. I done lost my other name a few years ago, and have no call for it. Just call me Print. Or Devil. Either one fits. I can sling type faster'n a cook can flip flapjacks. I've been known to set a headline and slide it into the form without even stopping the press."

"Print's exaggerating," Clegg said. "It's an offense to my olfactory senses. My dear Mr. Weed, Esquire, we're your faithful servants, men without colic or animadversion. My weekly stipend, sir, should be commensurate with my skills as a veteran captain of the fonts, the purveyor of the news, a knight and champion of the most illustrious interests, and a connoisseur of the English tongue. Put a font of Caslon in my fingers, sir, and you will be treated to music, to poetry, to wisdom, to colloquy, why, even to sage opinion, argued on the Socratic method, by means of inquiries, from the particular to the general or, if you prefer, from the general to the particular. I can argue backward or forward, as the case may be."

Weed eyed the bounder amiably. The man would do. He was obviously semi-educated and probably capable of writing any story Weed put to him without a quiver of rebellion or scruple. And if the man wasn't too far gone in booze, his vice would be useful—an amiable way to control the puppet strings.

"All right then, Clegg and, ah, Devil, we are going to try this out. You'll produce a biweekly rag, on Tuesdays and Fridays. We are going to charge a nickel, the opposition charges a dime. We are going to be for progress in every way, shape, and form. We will have industrial progress here, we will settle land disputes progressively, we will foster a progressive population."

"Ah, sah, how shall we make a profit at a nickel? You've two stipends to pay, and if it's twice a week we'd better have some flunkeys," Clegg said.

"Well, hire a flunkey or two," Weed said. "Don't worry about profit. I have other objectives."

"You don't say. Other objectives." Illumination filled Clegg's varicose face. "And what, sah, about the mother's milk of newspaper enterprise—the advertising? Have you a manager or a salesman? How will we snatch away the lifeblood from our non-progressive opposition?"

Weed was beginning to like the man. Clegg obviously knew what Weed wanted. "Don't worry about that. When I tell the merchants to jump, Clegg, they leap and dance. I'm going to pay my miners in company scrip, and it is absolutely elegant what scrip can do to bring a mining town to heel. Now, the miners may object a while, and you're to deal with that. And with a lot of things you'll learn about."

"A capital idea, sah. Scrip. Ah, it happens that editors and newspaper factotums and even devils are customarily reimbursed in the coin of the realm, however. Or folding money, whichever is more convenient. If you wish to purchase our everlasting loyalty, if you wish us to become knights-errant on your behalf, pursuing your Holy Grail like a true pair of Lancelots, then I suspect you'll need to pay us in greenbacks or specie, namely coin of the realm."

Clegg stood cheerfully, rolling the rim of his battered stovepipe hat through his hands. Weed didn't mind. Whatever it took to purchase these dunces, he would do.

"Very well, greenbacks. As a concession, of course. In return, you will study my position here as the principal force for progress in Oro Blanco, and you'll know my views and needs better than the back of your inky hands, and you'll proceed along certain lines without foot-dragging. Do that, Clegg, and you'll have seven dollars a week, three and a half for Devil there, plus bunks at the rear of the shop."

Clegg beamed. "We've struck a bargain. Yes, sah, this is a true Mayflower Compact, a Magna Carta, and a Baptist river baptism featuring total immersion, all in one, to commit us to the side of Divine Purpose. Now, sah, that done, how shall we proceed? I would suggest a small advance against future toil."

Perhaps he had gotten the right man, after all. It hadn't been easy. He had sent out feelers, made cautious inquiries. These vagabonds had last slung type in a Kansas railhead town on behalf of certain interests. They weren't exactly out of James Gordon Bennett's school, or Horace Greeley's either. It would never do to discover too strong a spirit of independence. He needed broke horses, not mustangs.

"That'll be arranged in a moment. Now, gents, on to the practical. I've leased the back of the Pepperdine Building. You'll have your own entrance on Weed Street, which the founders kindly named after me. Now, I've purchased a complete plant from Denver. It's set up and ready. If it lacks anything, anything at all, let me know and I'll take it out of the broker's hide. I haven't paid him in full. Examine the press, a new Hoe. Report to me in detail. Are there questions about that aspect?"

"New equipment, you say?" Phineas Clegg looked astonished. "A press that doesn't require love taps from sledgehammers? A modern engine of progress?"

"Brand new. I don't want breakdowns. You're going to rescue Oro Blanco from the troubles that plague it."

"A mighty mission, sah. Now how about a fiver for me and a deuce for the Devil?"

"You're about parched out, aren't you, Clegg? I can see it. A regular drought. Well, you'll have your advance in an hour. For now, pay attention. I'm going to describe the situation here. It's delicate. I could choose rougher means than print to wage my battles, but I choose not to."

"I understand, sah, but I listen better with a mug in hand."

"You'll listen without a mug," Weed replied, an edge to his voice. He wanted this pair to grasp the importance of all this. "If you follow my instructions, write carefully, and use your sotted brains, there'll be big bonuses coming along every little while."

"Bonuses, sah?"

"We shall establish bonuses, in the range of a hundred dollars for you and fifty for Mr. Devil, as certain objectives are met."

"A century note, sah? In company scrip?"

"No, in gold coin. It won't be easy. You'll earn every penny. The whole thing could blow up in your faces. If you rile up the miners and they walk out on me, you'll be on the next wagon out of town without a penny in your britches."

"Exactly, sah. A hundred, you say. You've whetted our appetites. When it comes to greenery, to pocket change, to capital, sah, I am a true apostle, and Devil here is a true disciple."

Weed surveyed the younger man. "Why did you abandon your proper name?"

"Ah, well, it was a common one."

"Or perhaps a wanted one."

"Well, I wouldn't go that far. Just a friendly saloon fracas was all."

"Until you pulled out the Arkansas toothpick."

Devil looked startled.

"I know all about you both," Weed said. "Remember it." Weed enjoyed the moment. If you were going to employ certain specimens of homo sapiens, it paid to get a report from Allan Pinkerton.

For the rest of the afternoon, Mason Weed described the precarious circumstances of Oro Blanco's mines and the town lots themselves. He explained the Escalante grant and where the matter lay in the courts, and the persistence of Baca, who seemed to have a mysterious source of funds. He described the appointed city officers and the forthcoming November election which could remove them unless a newspaper championed them. He described the delicate labor situation; the miners were just now finding their muscle. They needed to be divided and conquered. He described the efforts to drive away the greasers, which would permit the town to expand across Virgin Avenue and which might even undermine Attorney Baca's legal efforts.

And finally he dwelled on the largest menace of all, the recent appearance of *The Nugget*, edited by a man of firm conviction and education who was not in any circumstances to be taken lightly. Flint was on the wrong side, and it would be Clegg's duty to undermine Flint's credibility in every way possible, using every wile from ridicule to stories that contradicted everything Flint said.

"Ah, sah, I am a novelist at heart, and invention is the soul of literature," Clegg said cheerfully.

Weed nodded curtly.

"You'll obtain bonuses when you succeed in driving out the greasers, when you destroy de Cordoba's reputation, when you whip Flint, when it becomes clear that you have won the miners to your views, and when you've demolished Baca's case. You'll earn even more if the suit is thrown out of court."

"Why, sah, you are talking five hundred dollars," said Clegg. "For that we'll do anything."

24

When Sam Flint returned to his shop after the walk, he found his case boxes inside. Crawford and his pugs had returned them. Flint discovered his type in some flour sacks. It would take a day to sort it out and return it to the case boxes. The standing advertisements had all been demolished, and he would have to build each one anew. Some of the newsprint had been damaged, reducing his stock to dangerous levels, since his resupply had yet to arrive.

He surveyed the mess, knowing he would be lucky to produce any sort of edition by next Wednesday. But he would try. It might be just two pages, a single sheet printed on both sides, but it would be something. It would tell Oro Blanco that he was not beaten. And it would include a story about his jailing.

He was tempted to quit that evening; he had spent much of the day in jail wrestling with his own doom, and he wanted only to crawl into his own blessed bed and pull down the shades of forgetfulness. He was tired and angry. But he didn't give up. Instead, he lit a kerosene lamp, poured the scrambled type onto a counter where he could see it, and began to drop letters into their pockets in the case boxes. The labor was so automatic that he let his mind roam elsewhere, especially what he would say and how he would say it in the next issue.

He judged it was well after midnight when his hands and mind failed him. He had made a sizable dent in the pied type. Tomorrow, Saturday, he would have Libby sort the rest while he rebuilt the ads, using previous issues as his models. On the Sabbath he would set some stories, do the billing, and continue to rebuild the ads. Monday he would get what news he could. Tuesday evening he would print what little he had.

Melancholy beset him. What weapons did a newspaper editor have? Only truth and the printed word, and truth wasn't much of a weapon against thugs operating under the color of law and capable of locking him up, stealing his equipment, and intimidating his female employee. But just before he slipped off into deep sleep, he recognized that he was not alone in Oro Blanco. He had Mountain Jack Treat and his miners, and he had the intelligence and courage of Father de Cordoba. And he had other friends, too, such as Amelia Lowell.

Libby appeared early the next morning and proved to be a valuable help. She began sorting type and gained speed by the hour, her nimble fingers dropping letters into case boxes with unerring accuracy. He worked beside her, reconstructing the ads as fast as she restored the fonts.

"How did your mother endure, Libby?" he asked.

"The same, I guess. That big man helped her. All she needs is good food and sunshine each day."

"Was she upset?"

"Not for herself, for me. It was hard for her, with no word from me."

"Libby, what does she think about the paper? About me? Does she approve? Is this a job she approves of?"

"She just says for me to stick with you, that you're an honorable man, Mr. Flint. We've had food ever since you found me. Before, we just starved."

"But she knows I'm likely to create more trouble, Libby.

Surely you told her about Crawford's attempt to take the cabin from you."

"I told her. She just thought about it for a long time. Then she said, 'Libby, Flint's fighting for humble people. No one can hurt either of us much more, even if they take away our cabin. There's things worth doing, and fighting evil's one of them.' Then she made me promise to stick with you. She told me she would die soon. She said you'd look after me. And she said Mountain Jack Treat might help too—but to stick with you. I don't want my mama to die, Mr. Flint. You know what's keeping her alive? I mean, inside of herself? It's this paper. My ma's a scrappy woman. She'll hang on as long as there's a good fight and someone to root for. You've got to fight. If you quit fighting, she'll go. It's like she's got her life riding on you now."

Flint privately wondered why Maureen felt that way. It was more burden than he wanted.

They toiled past the nooning, and then Mountain Jack Treat barged in. "Got a story for you, Mr. Flint," he boomed. "Get your notepad and pencil and follow along."

Flint noticed a dozen or so stiffs from the mines outside, all of them with picks, pikes, shovels, and buckets. He had an inkling what this was about and turned the work over to Libby. Plainly he was going to get into the middle of trouble again, but he had a penchant for that. He doffed his smock, scrubbed up, and headed for the plaza, along with the miners.

"I had a time rounding up a bunch," Treat said. "Most of the stiffs want no truck with the greasers. But I collared this bunch and I told them, I sez, they're just folks like us and they need clean water. The town marshal stole all their tools, so it's up to us. We'll just go sink that well and line it, and if the constables complain, we'll just tear down that jailhouse until it's a mess of planks."

"Does anyone know? Like Bulldog Malone?"

"Not yet." Treat grinned. "I'm hoping they find out soon, though. I hate suspense."

They tromped into the quiet plaza, while the Mexicans watched with guarded expressions. They studied the pit, which was sunk several feet into caliche, and set to work. Some dropped down to the bottom, others rigged buckets on ropes. Every Mexican vanished; the plaza baked in the sun, foreboding and silent.

"All right, we'll go for water," Treat said. "We'll cut down faster'n a doublejacking contest."

"You gonna write this story up? You want my name?" said one.

"Yes, in fact I do."

"Well, I'm a bleddy Cornishman, and the name's Polgarth. Ed Polgarth, spell it the way she sounds."

"Why are you here?" Flint asked.

"Oh, just to raise hob."

"Not to help the Mexicans?"

"Well, I guess. I just hope the constables come around. I'd like an excuse to tear something apart."

The others laughed.

They didn't talk much, but equipped with good tools, they made swift progress. Four in the pit hacked loose the caliche and shoveled it into buckets; six above pulled up the loads. Several others patiently trundled wheelbarrows to the waste piles of the Golconda and brought back rock for the lining. Two men dressed the rock.

Flint watched patiently. The Mexicans, still smarting from their time in Crawford's jail, watched wearily from shadowed alleys and windows, ready to flee. But Treat's men hacked steadily downward, loosening the hardpan with pikes and picks, while working up great sweats and pausing only to suck water from a pail. Once in a while they exchanged jobs, as if one kind of toil was a respite from another. Flint found himself watching the alleys and streets leading to Virgin Avenue, from whence the minions of the law would come.

In time he had most of their names and a good bit of their philosophy besides. None of them would profess to being charitable, or to liking the greasers, or to following any dictates of conscience. But Flint did discover brotherhood. The greasers needed clean water; they were just like anyone else. Water was something anyone should have.

Flint was torn. He needed desperately to go back to the shop and rebuild the paper. He didn't have time to watch the sinking of a well. The miners had pierced to seven or eight feet, and the color of the caliche had grown significantly darker as they approached the water table. They had struck some moisture. It wouldn't be hard now.

"Treat," he said, "I'll come back at dusk and see what you've done. I've got a newspaper to put together. It's a mess."

Treat paused, sweat rivering from his brow. "We should have the hole dug by then," he said. "But lining it with dressed rock'll take a few days."

"You'll see it all in *The Nugget*," Flint said. "It'll be a mighty fine story." He turned to leave and discovered three lawmen striding toward the well, with Crawford in the lead. Flint decided to stay.

The lawman walked straight for the well, stood on its lip studying the operation, surveyed Flint sourly, and motioned his pugs to spread out a little.

"Treat, get your stiffs outa there. That's an order."

"Can't hear ya, Crawford," Treat said. At his nod, the miners continued to jab loose chunks of moist clay. Flint noticed that they were getting into shale now, and the digging would soon slow down.

For once, Crawford looked uncertain. He reddened, his hands twitching and then deflating, as if remembering word from on high, while the two pugs, sporting revolvers, sticks, and steel badges on their shirts, waited impatiently.

"The mayor don't want you digging a well, Treat. And that's the law speaking."

"Well, we thought to help the greasers, long as you stole all their tools, Marshal." Treat was grinning. His eyes had the feral look of a cat about to jump. "Tell you what, Marshal. I'll come on up, and we'll palaver."

He ascended the rickety ladder and loomed over the marshal.

"Now are we gonna build a well, or ain't we?" he asked.

"You're not."

"Why not?" Flint asked.

The marshal glared at the newsman, blank-eyed as an owl. "You write a word of this, and you'll be back in there," he said.

"Naw," said Mountain Jack. "Crawford, you gotta learn that next time there won't be a pokey to put Flint into. There'll be pieces of plank from here to Silver City."

"Enough of that," the marshal snapped. He pulled his navy revolver from its sheath just as Mountain Jack landed a hay-maker that drove Crawford ten feet back and into the clay. The marshal's revolver flew away. Treat lifted up Crawford by the back of the shirt and began a cheery bombardment of the man's nether regions.

The two deputies cocked their clubs but not fast enough. Treat's miners swarmed over them, enjoying every moment of the brawl.

Flint knew he was witnessing a great story, but he wasn't sure he would ever publish it.

25

Flint watched, enchanted and horrified, while the burly mining stiffs swarmed over the three lawmen. One pug gave good account, landing blows with the skill of a trained street-brawler and bloodying one of the miners. The giant Treat simply squashed Crawford, shaking him like a rag doll. But the deputies were no match for a bunch of big miners, and soon they were howling for mercy.

The marshal was, Flint reminded himself, a bona fide appointed law officer and what was happening was, in the eyes of the law, a major crime: resisting arrest or, worse, an insurrection. But that wasn't the whole story, as Flint knew; the law officer was a bully and a thief, engaged in grossly illegal acts that violated the rights of citizens.

Swiftly he scribbled notes in his pad; he would write this story even if Hell swallowed him. He would present all sides, including the marshal's. The story was going to be exact and credible. He glanced sharply around the darkening plaza and saw not one Mexican. But he felt eyes everywhere, a thousand eyes. Were they seeing more trouble, or liberation from Crawford's petty oppressions? Flint made a note to himself to find out from de Cordoba. Was the padre watching? He would learn about all this soon enough.

Treat now sat on a thoroughly whipped Crawford, whose lips leaked blood, whose nose had swollen, whose face had puffed up—and who glared up at the giant with murderous eyes while his chest heaved.

"All right, my dearie, we'll haul you dainty lads to the jailhouse," Treat said, enjoying himself. He and his happy colleagues marched the sullen marshal and his limping deputies out of the Mexican quarter, across Virgin Avenue, and up to the little plank jailhouse, while Flint followed gingerly, well aware of the marshal's black gaze.

Treat held the lawmen outside while a pair of miners entered the dark building and presently emerged with a handful of shotguns and revolvers and a few key rings.

"All right, in we go, sweethearts," Treat said, his massive paw steering Crawford by the nape of the neck.

One of the miners, Polgarth, fired up a lamp on the battered desk.

"Now, where are those picks and shovels you stole from the Mexicans a few days ago?" Treat asked. A blood-drenched miner pointed to a corner, where the work-worn tools had been stacked. At Treat's nod, some of the miners hauled them out the door. "They're going home, dearies," he said.

Flint noted on his pad that the tools were being returned to their owners.

Mountain Jack Treat herded his prisoners into the cell and swung the door shut. It clanged loudly, as if in protest. He found the keys on a ring and locked the cell with a snap of iron. The prisoners glared back at him, helpless and hurt and leaking hate.

"Well, how does it feel, Crawford?" he asked.

"You're all under arrest. We'll lock you up and throw away

the key," Crawford muttered through puffed lips. "Treat, we'll hunt you down and kill you like a dog. When I get out, your life won't be worth spit. And it won't be just me. This is an insurrection. I'll have coppers from six counties on you. I'll have the best posses in New Mexico hunting you, like coyotes after rabbits. I'll make sure there's a thousand-dollar award for any mankiller who wants it. If you live, after I've put some lead into you, there'll be judges and juries taking their turn. We'll build you a nice scaffold, Treat. And I'll do the honors."

Treat laughed heartily. "See that fella there? He's a newsman. He'll write this up. He'll make sure the whole story gets in. Now, Flint, you'll put in the marshal's words, won't you?"

Flint wondered whether Mountain Jack was relying too much on a little weekly, but he scribbled enough of the exchange in his notebook so he could reconstruct it when he set the story.

"You're in for three days and three nights, girlies. That's how long you locked up Flint, there, on no charges, and how long you jailed a little girl for the crime of selling newspapers. There's the pail. It'll do for three, and it'll stink soon."

The marshal glowered but said nothing. The two deputies looked sick. One's vest had been shredded, and the other's lapels had been yanked from their roots.

Flint recorded all that on his pad while he watched the miners go through drawers, looking for any spare keys for the cell. They found a second set in Crawford's desk.

Treat turned to the prisoners. "All right, girlies, pull your pockets inside out, and hand me your coats."

The prisoners didn't respond.

"Do you want some more? How about donating a few teeth to charity? We'll auction off your teeth, dearies."

Reluctantly the prisoners emptied their pockets and turned them out, loosing some change and a few greenbacks. They handed their coats through the bars; the miners poked around for weapons or keys and handed them back.

"We'll see you in the morning, dearies," Treat said, enjoying himself. "In three days we'll have that well dug and lined. We'll let you out for the grand opening. Maybe you can have the first drink," he said. "It'll be nicer than that fouled creekwater we'll be bringing you here."

The stiffs turned down the lamp wick, watched it blue out, and filed into the afternoon.

"I'll kill you," yelled Crawford as they closed and locked the door of the building.

"You gonna just leave them in there?" Flint asked, genuinely worried.

"They'll be fed and watered, Flint," Treat said. "I'll see to it meself."

"You're aware of what you'll be charged with?"

Treat turned serious. "Force is all Crawford understands, Flint. All we've done is lock up the worst crooks and bullies in town. Bullies don't think they'll get hurt until they get hurt. They'll learn they're not the only men around here who can use a little muscle. They'll stay there until we finish the well."

"You're dodging me," Flint said. "I asked if you're aware of the charges they'll level against you. Even your allies won't approve of this—taking the law into your own hands. Resisting arrest. Conspiracy. Insurrection. You didn't need to do all this. Those crooks can be voted out next November."

Treat said, "They'll push the greasers out before then, and half the town'll move over here. I'm not for or against the greasers, but that ain't right. I just figure they've got rights too. Look, Flint, old friend, when that bunch gets out of jail, they'll kill you and make it look like a crime."

"Kill me?" Flint asked, amazed. It hadn't occurred to him. But the more he thought of it, the more he supposed it could happen. Once the town marshal and constables got out, they'd come after him and silence him before they dealt with Mountain Jack Treat and the mining stiffs. The one thing they didn't want was publicity.

Treat threw a massive arm over Flint's shoulder. "You just write it up the way you saw it. Don't soften it on my account. Just get the facts down. That's all I want."

"All right. It'll be the lead story. I'll tell it all and hope I don't get shot. And it'll all be accurate. I'm funny that way. My mother always said I was stubborn."

Treat grinned. "I sure hope so," he said. "I'm counting on you, Flint."

Flint hiked back to his shop, through the strange afternoon, his mind awhirl. He doubted that the miners could keep the constabulary in its own jail for three days. Tonight, yes. But tomorrow morning, merchants would discover that no one was patrolling the town. Then they'd bust into the jailhouse, find the entire constabulary in the jug, get some hardware from the stores, and break out the prisoners. And the moment that happened, Crawford would descend on Flint.

It was an old familiar feeling to have a story burning so intensely in him that he had to compose it at once. He wanted to collapse in his bunk, but he knew he wouldn't.

Go to bed, he told himself. *Stop acting like a fool. You're in the news business, not the crusades.* He wandered to the rear apartment, stared at the welcoming bunk, and was pierced by guilt. Slowly, unhappily, his mind licking visions of his doom, he walked back to his shop and began setting the story, composing it in his mind as he went along.

By midnight he had finished the coverage. He had broken it into several stories: One dealt with the efforts of the Mexicans to dig their own well because of the fouled creek and how they had been stymied by Crawford—the men held without charges, their garden tools confiscated. Another story, under the heading DONNYBROOK IN THE PLAZA, dealt with Mountain Jack Treat's

efforts to build a well—an act of charity—and the brawl that en-
sued. And he wrote a third story—the one that would arouse
controversy—about motives. He offered some probable reasons
for the harassment of the original villagers and why they were
denied equal protection of the laws, and concluded:

> One can argue that the peace officers are duly appointed
> magistrates and the crime against them cannot be jus-
> tified by any line of reasoning. One can further argue
> that the marshal will be up for election in November,
> and any abuse of office could be dealt with by the voters
> at that time.
>
> But it can also be argued that the peace officers are
> themselves violating several laws with flagrant disregard
> for the rights and property of citizens. What is to be done
> when lawmen are the principal lawbreakers and peace
> officers are the first to disturb the peace? Wait until No-
> vember? By then it would all be over—the original citi-
> zens of Oro Blanco shamelessly driven from their
> ancient homes and fields. There is no law against dig-
> ging a well, especially in a public plaza given to the
> parish church by the grantholders.
>
> The marshal and his cohorts were the first to break
> law, by harassing the well diggers. The Mexicans, and
> later the miners who volunteered to finish the job, were
> entirely within their rights to resist the oppression of
> men who wore their badge of office while performing
> lawless acts.

He proofed and revised at the same time. It was a good chop
of work. The dry New Mexican air eddying through the plant
grew chill. Moths collected around the lamps, singeing their
wings. He felt the ghosts of the Escalantes gliding through their
haunts, and it gave him the jitters.

It was one o'clock when he hid the galleys in the cantina

oven and staggered to bed, wondering what madness possessed him. He scarcely knew any of the people he was helping, except for Father de Cordoba. But why operate a newspaper unless to bless the world?

26

Mountain Jack Treat plucked up three scatterguns and several revolvers and headed through the pre-dawn quiet to the Oro Blanco jailhouse.

He had never nursed a hard feeling for long in all his happy, rambunctious life, and he held no hard feelings now against the town marshal or his cohorts. It was just a mule-brained man like Crawford needed a little lesson now and then to keep him from swelling like a bullfrog.

The town lay quiet like a ghost-filled cemetery as he crossed Virgin Avenue and walked to the little frame jailhouse on the upper edge of town. He unlocked the door and let himself into the gloomy front room, which was chilly and musky with the smell of male bodies.

He peered into the cage and saw the three stalwarts staring at him through the murk, Marshal Crawford sitting on the bunk and the two porkers lying on the floor, getting their chalk-striped suits dirty.

"When do we eat?" Crawford demanded.

"After the lecture hour, my dainties," Treat said, depositing the arsenal on the desk with a peace-shattering clatter.

Their gazes followed the weapons. The pair on the floor sat up. "They're all empty," Treat said. "But oh, how ye'd like to hold a live six-gun or two in your hot palms."

"I want chow and I want water," Crawford growled, "before I shoot you."

Mountain Jack Treat lit the lamp and adjusted the wick so that the smoke wouldn't cloud the already-fouled glass chimney. He took his sweet time. "There, now I can see the Oro Blanco constables," he said amiably. "What a threesome. A pair of fat jailbirds led by a grafter and petty crook."

Crawford stood suddenly. "Treat, the reckoning's coming, and when it comes, you'll be six feet under."

"Well, now, I'm going to talk about that. As it happens, I'm about to let you out—if you promise to behave yourselves."

That brought them all to their feet. He knew he could lead them through avowals of virtue, promises of honesty, confessions of guilt, pledges of public service, and Bible-sworn oaths to conduct themselves according to the law of the land. They'd say anything he asked them to, if it meant his turning the key in the lock.

He watched them clutch the jail bars, their hands pulling and tugging the bars as if to yank them out by the roots or milk them like cow teats. "It's not a bad idea, pulling down the jail, long as you fellers keep stuffing innocent people in there. Now in your case, keeping the bars up makes sense, because you ain't so innocent."

"Treat, shut up or let us out."

"Ah, I'm getting to that, dearie. Now first of all, I stuffed you in there just to teach a little lesson. You get too high-and-mighty and the suffering citizens of Oro Blanco're likely to put you in there for keeps. There's a county full of semi-honest officials above you, and a Territory above that, and the federal government keeping an unblinking eye on you. But it's the six or seven hundred stiffs in the pits who'll do you in long before the officials. They've got the big, unblinking eye on you. And if you manage to bury me, ten others'll step in and keep the big eye on you."

They listened sullenly. Treat smiled. He always enjoyed a ruckus like this. In fact, there wasn't much about life he didn't enjoy.

"Now, dearies, you could arrest me after I let you out. You could go to the justice of the peace and say that you got locked up in the pokey for the night by Mountain Jack Treat. You could go whine to all the merchants that Mountain Jack and some miners locked you up. You could go whimpering up the hill to Mason Weed and tell him two hundred stiffs from the pits, armed with knouts and dirks and shotguns, disarmed you and threw away the key. Oh, sure, but you'd be laughed clear out of Oro Blanco. They'd either take you for three liars or three fools." He stared at Crawford. "You getting the idea?"

Crawford didn't blink.

"Now, if you arrest me, you'd better call in the militia, or the army, or a hundred or two lawmen, because the stiffs, most of 'em, they'll tear this little shack to pieces, and not all the scatterguns in the world'll stop 'em. They'd be mighty tempted to tear you to pieces too, but they're a pretty decent bunch. You leave them alone, treat ordinary people right, and obey the law, and they'll leave you alone." He stared again at Crawford. "You starting to hear my song?"

Crawford met Treat's gaze and said nothing.

"I won't make liars of you, at least not any more than you are already, by getting solemn, gold-plated, sworn-on-the-Book promises from you—unless you want to say them voluntarily. Now's your chance to make mighty oaths, dearies." He waited amid the silence. The sky was lightening from gray to blue outside.

"Now, if I was Mason Weed, and I heard that Jack Treat and a few miners put the three of you in the jug overnight, just for fun, I guess I'd fire the whole lot of you. Fine bunch of coppers you are. If I was Mayor Malone, I'd shake my head at you, and give you the boot—adios, amigos—and look for some lawmen who're worth their salt and don't start trouble. But of course it's all up to you. You can sing your sad song all over Oro Blanco if you want."

He waited for it all to sink in.

"All right," he said. "Don't dive for the guns. There's not a cartridge in 'em, and none in this dump. I guess you'll have to go home for some more powder or wait until John Strong opens his hardware. If it's fists you want, dearies, you just try out Mountain Jack Treat. We'll have us a ball."

He didn't wait for the response but slid the key into the large iron lock and slid back the bolt. Instantly, Crawford slammed into the door, intending to drive Treat to the floor, but Treat hadn't brawled all his life for nothing. He slammed the door shut, driving Crawford back into the bunk. The town marshal groaned, caught his breath, and rose shakily.

"Now," Treat said, "you dainties come out sweet and proper, and ye can go stoke up your bellies at the Elite beanery, just as you wish."

He let them out, and they stayed a respectful distance from his seven feet of height, his broad shoulders, and his three-foot-long arms capped by massive fists. None headed toward the desk and its pile of weapons.

"Think about it before you come after me," he said to their backs as they stepped into the glowing dawn.

He sighed, watching them scurry into the shadowed side-streets. This was the best way. No one in Oro Blanco would take it for more than a cheery prank. No mob of stern businessmen would collect around the jailhouse, demanding the release of the lawmen. There would be no arrest, inquiries, declarations of insurrection, and all the rest. Letting them out robbed them of the revenge they had been plotting all night.

He yawned—it had always been hard for Treat to bring himself to life so early in the morning, but he always managed to get to the shaft collar in time for the six A.M. shift. His new hours were more to his taste, tending bar in the saloon until the last stiff quit, usually around eleven or midnight.

He had one more mission this fine, summery, going-to-be-hot day in the Gila Mountains, and that was to tell Flint what he had done. It would put a different end on Flint's story if he chose to use it.

Treat reckoned it was still around six in the morning when he hammered on the door of the old cantina that housed *The Oro Blanco Nugget*. Flint didn't respond until the second battery, but eventually he opened to Treat, his face shedding sleep and taking on alarm, his body visible through the cracks in a gray union suit that had seen better days and too little soap.

"Need to talk to ye a moment, and then ye can get back to your slumber-bed, Flint," Treat said.

Flint nodded. Treat barged in, ducking his head. He had acquired long and painful familiarity with low Mexican doors and had several scars on his noggin to prove it.

"I let 'em loose. I figured the dearies got their little lesson, and it was best to keep it a little prank."

"Loose? Are they after you? Or me?" Flint hadn't arrived at full wakefulness, and he looked a ruin.

"Oh, they might be. That's a mighty embarrassing thing, getting run into one's own jail by a few stiffs. I'd guess they'd be embarrassed to see it all in print. I just wanted to let ye know." Treat grinned. Flint didn't.

"You're telling me not to print the story," Flint said.

"Not at all. I'm letting ye know what I did."

Flint sighed. "I set it last night. Set all night by lamplight. Too big to hold inside of me. That's why I'm not up."

"Go back to the blankets for a while, man. Your lass won't be along for a bit."

Flint nodded and turned away. Treat let himself out and meandered through the cool, sweet morning to the plaza. He passed a few early-bird greasers, who eyed him contemplatively. The plaza was empty and hushed, and no life stirred in the tawny adobe buildings around it.

Treat stepped to the lip of the well and enjoyed the sight of water in the bottom. It had seeped in during the night. There would still be some digging to do. The stiffs would sink the shaft deep into the aquifer, and the well that started all the trouble and brawling and fun would be a success. Treat thought it would take only one more session to deepen the hole and line it with stone.

A little brown girl slipped to the edge, stared down, and then up at the giant.

"*Agua,*" she said, smiling.

"*Agua,*" Treat replied, mighty pleased with himself.

She stabbed a finger to her breast. "Rosita," she said.

He jabbed his finger at his chest. "Jack—ah, Juan. Juan," he said. "Now don't you fall in there."

"Okay," she said, grinning. He watched as she skipped and leaped and flitted her way back to one of the low adobes, feeling the scores of eyes upon him.

Then the padre was descending on him, crossing the plaza from the church in great strides that stretched his brown cassock. The padre peered into the hole, saw water, and smiled.

"You're the giant," he said in accented, angular English, offering a hand. "I have heard of you. I think you are the Engine of God."

27

No coppers invaded Sam Flint's publishing emporium that day, much to his surprise. He was girded for more trouble, but it didn't come.

Libby worked hard, her determination and deft fingers making up for her lack of experience. He put her to rebuilding the ads while he worked on stories.

As that day lengthened, so did the story about the well, which had come to symbolize the right of Oro Blanco's Mexicans to live their lives where they had been born. He walked to the plaza during his brief nooning and found Treat and some off-shift mining brethren laboriously loosening underwater shale with their pikes and mucking it out. They were hip-deep in water.

"Flint! Behold a well," Treat yelled up at him. "It's good sweet water, and we're into a good vein. I guess the marshal'll be wetting his whistle here, same as anyone else."

"No trouble?"

"The poor dear's had enough." Treat laughed heartily and lifted an awesome chunk of shale from the murky water.

The Mexicans had come to the same conclusion. On the

plaza a dozen of them were dressing rock for the well's masonry lining. Others carried the rock to the lip of the well. If they all worked together, they would have a well very soon.

Even while Flint watched, Father de Cordoba approached.

"I have something for your paper," he said. "When the well is done, I will perform a blessing. Everyone is welcome while I celebrate the gift of water. Tell them that the well is for all people, *todo el mundo*; sweet water is a gift of God, and always for everyone. I wish to invite the mayor, the justice of the peace, the constables, and the prominent citizens. I will lift a bucket and bless it and let each enjoy its coolness. Flint, water is the most mysterious and necessary of life's gifts. It's so common but so precious. Let's make the celebration at twilight on Wednesday, the day you publish."

Flint nodded and scratched it into his notepad.

"And tell them that my people are grateful to the miners and have joined in the work. See how they sweat, Mr. Flint." The padre eyed him wryly.

Flint understood and noted it on his pad. He hastened back to his shop and added five inches of copy to the story that still lay hidden in galley trays in the cantina oven. He wondered if it would ever see daylight.

After spending three days as the marshal's guest he was short of news, but he wasn't short of opinion. Let an editor have a slow stretch, and it became the opportunity to express a little wisdom. He smiled. Some people wouldn't call it that. In fact, he would probably get letters announcing that he was as dumb as an ox and deserved to be horsewhipped. That's how the world viewed editors—useful but expendable if they got uppity.

Flint judged that he might just be able to produce the usual four-pager if he could fill a large news hole with opinion and add a few house advertisements promoting subscriptions. He put Libby onto the house ads after scribbling what he wanted to say on a pad, and he went to work on his weighty opinions.

The Nugget, he decided, would come out in favor of the

common-law rights of all citizens, the Bill of Rights, the equal protection of the law, and the civil liberties of all who were under the flag. He knew he would not need to name names. The stories on the well digging would suffice.

He began placidly, choosing subdued language because it usually had more impact. By the time he was winding up, he knew that he had composed a formidable essay, based on reason: pleading for an honest constabulary that didn't deprive any citizen of Constitutional liberties; an honest justice system; and an end to Star Chamber proceedings; equal protection for minorities; and the need for ordinary goodwill. At the last, he added a small warning: The unblinking eyes of the territorial government, the federal courts, and the federal government gazed upon Oro Blanco and its officials. It was a shot across the bow.

Satisfied, he boxed the editorial with ruler lines and slid it into the page-two form. He had not accused anyone of anything; he had merely spoken on behalf of basic principles needful in an orderly society based on common law and the Constitution. Readers would know whether the shoe fit any official in Oro Blanco.

That finished the edition.

"All right, Libby," he said, "I'll start to print. You've put in a long day. Tomorrow morning, you'll sell newspapers. Maybe you'll even be out of jail at the end of the day."

She gazed at him solemnly, not accepting his levity. "Is it that bad?" she asked.

"It's a true account of the entire controversy about the well. I hid the galleys. Do you want to read it?"

She shook her head. "I'll read it in the morning, before they arrest me. I must go to Mama now. She's had two bad days."

He watched her go and then slid the first form onto the flatbed press. Printing with his ancient press was always something of an athletic achievement. He hammered the type flat with a wooden block, inked the type with a chamois ink-ball, cranked down the massive platen to make an imprint, and then cranked it up again. By the end of the run, he would be exhausted and soaked with sweat.

But four hours later, deep into the night, he had two hundred fifty copies of a four-page edition, a miraculous thing after wasting three days of his life in Crawford's calaboose. He scrubbed away the ink from his blue-stained fingers, washed his face, and headed into the cool night looking for an open beanery.

The next day, much to Flint's astonishment, nothing untoward happened. Libby nervously hawked a hundred fifty copies at her Virgin Avenue stand, while Flint hand-delivered the rest, a few to the post office and the rest to subscribers and merchants. Just to be safe, he hid a dozen copies in an obscure corner of the old cantina and mercantile. The well-sinking story, including his reportage of the brawl, would not be suppressed.

Not that he wasn't watched. Crawford bought a paper from Libby, studied it grimly, and stalked into Bulldog Malone's emporium, no doubt to hatch plans to retaliate. But for one day, at least, freedom of the press had prevailed in Oro Blanco. The editor was not behind bars for saying things that its officials didn't want to hear.

It made Flint itchy. Crawford wasn't behaving like Crawford. Libby sold out by midmorning, brought her coins and bills to Flint, totted up her two-cents-a-copy share, and handed the rest to the editor. Flint placidly made out invoices for the advertising and delivered them, all the while wondering when the sky would fall on him.

The only hint of trouble that reached his ears was the sudden reticence of the merchants. Usually they complimented him and ordered another ad. This time they hemmed and hawed about another ad, saying they'd see about it. That worried Flint plenty, but he supposed they would soften in a day or two. He deposited his few dollars in Amelia Lowell's private bank and ate a quiet dinner at The Boston. He hadn't seen her for days, and she wasn't there that evening.

Thursday slid by so quietly that Flint decided that his foreboding had been merely the fruit of a fevered imagination. He and Libby broke down the pages all morning. That afternoon he hiked to the plaza and discovered a large crew of young Mexican men—he counted thirty-three—finishing the well. No one was bothering them. The mortared courses of the dressed-stone lining rose above the ground, and the toilers would soon complete a circle of rock masonry about three feet above the grade of the plaza. He made a few notes on his pad for a followup story.

Friday morning, Libby arrived for work in a state of wild excitement. "Look at this!" she cried, laying a handsome new paper called *The Oro Blanco Progress* in front of Flint. Blazoned in both upper corners was the price—five cents. A banner announced that it was published on Tuesdays and Fridays. "A man was selling it right where I sell ours."

"Did you buy it, Libby?"

"Yes!"

"I owe you a nickel," he said. "This is business."

"Oh . . ." she said, wrestling with that.

The masthead listed one Phineas Clegg as the owner and editor. The name sounded vaguely familiar, but Flint couldn't put a face or reputation to it. The man was operating from the Pepperdine Building. It shocked Flint. All of this had somehow transpired without his knowledge. He knew at once why the merchants had been so reticent: They had bought ads in a big new five-cent paper.

Flint dug in, looking at each of the four pages. Plenty of ads graced them, but new papers often ran free ads just to make it look as though they were doing a good business. A few firms he had never heard of had bought space.

He turned back to the front page: a long story about the well in the plaza; a lengthy interview with Town Marshal Crawford; a large-type, boxed declaration of purpose and principle.

Flint read that first, discovering that *The Progress* was first and foremost for Wholesome American Progress; for Prosperity and Sound Money; for Land Reform intended to break up large estates owned by privileged plutocrats and give all progressive people the chance to own their own parcels of land, whether a town lot, a mine, or a ranch.

The second plank in Clegg's statement of principle was America for Americans, and the Manifest Destiny of the English-speaking peoples to possess the continent.

The third was unqualified support of the town fathers and leading men, who were all deeply committed to making Oro Blanco a prosperous, peaceful, spacious, and lawful town.

The fourth was a direct challenge. *The Progress* intended to counter and rebuke the distortions and omissions of the opposing paper and show that its editor owed his livelihood to greedy Special Interests and reactionary elements such as the Catholic Church and greaser grandees that opposed progress and challenged the very foundations of progressive Protestant society.

Flint knew he had brutal opposition. This paper was the mouthpiece of Mason Weed, Bulldog Malone, and all the rest of the pirates. It would whip up resentment against Father de Cordoba. It would go after the original inhabitants of the town. And it would go after Flint as if he were a wanted man.

Flint sighed. It wasn't hard to see how the paper could survive while charging so little. It was subsidized. And it wasn't hard to see how a paper published Tuesdays and Fridays would exert a lot more power than *The Nugget*.

Everything in the edition confirmed that this was a venture intended to put him out of business fast. The story about the plaza well was loaded with fantasy and said nothing about the brawl that embarrassed the lawmen. Clegg had turned the whole thing upside down, turning innocent Mexicans into sinister rebels and law breakers, and Treat into a demented thug and gang leader. It was accompanied by a piece about Town Marshal Crawford, telling how the man had exercised restraint in the face of unstated provocations and upheld the law without fear or favor. There were veiled pieces on the virtue of town expansion, and a piece about squatters living on land they never owned—and an amazing piece about Sam Flint, hinting, just short of libel, that Flint had a shady past and was to be watched closely.

It all hit Sam Flint like a fist to the gut. And after he recovered, he got mad. He could become a swarm of hornets if the mood came upon him—as it did now.

28

Sam Flint had been in corners like this before. Sometimes he had been whipped, but once in a while his raggedy little paper achieved a breathtaking victory. Flint figured he always had the edge. He never had anything to cover up, and he never wrote anything intended to deceive. Truth was always the magic sword. The slick, subtle, insulting *Progress* would collapse on its own heap of falsehoods.

It hadn't always worked that way. Sometimes Flint, whipped and broke, had fled from a town without enough supplies to start somewhere else. Then he had become a job printer for a while, until he could build up enough to try a weekly again.

He slid his notepad into the pocket of his ancient tweed coat—which he wore out of sheer obstinacy in the New Mexico heat—and hiked across Virgin Avenue to the Pepperdine Building. He found the sanctum of *The Progress* around the side and let himself in.

He discovered a gleaming plant, with handsome wooden tables and counters just right for setting type, a shining press so new that its metal had not yet vanished under layers of scummy ink, and several cases of fonts.

An older gent with a boozy red face set type in the light of a large window, while a younger man, with the look of a pointed-nosed marsupial, broke down pages. Flint knew in an instant what sort of arrangement this was. Men with rheumy eyes and ruined faces didn't own expensive new printing plants.

"Ah, Mr. Clegg?"

The entrepreneur set down his type stick and smiled. "Want an ad, fella?"

"No, I came over to interview you. I'm Flint, owner of *The Nugget*. I thought I'd welcome the competition and let the world know a little about you."

Clegg smiled amiably. "Flint, eh? I've heard a lot about you. Rather a reckless fellow, eh?"

"Mr. Clegg, you know more about me than I know about myself. I found that out this morning. You must have done a lot of research to come up with all that news about me."

Clegg's cynical gaze settled over Flint like a fishnet. "Well, we'll have fun, you and me. Where you from?"

"Cincinnati, and I'll ask the same question."

"Oh, I'm not from anyplace, Flint. Been in so many I can't claim a place."

"Journeyman?"

"I hardly know the term, Flint. I've been slinging type since I was ten."

"It's bought you a nice new plant. A lot nicer than I could afford. You must have hit a streak of luck somewhere."

"Oh, yes, here and there, the fickle finger of fate."

"You're the sole owner and editor, I take it?"

"You don't see another mortal, do you? Except Printer's Devil. That's his self-anointed monicker. Call him Devil and he'll yelp."

"I'll guess I'll have to say you declined to answer my question, Clegg. You have a partner or two."

Phineas Clegg stared sharply, then smiled. "I'm the sole

owner and editor, Flint. I'm not beholden to anyone, least of all the forces of superstition."

"What're the papers you've owned or worked for, Clegg?"

"Oh, they're too many to count. It's vexatious, the way my noggin fails me when I need it."

"I'll have to say you declined to tell me, then."

"Yes, you'll have to say it. It's not anyone's business, least of all the opposing sheet."

Flint recorded it, and then tried again. "You're some miracle worker, Clegg. I can't publish for a nickel. How'd you manage it?"

"Advertising, Flint. Merchants are coming to my manger the way horses come for grain. Just good business. Volume advertising, volume sales."

"I'll quote you," Flint said, watching the minute flick of doubt sail across Clegg's ruddy face.

"Were you in the late war, Clegg?"

It startled the editor. "Why, I—why do you want to know that esoteric folderol?"

"Oh, just curious. I think I hear a little Southern in your tonsils. Maybe Arkansas. I fought for the Union myself."

"That's how I took you. It doesn't make us friends. The late conflict wasn't about slavery or about union. It was about federalism. The South fought for the sovereignty of the states."

"I sympathize. Arkansas, then, unless you care to correct me. I'll say you don't deny coming from Arkansas." Flint paused amiably, but Clegg didn't say anything. "Now then, let's discuss your impressive declaration of principles. I must say, Mr. Clegg, it resembles that of our preeminent citizen, Mason Weed. Amazing how much alike you think, although you've stated things coyly. I presume you've had a long talk with him?"

"Why, it's just coincidence, Mr. Flint. I'm always running into like-minded citizens. I abhor party and faction myself."

Flint scribbled. "I'll say you declined to answer, then, Mr.

Clegg, when asked whether you've discussed the matter with Mason Weed."

"Oh, I wouldn't say I declined. Mason Weed is an eminent citizen, and perhaps we agree on basic principles."

"Like shoving the Mexicans out and taking their land?"

"Ah, where did you read anything like that in *The Progress*?"

"I'll write that you declined to answer. Is Weed your silent or open partner?"

"You're a man after my own pious heart, Flint. Let's have a wash at Malone's emporium. I'll buy."

Flint grinned. "You declined to answer. I don't have time. But I'll take you up on it next time."

"*C'est la guerre,* Flint." Clegg stood there, rooted to the shiny floor, looking as though he had swatted a moth. That's how Flint remembered him as he slid into the hot street. Clegg had been around. He knew his business. With so much money behind him, Clegg could squeeze Flint's sheet to death in a few weeks.

But it wasn't that bad. Jackals made themselves unloved. Drunken jackals might even lose. And lying jackals could always be exposed, even by one wobbly little weekly rag with broken type and blurry pages.

It was time to sell ads. He worked his way up and down Virgin Avenue, stopping at the dry-goods store, the cobbler, the saloons, the hardware, the greengrocer, the bakery, and the freight yard. It didn't go well.

"Look, Flint," said Max Bardenwerper, a haberdasher. "I can put an ad in two issues of *The Progress* for less than I can put it into one of yours. They're cheaper. And I like their progressive stance. We needed someone around here to get this burg moving." Bardenwerper eyed Flint reproachfully. "I can't sell hats and shirts to Mexicans."

"How about a card? I reach a different set of readers, Max. Keep the company name before them."

Bardenwerper eyed Flint as if he lacked sense. "Sure, the miners. Three-dollar miners can't afford my suits either. No card. Waste of money."

"Want to trade? I'll barter."

The clothier turned frosty. "You're being bested by a better product, Flint. Cheaper, more news, better printing than your blurry rag. Maybe you should get new equipment."

Flint grinned, as he usually did in defeat. "Sure, Max. Got any news? Announcements?"

"Yes, I'm offering a new line of kangaroo-leather shoes, softest leather known, reasonable prices. You can announce it."

"I'll do it, Max."

That's how it went. At least he could count on Amelia Lowell— but at The Boston he found otherwise. "Mr. Flint," she said, "I'm obliged to place ads where my customers see them. It's a delicate thing, you know. I'm going to have to split your business with Clegg. It's really Weed, you know, but dear old Mason hasn't whispered it to me yet. Put me down for half, dear man. Whenever I have a Lyceum event, I'll buy an ad. Some of the miners are literate, and a few might even come."

He left The Boston disheartened and tackled the other merchants. By the end of a hard afternoon he had sold only about twenty percent of his previous take, and most of the sales were mere cards, boxed announcements, commonly used by politicians, seamstresses, and tailors to announce their services. At the last he stopped at The Miner's Home and found Treat willing to buy a first-time ad. "You write it, Flint. Just let 'em know that The Home's for miners. It's their private club. No tinhorns or doxies in here. Just honest, humble stiffs. You just say that and make it fit a three-column-by-one-foot ad, and I'll settle with you when it's printed."

"Mr. Treat, you've kept the paper afloat," he said.

He headed for the old cantina with a heavy heart, knowing he was going to have to do what he had to do. He found Libby hard at work. On her own she had set two or three small stories that had been left there by citizens—a christening, a dance given by the Odd Fellows, and an announcement of a revival.

"Libby," he said, "I didn't sell much advertising."

She stopped her typesetting and stared.

"I'm thinking, Libby, you might earn more money over at the other paper. They'll probably pay you a penny for every one you sell, twice a week, and it could come to more than the two cents you get from me once a week. That's a going concern."

"You're making me leave," she said.

"I can't pay you, Libby, and you and your ma desperately need cash money."

"You're making me leave."

"No, I'm saying that after today, I'll not be able to pay you. I'll scrape by. I'm in a fight, Libby, and the new paper holds all the high cards."

The girl set down her type stick and walked to the window. The low sun had gilded the west sides of the tawny adobes, turning them into molten gold.

"I read that paper when I ate my apple. I don't like it. I don't think it's honest. It said things about you—" She eyed him. "Are they true, Mr. Flint?"

"Not a word, Libby."

"Then I'll work for you forever," she said.

Her honesty hit him like a club.

29

Libby Madigan had no friends, and when she thought about it she wished she knew some other girls her age, just to talk to. She didn't know any boys, either. But there never had been time for friends. It was all she could do to stay alive and feed her mother. And besides, Mr. Flint was a friend, and her mother was too.

She hastened to her cottage, disturbed that Mr. Flint wanted her to work for that awful paper. He was trying to help her, she knew that. But it upset her anyway, and she needed to talk to her mother about it.

She found her mother lying in her usual place on the tick outside the door of the cottage, trying to blot up life-giving sun and breathe the healing air into her failing lungs. Her mother had tanned, but beneath the tan her flesh looked waxy.

Her mother's breath came in small gulps, and her eyes never ceased being feverish. Libby knew, desolately, that soon her mother would die. By age thirteen she would be utterly alone, grown up before she wanted to be. She stared at her mother, fighting back the terror and sadness that engulfed her and the tears that rose whenever she felt desperate.

"Mr. Flint says he can't pay me. He wants me to sell for the new paper. He says I'll earn more. Mama, I don't want to. I read it, and it's not true. It said things about Mr. Flint that aren't true. What should I do, Mama?"

Maureen Madigan looked at her daughter and then turned away. "You must do what you think is right," she murmured. She couldn't talk much; she murmured so quietly, Libby could barely hear.

"But Mama—" She realized her mother had drifted away. She realized also that from now on, she would have to make her own decisions without the comforting counsel of her mother, whose gaze was upon death, not life. "I need to earn money, but . . . I don't like that new paper."

Her mother slowly squeezed Libby's hand. "Take the hard road, if it's the right road. I like to think there's a guardian angel who's right there beside you. Or talk to Our Lord. Or respectfully ask the saints. Everything you need's inside of you, my darling girl."

The talking exhausted her mother, and she sucked air in small, fragile gasps.

"Do you really think there's a guardian angel? Two of them right here?"

Her mother managed a smile. "The promises were sealed to us. We are never alone. The worst sin is despair, Libby. Don't ever despair, not when you can ask for anything and receive it if it pleases God."

Libby felt comforted, and it amazed her that her dying mother could still comfort her. "I'll find a way to help Mr. Flint," she said.

"I think you've made a pure, beautiful choice," her mother whispered. "I love you and I'm proud of you. Maybe I can be your guardian angel soon." Her mother smiled. "I'll still make you read, and learn algebra, and write essays."

The thought of her mother as a guiding angel, an invisible friend, brought tears to Libby's eyes, and she bolted inside to cook some broth.

Through the next days she worked hard beside Flint to break down the old issue and begin the new. He didn't conceal a thing from her. He told her he had lost four-fifths of his advertising, that he couldn't pay for the newsprint when it arrived, and that he wouldn't quit.

He wrote up a long story that amazed her. He had interviewed the owner of the new paper, Mr. Clegg, and wrote about that, and how that tricky Clegg had dodged so many pointed questions.

Mr. Flint amazed her by welcoming *The Progress* to Oro Blanco in a cheerful, boxed front-page piece, containing some compliments and an expression of goodwill. She wondered why he did that when those new people were trying to destroy him. He smiled and told her that the paper that takes the high ground might seem foolish, but it wins the wars.

Mr. Flint had another exclusive story too. He had covered the blessing of the new well in the plaza. He wrote that not one Anglo had come to the blessing, or tasted the sweet water that was passed around, or stayed for the fiesta that followed. Nonetheless, Father de Cordoba had invited all people to use the well at any time; water was for everyone. That story pleased Libby.

When the Tuesday edition of *The Progress* appeared, Mr. Flint studied it closely, muttering to himself. Then he turned the paper over to her.

"Tell me what you think of it, Libby," was all he said.

She read a long piece on the front page about the need for Oro Blanco to expand: The white men's town was cramped into a narrow stretch between Virgin and the mines only because greaser squatters occupied the other side of the street on land to which they had no title. It urged the constables to drive off the squatters and recommended that the city confiscate the public land and auction it.

Another story dealt with vagrants. Town Marshal Crawford said too many people without visible means of support were loitering around Oro Blanco, sometimes begging or hawking worthless merchandise on the sidewalks. He intended to remove them as soon as the mayor and town fathers agreed. Libby had a terrible feeling that the statement was directed at her.

A third story was about Mr. Flint and *The Nugget*. It alleged that Mr. Flint was being paid by the greasers to present their side, that Mr. Flint did so with some cunning when he wasn't staring into a bottle, and that *The Nugget*'s editor had been known to publish papers devoted to special pleading on behalf of nefarious clients in Kansas and Nebraska and Colorado.

"But Mr. Flint!" she cried.

"It's the usual tactic," he said. "I rather enjoy it. It gets my blood up and my rusty brain working."

"But aren't you angry?"

He sighed. "I learned long ago that the first side to lose its temper loses the war. Actually, newspaper wars sell papers. There'll be plenty of people buying our paper tomorrow, just to see what I say—whether I can refute all the charges against me and come up with my own accusations. But I'll disappoint them. I'll write only a mild reply for now."

"You should fight back," she said.

"Ah, Libby. We'll win this war, even if it seems impossible. You wait and see. I have a weapon they don't have. People scoff at it, but it is the best weapon of all in our struggle with life. It's called a clear conscience."

"You sound like Mama."

He began printing that evening, after paying her fifty cents for the day. He said he would keep on paying her as long as he could. She watched him lock the forms, hammer down the type, slide the forms onto the bed of the press, and begin the inking. That was all man's work, but she wanted to learn anyway.

The next morning he had papers for her. She took an armload across Virgin to her usual corner and waited for customers. Two youthful bruisers approached, each carrying a load of papers. They posted themselves right beside her, grinning hugely.

The papers were yesterday's *Progress*. Both were hard-looking, with smirky looks on their faces. She had never seen them before, and she judged from their pale flesh they hadn't been in the Southwest long. She grinned wryly, acknowledging the competition.

The first prospect showed up, and Libby hawked her paper. "Buy today's *Nugget*," she cried. "One dime for the best news. . . ."

But the two pugs were drowning her out, and they closed between her and an approaching man, forming a wall. The man eyed the rough young fellows, eyed Libby, and walked by. He clearly had wanted one of Libby's papers.

Stunned, she realized this was how it would go. It seemed so unfair! All she wanted was to sell newspapers, but two big bullies were preventing it. She hung grimly to her job but failed to sell a paper, even though lots of people passed by. Each time she tried, the bullies hawked theirs, drowned her out, and drove off the customer.

Sick at heart, she realized her livelihood had come to an end. Then a big miner came along, a man with black hair and black eyes that burned in their sockets. The hooligans closed on him, but he barked at them to step aside. They didn't. He stepped forward, his massive shoulders pushing the bullies apart, and bought a paper from Libby while the bullies jeered and heckled.

"We'll take your dime from ya, sweetheart," one said.

The massive man collected his *Nugget* and turned slowly toward Libby's tormentors. "Picking on a wee girl, are you? Ye won't be called men among men. Ye be hooligans and thugs, and ye'll meet up with some fists sometime soon, when decent men gather to teach ye a lesson. Be off now, and don't trouble the lass."

Slowly her benefactor walked away while the bullies watched. But the moment the miner was out of sight their insolence returned, redoubled by their humiliation, and they began bumping her, sending her reeling and knocking her papers from her arm until she realized she could not hold the corner.

"All right," she said.

They laughed nasally.

She left, walking slowly down Virgin Avenue, desolated. She passed Bulldog Malone's gaudy Stamp Mill Saloon, and it dawned on her that she didn't need to sell papers on that corner. The customers were in the saloon. She ducked into the forbidden place and found lots of men at the bar and more around the gambling tables at the rear.

Slowly, her heart beating fast, she approached each man at the bar with a perky smile—and sold papers to almost all. She looked fearfully around for the mayor but didn't see him. She sold more papers to the tinhorns and gamblers and slid out, triumphant.

The bullies still lingered on her corner, enjoying their empty victory.

Libby slipped into the next saloon, The Good Luck, and sold a few. She did better at The Ritz Beanery, where lots of men slipped dimes and nickels into her hands and she gave them a paper and a grin. She tried The Boston, but the snooty lady drove her out at once, saying hawking wasn't permitted in the place. She sold a few in the mercantile, the hardware, and all the other shops, but the restaurants and saloons proved to be the best places, and by the end of the day she had sold out the edition.

She headed back across Virgin, her heart singing, knowing she had a lot to tell Sam Flint.

30

Juan de Cordoba read the first edition of *The Oro Blanco Progress* with care, grateful that his parishioners could not read a word of it. The paper had the toothmarks of his adversary Mason Weed, no matter that its masthead announced that it was owned and edited by one Phineas Clegg.

Most of the pieces on the front page raised his hackles. One openly invited the *norteamericanos* readers to seize the Mexican quarter, which was occupied, it explained, by squatters. In the name of progress, of course.

Another attacked de Cordoba personally. The padre had to admit it was artfully done and along the line of attack most credible to the readers of *The Progress*. The priest, it explained, was engaged in sedition aimed at restoring the territory to Mexican dominion. That had, of course, happened in recent history. A certain priest named Martinez at Fernandez de Taos had fought the Yankee intrusions all his life and may have fomented the insurrection in 1847, though the evidence was sketchy. Before and after the Yankee conquest and occupation, Martinez had seethed with resentment toward the *yanquis*, becoming a heavy cross to the bishops. To make matters worse, he had lived in open concubinage and had sired a son. No wonder the paper chose that line of attack.

It hadn't stopped with sedition, either. There was the usual melange of accusations: that the villagers were priest-ridden and destitute and kept in ignorance, that the Mexican church itself engaged in a secret conspiracy to oust the foreigners, that de Cordoba was engaged in a sinister legal enterprise that amounted to a giant land-grab based on fraudulent old land-grant claims.

That, at least, had a thread of reality anchoring it. The next piece, an assault on Flint's character and *The Nugget*, was as mendacious as the rest. Clegg had produced quite a newspaper.

The padre set aside the *Progress* and slid into the nave, which lay dark and silent and redolent with candle smoke and solemn with supplication. He genuflected and then retreated to the rearmost of the simple hand-hewn cottonwood benches. There he pondered, in the presence of God, what a poor parish priest might do against the mounting schemes and lies intended to dispossess him and his flock.

No particular idea came to him, but he decided it was time to act, even so. He hiked across the Avenida and then up the sharp slope to the Golconda Mine and Mill, which hissed and steamed and thundered like a creature from Hell. He had been to Weed's office several times, none of them a social occasion.

He announced himself to the pale clerk in the eye-shade. "It is a matter of charity," he said.

The clerk eyed him doubtfully, disappeared into Weed's sanctum, and reappeared. "He's busy, but he'll spare a minute or two. Be quick about it, please."

Weed's office reflected the man, the padre thought— red-flocked wallpaper, a massive beeswaxed walnut desk, heavy damask drapes. Not exactly the usual utilitarian office of a mine superintendent. A throne room, rather.

"Yes?" said Weed without pleasure.

The padre shrugged. "It is a little thing, Señor Weed. I am starting a bell fund, a dollar here, a centavo there. The mission church has never been able to afford one. There is that great crossbeam up there, but there is nothing to hang from it. An *iglesia*—a church without a bell is a church without a voice.

"It is an old church, you know. A century old. Great adobe walls, cottonwood vigas supporting the roof, something of a masterpiece of the art of my people. Some say miracles happen there. I thought perhaps you would like to be our first contributor. We will pray to God for your soul in the Mass. A gift for a gift. A great bell with a husky throat, a summoning bell, a wedding bell, a funeral bell, *y también*, a fire bell—cast in the great foundry at Durango by the Sanchez brothers. There is the need for such a bell for Oro Blanco. I thought you might be our *patrón*, with a gift of one hundred dollars for the bronze bell."

Weed looked discomfited, stared out the window, flicked lint off his suit, and smiled. "Later, Padre. I'm involved in some major financial operations just now. All tied up."

"Ah, Señor Weed, I understand perfectly." Juan de Cordoba laughed softly.

"Cordoba—"

"Ah, one more little thing, Señor. A much smaller charity. My people lack tools. They make the garden with hoes of the antler or the bone of a cow. They plow with wood made hard by the fire. I was thinking how good it would be if my people had the iron hoes and the rakes and the spades. Then there would be vegetables for all; Oro Blanco needs squash and beans and chiles and corn, *que no*? With fifty dollars I could give all my people the tools of the steel."

"I'm busy, Padre. Don't see me unless you want to call off Baca." He waved the padre out.

"*Muy bueno.* I will let the people know. We thought a fire bell might be a service. All of these buildings of wood here."

Weed motioned him away.

Juan de Cordoba retreated, laughing softly. It was a good sally from a humble parish priest. He hastened to the Pepperdine Building, found the side entrance that permitted entry to

The Oro Blanco Progress, and spotted two *norteamericanos* at home. The elder one—stout, florid of face, and acquainted with the bottle—he took to be Clegg. The editor looked up from his typesetting, saw de Cordoba's cassock, and retreated into himself.

"Ah, Señor Clegg!" the padre said. "I have come to see the man who edits this most esteemed paper."

"What do you want? I'm busy."

"Why, I've just come from a visit with your owner, Mason Weed. He had some things to say—*muy interesante*, very interesting things."

Clegg's hands stopped, a capital B in his fingers. "What makes you think he's the owner? Masthead says I own it. Can't you read?"

"All too well, Señor Clegg. But one must also read between the lines, *no es verdad*? I read more than words. Look at this fine shop with its new equipment. I do not suppose you own one stick of it. But somebody does, and that is the man whose opinions you trumpet."

"You're pretty smart, Padre, but not smart enough."

"I enjoyed my visit with Mason Weed. He is a busy man, but he listened. We talked about a bell for the church. It is an old church, Señor, but it never had a bell. And we talked about new garden tools—rakes, hoes, spades—for the people. Oro Blanco needs vegetables, is it not so? Beans, squash, corn, chiles . . ."

Clegg stared.

"Ah, Señor. A church bell is also a fire bell. What if a fire starts here? Poof! In *diez minutos*—ten minutes, *quizas*, this side of Oro Blanco would be gone. A bell is a good idea, I think, is it not? Now, you will give the support with our fund for a bell, will you not?"

Clegg muttered something unintelligible. "Weed going along with this?"

"Why do you ask, Señor Clegg? You are the editor and owner, are you not? Now, I have a little news. From now on, we're going to have a market day in the plaza across town, every

Saturday. The people will have good things—squash, the fruit in season. Good things for the tables of the *norteamericanos*. Hay and oats for the *caballos*. Maybe goat milk, cheeses, many such things. You write that up. It is a good thing for Oro Blanco, *verdad?*"

"Naw, I don't want to write that up. I got advertisers that'd be unhappy."

"Oh, you do not publish the news, then. *Por seguro*, Señor Weed keeps an iron hand on you. Then I will advertise the market. That way, it is not news. What is the cost, how much the rates, eh?"

"Don't want your ad. I got enough ads."

"Ah! No ads from the greasers!" De Cordoba laughed. "How about the one-sheet to pass around—*como se dice*, the flyer? You are the job printer, I think, no?"

Clegg was reddening with some sort of interior fires. Juan de Cordoba thought to fan the flames.

"*Claro que sí*, I will have to take the news and the advertising to your competitor. How do you expect to beat the competition when you will not accept advertising?"

"Likely you can't pay anyway," Clegg said.

"Now, one small matter, Señor Clegg. That little story about me."

"Vamoose, Padre."

"Now that was a most splendid fiction. Maybe it will win a prize for the best fable, eh? I wonder where you got your information. Is it true, all this you say about me? I am of amazement. I never knew these things about myself! Imagine, I am plotting an insurrection. I am disloyal. I am scheming with all my brother priests to overthrow you. I am burdening my poor sheep with all my expenses, living like a *rico*. This is all a marvel! I never knew I was so grand. I cast a long shadow, eh?"

"I've got informants, Cordoba."

"I have been found out! Now the authorities will come after me. They will jail me for this crime, *yo creo*. Pardon, Señor, but who was whispering in your ear? Could it be that man over there?"

Clegg looked at the other one. "Printer's Devil," he said.

"Ah, it all makes the sense. The printer's devil. Clegg, you may succeed in destroying me. Your people remember Padre Martinez of Fernandez de Taos. You will call me the new Martinez. It was clever, this attack."

Clegg smiled beatifically.

"And perhaps there will be a libel suit, *no es verdad*?"

Clegg smiled harder.

"*Bueno!* You will not accept my news or let me buy an ad or let me print posters. I am a poor country priest, and I do not understand the politics. Perhaps you will enlighten me. I will come by from time to time, and let you tell me how your *yanqui* world works. Maybe you'll educate a poor dumb padre." He cocked an eye, waiting for a response, but Clegg just glared. "I will go to your competitor, Señor Flint. I will remember you in the next Mass, if you wish. Would you like to be remembered?"

"Vamoose," said Clegg.

"I hear that much," the padre said on his way out the door.

31

Sam Flint expertly built a large ad promoting the Saturday market in the plaza. The padre had left the wording to him, saying only that the Mexicans would sell hides, fleeces, honey, goat's milk, cheese, tortillas, horse tack, fresh produce, grains, hay, and tables and chairs fashioned from peeled poles and leather. The market would run from sunrise to sundown and would do so every week.

Flint resorted to his sparse supply of display type and gradually filled the three-column page-length ad that would run on the rear page. He listed the food and products for sale in the most inviting fashion.

He would have run the ad for free, but the padre had other ideas. "Run this in each issue for a while, Señor Flint, and I will forget the rent."

That was welcome news. It would help the paper endure the advertising boycott. It would also make the paper look more prosperous. Nothing bespoke a desperate or dying paper more than the want of ads.

"We need you," the padre added. "Your paper is all that

keeps us safe. If *The Nugget* didn't exist, hard men would be riding through our side of town."

"I'll try to report all the news, Padre, including news that might hurt your people. It's a paper for everyone."

De Cordoba flashed a smile. "That's why we need you. A lot of the *yanquis* trust your little paper. Most of the miners, *sí?*"

"Trust is the only strength any paper has, Padre."

Flint set a story about the new plaza market too, with more detail in it, and featured it on page one alongside business news from the other side of Virgin Avenue, including the opening of a haberdasher and a story about the expansion of the Gold Queen Mine, which was sinking a shaft to a lower level.

Nothing calamitous interfered with his work, and he dared to hope that the worst was over. The town fathers would have their own mouthpiece and had probably pulled back from violence, intimidation, arrests, and threats.

But he worried. Libby's plucky victory over the bullies who crowded her off the street had set him to wondering about the future. Maybe Crawford would be primed this time and would chase her out of the saloons—where she was too young to be— and even the restaurants. Maybe they would start charging some impossible street vendor's license fee.

He stopped that night for a mug of beer at Mountain Jack Treat's saloon, noting at once that it had been transformed. The makeshift counter had vanished and a sturdy bar, the work of a cabinetmaker, had replaced it. Maybe it wasn't equal to the gorgeous, mirrored mahogany bars and backbars across Virgin Avenue, but it was good. The miners certainly made themselves at home at the one saloon where they could enjoy their own company, away from tinhorns, strumpets, and sporting types. The stiffs bought a few beers, settled into rowdy or quiet talk, cards, and even chess, happy to call The Miner's Home their home.

Treat himself was the mixologist that night.

Swiftly, Flint described Libby's troubles peddling the previous issue and his concerns about the next one.

"Well, we'll have us a wee say in it," Treat said. "You just tell her to drop off a hundred right here if they bully her. I'll put 'em on the bar, and she'll get her two cents for each. I'll spread the word among the stiffs. If they bounce our little Libby out of the other grog shops, the stiffs'll stay away from 'em too. If they want our custom, they'll welcome a girl doin' nothing but selling papers to feed her sick ma. Imagine, those bleddy sharks pickin' on a wee girl!"

"A declaration like that's worth another mug," Flint said, pushing his empty toward Treat.

"I'll go further, Flint," Treat said, drawing foam from a barrel. "If our little Libby can't sell *The Nugget* because they push her off the streets of Oro Blanco, then a few hundred stiffs'll march from one end of town to the other, selling every copy you print. And we'll make sure Crawford and his two thundermugs each buy half a dozen!" Mountain Jack Treat had that joyous look in his eye that Flint had come to respect.

"That'd be more than kind. It's good to have allies, Treat," Flint said. "But remember, I print all the news, including some that might not please your stiffs. I'm grateful but I can't be beholden—"

"Ah, there ye go again, Flint. All I'm asking is that the needs of the miners—all six hundred of us—reach grass. Reach topside. I mean sunlight. A paper that lays her out fair, she's gonna be trusted. That's why Clegg and his twice-a-week mouthpiece isn't respected by a soul, save a few politicians that sit around Bulldog's back room or eat fancy fodder at The Boston."

That reminded Flint to talk to Amelia. She'd shown Libby the door, but maybe she'd sell a pile of papers discreetly. He couldn't afford the fixed-price dollar-fifty dinners there, but he still did his banking at her wicket. He drained his sour suds and hiked across Virgin to The Boston to try her out.

"Why, my dear Flint," she said, "I'll sell your papers, but I'll also sell *The Progress*. I can't publicly take sides, you know."

"You publicly took sides in my first issue, Amelia, enough to land us all behind bars."

"Well, I'll have both papers or none."

"That's fair enough. I'm printing tonight. I'll have Libby start you with twenty-five tomorrow."

"Do spell better, my dear Flint. And use better ink. *The Progress* is so much easier to read."

Flint left, wondering where Amelia's loyalties lay.

He put the issue to bed and began cranking his press that evening, printing three hundred copies. He didn't much like the looks of *The Nugget*, which was miserable compared to Clegg's smart editions, but he had no choice. He was printing with worn and battered fonts on a press that should have been given a decent funeral years ago.

Libby arrived early the next morning, eager to start selling papers. Flint considered her gravely. He ached just to keep her safe. For months now, she had been out on the streets, wrestling pennies, selling flowers and now papers, fending off mashers and bullies, finding herself behind bars, having her papers and cash ripped from her by brutal males. And yet it hadn't seemed to darken her innate sweetness and courage.

"Libby, we may have a little help from the miners this time," he said.

She looked disgusted. "I don't need help. I'll sell every paper you give me."

"What about those two bullyboys? They're on to you now. Your trips through the saloons and beaneries caused some talk."

She considered that softly. Sun filtered through the small windows of the cantina, illumining her slim form. She still wore rags, still went barefoot. But she showed not the slightest sign of care; neither did she seem worn down or desperate.

"What's your secret, Libby? How can you face life so bravely with your father gone and your mother . . . so ill?"

"I don't know," she said. "Mama says I'm the only one left, and it's all up to me."

"What's up to you?"

She shrugged and smiled shyly. "Feeding two people," she

said. "No, more than that. Mama says to live up to everything. What Papa was—he was a happy man and he worked hard. Mama was the religious one, but not, well, you know, hidebound. She'd always take my side and let me do things that Papa didn't think I should do. Like reading a lot of stories."

"Where does your courage come from? Your Irish family? The church?"

"Why do you ask, Mr. Flint?"

"Because you've been punished so hard, struggled so hard to sell penny bouquets, but I don't hear any bitterness. And as long as you've been with me, you've never complained."

"Aw, I don't have time for that."

"That's true, but there's more, Libby. What is it?"

The girl suddenly clouded up, not far from tears. "Mama loves me, and soon she'll be gone. I have to do everything before she dies so she can die in peace. I mean, I have to *succeed.* Then she can let go."

"And then you'll be all right? Succeeding?"

"No, I won't be all right, Mr. Flint. I'll be alone. I mean, except for God."

"Is God your hope?"

"Mama told me that the worst sin is despair, because it denies the love of Our Lord." She slid deeper into her cloudiness. "But I can't always live up to that. When Mama dies I don't know, I don't know . . ." She glared at him. "You shouldn't ask me things like that."

"Libby, Libby, you're the first girl who ever worked for me. The first girl who ever became my printer's devil. You've done better than the boys, better than the men. You never rest. You're driven by fears and hopes. But Libby, why are you here? Why not on the other side, with *The Progress,* where it's safer?"

She was still glaring at him. "I thought you were so smart," she said. "It's safer here. I don't like liars, and I don't like mean people, and I don't like unkind people. I'm safe because you're— uh, I don't know the word."

He felt humbled. "I'm little different from them, Libby. The only difference is that I wrestle with life."

"If you were the same, I'd be selling flowers."

She gathered up a stack of papers. "I'll take these to Mr. Treat and to The Boston," she said. "Before those rats catch me and steal the papers."

"Good. He's offered to help if you get into a jam. Just let him know."

"I want to do it myself," she said.

Sam Flint watched her go as she strode up Virgin Avenue, a vision of loveliness not yet a woman, the sun making her glow, turning her gray rags into gossamer silk. He had never dreamed what powers might reside in the starving girl. He felt a strange medley of emotions: sadness, a sense of loss, admiration, awe, and simple gratitude. She had given him the courage to carry on.

32

Libby Madigan tucked a load of papers under her arm and ventured onto Virgin Avenue. Few people were about so early, but she would sell to anyone she could. Some mines had night shifts, and she would catch those stiffs as they went home.

The two bullies were on her corner, waiting for her, each with a handful of yesterday's *Progress* under arm. So they were going to try it again. She felt a flutter of fear course through her. She didn't know how old they were, but they weren't exactly boys. Both were beefy, broad-shouldered toughs, one with watery little blue eyes and a lantern jaw, the other with huge cheekbones and straight black hair parted in the center and pomaded down. They watched her progress and grinned.

She approached with dread, knowing how easily they could hurt her. But it didn't do to back off or show fear. She had her dander up.

"Well," she jeered, "you're selling stale news again."

"Beats the garbage you peddle," said the black-haired ape. "Beat it, sweetheart, or you'll be sorry."

"I'm not moving an inch."

Blue-eyes smirked. He edged closer and closer, grinning,

until he loomed over her, but she refused to budge. Everything inside of her started to scream silently. He glanced up and down the avenue, seeing no one, and with one swift blow he knocked her papers from the crook of her arm. They scattered into the breeze.

"Stop that," she snapped, reaching for the wandering sheets. But a massive blow toppled her into manure on the grimy dirt street. Then he pounded her shoulder, staggering her. She ached. Her temper flared. Black-hair was enjoying himself. She wanted to yell at him, pound on him, but that was just what he was waiting for. He'd bust her arm if he felt like it.

"I see you enjoy picking on women," she said, rising slowly. She started to gather the papers but was upended again with a shove from behind, this time by blue-eyes. She careened ten feet. The papers curled over, billowed under the breeze, and slithered away. She sprang up, snared a few, and then was catapulted twenty feet into Virgin Avenue. The blow robbed her of breath. The papers whispered and rattled and skittered away.

No one was in sight. She stood slowly, waiting for the next round, but the hooligans just stood there, enjoying their total power over her. She ignored the *Nugget*s for the moment and walked gravely up to them, eyes locked with theirs. "You're not gentlemen," she said.

"Not on your life, sweetheart. And you ain't a lady. You should be workin' up on the row. I'll come visit."

That made her boil. She snatched blue-eyes' papers and ran off. They laughed. They didn't care about the papers and weren't on the corner to sell the day-old *Progress*.

She watched glumly as her papers drifted away. She could not get them without starting another bout of trouble.

"All right," she muttered fiercely. She hiked toward the Pepperdine Building. At least she could let that Mr. Phineas Clegg have a piece of her mind. She might not have the strength of those bullies, but she had a mouth. She barged through the door and slapped *The Progress* on the counter.

"They're stronger than I am, so you win," she said.

The man paused in his typesetting and peered cheerfully over his gold-rimmed spectacles. "I'm glad you're a learner," he said. "Flint's so dumb about it."

"Mr. Clegg, this is not a good paper and you're not a good man," she snapped.

He laughed. "Doesn't bother me a bit, missy. You vamoose now."

"Vamoose! That's the big word around here. Anyone you don't like, you just say vamoose." She was yelling. "Well, I don't quit!"

Clegg nodded to the big printer's devil, who snatched a broom and loomed over her with it.

"Go ahead, hit me. Wait until I tell Mr. Flint and Mountain Jack Treat and every miner I can find. Wait until I tell Mason Weed. Wait until I tell that Pete Peters and tell him to fine you. I'll walk right up there."

Clegg shook his head, and the big man halted.

She was shaking so hard she could hardly keep herself standing up. "Your bullies told me I wasn't a lady and I should go work on the row. I'd die first. I want an apology from you, from him, and from Mr. Weed."

"You'd be a real attraction on the line," said Phineas Clegg.

It shocked her that a grown man would say that. "Words don't die," she said. "They leave your mouth and go somewhere. I've always believed that. You can say stuff like that and think no one knows, but it's there—out in the sky."

Surprisingly, he kept a sober silence.

She retreated into the clean, sweet air, and walked back to *The Nugget*. There, she picked up another armload, avoiding Mr. Flint's gaze, and hurried out. She tried the Stamp Mill Saloon first, but Bulldog Malone was waiting for her.

"Out! You're underage," he yelled.

She tried the Good Luck Saloon next and ran into one of the constables. "You git out and don't you come back," he said. "You come back and I'll pinch you."

Grimly she hiked over to The Ritz Beanery and found a dozen customers eating a late breakfast. She slipped up to one. *"Nugget?"* she asked. He nodded and handed her two nickels. She gave him a paper and headed for the next customer, who was mopping up biscuits and gravy. "Paper?" she asked, holding up the *Nugget*s. But the constable barged in. "Get outa here. Stop pestering the customers," he yelled.

"This isn't a saloon. I can if I want," she said, looking for the owner, who was back in the kitchen.

But the copper growled and chased her. A massive paw clamped her arm, pressing so hard it hurt her, and she felt herself being dragged bodily from the place.

Out on Virgin Avenue he towered over her. "You don't go in there. You don't go into any saloon. You don't sell papers, get it?"

"Why not? It's not against the law to sell papers."

"You don't get it. Then maybe you'll get this," he said. He slugged her arm. The fist landed just below the shoulder, shooting stunning pain through her. It radiated up her neck and down to her ribs and made her chest hurt. The papers flew all over. She stood, shocked and too dizzy to move, and then she started to pick up the papers. He booted her and she tumbled into the street. Tears came. She peered up at him through the blur and knew a black emotion she had never before known.

She clambered to her feet, holding her arm, which hurt wickedly. She knew he hadn't broken it, but he had pounded her enough to give her an ache for a long time. She stood, reaching for dignity, and finally faced him.

"I may be weak, and I may be alone," she whispered. "But your guardian angel and mine know what you did."

He laughed as if the world were coming to an end. She wondered what was so funny.

Ruefully, she walked back to the cantina, dreading to tell Mr. Flint she had lost forty or fifty papers and had sold only one.

"You should have slugged him," she said to her guardian angel. "That's what you're there for—to guard me."

Mr. Flint came to her the moment she walked into the old adobe room, his eyes sweeping over the dirt on her skirts and the smears across her face. He didn't need to be told. She handed him the two nickels, bitterly.

"I guess I better quit," she said.

"Quit! Libby, Libby . . ." He steered her toward the only chair in the place. "Tell me," he said.

She did.

He said nothing at first. He paced back and forth, and then grew aware of her again. "Come over here and wash up," he said. He led her to the alcove where he had a pitcher and basin and some gritty soap. "Nothing can ever dirty you," he said. She scrubbed her face and hands and brushed the street grit and manure off of her clothes.

"Don't blame yourself," he said.

"I'm not blaming myself. I'm just useless to you. I'm not strong like they are."

"You're very valuable to me," he said gently. "You're the best worker, the best typesetter, I've ever had. We'll find a way." He sounded doubtful. "I don't have time to hawk papers, but I can deliver them to The Miner's Home and The Boston when they open. They're trying to scare us off. They know how much that plaza market could mean to Father de Cordoba's parish, and how well it'd unify this town. If I don't get the papers out, no one'll know about the market."

She wondered how he could be thinking about the Mexican market when his paper was being strangled to death.

"Do you want to go home now?" he asked. "I'll pay you for the day."

"No, I'm going to work if you'll let me. I don't want charity."

He grunted. "You're as stubborn as I am," he said, but he let her don her printer's smock and start in.

She watched him set up the press, mix ink, and begin printing more copies of that day's edition. It annoyed her that he was doing it. Why didn't she work for someone with sense?

"You'll never sell them," she said.

"You may be right," he replied, levering the platen down. "I'm going to give most of them away."

"They won't let you."

"They won't know about it," he said, yanking the imprinted sheet out. "I'm going to deliver most of these tonight, one in every door until I run out."

"Give them away? You'll just lose more money."

"I'm funny that way," he said. "You know how to prime a pump? You pour water down it to get the suction. Then you can pump water."

"That's not why you're doing it," she said. "It's because you won't let Father de Cordoba down."

He grinned.

She wished Mr. Flint's guardian angel would tell him not to be crazy.

33

Market day went better than Sam Flint had hoped. He had gotten word out after all, and townspeople flocked across the avenue that divided Oro Blanco, eager to see what lay in the plaza. Miners especially wandered over to the Mexican side of town all that Saturday. But tradesmen and wives and mothers and children meandered across too, enjoying the new *pozo*, or well, in its center, and the array of goods. For many it was the first time they had crossed that mysterious barrier into a world they had been warned against.

Sam Flint wandered about, taking notes. He would have a fine story. Hostlers from the livery barns snapped up all the hay for sale and all the sacked oats and barley. Gringo women hovered over the early produce from those well-watered flats on that side of town, trying out a few Hispanic words on their neighbors. They bought beans and chiles and herbs and small sweet potatoes, carrots, radishes, peas, and cucumbers.

The *viejo* who made the peeled-pole-and-leather furniture sold out. The ranchers who had brought tanned fleeces and cowhides saw their piles diminish. A Mexican who braided gorgeous rawhide horse tack did a brisk business in bridles and reins and hackamores. Mobs of laughing children wheeled like flocks through the crowd; flies buzzed; families headed for the *pozo* and a cup of cool water.

Flint watched the padre slowly circle through the crowds, his face contemplative as he observed his flock. De Cordoba's face turned suddenly toward the side streets that led to the Avenida, and Flint watched Crawford and one of his bruisers as they each cradled a shotgun in the crook of his arm and stepped into the plaza, creating a pool of silence as they patrolled. A chill passed through the throng, but the marshal and his deputy passed and eventually vanished.

De Cordoba stepped over to Flint. "I feared things would be bad," he said. "But they were on a leash. I could almost see it holding them. The other end is held by Mason Weed, no? Señor Weed would like to sweep this market and my people into the desert, but he cannot do this so quick. He must be careful."

The priest laughed. "If you were not here with your press, printing truths and hiding nothing, we would be suffering now. It is *The Nugget*, *nada mas*. You alone stand between us and the *officiales* with guns who want to drive us away like sheep."

"Oh, it's not just the paper, though it helps. I'd say Mountain Jack Treat is most of it."

"Ah, how I bless that man. I thank *Jesucristo* for the eight knuckles of Treat. We have a little paper and eight knuckles."

Flint mulled that. "You know, Padre, it's not just the market that's important today. Something else. All those gringo men over there, and their wives and children, are seeing you for the first time, bargaining, laughing, eating those tamales over there. They'll go back across the avenue, but they'll be changed. Weed knows that. This market undermines his entire plan for Oro Blanco."

"It will go hard for you, amigo. He can do nothing until he destroys your paper. He will hear about this and make it worse. It is said that your young lady, Señorita Madigan, was actually attacked. It is possible, such a terrible thing?"

Flint sighed. "It happened. In broad daylight on the street.

In the saloons where she tried to sell papers. In a beanery. On the street again. One of those deputies nearly broke her arm. They destroyed about fifty papers and broke her heart. I can't let her go peddle papers again. I can't subject her to worse. I'm going to try something else, if I can."

"You will deliver during the *noche*—the night, *no es verdad*?"

"No, they're on to that one now. Next time, they'll be waiting for me. I can handle myself. I'm young and muscled up from jumping on that old press. But my weapons are words, Padre, not fists. If I try that one again, I'll end up bloody meat. I'm thinking maybe there's a better way."

"Tell me, Flint."

Flint didn't. "I don't suppose there's anything in your canon that forgives premeditated intentional sin, is there, Padre?"

"No, there is not such a thing. Not in advance. And, after a sin is committed, not without true repentance."

"Ah well, I suppose I'll just have to repent in a few years. Maybe on my deathbed."

"Señor Flint, *ten cuidado*—be careful." The padre sounded solemn, but his brown eyes danced.

On Monday, the editor spent a lot of time writing the story of the first plaza market. He described the items for sale and the bargain prices. He noted the fiesta atmosphere that brought together the two sides of Oro Blanco at last. He noted that now the town had a source of furniture, fresh vegetables, hay and grain, fleeces and hides, and Mexican delicacies.

He wrote about a little boy names James who tasted his first tamale, and a miner named Petersen who snapped up two handsome peeled-pole chairs, and a wife and mother named Annie who bought turnips and greens, collards, carrots, and cucumbers, and a few chiles just to experiment with. He described a miner's son who paid out all his pennies for a handsome rawhide bridle and reins for his pony.

But there was more to report. That Monday, John Strong sold three pointed hoes and a rake to the Mexicans. Horchhoff, the cobbler, got a pair of boots to repair, his first from across Virgin Avenue. Several Mexican ladies bought yard goods, lace, thread, needles, and ribbons from Hindenburg and Kaiser.

He talked to Twill, the hostler at the Goodenough Livery Barn, and learned that the hay and oats would relieve chronic shortages of livestock feed in Oro Blanco caused by the high prices charged by freight outfits to haul it from Silver City. He found several miners crafting their own beds and chairs from the fleeces and tanned cowhides they had bought in the plaza.

All of that went into his story. He stopped to get something from Father de Cordoba, and the priest obliged him with some pointed remarks about the wealth and plenty and variety that comes from neighborly trading, as well as the end of demonizing other people. Flint stopped at the mine offices and sought some remarks from Mason Weed, who refused to see him.

After debating the matter, he decided to write the story of Libby's ordeal at the hands of bullies and hooligan constables. He wrote it matter-of-factly, in a low key, but the effect was horrifying to read. Libby read it, glared at him, and sulked the rest of the day.

Tuesday he pounced on the new *Progress* and found not a word about the market day in the plaza, but instead all sorts of oblique remarks alleging that any one who traded in "strange places" risked theft, cheating, shoddy goods, disease, and, moreover, would rob progressive, honest Yankee merchants of trade.

Flint laughed.

That evening, after a hard afternoon printing his next edition, Flint headed wearily for The Miner's Home, wishing Treat had started on his plan a few days earlier. He found Treat behind the bar. The former miner made the bar—built to normal height—seem toylike.

Treat placed a foaming mug in front of Flint even before the editor could belly up.

"Treat," he said, "I'd like to take you up on your offer."

The giant eyed him cheerfully. "State the case, lad," he said.

"I'd like to hire a pair of stout miners as newsboys for an issue or two."

"Well, ye can't hire 'em, Flint dearie."

It annoyed Flint. "I know I can't pay much, two cents a sale, but—"

"Ah, don't you get your back up. There's not a stiff in the joint that'd take pay. I'll have twenty big newsboys for ye tomorrow, Flint me dear."

"Two will do, Jack." Flint sipped the awful stuff. No one in New Mexico had the foggiest notion how to make beer. "The fact is, I need a pair of tough fellows. I could brawl a little myself, but my weapons are words and type sticks. It makes more sense to hire the work. Miss Libby, she'll keep on in my plant. It's too much for her. She's been dark of spirit ever since."

Mountain Jack sighed, wiped his hands on an ancient towel, and shook his head. "No, Flint, I've changed me mind. I'll not find a pair of stiffs for ye."

"Why not? How do you expect—"

Treat was laughing. He flexed his massive paws. "I get a chance like this once every six months, lad, and you won't even give it to me. Where's the justice in that, eh? I'll just go park meself on the corner with those two bully boys, and we'll just see if *The Nugget* sells or not. But it's not fair, Flint. I need three or four to one to make it entertaining."

The editor stared in wonder at his salvation. "You wouldn't want to work every Wednesday, would you?"

"Ah, dearie, it'll only take one Wednesday. After that, our little Libby can sell all the papers she can, and nary a soul'll trouble her."

"Are you sure, Treat? What if Crawford shows up?"

"Ah, paradise!"

"What if the two punks from *The Progress* and all three lawmen show up?"

"Ah, thank ye for thinkin' of it. It brings tears to me eyes. I was feelin' a wee bit low today, just on general principles. Life's too civilized. The Miner's Home reminds me of an undertaker's parlor. A man like me needs a little elbowing room." He hoorawed at his little joke.

"Well, Mountain Jack, the sheet's printed and drying. It's got a front-page story about the Saturday market and a little article about what they did to Libby. It's got a boxed opinion piece in which I say that *The Progress* isn't progressive. And I remind my faithful followers that the other rag is the mouthpiece, and probably the chattel, of the owner of the Golconda mine and smelter, who desires to remove some equal citizens from sight. You think you can hawk the news?"

"Flint, me dear, I can hawk it and I can spit it," said Mountain Jack. "I'll be at your door at eight."

34

Mountain Jack Treat surveyed the quiet streets of Oro Blanco and knew this would be a rare Wednesday—maybe the best Wednesday ever. He sucked the still-cool air into his lungs and headed for the old cantina, filled with anticipation.

Flint was waiting for him. "Are you sure you want to do this?" he asked.

Treat beamed, feeling himself shed sunlight around the gloomy printing shop. "It's a fair day to be out on the streets, me friend. Now where's the rags? I'll sell the lot."

Flint took him to a stack of the new *Nugget.* "There's three hundred. I need to sell most of them, Treat. I've got a few hundred pounds of newsprint waiting in the Butterfield Forwarding yard, with an eighty-dollar shipping tag to pay. If you don't sell most of these, or if my advertisers don't pay, this is the last issue."

"Naw, it's not the last issue, dearie." He scooped up two large armloads and tucked them against his giant torso. "We're going to have a great sale of the rag, old friend. Mountain Jack's not gonna let this little howitzer run out of powder."

Treat hiked up the Avenida and headed toward the corner,

spoiling for a little warfare. Around him, Oro Blanco stirred. He hailed some of the nightshift miners heading for bed after maybe a gulp or two of spirits. Shopkeepers were opening their doors, which in these southern climes meant propping them wide open, so people could wander in and out at will.

At Libby's corner he discovered the two brutes waiting, each with a handful of the day-old *Progress*. They were a pair out of Hades, all right; bruisers by build, with the smirky, feral look of masterless men who would do anything for a nickel, up to and including murder.

"How be you, dearies," Treat said, muscling in beside them.

"Doing a girl's work are ya, pal?" said the black-haired ape.

"No, doing a man's work, dearie," Treat replied, feeling his juices begin to flow. He could hardly wait.

A stiff walked up.

"Well, if it isn't old Trenoweth," Treat said. "Ye need an honest paper that's a friend of the working man."

Trenoweth eyed the two bruisers but pulled a quarter from his dungarees. "I guess I do, Treat, me friend, but these here gents are disapproving."

"Let 'em, Harry Trenoweth. They're no friends of the stiffs in the pits."

"Right you be, Treat." He handed Treat two bits, and Treat handed him a *Nugget*.

"I can't make change, dearie, but there'll be a mug for ye in The Miner's Home."

"Hey, you don't wanna buy that lying rag," said the bruiser with the watery blue orbs.

"Lying rag, is it?" Treat said, his spirits lifting.

Trenoweth eyed the bruisers and Treat, muttered something, and hastened off. The pair grinned like apes and edged in, confident of their ability to punish the giant, two to one.

"Now just a minute, dearies," Treat said. He found a rock and placed it on his stack of *Nugget*s. But even before he stood up, the pair landed on him, one on his back while the other dove for his legs, toppling him like an axed sequoia. Treat hit the caliche like an earthquake, pain jolting through him. But he scarcely had time to contemplate that before he felt boots smacking his head and chest and heard the apes chortling. Each smack of those pointy boots laced pain through his ribs and head and shoulders.

"Ah, dearies, you're making a bleddy mistake," Treat said, rising amiably. Pain was his aphrodisiac; it was the condiment that spiced a fight. He needed a whiff of pain, and now he had it.

"Ah, my fine little newsboys, we'll have us a circulation war," he said, raring up like a grizzly. He boomed into the one who was flailing at Treat's gut and sent him catapulting out into the Avenida. He wrapped a paw around the other, who was smashing his fat knuckles into Treat's jaw and ribs. This one, the blue-eyed turkey, he squeezed with a clamp of his arm until the poor dearie began to howl.

The first fellow, the black-haired brute, sprang at him, and Treat felt an uncanny joy whoop up his throat.

"Ah, it's you, is it, me friend?" He threw all seven feet of himself into the mugger. They hit like a pair of locomotives, and the bruiser flew into the sky, knocked plumb out of his senses. Treat whirled toward blue-eyes, grabbed a handful of shirt, and popped the bruiser up and down like a posthole digger. The shirt surrendered, so Treat picked on the man's belt, lifting him a yard into the sky and smacking him into the hardpan.

"Ah, dearies, I was hoping for a brawl," he said as he lifted blue-eyes and tossed him into black-hair. They rolled around in the filth, groaning.

It was a pity. He had hoped for some fun, and these dillies hadn't supplied any. He was about to sell papers again when a deputy marshal jumped him from behind. All Treat saw was a flash of blue and a stick arcing toward him. The club smacked his ribs, shooting some honest pain through him, and Mountain Jack Treat reacted as he always did. He whirled, grabbed a fistful of blue uniform, and yanked Crawford's constable into him.

"Shall we dance?" Treat said. The man's club snapped into his shoulder and again into his neck, but Treat caught it as he would catch a fly and yanked it from the man's hands. The yank pulled the cursing constable past him and into the dirt, but this bruiser wasn't down. He shook his head and leaped at Treat, thrashing into his gut and neck.

"Ah, now you're getting serious, dearie," Treat said. He was finally working up some sweat, and his breath burned fire in his throat. The deputy marshal circled warily, ready to pounce again. Treat had to admire a man who didn't give up.

"Under arrest, Treat," the man mumbled from bloody lips.

"Oh, I am, am I? Fancy that, dearie." Treat ducked low, bulled in, lifted the brute onto his shoulders, and heaved him. The bullyboy crashed to the street like a loose cannonball. He hit with a sickening thud, gasped, then screamed in pain. He didn't get up.

Mountain Jack eyed the three groaning assailants and decided to let the constable lie there for a while. The deputy moaned. Treat collected the pair from *The Progress* and dragged them up the street toward the Pepperdine Building. People gawked. A woman shepherded a child away from the awful sight. Several merchants in white aprons appeared, staring. One wielded a broom.

"Go buy yourselves a *Nugget*, dearies," he called. "Leave the change on the stack. I'll be back directly."

They obeyed, edging toward the downed deputy even as Treat dragged his two assailants into the offices of *The Progress* and dropped them unceremoniously on the plank floor.

"Here's your newsboys," he said to Phineas Clegg. "Are we going to have any more circulation wars? Are they going to pick on girls?"

Clegg stared at the bloodied, groaning goons and at Treat like a calculating wolf. "Don't know what you're talking about, fella."

"Well, I'll just show you," Treat said. He advanced slowly

toward Clegg, who backed swiftly. "Are we going to stop pounding on girls? Are we going to stop picking on Flint?"

"I'll call a copper, you clown," Clegg said bravely.

"I already did, dearie. He's out there with a bruised shin, making peace with God. Why don't you get another, if any are on duty?" From the corner of his eye, Treat beheld the printer's devil, a much younger galoot, sliding forward with a murderous iron bar clamped in his hand.

Treat beamed. "Now, dearie, you don't want to get hurt, do you?"

But the sallow-skinned man—he looked as though sunlight was a foreign shore to him—waved that heavy pike back and forth like a gun barrel.

"You don't want to hit Mountain Jack with that, do you?" Treat asked softly. "It's not polite. We're going to have polite competition. You don't pick on girls. You don't touch the *Nugget*s. You don't rob a girl's purse or rip up her papers."

"Get him, Print," yelled Clegg.

The printer's devil lunged: the iron bar thrust straight toward Treat's gut. Mountain Jack laughed. He stood perfectly still and caught the rod, slowing the thrust. The bar smacked his gut, jarring him back a foot. Then he shoved. The printer's devil careened backward. Treat leaped. He caught the fellow a good blow to the chin and another to his chest, lifted him like a flag, and tossed him into some page forms resting on wheeled carts.

The heavy forms thudded into the planks like war axes, spraying type and lead everywhere. Treat sprang forward, found a barrel of mixed ink, and upended it over the printer's devil. Velvety black darkness slithered over the man and the floor. It mixed nicely with his blood and puddled on the floor. The printer's devil stared astounded at his jet-colored arms and chest.

"Ye look better that way, dearie," Treat observed. "Like a joker."

"Stop that!" cried Clegg. The editor ran toward a desk and

yanked open the top drawer. A shiny black horse pistol appeared in his hands.

"Ah, you're getting serious, dearie," Treat bawled, racing at the editor in two giant steps, knocking the revolver upward as it discharged. The noise deafened Treat, but a moment later that revolver lay clear across the room. Phineas Clegg started blubbering.

The printer's devil hadn't had enough and came at Treat again with his iron pike. Treat dodged and tripped him. The pike sailed into the press, clanging into the bed and then onto the floor. Gently, Treat plucked the dripping fellow from the floor and tossed him into the newsprint, scattering and inking the sheets.

"Now, dearies, are ye going to compete like gentlemen and ladies?"

They stared, glassy-eyed.

"I suppose ye haven't come to a decision yet. Well, I'll help ye along. It takes a bit of doing to stuff fairness into your skulls. And not even Jack Treat can bump honesty into them."

"All right," mumbled Clegg from the floor.

"All right what, dearie?"

"All right, we won't pick on the girlie."

"And what else, sweethearts?"

"Get out. Vamoose, Treat."

"What else, friends?"

They sulked silently on the floor.

"I'll tell ye what else. Ye'll be competing fair and square. Ye'll not be ripping up *Nuggets*. Ye'll not be stealing a girl's coin. Ye'll not be bullying advertisers. Ye'll be discharging those two hooligans."

Treat discovered townsmen staring through the windows and doors. He turned to them. "*The Progress* has just decided to compete fair and square, gents," he said. "They'll not be slammin' fists into the poor girl or knocking her into the dirt or stealing her papers or taking her coin."

A dozen awed and solemn faces stared back at him.

"Now, I'm going to sell *The Nugget*, me dainties. You can line up. I've got three hundred of this issue, and we'll get it done in an hour. She's a fine paper, with news about the market in the plaza and lots more."

They gaped at the spectacle in the newsroom. Blood leaked from the printer's nose and from the hooligans. The pied type and ruler lines made an awful mess. Black ink puddled outward and vanished through cracks in the floor.

Treat pushed into the street, heading again for the Avenida. "We'll bind up the copper and haul him to his home sweet home—the jailhouse. And then, my friends, I think ye should buy two papers apiece and give one to your neighbors."

But some citizens had already helped the deputy. Treat watched the constable limp away, supported by two citizens. "All right, step right up, buy *The Nugget*, best little rag in Oro Blanco," he bawled.

And they did.

35

Sam Flint needed a thousand dollars fast, and the only hope was Amelia Lowell.

Between the thirty dollars that Mountain Jack Treat had brought him, and the payments for ads, and the remaining funds he had in Amelia's private bank, he could pay the freight on the newsprint and keep on publishing. But the thousand dollars was another matter. He hiked up the Avenida de la Virgen to The Boston before noon and found the proprietress in her wicket.

"Why, it's you, my dear," she said brightly. "Causing trouble as usual."

"Mrs. Lowell, I need to clean out my account. And borrow a thousand dollars."

She paused, eyeing him as though he had climbed out of a swamp. Silently she dug into her ledgers, discovering what remained in his account, and laid forty-three dollars in greenbacks in his hands. Then she entered the transaction.

"Now, what's this about?" she asked. "I hardly ever see you anymore."

"I can't afford your meals," he said. "Not when I'm fighting for my life."

"It's best. My customers don't appreciate your paper, and I'd rather not lose them. It's all I can do to sell a few issues of *The Nugget* and keep that small ad running."

"You're inviting me not to come here."

"Well, dear, not during the luncheon or dinner hours. Now what's this thousand dollars about?"

"Bail money. Crawford and his other goon—that pair are brothers, Bugsy and Billy Bowler—arrested Jack Treat. They're throwing the book at him. Saint Peter set the figure high enough so that the stiffs in the pits couldn't meet it."

"Well, my dear, Mr. Treat did resist arrest, start a brawl, and break Billy's leg. I've heard it all."

"No, you haven't heard it all. Treat didn't start it. Those hooligans from *The Progress* started it, the same ones who pounded on my little Libby. And Billy Bowler wasn't acting as a peace officer. He wasn't trying to restore order. He didn't try to separate the fighters. He didn't threaten to arrest anyone. He's not really a peace officer at all—he's a paid hooligan for Mason Weed. He jumped into the fight to pound on Treat, to help the pugs from *The Progress*. It's as simple as that. If he wanted to stop it, he would have threatened them all with jail, including those two punks.

"I want to get Treat out. He rescued my paper. And I want to get a good lawyer. We have our own complaints. Billy and Bugsy Bowler and Crawford have denied my freedom of speech, abused a girl innocently selling papers, and a lot more."

Amelia Lowell looked annoyed. "I don't have a thousand to lend, and I can't fight your lawsuits for you. If you employ brutes, you pay the consequences."

"Mrs. Lowell—Amelia—our Mexican friends tell me that *The Nugget* is all that stands between them and being driven into the wilderness—"

"Oh, tut tut."

Flint paused, shocked. Amelia didn't sound friendly. "You're saying no," he said.

"Good morning, Mr. Flint," she replied.

Flint stepped into a day so hot that the clay under his shoes roasted his feet. Oro Blanco had become a harsher, meaner place. He was down to nothing now, with Treat in the jailhouse, the padre helpless, and the bail bond too high.

It came to him that now he was alone. He had no giant, like Jack Treat, to fight his brawls for him. Libby, back in the shop, depended on him. The padre depended on him. His reportage of everything that affected the Mexicans was all that kept them safe.

He headed upslope to the Butterfield Forwarding Company's yards and paid the shipping charges on the newsprint with his last cash and Treat's contribution.

"Have a dray deliver it," he told the clerk, named Boggs.

"Yeah, well, Flint, that paper's been ruint. Some joker come in here and tossed a few buckets of water on it. You got a few enemies or something?" He laughed. "Yeah, you do. It was that marshal, Bugsy Bowler. He just walked in here, plain as day, with a bucket and poured it. Then he went down to the creek and got him another, and poured it, too. I sez, 'Old Flint, he ain't gonna like that,' and the copper, he says, 'That's what I got in mind, and tell Flint I done it.'"

His chest constricted. "Ruined? Water?"

"Yeah. Do you want it delivered?"

Flint pushed past Boggs and into the warehouse, and the clerk followed.

"How'd they know the paper was here, Boggs?"

"One or another of them coppers, they look over the waybills every day, Flint. They allus know about this town—what comes in, what goes out."

"Why do you let them in? Do they have warrants?"

Boggs grimaced. "You want to try saying no to them Bowler boys?"

The sheets had been sandwiched between two board pallets wired together. One of the Bowlers had cut the wires, lifted off the top pallet, and drenched the paper, which lay pulpy and soft and wrinkled, still wet to the touch. Pure loss. It wasn't only the loss of the paper and the shipping costs; a newspaper had to be printed on something.

"Bring it to my place, Boggs. I'll try to dry this. But it's mostly pulp. Maybe there'll be some drier paper in the middle," he said.

"Sure, I'll get it over there, Mr. Flint. You sure pick your enemies, don't youse?"

Flint nodded curtly. He wasn't in a mood to talk. He plunged into the blistering sun, the oppressive heat as hot as his temper. He hunted Bugsy Bowler, intending to thrash the man, to pulverize him. It didn't matter that Bugsy and Billy were skilled brawlers—Flint was enraged.

The heat had driven everything off the streets, including the mutts and chickens. The air shimmered with it, making the distant slopes undulate. It matched his mood perfectly. He stalked to the jailhouse, eyed it speculatively, and then barged in. Bugsy Bowler wasn't around; Crawford was. Treat stared from the bench in the cell.

"I'm filing a complaint," Flint snapped at Crawford. "Your punk, Bugsy, dumped water all over my newsprint. That's a crime. You take it from there."

Crawford leaned back in his swivel chair, his eyes mocking Flint. "I told him to do it, Flint. You want to file a complaint on me?"

"I'll take it to Silver City. There's county law there."

Crawford sighed. "No you won't, Flint. You ain't going nowhere. I'm arresting you. You was in on this conspiracy to wreck *The Progress* and injure a peace officer."

White heat built in Flint. He did something he had never dreamed he would do: He leaped clear over the desk, landed on Crawford, and smashed a fist into the marshal's jaw, rocking the man backward. The chair skidded, smacking into file cabinets.

Crawford, taken utterly by surprise by a wordsmith, couldn't react for a moment, while Flint smashed him again, with fists and elbows. Then Crawford rallied, pushing Flint back and reaching for his sheathed revolver. Flint decked him, feeling pain explode in his knuckles. Crawford careened backward, and Flint landed on him, methodically pounding the man. The town marshal fought back, gouging at eyes, trying to knee Flint in the groin, but nothing could stop Flint. His rage fueled a madness that he couldn't contain. He bloodied the marshal's nose, cracked one fist after another into the man's ears and jaw, pulped his lips. Flint landed on Crawford, straddled him, twisted his right arm until the marshal howled, caught the man's thrashing hand, and smashed the man's fingers over and over.

"Hey, Flint dearie, don't kill him," Treat said softly.

Slowly, Sam Flint retrieved his senses. Beneath him, Delbert Crawford groaned, bled onto the planks, and clutched his hurt fingers, sobbing. Flint couldn't believe he had done it. He was a mild man, a scholar, without the slightest desire to brawl. But he had utterly lost control and had edged close to manslaughter—of a lawman. An alleged lawman. A crook in office.

The future flashed before him. Crawford was going to kill him. The man's dark eyes glowed murder.

Flint stood up slowly, undamaged except for a few smarting scratches, and breathed fire into his lungs. He resisted the impulse to boot Crawford until the man screamed.

"You've made an enemy, dearie," said Treat, radiating cheer. "It was a spectacle that elevated my soul."

"You want to get out of there?"

"Are you going to add jailbreak to it?" Treat asked, his grin stretching.

Flint didn't answer. He stooped over Crawford, who clasped his broken fingers, continued to bleed, and groaned. Flint pulled the revolver first and then unhooked the marshal's key ring.

"I'll get you, Flint," the marshal whispered through swollen lips.

"I'll write it up," Flint said. "We'll have a front-pager about how the editor beat up the marshal."

Crawford's eyes blazed pain and murder again.

Flint found the big key to the jail cell. "You sure you want to depart this vale of tears?"

Treat sighed. "They haven't given me a drop of water or a spoonful of vittles since they locked me up. Is that good enough?"

"All right," Flint said. He slid the key into the lock, threw the bolt, and swung open the jailhouse door.

Treat walked out. "There's something I want to do, Flint," he said, as he manhandled the cell door open as wide as it would go. Then he yanked and tugged, but the door didn't give. Iron rods proved too much even for Mountain Jack Treat.

"Help me carry 'im in," Treat said, going for Crawford. Together, they lifted the groaning marshal and lowered him onto the wooden bench in the cell.

"May as well lock the dearie up," Treat said.

Flint swung the heavy door around. It clanged into place, and Flint flipped the lock.

"I'll get you, Flint," Crawford said.

Flint didn't listen. Instead, he and Treat stepped into the blistering air, each wondering how long they would live.

36

Sam Flint hurt all the way back to his shop. Crawford had gotten in some good licks to the ribs and lips and shins. But his injuries didn't preoccupy him—his anger stunned him. Never in his life had he lost his temper beyond control. He was a pencil-pushing editor, not a brawler.

Crawford might be a crook, might be a bully, might jail innocent girls, might work for the mine operators, might be on the take—but the Territory had vested peacekeeping powers in the man. Flint knew he could spend years in the territorial prison for this one. He looked behind him, half expecting to spy the marshal and a wolfpack of deputized bullies. But the Avenida de la Virgen slept under the blistering sun.

He could pack up and be out of town, out of the county maybe, before Crawford recovered enough to come after him. The man had taken a beating; Flint had heard the man's fingers snap. Flint realized that operating his handpress required muscle and endurance. He probably was in better shape than the constable.

Flint was tempted. Jail would be hell. There'd be nothing to return to. He'd never see his press or fonts again. If he acted now, he could harness up Grant and Sherman, load up the old wagon, and drive out, and no one would stay him. But the instant he left town, the cabal of mining magnates and town fathers would drive every Mexican into the desert, starting with Father de Cordoba, and hush it all up. By the time the court settled the Escalante grant case, there wouldn't be a Mexican in town to celebrate it. The cabal would win anyway.

No, he'd stay and fight. He'd risk everything he had. But that wasn't an easy decision. He entered the cool of his shop—almost chilly behind its adobe ramparts—knowing that the temptation to get out while he could would stalk him, wake him in the night, seize him every time he saw a deputy on the street or heard someone enter his place of business. Staying on to fight might be the idealistic thing to do, but from now on his life would be filled with terrors. And his freedom might come to an abrupt end.

Libby was working quietly on a story about a family reunion she had gotten from one of the mining stiffs. She eyed Flint's limp and disheveled appearance and stopped setting type.

Flint grinned, feeling feisty. "I got Mountain Jack Treat out," he said.

"You did?" The news utterly amazed her.

"I don't think Crawford will ever forget it," he said, ducking into his private quarters to wash up.

He poured water from the pitcher into the basin and splashed it over his face. He ached in a dozen places. He would need a week to feel himself again. But some ebullience welled in him as he remembered pulping the town marshal's nose and boxing his ears, even as the copper writhed under him, kicking and striking back.

He flexed his fingers. They had been bruised, but he could set type. They would stiffen up tonight, but as long as he could set type he would be all right.

He returned to the shop, donned his printing smock, and set to work. But he scarcely knew how to begin or what to say. He finally settled on humor.

Rumor has it that a meek and peaceable citizen rearranged Town Marshal Delbert Crawford's nose the other day and temporarily expanded other body parts, including ears, lips, hands, shins, arms, neck, jaw, eyes, and ankles.

We don't know for sure, but the marshal hasn't been making his rounds of late and is said to be in a pet. The perpetrator of these rearrangements of the marshal's flesh is said to be a gentle-mannered businessman wishing only to engage in commerce without hindrance. The event came as such a surprise to the law officer that he was entirely unprepared for it.

We have it that the marshal is wishing the story would remain buried, following as it does upon another episode in which a *Nugget* salesman was accosted by rivals and then by the marshal's deputy, Billy Bowler, whose flesh was also rearranged, even though the salesman was battling three-to-one against his tormentors. That leaves only Deputy Bugsy Bowler to keep peace for the next week or so, the rest being *hors de combat*.

Having rearranged the marshal's nose, the unlikely victor in this affray released his salesman from the town jug, where said salesman had been unlawfully kept, there having been no charges ever filed, and no evidence that selling items on the streets violated the Code Napolèon or any other, or that said deputy was engaged in keeping the peace rather than siding with the salesman's rivals. In any case, the salesman is back at his usual post, cheerfully inviting the minions of law to his lair.

With two-thirds of the town constabulary currently

on the mend, and considering lessons learned, we suspect there will be no further action in the matter. . . .

Flint carried on in that manner until he had a fine, wry story
that no one would misinterpret. Treat was already spreading the
tale among the stiffs, and it would soon wend its jolly way across
town. The glare of public knowledge was, as always, his shield
and armor.

Still, he wasn't the only paper in town. *The Progress* would
do what it could to undermine Flint's effort, and it would howl
hysterically for vengeance.

Which reminded him of that miserable heap of soaked
newsprint sitting in his shop. He turned to assess the damage,
peeling off a half inch of worthless sheets until he hit ones that
were dry in the center, albeit wavery and wet around the edges.
Those would dry. He would be printing on wrinkled sheets, but
the damage had been less than he had supposed when he looked
at that soaked stack in the warehouse.

"How did that happen, Mr. Flint?" Libby asked.

He told her.

"Why do they hate you so much?"

"Because there's so much at stake, Libby. The land-grant
swindle could be worth millions of dollars to them. We're keeping some ruthless schemers from a bonanza—and from causing
misery to innocent people. This little paper, this weak, impoverished, broken-down rag, with just you and me to operate it, is
holding the wolves at bay. What a paper prints doesn't just reach
buyers and subscribers, the news finds its way to officials and
politicians and ministers and men of goodwill. That's why
they're trying every way they dare to destroy us."

She eyed him solemnly, as if seeing something about him
she had not seen before. "They'll kill you," she said. "And
maybe me too."

"Libby, they won't go that far. The finger of law would point
straight at them."

"But they *are* the law."

"A part of it." He saw the fear in her eyes. "Libby, you have a powerful friend in Jack Treat. If anything should happen to me . . ." He couldn't finish it.

She smiled suddenly. "We're in it together," she said. "My mama's proud of you, and me too."

"You have a rare woman for a mother, Libby. Instead of worrying about her illness, she blesses our struggle. I pray to God for her health and recovery."

"She's poorly," Libby said, and Flint sensed there had been another downturn. "Praying doesn't do any good," she said.

Flint had no answer. He thought of telling her that the will of God was unknowable, but he didn't. He wrestled with faith himself.

He turned to another of the stories he had in mind about the current conflict. This one, he decided, ought to be told straightforwardly, naming the name and explaining the circumstances in a way that any reader could examine for himself.

> Readers will notice that this edition is printed on water-stained and damaged newsprint. This circumstance will continue for several months. The paper was not damaged in transit from our supplier in Denver but at the warehouse of the Butterfield Forwarding Company here in Oro Blanco. And not from any accidental or intentional damage done by that excellent company but by the design of parties intending to put this paper into its grave. . . .

Flint recorded the whole story, just as Boggs had told it to him—every detail of the daily visits from Deputy Marshal Bugsy Bowler—and in the end he had a damning study of the abuse of police powers and deliberate destruction of property by law officers on behalf of interested private citizens. He knew it would raise the tempers of all the fair-minded citizens of Oro Blanco.

Law that would do that was law that could not be trusted by anyone.

Flint turned then to the most important of the stories, the one he had been waiting weeks to discuss. The time had come to discuss the lawsuit and its consequences. He only hoped he wasn't too late. He was not at all sure this issue would ever reach the streets or even that he would live long enough to see it in print. But he had to try. He had not yet interviewed the attorney for the Escalante estate, Alonzo Baca, but he couldn't wait any longer. A thundercloud had been gathering over the town, and he could no longer control events.

It will come as a surprise to the many peaceful and law-abiding citizens of Oro Blanco to learn that a lawsuit, now before the federal district court in Albuquerque, will probably result in the invalidation of all deeds to real property in the Oro Blanco district. . . .

When bonanza gold was discovered here a few years ago, territorial officials simply declared the Escalante grant invalid. Claims were filed on mining lodes as if it were public land, and the town-lot company filed for a town-lot patent, also on the presumption that the land here was public domain. The elderly Escalantes were harried to an early grave, but not before willing the grant to the Parish of Saint Joseph.

Father de Cordoba, unlike his opposites, has no desire to uproot citizens whose deeds may be found invalid by the federal court. He would simply grant merchants and private holders the right to their holds by deeding the land to the town-lot company.

The mines are another matter. Father de Cordoba seeks the traditional twenty-five percent royalty for minerals extracted from the several mines on the Escalante grant, not only from current production but from past production as well. These claims were illegally filed on private land. . . .

There was a lot to explain, and it took Flint several hours and a long column of type that filled two galley trays before he had described the entire situation to his satisfaction. He ran two proofs and gave one to Libby. Together they corrected the errors. Then he hid the galley trays in the old cantina oven, just as he had always hidden his most sensitive material.

"I'm scared," said Libby.

"So am I," Flint said. "If you want to stay away for a while, I'll get along."

"No. We've got to get this issue out, no matter what."

"No matter what," said Flint.

37

When Mason Weed slid into a certain snaky mood, he knew he was as dangerous as a silent rattler. He had a way of terrorizing people, though he didn't know quite why he possessed such a gift. A cock of the eyebrow, an icy glare, words that ground like shattered glass—these and an ability to convey mortal menace were his weapons to impose his absolute will upon a refractory world.

Such was his mood when he walked smartly down the grade from the Golconda mine in the middle of the afternoon, through a furnace heat, en route to The Boston. He intended to have a little heart-to-heart with Amelia Lowell, and he was sure dear Amelia would never be the same again. He had suffered some calamities in the past few days, but none matched the black epiphany he had received by post that morning from Detective Egbert Wallheim in Albuquerque. Fortunately there were means to deal with the situation. For a man of Weed's prowess, there were always means.

For months, Mason Weed had worried the bone of a puzzle: Where did Alonzo Baca, attorney for the Escalante estate, acquire the means to pursue the case? Surely the priest, de Cordoba, hadn't a peso. But the little greaser lawyer had met thrust with thrust and had recently prevailed. As a result of Baca's pleading, the court would soon entertain a motion to put all earnings from the district mines into holding pending the verdict on the Escalante grant.

The greaser's success had puzzled Weed. The man had a few Hispanic clients, handled some business for the Church—which, until now, Weed had supposed was the financial engine supporting the slippery little devil—and lived in a modest adobe along with his wife and family. He obviously was a man of precarious means.

It had dawned on Weed to hire an investigator. Egbert Wallheim had filled the bill perfectly, being a man as relentless as Weed himself. The man charged too much—five dollars a day—but Weed suspected the cost would be well worth it, and it was. While the Baca family was attending a requiem mass and funeral for a hidalgo, Wallheim availed himself of the opportunity to walk into Baca's office, situated at the rear of his lengthy adobe and barred by the formidable Consuelo Baca. But on this rare occasion, Detective Wallheim merely trotted through the unlocked front door, picked the simple deadbolt arrangement protecting the office, found Attorney Baca's brown morocco ledger, and discovered regular monthly payments of one hundred dollars, beside which stood the initials A.L.

A.L.! Weed cursed himself for not guessing. The dotty woman had been busily undermining the whole town, invalidating the deed to the very land her building stood upon. Well, he knew exactly how to deal with idiot women, and it would not be by any civilized code she might subscribe to. He would deal with her first. Then he would deal with the rest. By the time he was done with today's piece of nasty work, he would put the whole matter to rest. If he couldn't trust Crawford and the

Bowler brothers, or Bulldog Malone and Saint Peter, or Clegg and his two hired pork chops, then he would have to do it all himself, which secretly gave him a certain satisfaction. Mason Weed understood his superior intelligence, his superior will, and his superior cunning, all of which transcended brute force, muscle, and mayhem. All they had to do was silence that rag, *The Nugget,* and they could complete the business in peace. That's all.

He felt an odd moment of sadness, as if he were about to commit sacrilege. Flint was a man of rare courage. De Cordoba was a brave priest tending his flock. Amelia had her graces. He admired each of them, along with their principled lives. And yet they stood in the way of human progress. He couldn't stop history. Europeans were bringing civilization to, and wrestling wealth from, a land that had lain fallow in the hands of red and brown men. These brave adversaries simply were on the wrong side.

By the time he reached The Boston, his starched collar had wilted. He had raised no sweat; the cauldron of the sun had evaporated it. He pushed inside, letting his unblinking eyes adjust to the gloom. The hour was perfect. The lunch crowd had vanished; the dinner-and-drink crowd had yet to arrive, and the only possibility of unwanted company would be someone transacting business at Amelia's wicket. But he saw no other than Amelia herself, bent over her ledger.

"Why, my dear Mason," she said, surprised.

He grunted. Why was the woman so attractive? Silver-haired, lovely, with eyes as innocent as a child's, she was clearly the most patrician and enchanting woman in these rough precincts.

"Why, you're disturbed about something. We shall have tea," she said, rounding the wicket. He followed her to one of those linen-covered tables. She ran a silver bell and signaled for tea. "Now, tell me, my dear."

"I should have known it was you," he said as soon as they had settled. "You've been financing Baca. Thanks to you, we stand a good chance of losing everything."

"Why do you say that?" she asked blandly.

"Amelia, I have my ways. You send Baca a hundred a month to prosecute a suit that would take the very ground you're on away from you. I've always known you were daffy, but I didn't quite expect you to destroy Oro Blanco."

She didn't respond for some while. "You're a snoop," she said at last.

"I'm what I have to be, for the good of everyone here."

"Not for the good of the Mexicans or the parish."

He didn't reply. He didn't come here to get into an argument. "You, of all people," he said, "betraying your customers. Everyone who walks in here."

She smiled. "If the Escalante estate wins—and it will, my dear—Father de Cordoba intends to deed the very land the town-lot company tried to patent to the company. Every freehold in town'll be safe. Unlike you, my dear Mason, he doesn't wish to dispossess people from their freeholds. The mines are another matter. He wants the parish to receive its rightful royalty, retroactive to the beginning."

A waiter set a pewter tea service before them and vanished into the kitchen. She poured. "There you are, Mason. It's Earl Grey. It's lovely, in this greedy, grubbing world, to see a man like Father de Cordoba, willing to be charitable to all, even those trying to uproot his people—and him."

That news appalled Weed rather than mollified him. If the deeds of all the merchants and artisans were safe, and the dwellings of all the people in town were safe, they wouldn't side with him in the showdown. Why would they? Those who knew about the Escalante case would rejoice in its outcome. Scarcely a soul in Oro Blanco would mind seeing the mine operators paying that royalty to the Escalante grant.

"Does Flint know that?" he asked, his mind leaping ahead.

"Why, of course he does, Mason. He walks with Father de Cordoba most evenings, as soon as it's cool. They're brothers in a way. Each has a large vision of what a good world should be like. I rather admire Mr. Flint, even if he's a bit headstrong and not quite acceptable. He can't spell, you know. A headmaster's son, but he offends Webster. And the good father's able to live on a lofty plane. Not every parish priest would consider the Golden Rule in such circumstances."

Something almost murderous slid through Weed's mind. This madwoman had almost defeated him. But Baca still needed her money. The greaser had employed attorneys in Seville and Mexico City to come up with a copy of the grant. That cost money. And the result would probably devastate Weed and his colleagues. In all likelihood, this madwoman had cost him and his colleagues several million dollars.

He sat there, sipping her tea from a Haviland cup, staring at this coiffed, groomed, fragile, privileged, overeducated, spoiled Boston Brahmin, feeling a loathing that slowly spread from soul to body to fingers. He would gladly strangle her and enjoy her last choked gasp.

"Well, Amelia, what are we going to do?" he asked tightly. "You've cost me a fortune."

"You could grant Father de Cordoba his rights. Withdraw the suit. Agree to a royalty."

He laughed softly. "I expected just such an answer. Here's what we're going to do. We're going to shut down The Boston, and you're going to leave here. Immediately."

"Why, Mason, I've come to civilize Oro Blanco. Perhaps you're the one to leave. You're the only barbarian here."

"I think you're pretending not to understand me. You want me to state it plainer, Amelia?"

"Yes, my dear, state it."

"You'll leave New Mexico whether you want to or not. You'll find no future in the Territory."

"You're still not saying it plainly, Mason."

"It doesn't need to be stated. You understand perfectly."

"Why, my dear, you're politely leaving the threats out of everything you say. What you really mean is that you'll drive me out by foul means. You'll find ways—you and Marshal Crawford and Mayor Malone and perhaps the Santa Fe people who misgovern this lovely Territory—to remove me by force."

"You haven't heard me say it, Amelia."

"Oh, but you're saying it. I'll put it to the test and stay on. Then we'll see."

Her resistance irked him. He peered about the dining room, seeing her man cleaning the tables. Weed waited until the man vanished into the kitchen.

"So many sad things might happen. The Territory might discover that you run an unchartered bank. The city might discover you lack a proper license for selling spirits. The courts might rule against you in ruinous suits. You might find yourself in trouble about back taxes. You might find yourself facing criminal charges and prison. You might be compelled to deed over the building to your creditors."

She smiled, her eyes dancing. "Ah, Mason, I wasn't mistaken. You're behaving exactly as I knew you would. But my answer is no. I shall stay. I shall finance Father de Cordoba's suit. Now what are you going to do about it?"

He sighed. "Remove you. Break you. But it doesn't have to come to that, Amelia. You can leave here unscathed and financially sound—or not."

"Forcibly removing me would be a nice scandal. Mr. Flint would enjoy writing it up."

"Flint won't be around to write it."

She laughed melodically. "Surely, Mason, I possess certain rights. One of them is spending my money on any lawsuit I

choose to prosecute. Another is to live here peacefully and conduct a lawful business. Put me out of business if you must. Put
Mr. Flint out of business if you must, but do you suppose that
will silence him—or me?"

He cut that off. "Amelia, you're going to be on tomorrow's
coach to Silver City and out of the Territory in two days."

"We'll see," she said sweetly.

He stared coldly at her, knowing the formidable woman
would yield only to brute force. "I'm shutting down your
bank," he said. "You've cost me a young fortune, and now I'll
pay myself back. You're no longer in the banking business.
You've gone bankrupt. Let's say there was a run on your
reserves."

She stiffened. "Most thieves find excuses for what they do,"
she said. "There are always excuses for crime, aren't there,
Mason?"

He didn't reply. Instead he rose, walked to the safe, scooped
its contents into a canvas bank bag, and studied her ledger. He
knew he had taken several thousand in cash and coin. He decided it would be helpful to take the ledger too, so he stuffed it
into the bank bag.

She rang a silver bell furiously, and her man appeared.
"Mr. Weed is robbing my bank. Stop him," she commanded.

The young man hesitated. "This is a joke?" he asked. "Mr.
Weed, sir . . ."

"Oh no, I'm doing some business," Weed said cheerfully.
"Amelia's having fun with me. It's a little transaction that's long
overdue. You're dismissed. Everything is fine. Go on back to
work."

The man stared uncertainly at him and at Amelia. "I don't
know . . ." he muttered.

"Stop him," commanded Amelia, but the man was obviously
hesitant to confront Oro Blanco's foremost citizen and The Boston's most important customer.

"Thanks for the tea, Amelia," Weed said. "Be sure you're

out of here by tomorrow. Marshal Crawford's a hard man to control, you know. He'll be eager to lock the doors."

Weed walked out calmly, carrying the satchel, while the waiter hesitated. The gold-mining magnate felt bad about it all, but some things couldn't be helped.

38

Amelia Lowell watched the town's foremost citizen depart with her entire bank while her kitchen man hesitated.

"It was a robbery," she said to him.

He gaped at her. "Ma'am? Mr. Weed?"

"Oh, go back to your work," she said. "I'll take care of this." She could hardly blame the youth.

He sidled away, mystified and ill-at-ease.

Her mind whirled with questions: Should she go to Crawford? How much cash had been lost? Could she ever repay it? Could she hire an attorney? Would her little stipend from Massachusetts get her through all this? Could she and Mr. Flint make enough of a fuss to get it back? Might this awful theft be just the thing Attorney Baca needed to win the case?

Mason Weed, she thought, was a loathsome man. When it came to money, his civilized veneer had fallen away. He could have concluded the matter then and there, agreed to end the lawsuit, given Father de Cordoba's church its rightful royalty, and gone on making a fortune.

What good would it do to go to the police, when they were the henchmen of that awful Weed? Or the mayor? Or the justice of the peace? She didn't know, but the more she pondered it, the more she decided it was absolutely necessary to make the matter known to officials, to file a complaint, to press charges. She would make a public record, and if they hid it, all the worse for them.

She pinned a straw hat onto her silver hair and made her way through the heat to the little jail and marshal's office at the upper end of the Avenida. She was all too familiar with this place, having recently been an involuntary guest here. Maybe she was about to be such a guest again. She entered, her nostrils assaulted by the odors of tobacco and sweat.

Within she beheld Town Marshal Crawford in his chair, his face multicolored—green, blue, black, angry yellow, red. She didn't have much to crow about at the moment, but the sight gladdened her. He eyed her sourly.

"I wish to file a complaint. I shall expect you to bring the party to the bar of justice."

He eyed her skeptically.

"You may bring charges of robbery against Mr. Mason Weed," she said. "It happened a few minutes ago in my place of business. He stole my entire bank, every penny left me by my depositors, as well as bank funds. I don't have the exact amount, but it was around five thousand."

Crawford's eyes retreated into their black sockets.

"Well, be about it," she said.

"Weed?" he asked. "Were there witnesses?"

"Yes, my man, name of Gabriel Stoughton. I'm filing the complaint. How shall I do it?"

"You won't," he said.

"I will. What are you, some lackey of his? Have you no manhood?"

"Vamoose, lady," he said.

"Very well, when I contact county officials, they'll hear that you refused to act on my complaint. And you're running for election too."

He stood suddenly. "Get out before I bust your arm. And if you say a word about this, you'll be swallowing your teeth."

Her head throbbed. She was getting a migraine. She smiled sweetly and departed under his murderous glare.

She walked wearily through a wilting, suffocating heat so intense she could scarcely breathe, turned onto Weed Street, and pushed through the door of *The Oro Blanco Progress*. There she discovered that Clegg man glaring at her from eyes set on either side of a mountain of red veins.

"I have a story," she said.

"I am always an eager partaker of the feast of news in our fair metropolis," he replied in a mellifluent whiskey voice.

"Will you run it?"

"*The Progress* is a fearless, impartial beacon of honor with a sacred trust to inform our community," he said.

"Good. You shall print this. An hour or so ago, I was robbed by the owner and superintendent of the Golconda Mining Company, Mr. Mason Weed. He stole every penny in my safe. I've taken the matter to the town constables and made a formal complaint." She smiled.

His carp lips puckered a while, and his bright blue eyes flicked toward her and away.

"Ah, madam, we must verify everything, you know."

"I'll verify it. Come with me and I'll show you my empty safe and let you talk to my man."

"Madam, I don't doubt your veracity and your sterling honesty, but it will take me some little while to corroborate your remarkable story."

"There's more to it, my dear," she said relentlessly. "Our friend Mr. Weed also told me that I must leave town. If I don't, it seems that all sorts of misfortunes will befall me. I shall be hauled before courts, made to suffer, reduced to poverty, driven from my place of business and home. Be sure to print that too. I'm taking it to the other paper, you know. You wouldn't want them to scoop you."

"Remarkable! This is a rich vein. Pray tell, madam, what prompted this alleged display of distemper in the estimable Mr. Weed? It seems, ah, a bit odd?"

"Oh, I'm sure Weed'll tell you in his own way, just as he'll dictate what a newspaper toady must write. But I'll tell you this, Mr. Clegg: I've been supporting a good and just cause, which I am perfectly free to do."

"A good cause, eh? I don't suppose you resist progress."

"Of a kind, yes. I wouldn't call theft of a land grant progress. You might, but I do believe that its owners ought to get something for it, wouldn't you say?"

"If they own it. There's the rub, madam."

"They've owned it since 1752, Mr. Clegg. But I imagine you'd like for them to own it a thousand years before they call it their own."

Clegg sighed. "I'm afraid, madam, that our standards prevent us from publishing unwarranted gossip. If you'll point to a few witnesses, we would make it our civic duty to bring this prominent citizen of Oro Blanco to an accounting. We'll get his side of the story and proceed."

"Proceed to hush it up, I'm afraid, my dear Clegg. You're a very impudent person, calling yourself an editor."

"At your service," he said gallantly. "No matter what a lady chooses to call me, I return only bouquets and compliments."

She left, trembling slightly. She had thoroughly violated Weed's command to hush it all up. And she wasn't done, either. Her head renewed its throbbing, and it reminded her of the trouble her cast-iron puritan conduct was generating. She yearned to retreat to her darkened bedroom and place a cool, damp towel over her forehead.

She walked slowly across the Avenida de la Virgen. It always seemed to her as if she were penetrating a foreign country when she did. She had nothing in common with these simple Papists and superstitious peasants and couldn't even bear the company of any of them except the ironic, dour padre. She certainly wouldn't invite them to her salons. But their cause was her cause, and the injustices visited upon them had outraged her.

The Miner's Home Saloon beckoned to her. That brawler, Mountain Jack Treat, was a man she might call on if she must, but she avoided relying on tradesmen if she could. She didn't need that ruffian. The steel in her spine—along with the whale-bone in her heart—would suffice nicely to deal with trash like Mason Weed. Headache or not, she was moving smartly along, like a good Yankee clipper ship with wind in its sails.

She turned the corner and found her way to *The Nugget*. And there, before Mr. Flint and young Miss Madigan, she told her entire story, rather enjoying it in spite of the appalling headache.

"We'll publish it all," said Sam Flint quietly.

39

Amelia Lowell closed The Boston. She could not pay her cooks or waiters or her manservant. Sam Flint generously offered to run an advertisement for free, announcing the closing and the reason: robbery. His news story would go into all that, he said. She thought it was wondrously brave of him to write the story at all.

She intended to open The Boston again as soon as she could get some money from the East. It would take time. Her next quarterly stipend wasn't due for two months. Oro Blanco was two hundred miles from a telegraph, and even if she wired for money, she feared her Boston bankers would hesitate and verify before acting.

She was penniless, but she had property she might barter for the things she needed, and the restaurant kitchen contained tins and bins of food.

For Amelia Lowell, all this was her just dessert. Her conscience tormented her. She did not approve of her recent conduct; she had been spineless. When *The Progress* had opened, she had shifted most of her advertising. It had been the expedient thing to do. She had thought the way to keep her elite customers was to show some solidarity with them. Weed's nasty, lying rag had been prominently displayed at her wicket, available free to anyone who wished to read it while eating lunch. She hadn't entirely abandoned Flint's *Nugget*—there were copies of that too, but hidden from view. One had to ask for them. She had even chased away Flint's perfectly innocent urchin, who was only trying to earn a few dimes.

Amelia sat desolately in her quarters above the restaurant, rebuking herself. But it was a pointless exercise, and after an hour of flagellation, she turned to the future. She intended to start up her Lyceum events again, just as soon as she opened, and the first two speakers would be Samuel Flint and Juan de Cordoba, addressing the issue of Oro Blanco's future. She would print up flyers and advertise the event and perhaps, through public education, alter the soul of Oro Blanco.

She had deliberately defied Weed and expected more trouble from him, but she knew that most of the ladies and gentlemen of Oro Blanco were perfectly honorable souls, reasonable in their judgments. When they learned that the heir of the Escalante grant had no wish to take the land from under them and would grant his own deed to the town-lot company, they would come around. Most people were against theft on principle, whether theft from themselves or theft from others.

She sipped some tea and then reached for a pencil. Mason Weed was going to find out that threats of ruin, banishment, imprisonment, and lawsuits would not stop a New England Brahmin or even slow her down.

It was in such a mood, nursing her soul, that she was summoned to her apartment door by an imperious knock. She opened to Mason Weed, who pushed in without invitation.

She followed him into her parlor, which he surveyed with an owner's eye, and then settled himself on the settee.

"Well, Amelia," he said, "you didn't follow my direction."

"Get out. This is my home," she said.

He smiled wryly. "I must admire you, madam. But admiration doesn't stop me from doing what I have to do. You've made the matter public. Of course, not a soul believes you. They enjoy your inventions. But I did caution that certain things would happen. We discussed your future. Your ruin, as a matter of fact. And now I'm afraid it'll come to pass, just as you were warned it would."

He smiled at her, and she studied the man. He had dressed himself nattily, in a cutaway coat, striped trousers, starched collar, and broad cravat. He looked the magnate that he was, but he also looked somehow weak to her. Some aura clung to him, not of softness—he was the hardest of men—but of vanity and indulgence and excuses to paper over his conduct. She knew at once his vulnerability: He needed to feel he was a perfectly honorable gentleman. He found lofty excuses for all that he did—such as Progress, for disfranchising the original settlers of Oro Blanco.

"Do what you will; I won't change an iota. I will resist every inch of the way, Mr. Weed."

He surveyed her blandly, perhaps to learn whether this was bravado or serious talk. Eventually she detected a modicum of respect in his eyes.

"You seem to enjoy pain," he said too easily.

"Mr. Weed, I come from a long line of Congregational ministers. If there's one thing that makes a Puritan happy, it's to suffer on behalf of a principle. If the principle is a divine one, a good Puritan will go smiling to the gallows. My principles happen to have divine origins: Thou shalt not steal. And the Golden Rule, requiring us to treat others as we would wish to be treated. All right, you have a middle-aged lady at your total mercy. Proceed, bring out the bullies. Show us both what a man you are, what power you have over my frail body. You have no power over my mind or soul. I will tell the world about it."

A tic developed around his mouth. He sighed, pursed his lips, and got down to business. "You're being a bit melodramatic, Amelia. I've come to have you sign the deed to The Boston. I'm taking it in payment for the costs I've incurred fighting to hold what's mine."

"There you go, papering your theft with your self-justifications. No, Mr. Weed, you can't escape your conscience. You aren't a gentleman. You aren't even a man."

Weed laughed softly, perhaps because he couldn't think of anything to say. He pulled out a deed, a bottle of ink, and a nib pen and set them on the escritoire beside her.

"Sign there," he said.

"I won't sign anything."

"Sign or you'll suffer worse."

She refused to budge. "Mr. Weed, you may as well prepare to commit murder."

A tic began stabbing at his lips and then his eyelids.

"Go ahead and forge my name," she said. "You'll have an excuse at hand for that too. If I live, I'll tell the world about it. Maybe even Mr. Clegg, who strikes me as a man devoid of anything resembling a conscience, will decide you're too much for him. I suppose that's the litmus test, Mr. Weed. Let's call it the Editor Clegg Test. Here's a man without a bone of truth or honor or mercy in him. If Mr. Clegg is appalled by you, then you'll know you've reached the seventh layer of Hades."

He blinked, and she sensed she had won something through sheer will. "I'm going to reopen when I am able to get funds. You will not stop me. I will make sure everyone knows of this episode. I did well, didn't I? I started with your sterling officer, Marshal Crawford, and then I told your sterling editor, and then I told a few others, including Mr. Flint. I suppose you'll murder him too, for the sake of the gold you're stealing from its owners." She stood. "If you're going to kill me, sir, be about it. Otherwise, you'll kindly depart from my private home."

She came up only to his chin, but she stood there, prickly with anticipation.

"I've better ways," he said at last. "As I told you, you will be leaving town at once. You'll go where you will, but you'll not return to Oro Blanco or New Mexico. It doesn't much matter whether I have your signature on the deed or not. Once you're gone, you'll never possess The Boston again. The stage leaves for Silver City in half an hour. I noticed that the team's already in harness. They're friends, the Butter-field Forwarding Company. I've already had a little talk with the driver. In fact, I gave him a good tip—twenty dollars. He won't let you off the stage until Silver City. Now, Amelia, you may pack a bag if you wish, or not if you wish. It doesn't mat-ter to me. Once you're gone, I can conclude my affairs in peace."

She responded by sitting down in her wing chair.

He understood at once. "All right. You choose ruin."

"What a man you are," she replied.

The self-rebuke flickered in his eyes again.

"If you're going to ruin me, be about it. If you're going to get some louts to carry me out and put me on that stagecoach in front of everyone on the street, be about it. I do believe there'll be twenty or thirty people there. Maybe you can show them my violated body."

Weed smiled again, and she saw that she had won.

"You're the sideshow," he said. "I'm sorry my attention was diverted. You've done me a favor, Amelia. You're a woman of great courage and strength. If things were not so painful between us, I'd propose wedlock."

He smiled. She smiled back. He bowed graciously, swept up his papers, and descended the long stairs at the side of the building. She stood at her window, watching the magnate of Oro Blanco go.

He would begin his real business now, Amelia knew, which

was destroying *The Nugget.* As long as the little paper survived and published the real news, a mantle of protection lay over even the humblest souls in Oro Blanco. Poor Mr. Flint, she thought.

40

Sam Flint set the story of Amelia Lowell's ordeal, being careful to ascribe each assertion to her. He didn't doubt her, but there was always the possibility of exaggeration. An innate caution, honed on years of reporting the world's events, prompted him to write in a guarded fashion. He composed as he set type, which was the way most veteran editor-compositors did it, and before long the story filled his galley tray. He proofed and corrected it and then slid the tray into the cantina oven, along with the rest of the explosive material that would make the forthcoming issue of *The Nugget* memorable.

He wondered if it would ever see print. Surely Mason Weed and his crowd would know that this issue might well arouse every decent and honorable citizen of Oro Blanco. Perhaps they thought they had destroyed his stock of newsprint and there would be no more editions. But, he mused, were he in Mason Weed's shoes, he would make sure that *The Nugget* was done for.

Flint would print that evening, but before then he wanted to see what *The Progress* was saying, if anything. He left the plant to Libby, who was breaking down type, and hiked over to

Phineas Clegg's sanctum. The famous editor wasn't around, but Printer's Devil was, returning type to its case boxes.

"What do youse want?"

"A paper," Flint said, plucking one from the counter.

"Five cents."

"I have a two-year subscription," Flint said and walked out. That was about right, he figured. Those bullies had demolished a whole stack of Libby's papers.

He stood in the street and studied the paper. Phineas Clegg had not covered any of the embarrassing events of the week. The constables' absence on the streets went unreported. The black-and-blue color of Crawford's mug occasioned no comment. But Flint did discover a lengthy plea for law and order, a savage diatribe against hooligans, muggers, footpads, foreigners, and undesirable elements who were disturbing the peace and tranquility of progressive white citizens. Clegg called for a sheriff's posse to restore order.

Amused, Flint peered up and down the tranquil streets of Oro Blanco. Rioters were nowhere in sight.

Advertising ran chockablock through the whole paper. One way or another, Weed's minions had bullied every business in town into advertising in *The Progress* and pulling ads from *The Nugget*, no doubt with threats. His own had fallen off to nothing, save a small ad for The Miner's Home Saloon. Amelia hadn't a cent to pay for an ad. He no longer even published cards from the milliner or from politicians. The promoters of progress had obviously visited each and every advertiser in *The Nugget* and twisted arms. Weed knew just what to do.

The Progress that week was devoted largely to filler. Clegg reported no burglaries, injuries, weddings, funerals, sales, baptisms, or any other events. The only local story of any consequence was one devoted to the mines. The Golconda was pushing its expansion to a new level; the Gold Queen and Pandora were reporting record yields.

All that suited Flint just fine. If Clegg wouldn't report local news, Flint surely would. And people would read *The Nugget* because Phineas Clegg's paper remained silent about all the important things.

It was worth a jibe. Back in his sanctum, Flint composed an amiable little barb aimed at *The Progress*. Why, he asked, was that rich, biweekly paper so devoid of local news? Was its editor too lazy to gather it? Did the paper exist to serve the community, or did it exist merely to promote a certain agenda?

He showed it to Libby, and she smiled. "I haven't been here long, Mr. Flint, but you've taught me what a good paper should do. I think I want to edit a paper someday. Do you think a woman could do that?"

"Of course I do! Maybe someday soon you'll be editing *The Nugget*. I think you'd do a mighty fine job, Libby."

"Do you really think so?"

"Libby, whatever you set your heart on, you'll do. This is a good place. You'll grow up with the town. Clegg's rag'll blow away. All this trouble, it'll pass, and Oro Blanco will be a civilized place to live."

She frowned. "But how'll I get a press and all this stuff?"

He didn't really have an answer, but he had hope. "Sometimes, the good, sound businessmen in a town know they need a paper—especially if they've had to deal with a bad one. Sometimes they'll form a company and get a plant and then look for the right person to edit the paper. Maybe they'll do that here, and maybe they'll choose you."

She scowled. "They won't choose me," she said in a way that closed the discussion.

He nodded to broach another matter. "Libby, I'm printing tonight. Tomorrow, I'll get Jack Treat to sell papers. I don't think it'd be safe for you."

"I need the money," she said. "I need it for a doctor. Ma doesn't get out of bed very much. It's bad."

It tugged at him. "But Libby, this issue—this issue . . ."

"I'm not afraid of them," she said.

"You should be. Those pugs of Clegg's might show up again. Maybe Crawford'll show up. Then what?"

"I'll walk away. That's all. They won't hurt me now. Not after Mountain Jack."

"You're more trusting than I am."

"Please let me try. If there's trouble, I'll just leave, and you can get Mountain Jack."

He fought with himself and surrendered. "Libby, at the first sign of trouble, you come back here. If Crawford or his bullies come, just walk off. If you'll do that, it'll be all right. Your mother needs to see the doctor again. We'll find a way."

"Her breathing's bad, Mr. Flint. She's so . . . like wax in her bed. Just like wax."

He sighed, wondering if Maureen Madigan was closer to death than Libby knew. The girl had seen death but might not be letting herself see this one. "I'd like to come and visit after we get this issue out," he said.

"She can't talk much."

That's why he wanted to visit, but he said nothing of that. "Maybe tomorrow afternoon, after we get the paper out. If you'd be willing," he said.

She looked at him somberly. "You think she's dying now," she said.

He nodded.

That afternoon he slid the galley trays from their hiding place and built the pages. He had no paid ads, so he ran a few free ones, knowing that the merchants wouldn't like it—not if Weed had threatened them. But he had to fill great holes of space with something. *The Nugget* would again be a single sheet, printed on two sides and folded. This issue would appear on water-stained, wrinkled newsprint.

Libby left for the day, and Flint set to work printing the most important edition of any paper he had ever edited. It worried him. A few thugs could jump him now, destroy his finished pages, steal his type, destroy his newsprint. He had no way to defend himself.

He cranked out paper after paper that afternoon, pounding on his handpress, yanking sheet after sheet from the bed and laying them on a growing stack. His eye was on the door. They knew when he printed. They knew when to strike. He sweated a river in the heat but didn't quit. He knew what he would do: Two hundred copies would dry overnight in plain sight, just as always. Two hundred additional copies would lie in the rear of the *mercado* part of the old adobe building, well hidden from sight. Four hundred copies.

He finished the first hundred and carried the whole inky stack to its hiding place. He printed another hundred in the evening dusk and hid them also. Then he set to work on the decoys, slapping the most-wrinkled paper into the tympan, lowering the platen, inking the type with his chamois ball—page upon page until the heat dehydrated him.

He had printed more than a hundred when the Bowler boys walked in. Billy limped. Grins split their faces. One brandished a revolver. The other twirled a long hickory stick.

"Up to your old tricks, Flint?" asked Bugsy.

"What do you want?"

Billy chuckled. "We want you," he said.

"What have I done now?"

"Oh, whatever we thunk up. Get away from that press and put your hands up."

"You're asking for trouble," Flint said softly.

Billy got serious. "Flint, we'd just as soon leave you in a puddle of blood. Only Delbert, he says don't make meat unless you have to."

"I suppose the First Amendment doesn't matter," Flint said.

"Never heard of it," Bugsy said, examining the pile of newly printed papers. He plucked one up and studied it. "I'll keep this for a souvenir," he said. "Wrinkled edges. I shoulda dumped more water on that heap of paper. Well, live and learn."

"The old *Nugget*, she just went outa business," Billy said. He prodded Flint away from the press with his club.

"I think a person has a right to know what the charges are," Flint said.

Bugsy laughed and leveled the revolver at Flint's belly. Flint stared up at the bore, taut as a fiddle string, and wondered how long he might live.

Billy set to work. He yanked the heavy forms from the bed of the press and let them crash to the floor. Type flew in all directions, along with ruler lines and the wooden blocks called furniture. The pair laughed.

Next he heaved the case boxes to the floor. They cracked open, spilling their type.

"My oh my," said Billy. "What a mess."

Flint thought of a lot of things to say but kept his silence. A revolver leveled at a man had that effect.

Billy lifted a fistful of *The Nugget* and dropped it. "Hey, the ink's still wet. You done dirtied my fingers, Flint."

Flint kept quiet.

Billy spotted the old cantina stove. "Ah, there's the answer. We can't have inky paper around." He grabbed fistfuls of newspapers, shoved them into the cast-iron oven, and lit them with a lucifer. They didn't burn well. He spotted an oil lamp and poured the contents of its reservoir into the stove. The smoking paper flared into flame.

"Ah, that's better. Takes some doing, don't it, Flint? How does it feel to see your filthy sheet die?"

He fed paper into the blaze until *The Nugget* had vanished—save the one copy they would take back to their masters. Then, for good measure, he kicked the case boxes until they split apart.

"Flint, get out of town. You hang around, you're dead," Bugsy said. "That's not from me; that's from Weed. Thought you'd like to know."

Flint watched them leave. His heartbeat slowed. He still had a press, type scattered from one end of the room to the other, and some water-damaged paper. And two hundred copies of this edition hidden from sight.

It was time to recruit Mountain Jack Treat.

41

Libby arrived early and studied the pied type scattered from one end of the shop to the other.

"Did they hurt you?" she asked.

"Told me to get out of town," Flint replied.

"Who was it?"

"The Bowlers. One held a revolver on me; the other threw everything to the floor and burned the copies I'd printed."

"Oh, Mr. Flint. I guess I don't have a job." She sounded so downhearted he thought he'd better tell her the rest.

"Libby, I'd like you to pick up type and sort it into piles on the bench. They wrecked the case boxes, so all we can do is make piles of each letter, upper and lower."

"I was hoping to sell papers—I need to earn something . . ." She sighed. "I guess I never will."

"Libby, come here." He walked through an arch into the old *mercado*.

She followed, puzzled.

"Up there, I printed two hundred and hid them."

"What?" She could scarcely believe him.

He clambered heavily onto a counter and reached toward a top shelf, pulling papers into sight. "Here. I printed these first and hid them. Glad I did. They caught me when I was printing the next bunch."

"Oh, Mr. Flint," she whispered. "I knew you'd do something. Now I'd like to go sell them."

"Libby, it's too dangerous for you. Oh, it'd be all right for a while—they think they destroyed this edition and my shop. So they won't be waiting around. But they'd find out fast enough."

"But I'll just run if I see them." Desperation filled her face.

"I can't let you, Libby. I need you here. There's a day's work just getting that type organized. And I can't let you onto the streets with this edition. They'll hurt you."

She swung reluctantly into the cantina, defeat etching her body.

"Libby, the first twenty papers I sell, I'll have two dollars. It's yours for your mother."

She nodded, unsmiling. "I wanted to sell this paper so bad."

"No. They might hurt you."

"Oh, they wouldn't," she mumbled with doubt in her eyes.

He watched her begin picking up type. He had ruined her day and assigned her drudgery.

Flint and Jack Treat divided the papers. They had worked out an elaborate plan to distribute *The Nugget* and also to preserve a few copies. Treat would hide a handful in his Miner's Home Saloon and sell the rest on Libby's corner, perhaps before the constables got wind of it. Flint would take his armload to the Golconda minehead and sell it to workers arriving for the day shift. It would go down the shaft in lunch pails and come up again at the end of the shift, finding its way into the homes and boardinghouses of Oro Blanco.

"They're itching to shoot you, Treat. If they pull a sidearm, don't resist."

Mountain Jack guffawed. "Nothing like a lead pill to heat up my temper," he said. "I'll peddle the whole lot. Should fetch you ten dollars."

"You take your two out of it."

"Naw, Flint. You're flat busted. I got cash coming in every day. You pay Libby and buy yourself vittles. We need you here."

Flint didn't argue. He had little. The sale of all two hundred would net him around twenty dollars.

He turned to Libby, who was on her hands and knees, plucking type from the floor and dropping it into a pail. "If they come in here, Libby, go out the rear door through my apartment, if you can. Just avoid them. Don't try to protect the equipment. You're much more valuable than pieces of iron and type metal."

She looked annoyed. She wanted to fight. Her Irish was up, and he wondered whether she'd look after her own safety.

"Libby, me sweetheart, you give 'em bleddy dickens," Treat said, his eyes alight with joy. Anything resembling a fight animated him. "Ye are a terror of a child. I'd hate to be your paw."

This time she grinned.

Flint and Treat slipped into the deserted streets and walked the Avenida as far as Treat's saloon. He vanished inside and emerged again, carrying a few less papers. Then Treat hiked across the Avenida and established himself on Libby's old corner. Flint didn't like the way the red sunrise poured blood over the cheery face of Mountain Jack.

Flint hurried toward the Golconda, climbing the steep grade alongside quiet miners heading for the collar of the shaft and the cage that would drop them into tiny tunnels far under the surface. He posted himself on the path and began selling.

"Read *The Nugget*," he said. "Read about Mason Weed."

That was all it took. "Read about Mason Weed" would be his line. Half a dozen miners crowded up, bought papers, and headed for the gallows frame above.

"Read about Mason Weed," Flint said conversationally. He hardly needed to shout to men walking right by him. "Read about Mason Weed."

They bought. Some didn't want change for their two bits. A few bought two copies. This was their paper—Mountain Jack Treat said so. The pitiful, thin, one-page edition cost twice as much as the fat *Progress* with all its ads, but it didn't matter. Flint's paper had all the real news.

It amazed Flint that in ten or twelve minutes he had sold out, save one copy he intended to hide somewhere. He knew he had more than ten dollars too, perhaps twelve. It heartened him. Men stood at the minehead above, reading. More would read during their lunch break deep underground. In the bottom of Weed's own mine were scores of copies of a paper that described the ways he and his bullies had brutalized Oro Blanco and the nature of the lawsuit over the Escalante grant. Most of them would be learning of that for that first time. Many would side with Weed on that one, but the fierce court struggle to wrest the Escalante land from the parish would no longer be a secret known only by the town's ruling cabal.

Flint saw no sign of a constable and doubted that Crawford or the Bowler bullies were out prowling. Why should they? Hadn't they destroyed *The Nugget*?

Selling had been easy. He hiked down the slope, his pockets jingling with coins. He knew where he would hide that last copy, and he headed for the dark, lifeless bulk of The Boston. He knocked at Amelia's apartment door. She responded with fear in her eyes.

"Take this," he said. "Read it and hide it. We did it. They tried to destroy the edition last night, but I'd hidden some."

"Oh, dear man, come in for tea—"

"Not now, Amelia. I have to check on Treat; keep an eye on our Libby."

"Of course, my dear Flint. Of course."

He hiked down the Avenida and found Treat selling to early risers, mostly merchants and tradesmen. Deering, the coal-and-ice dealer, bought a copy, surveyed the avenue, and tucked it under his wagon seat.

"Deering, pass the bleddy rag on after ye've read her," Treat said. "She's like a barrel of powder."

Deering hawed his team away, as if afraid even to be seen with the town's troublemakers.

"We're going to do it. We'll get this edition out," Flint exulted.

"I wish a copper'd show his puss," Treat said. "My poor old fist needs company."

But they spotted no blue uniforms, nor Marshal Crawford's black suit in the glowing morning.

"I'll take a copy to the padre," Flint said, plucking one from Treat's armload.

"You want your cash?"

"No, keep it at the saloon. I expect the wrecking crew'll tackle my shop again—a lot more carefully this time. They'd find it."

Treat hoorawed and advanced on a pair of ladies perambulating their babies.

Flint watched the man gravely—the danger seemed to be mounting by the minute—and hastened across the Avenida and deep into the Mexican quarter. He circled across the plaza, admiring the new *pozo*, and headed for the padre's little adobe room—it didn't deserve the name rectory. But de Cordoba wasn't in, and the plaza still slept in the cool light of the morning.

Flint tried the church and discovered the father in a chasuble mumbling the morning mass, his face to the altar, his back to a congregation of half a dozen old women and a boy in the nave. The padre recited the familiar Latin by rote, as he had most of the mornings of his priesthood. Flint listened quietly. Something ancient and true permeated the tranquil, shadowed room, largely lit by altar candles that cast a dim orange glow on the wrinkled faces of the old women.

Maybe this day these people found the safety they sought, he thought, sliding out into the morning light. He left *The Nugget* inside the padre's door and hastened back to his shop. He was worried about Libby.

But she was all right. She had all the type off the plank floor and had mounded it on the worktable.

"We did it!" he said. "It's out. Here." He dug into his pockets, counted out two dollars, and set it before her. "This is for you."

She looked blankly at him. "But I didn't earn it."

"I wouldn't let you earn it out there," he said. "Take it. We can go another week if they don't destroy us."

"You sold out?"

"I did, at the mine. Treat's sold more than half of his. It's out. They'll never hide their secrets again."

She smiled, the first real smile he had seen in days. "How's your mother?" he asked.

Her smile vanished.

"Libby, I can do this sorting. That money can buy her some medicine—"

"Oh, no! I have to work! I want to."

Flint headed restlessly toward the door and squinted into the light. He saw no constables coming, no deputized posses, no murderous crowds. But that didn't mean he and Libby were safe.

"Libby, I'm going to bolt this door. It won't keep a crowd out of here for long—any copper could kick it down—but it'll give you a moment. If trouble comes, don't wait. You run out the back way as fast as you can. Promise me that."

She nodded slowly and began dropping type into tiny piles again. She seemed so haunted, not like other young girls her age. Fear and desperation had settled in the hollows of her eyes, and she slumped over her task as if life would never relent, never give her a portion of goodness. "I wish I could be someone else," she said absently.

"Libby," he began hoarsely, though he couldn't finish what he needed to say—that she was a small, sweet saint touched by sorrow.

42

Sam Flint sensed that something had changed in Oro Blanco. He couldn't quite put his finger on it. That explosive issue of *The Nugget* had vanished into the town without a trace. He knew that his paper was being read, passed from person to person. And Jack Treat reported that the miners in his saloon were arguing about the Escalante grant, the abuse of Amelia, and the rights of the greasers.

He expected trouble all day Wednesday, but none visited him. That afternoon, while he and Libby were sorting type, the padre appeared in the shop. He surveyed the mess but said nothing.

"Those are the case boxes, *sí*?" he asked, pointing to the demolished type chests. "I would like them if you do not want them."

"Sure, take them," Flint said. He didn't know what he would use to store his fonts, but the boxes were beyond repair.

"I will give them to Bartolomeo," he said.

A few minutes later the padre loaded the shattered wooden chests onto the back of a burro and led the animal away.

Flint and Libby continued to sort type into little mounds. He was fearful that a Bowler or two might wander in and scatter the whole day's effort to the floor again with one sweep of the arm. But no one came. Flint dared to think that no one would. Something as common and powerful as public opinion was staying the hand of Weed's men. However much the Anglo citizens of Oro Blanco might disagree with Flint, he knew they would rise up in rage at further efforts to railroad him out of town, suppress the paper, or abuse generous citizens like Amelia Lowell. Public opinion was the great explosive loosed by a truthful little paper. Public opinion could curb even such a ruthless mogul as Mason Weed, at least for a while.

The next day, Flint received another clue to the shift of mood. John Strong, the hardware man, stopped by and bought a three-column-by-ten-inch advertisement. He wished to promote his gardening tools in *The Nugget*. Mrs. Duffy, the milliner, restored her one-column card. Neither of them said a word about their reasons. Flint would need a lot more advertising to stay afloat, but the change heartened him. He had been on the brink of starvation.   •

All that day Flint wondered what he could do about type chests. He couldn't afford new ones and he couldn't think of a substitute for the shallow drawers criss-crossed by the wooden grid that made pockets to hold the type.

He had to start over, and he began with the masthead. He gathered the sixty-point display type that had gone into the mast and created THE ORO BLANCO NUGGET anew. He added the ten-cent price and a line of his regular Caslon type naming himself as editor and proprietor. Then he cut a ruler line and pushed the new mast to the top of the chase, where it had always stayed. It heartened him. He had rebuilt the mast, the name, the flag of his leaking ship.

Libby had slipped into deep silence that day, and he wondered what had deepened her gloom. She seemed desperate. He waited for her to tell him, but she didn't.

"Libby, how's your mother?" he asked at last. "Did you get the doctor?"

She glanced at him darkly. "I got Dr. Worth. He listened to her chest and looked in her mouth and that's all he did. He just talked to her."

"What'd he say?"

"Oh, I don't know. He talked about me. He said I was coming fine; I was strong as a horse. He said I could make my way in the world; I was plumb grown up now. He said I had some sense."

Flint's heart sank. "That's all? He didn't leave any medicine?"

"He said he would give her some opiate to kill her pain."

"How did your mother respond?"

"She cried, and then she slept. He didn't charge me, so I have two dollars."

"Libby—"

"Just let me work!" she cried, turning away.

That day Flint rebuilt the ads and collected some news from merchants who eyed him seriously. When he returned late in the afternoon, he found Father de Cordoba waiting in the shop. And he found a miracle: One of the case boxes had been mended.

"Ah, Señor Flint. I have a magician among my people, old Bartolomeo. He makes the furniture that the gringos buy at the market. I told him to put these together for our friend, and he shook his head. But he started at once, with his glue from the hooves of horses and his rawhide bandages. It is not pretty—see how the rawhide holds it together—but it is a case box, *que no*?"

Flint slid open the drawers, amazed. The pulverized, wounded wood had been patiently assembled piece by piece and glued together. The box had an abused look about it, but it would hold the letters. Joyously he began dropping the piles of type into their pigeonholes.

"The other box, it will take longer, Bartolomeo says. He must whittle some new pieces and glue them in. But he will have that one *muy pronto*."

"I—I'll try to pay as soon as I can. . . ."

"It is—*un regalo*," the priest said. "A gift. A little mended wood, a lot of prayers for you, for the paper, for your soul."

Flint nodded, moved by the padre's words.

"Now, amigo, if you have an hour, follow me to the rectory."

Puzzled, Flint left the work to Libby and followed the silent padre as he led him across the plaza and around the old church. Within the cool adobe walls of the rectory, he discovered Amelia Lowell, much to his surprise.

"I have a letter from Alonzo Baca," the priest said abruptly. "It is in Spanish. I will simply tell you what it says." He studied the first of three handwritten pages that lay on his chest of drawers.

"Our attorney, Baca, employed lawyers in Seville and the City of Mexico to find the documents supporting the Escalante grant. Seville, you know, is where the New World was governed by the Spanish. Our man there, Raoul Torres, *ai, cual es la palabra*, ransacked, *yo creo*, the Archives of the Indies—the place where all such records are kept—and came up with the empty hands. He wrote Baca that there is no evidence at all of a royal grant to Antonio Escalante, the great-grandfather of Ramon. *Nada. Nadita.*"

That didn't sound good to Flint.

"At the same time, Baca employed another attorney, *muy distinguido*, Arsenio Segova, in the City of Mexico. Maybe, you see, the grant came later, after the *revolución*. Mexico rewarded its soldiers with land, and Antonio Escalante was a *capitán*, *verdad?*"

The priest smiled faintly. "Now Baca has heard from Segova also. There is no Escalante grant. *No hay.* There never has been."

"No grant?" Flint felt an arrow pierce his soul.

"It was the invention of Antonio Escalante. Baca's man, Segova, had to dig deep in the archives and pay much of the *mordida*, the bribe, to officials to find out. He found nothing among the grants made by the federal government of Mexico and no copy of any grant awarded by Spain. But *finalmente*, in letters between the *el gubernador*—the governor—of Chihuahua of the period and officials in the City of Mexico, he found the thing.

"While Antonio Escalante was a captain in the army of New Spain, he committed some indiscretion—it is unknown now— and resigned. He took his Isabella with him and came here and became a *hacendado*. Soon he had attracted peons to his hacienda and made Oro Blanco a frontier bulwark of the Spanish Empire. Sometime very early, he claimed that he had a royal patent on this land, three leagues square, and he produced a document that looks very like a royal grant. But it is a forgery.

"The letters of the governor, which were written in the revolutionary period following the *Grito de Delores*, clearly indicate that the governor knew the grant was a forgery. They questioned Antonio's loyalty to Spain, and rightly so—the man became a revolutionary. But at the time, nothing was done because it was so important that a strong, defensible town like Oro Blanco occupy the frontier. The continent was being settled by English and French, and Oro Blanco helped secure Santa Fe and Albuquerque." The priest sighed. "There never was a grant. I have given you only the outline. Baca must take his new evidence to court. Under the English system, he is an officer of the court, obligated to tell the magistrates of such new evidence, even if it destroys his case. He will give the court fair copies of the correspondence.

"But he is like the bulldog. He is now preparing a new pleading. He believes that under your English and *yanqui* common law and equity law, a court may recognize title by ancient occupation—the justice of letting people stay where they have lived and farmed for a century. He tells me that the holdings of the people will probably be validated; the parish church will probably rest on its own ground. But the court will probably validate the titles of the mines and all the gringo properties across the Avenida. . . . Maybe we have not gained wealth, but we have not lost our homes."

The padre stopped talking. A thousand questions and details teemed in Flint's mind. The priest held a sheaf of papers that Flint ached to read in translation.

"I seem to have paid a lot of money to defeat myself," Amelia said.

"Ah, no, Señora. We have only been led to the truth, and the truth is best. *Sea feliz*—be happy that Baca's agents discovered this first, before Señor Weed's lawyers found out. We have a better chance this way. Ah! We have faced worse troubles. I tell my people to be thankful for all things, for they are the blessings of God."

Flint knew what he had to do, and he dreaded it. "I am compelled to write an account of this, Padre."

"But Flint!" Amelia cried.

De Cordoba pondered that. "I would prefer that you wait, Señor Flint. It is not yet news. It could harm my people."

"You're not going to write a word. Not one word," Amelia said in a voice that brooked no argument.

"I have to."

"But why?"

"It's the thing to do."

"But Señor Flint, Baca has yet to present this new information to the court," she said.

"A paper wins trust when it publishes all the news, not just some of it. Even news that might hurt its own causes. If you want *The Nugget* to be a respected voice in Oro Blanco—to be trusted—I *must* print this before Clegg does. If he gets wind of it . . ."

"I cannot persuade you, then," the padre said.

"No. You can help me. I need to take notes, get it right."

"You have the madness and cunning of a god. Things that make no sense are our salvation," the priest said.

"Help me. Translate this and interpret."

Amelia Lowell closed her eyes and then spoke very slowly. "No one can stop you, Mr. Flint. So whatever happens is going to be your burden—your triumph or disaster. Are you prepared to assume a burden so grave?"

"I'm going to set type all night and run a one-page *Extra*," Flint said. "These things that look so bad can be miracles."

With that, Flint set to work. He would stay up most of the night, set the story, crank up his press, and have an *Extra* to sell at dawn. He would do what he had to do.

43

Mason Weed surveyed his troops and wished he had better men. He summoned them to his office at the Golconda in the dark of the night to deal with the crisis at hand—the publication of an edition of *The Nugget* chock-full of damning material, not the least of which was the piece on the Escalante grant litigation that made everything public knowledge at last.

He could wish for better men, but his only option was to work with those who stood before him. Town Marshal Crawford, Mayor Bulldog Malone, and Justice Pete Peters were all political appointees of the governor, filling offices until the next regular election. Phineas Clegg alone was truly Weed's man, but that didn't make him any more acceptable than the others.

If anything, Crawford had turned even more sullen and hair-triggered since his whipping at the hands of Sam Flint, of all people. Malone had the brains of a gnat. Clegg had brains and cunning, but his newspaper was so cynical that *The Progress* was a laughingstock. Clegg didn't believe in anything. It would have been better to find an editor filled with visions of Manifest Destiny—anything that made the paper less transparent.

Weed saw no respect for his leadership in any of them. Even Clegg, dependent on Weed for every penny, would just as soon pack up his carpetbag and head down the road, like every other gypsy printer. Bumblers and boneheads, the whole lot. But Weed would change that. He intended to run his own candidates in the November election, and they would win.

"All right, we're all here," he said. He stared at Crawford. "I understood that your Bowler boys would spike that issue of Flint's paper. They weren't very bright."

"I'll fire them," the marshal said. "They can't do anything right."

"No, they can't. But get some replacements first. Clegg, how are you going to handle this mess?"

The editor grinned and shrugged. "I'll say the lawsuit's a good thing. It'll bring progress."

Weed sighed. "That won't do it. The trouble with you, Clegg, is that no one believes a single word you write."

"That's what you hired me for."

Weed grimaced. "No, I want a paper that's gospel to everyone. You're making a joke of the news."

Clegg grinned. "You firing me?"

"No. The damage is done. There's a change in this town, I can smell it. It doesn't matter what you print. You're a joke. Just write what you want and keep the rag going. I'll get a serious editor when I'm ready."

Clegg didn't even wince. The crusty old bum had probably heard this sort of thing fifty times in his life. Weed loathed him, loathed them all. He needed good men, men with vision, men who shared his dream of a fabulous town growing richer and more comfortable daily, with plenty of space to grow—its citizens all white, all progressive, all law-abiding and hard-working.

"All right," he said. "Flint's narrowed my options. He got that issue out, and now I can hardly maneuver. I've been wanting to pay my help with scrip—it's a way to keep the lid on a place, and a way to keep merchants in line. But Flint stands in the way. I want to get the greasers out. We need that land across the Avenue. And I want to get rid of that priest. He holds them all together over there. If I could get rid of him, it won't matter if we lose the lawsuit. That parish wouldn't exist. But Flint stands in the way." He turned to Crawford. "You told me you'd put Flint out of business."

Crawford glared.

Weed felt his old melancholy worm through him. He didn't like unpleasantness. He really was a gentle, respectful man, and it saddened him that the most admirable people in Oro Blanco were those who opposed him. But it couldn't be helped. He would do what he had to. He was the future; these people were the past. No mortal could stop history. He didn't hate Flint or de Cordoba or Amelia or even Jack Treat. They were people he might have enjoyed socially had they been aligned with historical forces.

"Thanks to your blundering," Mason Weed said, staring first at Crawford and then at Malone, "my back's to the wall. Busting up Flint's shop will work against us. Everyone in town is aware now and watching." He paused, annoyed all over again with his cohorts. "There's one option left. The town won't like it, but memories are short, and in a week it'll be forgotten. Crawford, you're going to put all four—Flint, de Cordoba, Amelia Lowell, and Mountain Jack Treat—on the four-o'clock stage to Silver City."

Crawford inhaled sharply. "How'm I going to get Treat on that stage and keep him there?"

"That's up to you. I would imagine that fowling pieces with buckshot would do it."

"How'm I gonna keep him on that stage after it leaves?"

Weed smiled. "You're a competent lawman. You figure it."

"How'm I gonna keep any of them from coming back?"

Weed smiled.

"The greasers won't like this," Malone said.

"That's why we'll do it." He turned to Malone and Pete Peters. "You'll let the bishop in Santa Fe know de Cordoba's a seditionist and is not welcome here. A parish in Old Mexico would be nice." He addressed Clegg. "A piece about de Cordoba's seditions in the next issue."

Clegg belched. "First you say no one believes *The Progress*, and then you assign me the onerous and dishonorable task of writing the unbelievable. Ah, my dear and noble Weed, you're a prime specimen."

No one laughed. Weed smiled.

"You want me to lock 'em up tonight or in the morning?" Crawford asked.

"No, that'll draw a crowd. Round them up at three or three-thirty. Put them on the stage, I'll deal with the Butterfield Company. Avoid crowds, do you understand? Avoid crowds. Avoid a scene."

"How're you going to deal with Butterfield? Treat'll be off that stage in two minutes."

"Delbert, have you ever heard of manacles and irons? You'll put him in irons and escort him to Silver City. You'll be armed; they won't."

"Pardon me, Weed, but do you know what Treat, in manacles and leg irons, could do to that coach—assuming we can put irons on him?"

"No excuses, Marshal."

"And what if we can't find some of them?"

"Are you a competent lawman or not?"

The marshal subsided into sullen glaring.

"Flint's got a wagon behind his place and a pair of big mules the greasers are pasturing," said Malone.

"Send him out on the stage with nothing but the clothes on

his back. The city could use some mules and a wagon." Weed turned to the marshal. "As soon as you've got him, clean out the shop. Take everything in it to *The Progress*."

"What about the girl?"

"Well, what about her?"

"She'll go yelling."

"I suppose a barefoot girl is a big problem for the police," Weed retorted testily.

"Yeah, but the town likes her," said Bulldog Malone.

"Isn't that nice," said Weed. "She can sell flowers or go have a talk with the sporting houses."

"Well, she's become sort of a symbol. I got miners coming into my joint all the time; they say to me, 'Don't hurt that girl or we'll hurt you.' I been hurt enough. Treat's made off with half my business."

"You buy her first bouquet, Bulldog. Or talk her into hawking *The Progress*. She'll probably sell more of my sheet than those bums did. Clegg, you go hire her after we get Flint out of town. She doesn't have a nickel. It'll be easy. And you, Crawford, leave her alone. Shut down Treat's joint."

He watched the town marshal sink into silence. "Marshal, if you're not man enough to run Treat out of town and keep him out, why I'll wire the governor about a new appointment."

It struck Weed that he was being unfair. About the only way they could get Mountain Jack Treat out of town was to kill him—which wasn't a bad idea, but he wouldn't say it. He had learned not to say certain things. And he knew Crawford got the message.

"Pardon me, Weed," said Pete Peters. "Amelia Lowell's got money and a mouth. Flint's got respect. They'll go to Santa Fe and make a stink."

Weed didn't bother with a reply. The Santa Fe Ring had ways of protecting its colleagues and friends, silently and cleverly, without a ripple on the surface. They ruled the Territory without a breath of trouble. Weed stood—the signal for them to get out—and watched them depart into the night. He needed good men, not these swamp creatures. But it would all pass. That very day, his day-shift foreman had reported that the new workings on the third level had hit incredible ore, running five thousand dollars a ton. There was no point in giving the greasers any of it.

44

Miraculously, Maureen Madigan had rallied. Her flesh showed some color, and the bright fever in her eyes had diminished. Libby stared at her mother in astonishment, feeling a burst of hope.

"Help me get some sun, Libby," her mother whispered.

Libby supported her mother through the door and into the brilliant morning light and seated her in a battered chair beside the door.

"The light heals," Maureen said. "The light gives me strength. It's like medicine."

Libby tucked a light robe around her mother, who smiled at the attention.

"What happened?" Libby asked, in wonder.

"I refuse to die," Maureen whispered. "The spirit rules us. I make myself live."

"Oh, Mama!"

"Despair is the enemy. When we were alone . . . starving . . . desperate . . . I surrendered." Maureen smiled, and Libby cherished the sight.

"We have help, Mama. I've a good job. Mr. Flint really cares about us. He spares us all he can."

"Yes, and Mr. Treat too," Maureen said. "We have food and hope."

"Food and hope," Libby echoed.

Maureen closed her frail hand over her daughter's. "Hope for you. I see sunlight bathing you. The worst is past."

Libby returned the pressure of her mother's clasp. Even in her desperate illness, her mother was giving rather than receiving. Libby felt energy, a life force, flowing from her mother's frail fingers into her—strangely and sweetly beautiful.

"I'm growing up fast, Mama. Mr. Flint, he teaches me things. He's like a father."

Her mother smiled. "The light, the light," she whispered through her ruined throat.

The words frightened Libby, though she didn't know why. She sat with her mother in the morning sun, knowing she would be late to work this day. But it didn't matter. This moment was so precious and so filled with hope that she would not abandon it. Mr. Flint would understand.

Her mother studied her and smiled softly, sharing some sort of joy this morning.

Maureen Madigan's face caught the light and held it, as though she had triumphed over death. She was beautiful. Something like a glow had transformed her. Light filled the space around her mother, as if she wore a halo. Her mama was the most beautiful woman Libby had ever seen—more beautiful even than the Virgin.

"I've had enough sun now, Libby. Help me in, dear."

"Yes, Mama." Libby did, settling her mother upon her pallet once again.

"Run to work now, Libby. I'll rest," Maureen whispered.

Libby trotted down the slope to the newspaper, though she was filled with joy and terror. Something was strange about her mother's rally.

She found Mr. Flint unshaven and haggard. He eyed her sharply. "Is something wrong, Libby?"

"No. Mama's better."

"You looked so worried. Do you want to spend the day with her?"

She shook her head. "I'll work. But I might leave a little early. I just need to be with her."

"Of course," he said. He looked so tired it made her wonder what was wrong. "Libby, are you up to selling an *Extra* today? We have news so important it couldn't wait."

"Sell an *Extra*?"

He nodded. "It's just one story, part of one page, but I think my whole issue'll sell. You'll make a few dollars."

Bewildered, she eyed a stack of sheets printed on one side. "Read it," he said. "It's about the Escalante grant. It seems it never existed."

She hesitated, and he misread her feelings.

"You'll be safe, Libby. This is a story all those people—Weed and Crawford—want published. And anyway, the feelings in this town have changed, ever since that last issue. Things are better."

"But—" she began. He had utterly bewildered her.

"Read it," he said.

She did—twice—not comprehending why he was running an *Extra* based on this bad news. It meant the Mexicans wouldn't get anything.

"But why are you publishing it? It should be a secret."

He smiled, and suddenly she understood more about Sam Flint than she had ever before.

"But it'll hurt the Mexicans!" she cried.

"They never had the land that had the gold, Libby. Let me put it this way: It's much better for Father de Cordoba and his parish that we publish this first. It'd be much worse if Clegg publishes it before we do."

She wasn't so sure of that. "Maybe Mr. Clegg would never find out."

"It's only a matter of time, Libby. Weed's lawyers are re-searching too."

"Well, all right," she said, hefting the thin sheets. "You're gonna charge ten cents for this?"

He grinned and nodded.

She brightened. "I'll sell these on the corner. Then I'll go look in on Mama."

"That's a good plan, Libby."

The girl stepped into the blinding sun. A cruel heat made the air shimmer. She walked blithely toward her corner, wondering about Mr. Flint. Maybe he was crazy, making a big story out of a tragedy for the greasers. Maybe he was on the wrong side. But she knew he wasn't. He was driven by strange ideals she didn't always understand. He was always making her rewrite stories to make them more accurate. He was always telling her to spell the names of everyone just right, and not to exaggerate, and never to guess at things, and always to have sources for everything. He was always saying that everyone was good and bad—including himself—and just because he was siding with the miners, or the Mexicans, didn't mean that they were always right. Once, he had eyed her and said that Original Sin was the best perception of mankind he had ever heard of. She hardly knew what he was talking about. Why did he side with anybody if everyone was bad?

She reached her corner on the Avenida and stationed herself there in the silent heat. It'd be a bad day, but maybe she could sell out before it got too hot. She saw the night-shift miners drifting home or into saloons and chophouses. One stopped.

"What's this, Miss Libby? Selling the sheet on a Thursday?"

"*Extra,*" she said. "There never was the Escalante grant."

"That's odd," he said, handing her a dime.

He stood beside her, reading the strange story and muttering to himself. Then, instead of continuing home, he headed for knots of other miners, and soon a bunch of them were buying her little one-page paper. The coins began to weigh in her pocket.

"Flint sold out?" one man asked her.

"No, sir. He says he has to publish whatever's news. He says this is news and shouldn't be kept secret."

"Flint's quite a fellow," the miner said.

That's how it went for a while. She did a brisk trade. First the night-shift miners, and then businessmen, and then all sorts of people. No one complained about paying a dime for one tiny half-page of text.

"Where'd he get this?" one man asked.

"It's in the story. The lawyer wrote Father de Cordoba."

For an hour, people crowded around her, asking questions. "Go talk to Mr. Flint," she finally said, unable to answer all the things they asked her.

"It shoulda been in Clegg's rag, not Flint's," one man said.

"Well, I've got to give Flint credit. He got all the gringos mad at him, and now he'll get all the greasers mad at him."

The man was grinning, and Libby managed a grin too. For a little while, at least, she had put her worries aside.

"He prints all the news, sir," she said.

The man nodded. "It sorta separates the two outfits, I'd say. One's a real newspaper. The other . . ." He winked at her.

Oro Blanco had never seen an *Extra* before, and it sold out. The selling enthralled her.

She saw Town Marshal Crawford huffing up the Avenida like a steam engine, and she wondered whether he was mad. He couldn't be. If he'd read the paper he'd know this was good news for his side. But he kept right on, his long hickory stick in hand, and began to push through the people who were standing around, discussing the news.

She saw the look in his face and knew she was in for it. Her knees shook. Then she bolted, clawing her way past people.

"Stop!" he roared.

She didn't. She raced as fast as her skinny legs would take her. He gave chase, lumbering along behind and roaring at her as though she had committed murder.

She glanced back. He was gaining, waving that stick in brutal sweeps.

She burst ahead, but he loomed up behind her. She turned to see the club arc through blue sky. She tried to duck. A violent blow on her head shattered her thoughts and sent her tumbling. She saw white. She saw streaks. She felt her papers scatter from her arm. She felt herself hit the clay of the street. Then she felt nothing.

45

They did the girl," shouted old Polansky.

Ice rose in Mountain Jack Treat's veins. He dropped the mug he was washing into the soapy water and lumbered onto the Avenida. A cluster of people had gathered a block up the street.

He pushed through a silent mob and found himself staring upon a sight so obscene his gorge rose. Libby lay crumpled in the dirt, twisted like a rag doll, her skirts hiked above her calf. He saw no movement. Something had caved her skull behind behind her right ear. A little blood mixed with her brown hair. Her mouth formed an O. Her innocent eyes saw nothing.

People gaped. Crawford held them at bay with his drawn navy revolver. "Get away," he growled. "Police business."

"Murder," a man yelled from the sullen crowd.

The revolver swung toward the man, who backed away and slid behind others. "Resisting arrest," Crawford said.

No one said a thing. His words were obscene.

"Get going now, or I'll have you for rioting."

People read the one-page *Nugget* and passed it to others.

"Gimme the paper," Crawford said.

A miner handed him one. Crawford didn't read it.

"Read it, Crawford," said a young man.

"It's all lies," Crawford said.

Someone laughed. The bore of the navy turned in that direction.

"Is a doctor coming?" asked a man in pince-nez.

"Too late for that."

A copy of the *Extra* reached Treat. He read it, amazed. Something icy and hard filled him. Usually when the itch to brawl overcame him, he felt a swift joy and a shot of excitement coursing in his blood. But this time he felt still and cold and deadly.

"I'll take the girl," Treat said.

Crawford noticed him for the first time. "It stays there. You get out of here before I shoot."

"I'll take the girl." Treat stared levelly at the town marshal and stepped into the no-man's land inside the crowd. He stuffed his paper at the marshal. "Read the bleddy story."

The marshal took it. The revolver didn't waver.

Treat stood quietly, his arms hanging loose, waiting. Around him the crowd grew, and he saw darkness and horror upon faces. He would always remember that moment. Libby, battered to death at age thirteen, sprawled there. The crowd radiating something so terrible it blotted out the sun, and Crawford waving his blued revolver and daring himself to read the *Extra*. In the end, the marshal chose not to read it. Instead, he watched the silent mob as a rabbit watches wolves.

A doctor—this one was young Bulwer—in gold-rimmed spectacles, pushed through with his black leather bag. He stopped at the sight of the thin, twisted child. He eyed the navy warily and then stepped forward.

It took him only moments. No pulse, no breath. He turned Libby's head, examining the wound that had dented the rear of her skull.

"How did this happen?" he asked the town marshal.

"Resisting arrest."

"Arrest for what?"

"That's no one's business."

"She was selling the *Extra*," a spectator volunteered. "He came after her. She ran; he chased her. Hit her from behind with his stick. We all saw it."

"Was she armed and dangerous, Constable?" the doctor asked malevolently.

Their gazes locked. The doctor didn't flinch.

"Get out of here. All of you," Crawford demanded. No one moved. "Get out!" he yelled, firing into the air. The crack of the revolver seemed puny, almost like a popping cork.

Treat wondered why that was so, and then he realized that the crowd's presence had become thunderous. The unspoken noise, mysterious in its power, drowned out the revolver.

The doctor stood. "She's gone. Someone get Theo Parnassus."

But someone had already gotten the undertaker. The man, wearing his black-silk stovepipe hat over his jet hair and draped in a gray cutaway coat, was wheeling a pushcart up the Avenida.

"I'll take her," said Treat. "She'll not be getting a pauper's grave."

Crawford seemed to gain strength with the arrival of a doctor and undertaker. "No, Treat. This is city business."

"Read *The Nugget*, damn you, Constable," yelled one of the onlookers.

"There's nothing worth reading."

"The Escalante grant don't exist! Never did! That ain't worth reading?"

The marshal gaped, studied the *Extra*, and stared into space. The crowd waited.

"What was it you arrested her for, Marshal?" asked Strong, the hardware man. "Sedition? Riot? Or maybe peddling an honest paper? Sort of beats *The Progress*, don't it? Maybe you should hang. A lot of folks here saw you do murder."

Crawford stepped back a few paces.

Treat edged forward, blocking the undertaker's progress.

Slowly he smoothed Libby's skirts, folded her arms, and then lifted her onto the cart. She felt so light, as if she were a bird.

"She's a bleddy saint, Parnassus. Treat her like one. Don't you spare a nickel."

"Who'll pay?"

Treat grabbed a fistful of shirt and cutaway, lifted Parnassus to the tip of his polished shoes, and let him slide slowly to the clay. "Those who loved her," he said.

The undertaker nodded, bug-eyed, and grasped the twin handles of his ebony pushcart, eager to escape this silent, menacing crowd. He rattled away with the child; Crawford chose the moment to retreat also, his revolver leveled as he backed away.

Treat stalked Crawford step for step.

Crawford cocked his weapon. "Try it," he said.

The bore of the navy pointed straight at Treat's chest. Treat kept pace, as if in a strange trance. No bullet could pierce him. He could see only the marshal. Vaguely, from a distant shore, he heard shouting.

Treat kept pace as Crawford backed up Virgin. Crawford stopped, and with his free hand he extracted a hideout revolver from his breastpocket and leveled both weapons at Treat. "Stop now," he said softly.

Treat did. He looked into two muzzles of two revolvers. The trance ended. Treat stood stock-still, aware of everything.

Crawford enjoyed his moment.

Treat watched the marshal back his way toward the jail-house. It wasn't over. He turned to discover he was alone on the street—the crowd had fled for cover. Ahead half a block, the marshal spun forward and trotted to the jailhouse.

"It's not over," Treat said aloud to no one. He walked back to the place where Libby's life had ended. Not a spot of blood marked it. She left nothing behind her but a few fragile memories that would soon ebb away in Oro Blanco.

"It's not over," Treat said, this time to the crowd, which had materialized again, out of range of Crawford's bullets.

Slowly, Treat's daze left him. John Strong, the hardware man, was voicing an opinion. "We need a new police force. It isn't just Crawford, it's those thugs, the Bowler boys. Murdering a little girl and calling it resisting arrest! And for a story that Clegg would have been glad to trumpet all over his front page too. They should be tried, I say."

"It's not decent," said Sorley Mulligan, who owned the Good Luck Saloon.

"We've had enough of their bullying," a rough miner growled. "I can build a noose as good as any."

"No, that's not the way," Strong said. "Crawford should be tried, the rest run out of town—Bulldog Malone, Pete Peters, and those constables."

"I'll get on the jury. I won't let him get away with murder," said the miner. "Murdering a wee girl for nothing."

Treat watched Phineas Clegg push into the crowd, a pencil and writing pad in his hand.

"What's all this?" the man asked, smiling. "Was the competition at it again?"

Strong stared at Clegg. "Crawford killed the girl with his stick."

Clegg's smile vanished. "Oh, a pity, a pity. Poor waif. I am mindful of a sweet countenance and lovely eyes. A fine child lost to the living. I do suppose, though, she was peddling some more of that horsepucky that irritates the town fathers."

"Cut it out." The hardware man's voice cut like a dagger through Clegg's oration. "It's murder. And you're a part of this. You all are, starting with Weed. You, Malone, the JP, your thugs and hooligans. You're on your way out."

"Oh, a man of passion. May I quote that? It's a splendid lead for my story. 'Strong calls for mass resignations.' "

But no one responded. Clegg studied this crowd and swiftly

turned funereal. "Oh, a most inappropriate remark. Levity uncalled for. Now, if you will, recount the events for me, in detail and chronological order, and I shall record them in precise and faultless fashion for tomorrow's *Progress*."

The men stared at the bulbous-nosed editor with obvious disgust. Silently, one shoved a copy of the *Extra* into Clegg's pudgy paws. The editor unfolded his gold-rimmed spectacles, donned them, and studied the paper, clucking, eyebrows bobbing like waves crashing upon a shore.

"A great mystery," Clegg said. "Flint's mad as a hatter."

"Maybe Flint's honest enough to print the news," Strong said, his voice rough.

Treat felt too desolate to say anything. There wouldn't be a hanging, because Treat was going to get to Crawford first. But he owed things to Libby and Maureen Madigan. He wanted the girl decently buried. She and her folks were Irish, they'd want a priest. He would fetch de Cordoba. He would have to find Flint too. The editor had missed all of this.

He left the whispering bystanders and hiked toward the greaser side of the Avenida and around the corner to Flint's adobe shop. He pushed in, finding silence and no sign of the editor.

"Flint?" he bawled, but no one responded.

He eased through the silent place toward the rear apartment and spotted Flint sprawled on his pallet there. Treat thought for a moment that the man had been murdered too, but Flint was breathing. He had obviously toiled over his *Extra* all night, and sleep had overwhelmed him. Treat decided not to wake him. Let the man who had saved Oro Blanco from itself have his rest.

Treat eased out the door. The heat belted him like an uppercut. He needed the priest. De Cordoba had to learn about this, had to tell Maureen Madigan. Priests were used to that.

He found the padre in the sacristy, listening to two of his parishioners, his face wreathed in pain. He glanced up at Treat.

"The girl is dead," the priest said. "God have mercy. That is why you have come."

Treat nodded.

"I have seen too many sorrows, but I have not seen a sorrow as dark as this," he said.

"Padre, her mother—someone's got to tell her mother."

"By someone you mean a priest."

"Yes."

The priest nodded. "It is a hard duty. I have done this thing a few times. I managed only because"—he smiled deprecatingly—"my faith permits me to see this a little differently."

Treat nodded. The padre spoke in Spanish a few moments more to the Mexicans, who listened intently, nodding. One of them handed the padre a copy of the *Extra*. De Cordoba read silently.

The padre turned to Treat. "This is what a girl dies for?"

"Crawford didn't read it. He just saw her and started swinging his stick."

The priest stared out the window into a brassy sky. "I do not always grasp the will of God," he said.

He motioned Treat forward, and together they started for the little cottage near the Golconda mine where Maureen Madigan lay.

46

The padre walked resolutely toward the Madigan cottage, but the giant beside him lagged and fretted.

The priest understood. "Señor Treat," he said, "I will do this thing. You are needed on the Avenida. Bad things might happen there. A mob can turn into a wild animal. You go back, *por favor.*"

Treat didn't need any more invitation. "I'll do that. Thanks, Padre."

De Cordoba watched the big man turn and flee as if escaping the jaws of hell. In his years of ministry, the priest had seen many kinds of courage and many kinds of cowardice. He had always marveled at it. This giant, this happy brawler who faced fists and knives with a wild cheer, could not bring himself to tell terrible news to a mother.

But the padre had seen the opposite too. Meek men who avoided trouble suddenly turning into tigers for the sake of their families or a sacred belief. Shy and reticent women braving childbirth with a courage that wrought wonder. The doomed sick, summoning cheer and laughter. How wondrous and diverse was the human race.

It would be hard, telling Señora Madigan about her daughter. But a faithful priest might see these things from the standpoint of eternity. For this sweet child was surely safe in the bosom of God, and death might be a cause for rejoicing. And as a priest, he would remind her of these things and then share her grieving. He had held many a hand of the bereft, who found comfort in the simple knowledge that they were not alone.

He walked patiently upslope to the cabin and knocked on the door. He heard no answer, but he knew she lay within. He ventured to open the door a crack. Light streamed through the two small windows.

"Señora? Señora Madigan?"

He saw a faint stirring on the pallet in the corner. Motes of dust caught in the glare of the sun.

"It is I, Father de Cordoba. I wish to see you."

He heard something like a whisper scratching from her throat and took it for a welcome. He pushed the door wider and padded across the barren plank floor to her bed. The sight of her shocked him. She had sunk into the final, skeletal economy that marked the last stage of her disease. Her flesh stretched tightly over her skull. She peered up at him from eyes sunk in dark caverns. And yet she smiled at him from a face flushed with color. She was living by spirit alone.

"You came to visit. Libby sent you," she whispered, and then gasped wildly. She raised herself a little on her pillows and pulled up the coverlet.

"Ah, Señora—"

"I thought she might. I'm a little better, you know. I took some sun this morning." That was as much as she could say for a moment. She studied him. "So we meet at last," she whispered. "You'll be a comfort. Perhaps, if you're willing, I might receive the sacrament." She smiled expectantly.

"Señora . . . the sacrament. Indeed, yes, it shall be done. I've neglected my duty. I failed to bring it."

Her smile faltered a moment. "Next time, then," she whispered.

"Madre de Dios," he whispered. He needed a moment to think. Sitting down on the edge of her bed, he clasped her thin, cold hand in his, while his mind whirled. She stared at him from those black pits, the tentative smile frozen on her face.

"Father?" she whispered. "Is something wrong?"

A heaviness clamped him, and he knew what he must do. "Señora, I bear news for you. Your dear child is in the hands of God."

She stared, her mouth open. A thin slick of saliva collected at the corner of her lips.

"Where is Libby?" she asked.

"She—went away this morning." He felt the horror of it and wished he had kept quiet. He should have brought her communion, blessed her, and delayed this moment a while.

"The marshal," she whispered.

"Sí, sí, it was that one."

Maureen Madigan groaned, a sound that welled up from the shreds of life within her, something eerie and terrible, the cry of a betrayed soul. She groaned as one who had suffered the last wound. De Cordoba could not remember a more awful moment in his priesthood.

"Libby dead?" she whispered.

"No mortal can know the will of God, Señora. Maybe he loved Libby so much he wanted her with him."

Unbelievably, the woman began laughing at him, coughing, wheezing, mocking. Then she brought her spasm under control. "And so God made the constable shoot her," she gasped. "For what? Selling a paper for her two pennies?"

He didn't correct her. There was no need to tell Maureen Madigan that her little girl had been clubbed to death.

"Does God cause evil? Oh, you priests and your lies!" She coughed desperately and drew in air as if she were drowning.

"I am but a poor priest," he said. "I have no answers."

He waited for her while she wrestled the paroxysms of her

lungs. Finally, she settled back into her ancient blankets and stared up at him again, something hard and bleak radiating from her eyes. The rest of her seemed dead; her hands were lifeless. But hot coals of life burned in those eye sockets.

"Nothing left," she whispered. "Garth gone. My sons. Now Libby. I gave nothing to the world." The sorrow in her voice sent chills through him.

"Señora, you bore them, nurtured them, gave them your milk."

"Leave me," she said.

"Leave you? But Señora—"

"Go."

"But Señora. You wish to be shrived. The sacrament—"

"I don't want the sacrament. I don't want your lies. I don't want your . . ." She coughed softly. Tears rose in those caverns. "I don't believe in anything."

She closed her eyes and lay so still that he feared she had slid away. He wanted desperately to rescue her from this, from mortal sin. And yet he knew that he could not. And he knew also—some blessed faith guided him here—that all this would not keep her from her glory.

He would not argue with her. Instead, he watched her closely, sensing that life lingered even though her hand felt cold within his.

"Señora Madigan," he said gently. "You will soon come to your glory. You are a beautiful woman. I have learned something of you. I saw you in your daughter. She had courage. You faced a hard life with faith and joy. So did she. You suffered as few mortals ever do, and now you are beautiful. I have never known a woman as beautiful as you. You are beautiful before the world and beautiful before God. You and Libby will fill us with beautiful memories. You will never be forgotten in Oro Blanco. . . ."

He felt helpless. His words were probably tumbling into unhearing ears. But she opened her eyes and peered at him. He swore the pain had vanished from them. He swore he saw angels and archangels and all the hosts of Heaven in them. He swore he peered through those eyes upon a landscape so sunny and infinite and golden that it was not any place on Earth.

Then she closed her eyes and died.

He had glimpsed Heaven. He held her hand for a moment. Spirit was all that mattered. A great peace had embraced her. Everything had softened. He saw no pain or desperation. Maybe this was a miraculous death, he thought as he studied her hands for signs of the stigmata. Maybe she was a saint. Maybe she had lived to be an example, a byword for the women of the church. Maybe some achingly beautiful vision of God had willed that she and her daughter would live and die and live forever, only minutes apart. He did not know these things. No seminary or catechism could ever prepare a simple priest or any other mortal to understand divine beauty. He felt refreshed, as if everything in his soul had been cleansed or made new.

He prayed softly for a while that she and Libby and her husband and sons might have a joyous reunion up on the mountaintop. The vision of them filled him, and for a while the cabin seemed bathed in white light. At last he leaned over her and made the sign of the cross.

Father de Cordoba emerged into a blistering morning. All this had happened in the space of an hour. The path took him downslope toward the Avenida de la Virgen, and he was struck by something he hadn't thought of before. It wasn't just the gringos who had drawn a line down the middle of that broad street. He and his parish had drawn the line too. He had never welcomed the gringos into his congregation, never invited them in English. He had always supposed that his was a Mexican parish, and his task was to serve his own people. But now, suddenly, he knew what he had forgotten. The church was universal, and he had failed in his duty to make others welcome. He had not welcomed the Irish Madigans, and they had not come on Sundays and holy days, and thus he had failed in his mission.

He sighed, knowing he had a formidable task ahead. From this sad and instructive day forward, the parish of San Juan would reach across the line that made Oro Blanco two cities. He would knit the two cities together—if it was not too late.

47

Town marshal Delbert Crawford felt like he had a nest of baby rattlesnakes in his belly, and any moment now they would wriggle up his esophagus and slither out of his nostrils and mouth and ears.

He was mad at himself and everything else. He hadn't meant to kill her; it was a stupid, dumb stroke of bad luck. The smart-mouthed little brat had goaded him into it, and all it had taken was a single swipe of his hickory stick behind her ear. Now he was in a corner, the worst he'd ever known. They would come for him and string him up.

He stomped into the jailhouse. He didn't want to see what he had seen, that crumpled girl dead as a stump while a hundred gawkers gathered. She wasn't a bad little thing. The miners liked her. He sure didn't mean to knock the life out of her.

He knew he couldn't undo it, knew that he'd live all his life with the death of a half-grown girl. He'd sleep with that in his brain; he'd sit in the outhouse thinking about her. He'd live with it the way some men lived with cancer or a prostate that slowly shut off their water. They'd whisper at him, point their fingers. But it was fact; it was over. He couldn't change a thing. He sighed, knowing he'd have to tell Libby's sick old lady. Or maybe he wouldn't. He'd send Bugsy up there, let him suffer. He needed some suffering.

Maybe he should get out. It tempted him. He could pack his warbag, get hold of a saddler, and vamoose in half an hour before it all came tumbling down on him. Jesus, it was bad. He could ditch this rotten little burg, head for the lights. What did he ever get out of Oro Blanco anyway but grief and fifty clams a month and whatever he could twist out of the madams?

They would all say the same thing: He hadn't even read the paper. If he had bothered to peruse a few paragraphs he would have known that Flint was throwing in the towel; the greasers had quit. They never had a leg to stand on. He cursed himself for not even taking a quick squint at the lousy little *Extra*. He'd seen that little harpy and gone for her like a snorting bull.

He poured a cold cup of the viscous coffee he let sit around for days at a time and sipped it. The brew was as bitter as his bowels. The day's heat stabbed him, drew sweat from him, and then scorched it off in air so fire-sharp that it was hard to breathe. He needed to do something—anything—before the town's firebrands started building hemp nooses. The day-old coffee tasted as rotten as Oro Blanco, and he splashed it at the empty cell across from his battered desk. It pooled on the plank floor.

That damned little snip deserved it. By God, he wished he had laid the club to Flint's ear too, and Treat's thick skull. He wrestled himself into a calm. He had to think. He was tough as an oak post, and he could ride this, just as he'd ridden out of other messes.

Resisting arrest—that's what he told that sullen crowd. They'd scowled. They thought he was talking about selling papers he didn't like. That was the reason he'd chased her, but now she was a corpse, and he needed better reasons than that. Still, it wouldn't be hard to come up with one. He was going to arrest her, all right—for picking pockets, that's what. He'd caught a pickpocket. He'd suspected it half a dozen times; people had reported her. But this time he'd caught her with her skinny fingers in that miner's pocket. He liked that. It'd be his word, and it'd stick.

He was required to record all these things, so he found his buckram-bound record book, noted the time on the big seven-day clock, and dipped the steel nib of his pen into the ink bottle.

"Approximately nine-fifteen A.M. caught a female minor, one Libby Madigan, Oro Blanco, lifting purse from pocket of man she was selling an alleged *Extra* edition of *The Nugget*. Told her she was under arrest for theft and not to move; she ran. Pursued criminal escaping justice. Shouted to her to stop. Suspect didn't. Applied stick just as she turned; inadvertently causing routine blow to have mortal results."

That looked good. His bilious stomach calmed down. An official record had its own austere authority. Those inked words carried with them the majesty of official purpose and lawful scruple. He could weather this if he tried. His mind swarmed with possibilities and plans. The next step was to enlist Clegg. The step after that was to proceed exactly as planned. Weed wanted the town's troublemakers on the afternoon stage, and that's exactly what would happen. He'd get Flint, Treat, de Cordoba, and that Lowell witch on the stage. There wouldn't be anyone left to cause trouble.

He peered through the streaked glass window onto a deserted street. The vicious heat made the Avenida undulate, along with all the buildings along it. But the searing sun had chased away the crowds. They weren't gathering into an angry mob outside the jailhouse. From his window he could see the two blocks to the corner where the Madigan girl had hawked her sheet. No one remained there. The sun had blistered away the whole affair. Good enough. It'd pass once he got the rabble-rousers out of town.

He collected a double-barreled shotgun from the wall rack, broke it open, and checked the buckshot loads. That would be his riot protection. The weapon felt so hot he wondered if it had just been fired. But that was the illusion of a murderously hot day. He tucked it under his right arm and slid into a glare so blinding that he had to yank his hat down and squint into the whiteness.

Moments later he shoved open the door of *The Progress* and confronted Clegg, who greeted him with a leer. Sweat had beaded on the editor's brow.

"Kill any more little girls for breakfast?" the man asked cheerfully.

"Shut up or I'll butcher you too, Clegg."

Clegg leered. "It's such a good story. Best news story I've written in years."

Crawford felt like ripping the tongue out of Clegg's foul mouth. Instead, he walked around the counter and loomed over the porcine editor until Clegg was blinking back terror.

"That girl was picking a pocket. I saw it. I've been suspecting it for weeks. Little tramp, selling papers and dipping her skinnies into every pocket she could. But this time I caught her, plain as the hair up your nostrils. I told her I saw it, told her I was pinching her, told her to stand still. But she ran. I told her to stop. She didn't. I could have shot her—escaping prisoner—but I didn't. I went after her. I didn't hit her head; she turned into the swing. Now print it right or I'll cut your guts out."

Clegg smiled sweetly and nodded.

"If Weed comes boiling down here, tell him what happened. That *Extra* had nothing to do with it. You get me, Clegg? That's how it is on the official record. They can run any kind of inquest or grand jury they want, and it'll still hold. I saw the snatch; I went after her. I was planning to throw the book at that little parasite."

Clegg's face filled with such amusement that it was all Crawford could do not to smack him with the butt of his shotgun.

"Sublime," said Clegg.

Crawford stomped out into the furnace of the midday and

hiked upslope to the plank cabin where Billy and Bugsy bached. They weren't supposed to be on duty until two, but he was going to put them to work. If he had to deal with a mob, he wanted two seasoned pugs with double-barreled shotguns beside him. He could hold a few hundred miners at bay with firepower like that. But it would never come to that. The insane heat was working for him.

He pounded on the door and didn't wait for an invitation. He barged into the cool and let his eyes adjust to the darkness. When he could see at last, he found himself staring into the bore of Billy Bowler's Walker Colt.

"What the hell do you want?" Billy said from his bunk.

"We got trouble. Get dressed and report to the jailhouse. There might be a mob to deal with."

"What kind of trouble?"

"Caught that Madigan girl picking pockets. She ran; I stopped her. Parnassus has her."

"Jaysas, Crawford. And you want us to protect your pink hide?"

"Get down to the jailhouse or get another job."

From the other bunk, Bugsy grinned. "Ought to be a carnival," he said. "I allus liked scatterguns. We got some sawed down to fifteen inches. They'll spray buckshot like a scythe in wheat."

"Well, be about it. We can ride this thing if we put the troublemakers on the stagecoach, just like Weed wanted."

"Does he know?"

"Probably. If we clean Flint and that bunch out, he won't say much."

Bugsy laughed nastily.

Crawford slammed the door and headed down to the Stamp Mill Saloon for a talk with Mayor Bulldog Malone—who wouldn't yet be up. Malone liked to rise about noon and retire in the wee hours, after a sociable evening pouring libations for his customers.

It had turned so hot that Crawford was losing his breath. He was walking into a flaming wall, sucking air that didn't satisfy the lungs. He hit the Avenida and turned right, finally pushing into the beer-sour darkness of the Stamp Mill. The place never seemed right by day, but by night it turned into a glittering palace that could satisfy any appetite. He nodded at the yawning bartender, pushed into the rear poker parlor, and then exited through the door into an anteroom. There he hammered on the mayor's door like a flat-wheeled freight train.

Malone opened the door and surveyed Crawford. The mayor was up and dressed. He held the *Extra* in his meaty paws.

"Delbert, now you've done it," he said. "You're solid bone from ear to shining ear. A child butcher."

"I've got it licked," Crawford growled, ignoring the insult. "Let me in and I'll tell you about it."

48

Sam Flint slumped into his cot, his head buried in his hands, utterly numb. The padre had awakened him from his fitful rest and told him how Libby died. And Libby's mother. The priest had stayed a while to comfort him and see him through the shock.

Flint tried to envision Libby at her work, but no image came to mind. He tried to remember her voice but couldn't. It was as if his memory of her had vanished along with her life. Maybe when he wrote her obituary it would all flood back, and then he would grieve at last.

He accused himself of sending her to her death. He should have known better. The sight of her peddling papers was all it had taken to turn Crawford berserk. Flint had supposed that the *Extra*'s contents would protect her—and he had been wrong. He knew his self-accusation would haunt him the rest of his life.

Odd that he couldn't weep. He needed to, but all he could do was stare into the gloom of the adobe-walled cantina. It was as if this thing was too monstrous to permit feeling. Her life had been as short as any he could remember. It didn't make any sense. Why had she been born to hope and love and promise in the first place? Why had it come to this death in a cruel little town, at the hands of a brutal constable?

And Maureen Madigan too. She had expected to die sometime soon, but not upon the news of her daughter's murder. Her last moments had been filled with desolation, not hope; defeat, not triumph. The priest said she took the news, closed her eyes, and surrendered life. He said he would take care of funeral matters; he would have his own people pick up Maureen and get the girl from the undertaker. He said old Umberto would build two boxes, and his congregation would see to the rest of it.

The priest was used to death. Flint wasn't. He had seen enough of it in the war, but he had never gotten used to it. He would have to write this story too. He struggled to his feet, glad to be utterly alone. The priest had gently pressed his hand over Flint's bowed head, prayed, and left, his huaraches flapping on the terra-cotta floor of what had been the Escalante residence.

Flint sipped some tepid water from a sweating olla, and ventured into his sanctum, looking for a copy of the *Extra*. He didn't really know what to do, but he thought to start at the source of Oro Blanco's grief and his own pain. He stepped from the cool adobe into a stunning wall of heat, which struck him with physical force, like the blast lancing from the firebox of a giant boiler.

The heat had boiled the life out of Oro Blanco. He didn't see so much as a burro or a dog. Even the ants and birds had fled. No wonder the Mexicans took their siestas now. No one but mad, money-grubbing Yankees would be out under this murderous sun. He pushed through heat as if he were pushing through nets, passing the place where Libby had been clubbed down and then upslope toward the sullen Golconda mine, the monument and empire of Mason Weed. He watched lethargic mules draw an ore car to the slack pile and spotted a lethargic topside man releasing the rhyolite wastes. The heat swallowed the noise and turned it into a whisper.

Weed's administration building, a frame structure, radiated heat like a stove, and Flint supposed that those inside were baked—which suited Flint fine. Let them enjoy the hell they made. Flint wasn't sure what he would do when he corraled Weed. He had come with no plan; he had come because he wanted to see Weed squirm. Weed had pulled all the strings with the territorial officials. He had gotten Crawford appointed, along with Malone and Peters. Flint intended to lay the deed at the mine owner's feet. Libby had been clubbed to death. Weed was going to be clubbed with the responsibility for it.

He opened the door, and the heat muffled the chatter of its hinges. He entered into suffocating silence. Outside, at least faint breezes stirred. In here, the fiery air had been boxed and stilled.

A clerk under a green eyeshade pretended to work.

"I want to see Mason Weed," Flint said.

The man slowly surveyed Flint. "The *Nugget* editor," he said. "He's not here."

"He's here and I want to see him. He's on that quilted couch in his office taking his siesta."

"Vamoose, Flint."

"How's Weed going to celebrate his victory?"

"Victory?"

"There never was an Escalante grant."

"There wasn't? How do you know that?"

Obviously, Weed hadn't heard a word. He sure wouldn't hear about recent events from Crawford. Flint shoved the *Extra* at the man. "Take this in to him."

"He doesn't want to be disturbed. Especially by you."

"Take it in to him." He waited for the man to read the top paragraph of the sensational story. "I think his eminence would like to know."

The clerk rose slowly. In such heat one reduced motion to the most languid, economic movement. He sighed and vanished through the door into Weed's office, carrying the paper.

Flint felt an odd power coursing through him. It was too hot to be angry, too hot to feel anything but heat. It made him calm and merciless.

The air didn't stir.

The clerk reappeared. "He wants to see you," he whispered.

"Why don't you open the windows?"

"Mr. Weed likes the quiet, especially during his siesta."

Flint followed the clerk into the office, noting once again the luxury that surrounded Mason Weed. Redflocked wallpaper. Brass spittoons. Beeswaxed desk. The room stank of used air.

A shiny navy Colt lay on the desk. Behind it stood Weed, looking rumpled in his suit and vest and gold watch fob and iron-collared white shirt and cravat.

"We won," said Weed. "Baca caved in."

"Not entirely."

"Dumb little greaser. He could have kept quiet. Why'd you print this?"

"It's the news. I publish news."

"You're daft, that's the only word for it. Baca's daft, making this public. What did you gain by telling the world you've got no aces in your hand?"

Flint grinned. "We gained something you don't know anything about, Weed."

Weed poured tepid water from a carafe into a cutglass tumbler. "What did you gain by it?"

"Trust."

Weed laughed shortly. "Yes, a rag needs that. Clegg's rag could use some. Why're you here?"

"I don't know. I just wanted to see your reaction. There's something else you don't know about. Crawford clubbed my newsgirl to death in front of a score of witnesses. She was selling this *Extra*. Clubbed her to death, Weed, with a blow behind the ear. His stick. He was going to arrest her for selling this *Extra* that was so full of good news for him, and you. She's dead, Weed. Her life over at age thirteen, like a rose than never bloomed."

A tic spasmed the flesh around Weed's soft lips. "I'm sorry," he said. "He shouldn't have done that."

"You're the spider in the middle of the web, Weed. People will think he was following your commands. They think that everything the marshal and his deputies do is what you want them to do."

"That's nonsense. They're appointed public officials."

Flint felt testy. "Don't start boxing with facts," he snapped.

Weed squinted out the window. Heat waves made the whole white world outside dance like a body on a gibbet. "I had nothing to do with it."

"They'll blame you." Flint felt his own power and was amazed, but he was finding savage pleasure in it. "Looks like I'll be setting another *Extra* tonight."

"I'm sorry. I'm deeply shocked and sorry about your newsgirl. She was a little vagrant, I take it. It's a pity. But what chance did she ever have at life?"

"The news killed her mother."

"Two dead? This is a tragedy. I don't know why you came to me with it, though. The constable will no doubt have his own official version of these events. I'll wait until I hear it before coming to any conclusions. Rumors don't always match what's in the official books."

Flint grinned sardonically. "It happened this morning. He hasn't told you. He's obviously afraid to, or concocting some excuse. He's your man, you got him appointed. Crawford and Malone and the JP. The streets might be empty, but that doesn't mean anything, Weed. People think the blood's on your hands too."

The tic deviled Weed's cheek again. "And you're going to print up the story."

Flint shrugged. "I print the news," he said.

"All right," said Weed. "I'm going to give you a quote for your paper. 'This is a tragedy. I'm deeply sorry. I'll contribute to the funeral of these two women.' There. Print that."

Flint knew he had been dismissed. "It'll be in *The Nugget*," Flint said. "Should scoop Clegg. He can't print anything, because you won't let him."

Weed sipped the tepid water, wiped his pulpy lips, and smiled. Flint wondered why.

49

After Flint left, Mason Weed gazed out his office window onto a cruel world. He could see the wide Avenida de la Virgen, which cleaved Oro Blanco, and the polluted creek that cleaved the avenue. The heat had harried every living creature to shelter. He had never experienced such a blistering day. Nothing could endure such a bombardment of furnace air and unbearable light.

Behind him, at the Golconda, topside men wearing wide-brimmed hats trundled ore cars that carried cold rock from the bowels of Mangas Mountain. He hoped they were drinking enough water. But below him, Oro Blanco looked deserted. No women shopped. No dogs sniffed at the corners of buildings. No children caromed through the alleys. No wagons stood before the mercantiles, and no saddle horses sagged at a hitch rail. Under the heat waves, the city made motion where there was none.

A terrible sadness seeped through him. He wanted to sit down, go to sleep, start a different day. He wished he might snooze, but that would set a bad example. If he took a siesta, word would get out, and all his employees would too. He would resist the siesta; that was no way to fight the melancholia that pervaded him and turned the day bleak. For as long as he had been in Oro Blanco, building the mine and bullying gold out of the reluctant rock, he hadn't really thought much about anything but wealth, profit, and gain. But now he could not think of those things. He knew there were more important things in life, things he had neglected; things in his soul he had tried to strangle to death, such as love and honor.

The girl had been clubbed to death by his bought lawman. The fact ate at him. It focused a small, mean light upon himself. He felt pity for the girl. How awful to die like that, so young, so fresh with life's beginnings—for nothing. He hadn't swung the club, but that fact didn't lift his sadness. Nor would he pretend that he had nothing to do with the miserable business. He had selected Oro Blanco's appointed officials and used them all to further his obsession. Delbert Crawford had been his man.

Poor girl, struggling with deuces and treys but struggling just the same, earning the pennies that bought her food. Her death desolated him. He ached to flee his soul, be something else less burdened with self-loathing. Poor child, shoeless, desperate, too busy staying alive to have friends. He wished he could do something for her, but it was too late. His numbed conscience hadn't awakened from its long sleep until this very hour. And now it pricked him.

He knew he had arrived at a great turning point in his life and knew that the things he did now would mean the difference between a rich and miserable man or a somewhat less rich man who might come to like himself. What good was all the wealth in the world if he hated himself and couldn't stand the sight in his own mirror when he shaved his face each morning?

He couldn't repair what had happened to the Madigans. Mother and daughter lay dead. His had been the invisible hand that had brought them low—that and disease. Remorse found him at last, at just a time when remorse wouldn't help. He buried his face in his hands.

"Oh God, oh God," he cried. He slumped into his tufted-leather swivel chair and wondered if anything would save him. Some men could have ridden this easily; he couldn't. Some men seemed to be born without the promptings of decency. He had made wrong turns long ago, grown more and more worldly, sought the glittering prizes without any thought of how others might be hurt. What good did it do to gain the whole world if it cost him his soul?

For an hour more he sat, his door closed as his clerk, Willard Beam, fended off callers. Then at last he stood. He doffed his suitcoat. He would appear in public in his shirt-sleeves for the first time. It felt odd, shedding the coat that had armored him and spoke of his position among men. But he took it off quietly and hung it on the antler rack. He would leave his vest on; one couldn't just wander about in one's shirt.

He couldn't bring back Libby Madigan, but maybe he could give meaning to her death. Maybe he could turn this terrible tragedy into the beginning of something good in Oro Blanco. Or maybe it was simply too late. It occurred to him that he probably couldn't undo what he had spent two years doing. But he could try.

He opened the door and walked past Willard, ignoring the clerk's shock at seeing his employer in his shirtsleeves.

"It's the heat, eh?" said Willard.

"No, it's the armor. Too much armor," Weed said, heading into the glaring afternoon. The heat sucked his breath from him. He trod resolutely down the hill in a hushed afternoon, passed several shops, and reached the Avenida de la Virgen. He crossed it, walked over the single bridge that connected the two halves of Oro Blanco. He entered the Mexican side of town, an area he had rarely seen. Nothing stirred. He passed decaying adobes, smelled strange cookery, and finally reached the plaza with its new *pozo*. The adobe church rose solemnly at the west side. It had a bell tower and no bell.

He wanted to find de Cordoba. That was the place to begin. He surveyed the empty square, the church, and the little adobe on the church grounds that Weed took to be a rectory. He would try the church first, if only because the heat was frying him and the interior would be cool behind those massive adobe walls. He entered and found no one in the cool gloom. The silence caught and held him. He beheld the *santos* in their niches, the simple altar devoid of the riches he had expected.

"Father de Cordoba," he called, though no one responded. He checked the sacristy, finding no one. He found his way out a rear door, followed a worn path that took him to a one-story square adobe. He knocked, and again no one answered. He found a window and shouted into it, but no one replied. The priest wasn't there. Weed was disappointed. He had come to do good and had been thwarted. It occurred to him that nothing is more painful than to be unable to do a good thing. He looked for something with which to leave a note, but then gave up. The priest was elsewhere.

"I need you, Father de Cordoba," he muttered. He remembered the patient, wily man who had visited him on occasion and he knew it would be a long while before that intelligent priest believed a word of what Weed intended to say.

He walked patiently across the plaza and headed toward the Avenida. The next person would be Flint, who wouldn't believe him either. He hiked down the Avenida, staying on the Mexican side, until he found Calle Escalante and the copper-roofed cantina. He entered into cool once again and found no one.

"Flint. Mr. Flint," he cried into the gloom.

The apartment, then. The heat was probably too much for the editor. That and Miss Madigan's death. He threaded his way to the rear. The door to the private quarters was open.

"Flint," he said into the quiet.

Boldly, he entered the apartment and peered into Flint's bedroom. He felt thwarted again. Flint, more than anyone else, had reminded him what it was to be an honorable man. Every morning Flint could look into a mirror that reflected an earnest and likeable person. He envied Flint. He was troubled. He had come to a great crossroads, prodded by his own bad feelings, and yet he hadn't been able to contact anyone. Were they somewhere with the remains of the Madigan women? Some vigil?

He closed Flint's front door. Why had it been open? Some imperceptible sadness clung to the place. Was it the ghost of that child come to haunt it? Was it the desolation of the Escalantes in their last trouble? The thoughts stabbed at him.

He remembered that Treat's saloon, the Miner's Home, was on this side of the Avenida, so he hiked down a block and paused at its bat-wing door. The smell of beer seeped out from inside. He wanted badly to talk to Treat, not only about this tragedy but about the mine and its workers. He wasn't sure that Treat would believe him. Who would believe a sudden change of heart? But it hadn't been so sudden. For weeks, Flint's courage had stirred something in Mason Weed's heart. All he could do would be to tell Treat about it.

He stepped into the gloom and found no one behind the bar. That seemed odd. No customers, either. It was the one thing he hadn't expected. He'd steeled himself for the other: the rank hostility of the mining brotherhood. They would resent his invasion of their club.

"Treat," he yelled, "I want to talk."

No one replied. Weed pushed through a pair of curtains into a rear storage area that contained a crude desk where the giant kept his ledgers. Empty. Very odd. A saloon was always manned. The place could be robbed. Something sinister hung in the dead air, as if these walls had just witnessed an obscenity. It disheartened him.

He stepped into the blinding heat again. Maybe The Boston. He ought to let Amelia know. She'd laugh at him in that snobby way of hers. He traveled two blocks up the Avenida, staying in the shade of buildings on the Mexican side as much as possible. His meandering had dehydrated him, but he could get some cool water from Amelia. He crossed at the bridge and walked to the rear of the shut-down restaurant and lyceum. He climbed the hot stairwell to her apartment above and found the door open. Surely she was seeking air. The murderous heat was making it hard to breathe in closed spaces.

He tapped. "Amelia," he said.

He tapped again but got no answer.

"Amelia!" he bellowed. His lips were parched and his tongue had turned to cement.

He entered uneasily, repeating her name every few steps. He peered about, finally daring to peek into her bedroom. Everything was in perfect order: her clothing in the armoire, the bed made up, her several pairs of shoes in a neat row.

He heard, at last, some noise on the street, the clopping and snorting of a team of horses and the rumble of a heavy vehicle, almost deafening in the silence. The four-o'clock stage for Silver City was being brought from the Butterfield yards to the depot on the Avenida. And then he remembered.

50

Early that afternoon, Flint huddled in an ancient rocking chair in his quarters. Even in the heat he felt cold, and he had drawn a shawl over his legs. His blood wasn't pumping, and the warmth had fled his body. He was no longer conscious of time and temperature. Libby had been murdered. He had no other thought in his head. Libby was dead.

He heard his shop door open, but he didn't respond. Let them leave. He didn't want to see anyone. He heard footsteps and then saw Billy and Bugsy Bowler filling his doorframe. They grinned. Their steel deputy badges glowed on their vests. Both wore revolvers and carried hickory sticks as long as ax handles.

"Flint," said Billy, "you're leaving town. Pack a kit or not. We're putting you on the four-o'clock stage."

"Get out," said Flint.

Billy loomed over him. "Get up and pack a kit."

"What if I just stay put?"

Billy waved the club menacingly. "You'll wish we'd just shot you. Himself there is an expert with the stick. He can make you hurt in places you never knew you had."

"I'm tired. I'm grieving. You butchers killed Libby. Get out."

Bugsy grinned. "Is he resisting, Billy? Don't it sound like he's disobeying the law?"

"He's sure disobeying us, Bugsy." They edged closer. Billy still limped.

Flint watched them. "Kicking me out, eh? Out of town by sunset, isn't that the old bromide?"

"We ain't waiting until sunset, Flint."

"Who's paying the freight?"

"It's all arranged."

"What about my stuff?"

"Sorry, Flint. It's been confiscated."

"Where's your warrant?"

"This is our warrant," Bugsy said. He popped Flint's head hard with the hickory stick. It shot a bolt of pain through him, blinding him a moment.

Flint clasped his hand to his ringing ear and slowly set aside the shawl. He felt colder than ever. He hadn't shaved; he hadn't even washed his face. He stood, hunting around for his tweed suitcoat. He felt so cold his teeth chattered. They watched him, itching to speed him up with another pop of the stick.

Flint wished he could turn into Mountain Jack, bull into these two pugs and smash them. But he knew better. He fumbled around with his baggy coat. He didn't feel like packing a kit. Who needed anything in exile?

"Move, Flint."

He walked into the shop and eyed his equipment. "Who gets this? Weed?"

"It ain't worth spit, Flint."

He stepped into an awesome blast of heat that stabbed into his woolen coat. It wasn't enough to warm him inside. He still shivered.

They started up the Avenida toward the Butterfield Forwarding Company office. The street was deserted. Oro Blanco turned giddy to his sight.

They passed the Miner's Home Saloon. "It took two sawed-off shotguns and Crawford's navy to persuade Treat," said Bugsy amiably. "Now there's a man I respect."

"Who else is going?" Flint asked.

"Take a guess," Billy said.

They rounded the door into the stage station. Flint discovered Treat sitting on a bench in leg manacles, under the bore of Crawford's revolver, which the marshal held in his left hand. His right was still swollen. Next to him sat the priest, unshackled.

"I'll get the biddy," said Bugsy.

"She's the most trouble of all," said Town Marshal Crawford cheerfully.

Billy prodded Flint to a seat next to de Cordoba. "Don't move, or I'll make your kidneys hurt for six months."

"Señor Flint—" said the priest.

"Shut up," Billy said. "One word out of any of you, and you'll think that Madigan girl got off easy."

"You can't hide murder," Flint said.

The blow across his arm knocked him into the priest. A rage built in Sam Flint.

"Resisting arrest," said Crawford.

They waited silently. Even in the shade, the merciless heat suffocated them. The clock ticked toward four.

Amelia showed up, prodded by Bugsy. Her hair needed a brushing and she wore no ornaments.

"Get your stick out of my liver," she snapped.

He jabbed her with it.

She grunted and collapsed onto the bench beside Flint. "They forgot the tar and feathers," she said.

"Shut up," Crawford said.

"I will not. My tongue is one muscle you have no control over."

He rapped her arm.

"Oh! You think you can control one muscle by offending another," she gasped, clamping a bony hand over the insulted spot. "Mr. Crawford, you will need manners if you wish to be a success."

He laughed and jabbed her again.

"Cut that out!" Flint snarled.

The knock on his head again blinded him a moment. He heard the slow clop of the team and felt the rattle of the Butterfield mud wagon, a coach with open sides and pull-down curtains to fend off weather.

A jehu halted the team. Beside him slouched a shotgun messenger who worried a huge lump of tobacco in his cheek.

"All right, you first, Treat."

The subdued giant rose, clanked his way slowly to the iron coach step. Billy and Bugsy helped him up. Flint thought Treat smart not to say a word. The Bowler boys were itching for an excuse to pound him to pulp with their hickory sticks. The lesson came hard to Amelia. They jabbed her mercilessly with her every word. The priest followed, silent and tight-lipped, his gaze shifting from one to another of his captors. Then they jabbed Flint, the tip of the stick thumping hard into his ribs. It hurt. It was intended to hurt. Flint could barely control his exploding rage.

Crawford stood in the door, looking satisfied. "Don't come back. You'll be shot like snakes. Whine all you want in Silver City. It won't do you any good." He turned to the priest. "Greaser, head for Mexico. I'm filing sedition charges. You're a wanted man."

"The church is an outlaw. So it must be," said de Cordoba gently. *"Cristo el Rey!"*

Crawford eyed them all. "Treat, don't try it. That shotgun guard up there, he'd like nothing better than to have you try it."

Treat didn't dignify the words with so much as a nod. Crawford closed the veneer door.

"Marshal," said a quiet, commanding voice. "I've changed my mind. Release them."

Flint and the others gawked at Mason Weed, who stood before the three Oro Blanco peace officers in his shirtsleeves and vest. Weed's lips were compressed into a grimace. A tic twitched his cheek.

"Release them? What are you talking about?"

"Release them," said Weed, his voice knifing through the heat.

"Weed, I happen to be the law here, not you. This town happens to have a mayor, a town marshal, and a JP. And I happen to be getting rid of the troublemakers. Minute they're gone, Oro Blanco'll be sweet as sugar."

"And ashamed," said Weed. "Let them out or I'll take the matter to Sante Fe."

Flint had heard something he had never expected in Weed— an expression of principle. He glanced at his fellow passengers, who listened raptly.

Crawford ignored Weed. "Murray, git," he said to the jehu.

Flint heard rustling above, and the snap of lines, followed by soft oaths barely audible within the coach. He heard the harness tense, and the coach rolled slowly away, into the unknown.

"Mr. Murray, stop." Weed's voice again.

Flint heard voices above, and then the wagon creaked to a halt. Weed strode toward the door and opened it.

"Get out," he said. "I'm sorry this happened."

No one within the coach moved.

Crawford caught up with Weed, spun him around, and slammed the coach door shut. "Beat it, Weed," he snarled.

Weed stood stock-still, and only the reddening of his face and the slow clenching of his fists betrayed his mounting rage. "Give me your badge," he said.

"I'll kill you, Weed."

"Then be about it," Weed said. He stood waiting, unbudging, as solid as Gibraltar.

They locked unyielding eyes until at last Crawford caved in. Flint had never seen this hard, implacable side of Weed, and he was impressed. Weed held out a hand. Slowly Crawford unpinned his steel badge and dropped it into the waiting palm. Silently Weed extracted the deputy badges from the Bowler brothers.

He addressed one of the men on the seat above. "The key, please," he said.

A ring of keys dropped into Weed's hand, and he tossed it to Treat. "Free yourself," he said. "And then step out, all of you."

They did, silently, while the former constables stood sullenly.

"You won't believe me until you see it happen," he said to the prisoners, "but I want to heal this town. It's the only way I will ever find meaning or purpose in the death of Libby Madigan, God rest her soul."

51

Something as cool and sweet as springwater began percolating through Mason Weed's soul, filling him with a heady joy he had not experienced in a decade. But it was too soon to think about that. Fate still hung in the balance.

He eyed the Butterfield men atop the coach. "Gentlemen, be off now. You've lost some passengers."

The shotgun messenger eyed him from the deep shadow of his straw hat, spat some chaw into the dust, and nodded. The jehu muttered something gentle, and the team pushed lazily into its collars. The coach whispered away, raising eddies of dust in its wake.

He turned first to Crawford and the Bowlers, fully armed and dangerous, their minds feverishly weighing their options. "Be on that coach tomorrow," Weed said.

"Who's gonna make us?" asked Bugsy Bowler.

"You're going to make yourselves get on. You're going to pack your warbags, return everything that's been stolen from the citizens of Oro Blanco—especially what you've taken by shaking down the Mexicans—and you'll leave the Territory. If you leave New Mexico, you'll be . . . safe. If you stay . . ." He let the rest go unspoken.

They stared at him coldly.

"The shotguns belong to the city. Put them back. Clean out the jailhouse. Do it voluntarily, and you'll come to no harm."

"What makes you think you can get away with this?" asked Crawford. "I could come after you."

"I've had an attack of conscience. It's a trait that seems to be lacking in you, as it was in me. But you'll heed power, and it's within my power to turn you into wanted men."

"We were following your orders."

"That's correct. And that's why I didn't simply put you on that stage. You'll have a day to get your affairs in order."

"I oughta shoot you, Weed."

"If you're going to shoot me, be about it."

Crawford glowered at him. He motioned to Billy and Bugsy, and the three walked away. Weed watched them go.

He turned to Father de Cordoba. "I am the source of all your grief. I will make amends as far as I am able, with deeds, not words."

"It is said that Heaven rejoices when the lost sheep is found," said de Cordoba.

"I'm an agnostic, Father, but I will give you other reasons to rejoice."

"Let's get out of this awful heat," said Amelia. "I have some tea and a little ice left in my cellar."

Wordlessly they followed her along the Avenida, up the stairs, and into her front parlor. It wasn't much cooler, but at least the sun was held at bay.

She puttered around in her kitchen a long time, while Treat, Flint, and the padre sat silently. Weed could not read what was upon their minds, but he knew their thoughts were not kind, even though he had taken some initial measures to atone. They all knew it had been by his command that they had been

rounded up to be driven out of Oro Blanco like the worst unde-
sirables, their property up for grabs, their life-work halted.

Amelia returned with a tray bearing the iced tea. The drink
would be a rare treat on a day like this—on any day in Oro
Blanco. Silently she handed the sweating glasses to her guests.

Mason Weed sipped and then cleared his throat nervously.
"It's been a terrible day," he began, the words catching and
making him hoarse. "It began with the murder of a half-grown
girl. Here we are, not yet five o'clock, and so much has
happened.

"It's true I didn't strike that child, nor did I command it, nor
would I have approved. But that doesn't exonerate me. When I
received the news of that awful death, I tried to shift responsibility away from myself. I couldn't. These hands are as bloody as
the town marshal's. My ambition, blind and terrible; my self-
importance; my lust to be a great man of the Territory—these
things bloodied my hands."

He held them up and stared at them, despising his own
body. "My ambition destroyed a child in the springtime of her
life. The very last thing her mother experienced from this life on
Earth was the news of her child's death. I gather there are no
survivors. With her sole remaining child dead, her spirit died. I
killed not one, but two."

They stared at him impassively. The priest's brown eyes
fixed on him intently, alert to confession, sin, repentance. But no
repentance could be enough for this, Weed thought.

"I am not a religious man, but I believe in a moral law and
in virtue. The problem with moral law without religion is that it's
so easy to discard. I did, and my spirit cries out against me. I
will carry this agony the rest of my life."

It came out of him in anguish, like pain searing through him,
like a man walking to the gallows knowing that he deserved the
noose.

"I cannot bring a girl to life or make her mother's last

moments on Earth peaceful. I am lost. All I wanted was gold, and wealth, and importance, and power, and a say in the Territory, and the luxuries. And I never thought of my soul. Through it all I simply became more miserable, more alone, more angry, and more willing to commit evil against everyone around me."

They stared. He peered from one to another and couldn't fathom their thoughts—except for the priest, whose faint smile seemed like an island for the shipwrecked.

"I am a broken man. On the day I die, I will be remembering Libby Madigan and my part in her fall." He sighed. "I don't mean to trouble you with my ordeals. They are nothing compared to yours. I've consciously inflicted suffering on each of you, turned my wolves upon you, let them maraud through you, devouring what was yours. I am looking at each of you, knowing that your courage and virtue have given you good lives and that you won't have to live with the horrors that I have visited upon myself."

They sipped the tea. He sipped too, gathering his thoughts.

"You don't need to hear my self-pity," he said.

"What does our Lord require of thee but a broken and contrite heart?" asked the padre.

Mason Weed felt weary. "Restitution," he replied. He ached to make things right, as much as possible. "I'll contact my attorney, Catron, to support Baca's petition. The court'll go along with it. I want every Mexican in Oro Blanco to be secure in his property. And if the rest of what was called the Escalante grant is made public land, I'll help your people file homestead claims on it at my expense. Enough land for their livestock."

"That is a good thing," said the padre.

"It's hardly a beginning. You wanted a bell, Father. Order the finest bell in the world, the bell with the sweetest tone, the deepest resonance. Order a bell, order a carillon if you wish."

"It would be a blessing," said the padre.

"I won't let this town be cleaved in two. I'll heal this—this gulf, any and every way I know how. There'll be jobs in the mines, and if any of my employees troubles your people, he'll find himself discharged. If your merchants wish to sell on the gringo side of the Avenida, I'll find space for them and protect them."

"My ears hear things I never thought possible," the priest murmured.

"This is only the beginning," Weed cried. An odd joy crept through him, so strange and heady that he could barely put a name to it. "Amelia, open up The Boston. I'll help you. I'll repay your every loss."

"I'll think about it," she said.

He sensed the reserve. They weren't exactly certain of his change of heart. That was all right. Scarcely seven hours had elapsed from the murder of that poor girl to this moment. How could any mortal shuck his past and assume a new life in such a short time?

"Mr. Treat, you've fought heart and soul for your brothers in the pit and for your friend here, Mr. Flint, for the people who were being pushed around—by men I selected or employed. You were my nemesis. And you've won my respect. I've two things to ask of you: The first is that you be town marshal."

Treat growled something, but Weed cut him off.

"Just for now. The town has no one. You're respected on both sides of the Avenida. You'll be a symbol of change for the Mexicans. I haven't the power to appoint you, but Mayor Malone does, and I'll see that it's done."

Treat smiled. "I always fancied wearing the badge," he said. "Then I can have me a brawl without getting pinched." He laughed. "But just for a while. Mr. Weed, I'm your . . . adversary. I want my brothers in the pits to have a fair wage, good air, plenty of timber holding up the rock, and a little spare time to see some sunlight."

Weed had expected that. "That was my second request, Mr. Treat. Look after your own. When you come to me—and the door will be open—I'll listen. That's one thing I can do."

"You much of a hand at arm-wrestling, Mr. Weed?"

"I've never tried it in my life."

"Well, we're going to try 'er," said Mountain Jack Treat.

Weed turned to the third man. "Mr. Flint, at first I loathed your courage. And then your courage and integrity made me ashamed, because I had none. And I'm here now to tell you that you're the better man. If it weren't for you, for your paper, for your stories, I'd be in total control of Oro Blanco. I'd be driving out the original settlers. I'd be rich and powerful and filled with such self-loathing I'd probably end up a suicide."

Flint didn't smile, but he nodded slightly.

"I've all but destroyed your paper and your equipment. I'll give you anything you need from *The Progress*. I'm closing it down and discharging Clegg along with his bunch. I won't ask you to be its editor. I honor your independence. Now, what would repay you?"

Flint blinked a moment. "Some paper and some fonts and a case box."

"Is there anything else you need?"

"My First Amendment rights and the freedom to sell ads without interference. You can keep your paper alive if you want. Competition whets the appetite. It's good."

Weed sighed. "The credibility of *The Progress* is beyond redemption. Clegg's reputation is beyond repair. Those bullies he hired to destroy your circulation give the sheet a black eye. No, I'll shut it down and send them packing."

"I lost some revenue too. The town marshal cleaned out Libby's purse more than once."

"Mr. Flint, you'll have the equipment and a new press too, and a draft before this day has passed."

Flint finally smiled. "We'll see," he said.

"One thing more," Weed said, this time addressing them all. "I want to pay for the funeral. That won't make anything right, but it's an offer I must make."

Father de Cordoba shook his head.

52

Theo Parnassus needed to bury Maureen and Libby Madigan as fast as possible because of the heat. The very next morning Flint found himself at the gringo cemetery, where the graves had been chopped into the caliche beside Garth Madigan.

There weren't very many people. Treat had corralled half a dozen pallbearers from among the off-shift miners in his saloon. They looked eager to get on with it, fidgeting where they stood. The miners would pay for the funeral. Libby and Maureen rested in two wooden boxes, as honest and unadorned as their lives. Father de Cordoba, in his black cassock, would lead a prayer and say a few words. Flint thought to himself that de Cordoba looked restless and uncomfortable among strangers and Protestants and Yankees.

Among the handful of black-clad spectators were a few curiosity seekers and one businessman, John Strong. Flint had his notebook and pencil ready. Treat had asked him to speak, but the editor couldn't bring himself to do that. He was a chronicler, not an orator. He could express his grief better by writing of it than declaiming it.

It would be, all in all, a humble ending for Libby and her

mother. There would be no stately ceremony, no dirges and hymns, no eulogies this morning. Flint wasn't sure he could find meaning in it, and he knew he could find no solace at all. Parnassus and his black-suited assistant would shovel the hard caliche over the coffins, drive their ebony wagon back to Oro Blanco, and collect a few dollars from Treat, who had passed the hat.

Absent also was Mason Weed, but Flint took that as a sign of decency. It would have been ghastly for Weed to show up, even though he had plainly come to his own abyss because of Libby.

It was early on another blistering day, but the sun had not yet blasted away the faint cool of the night. De Cordoba read a burial liturgy, recited the Lord's Prayer in Latin, and nodded. The miners, wearing their stiff suits, lowered the two pinewood boxes.

Father de Cordoba peered at those around the grave, one by one, as if to bond them all together in their grief.

"This child and her mother are surely with God," he said gently. "They brought him a gift: all the evils and sins of Oro Blanco. We are all transformed."

Flint listened impatiently to the priest's dubious theology and to the benediction. Then the grave digger set to work as the small crowd disbanded in silence.

Flint turned away empty. Two mortals had unceremoniously been committed to the earth, and their souls to whatever lay beyond, if anything. He stuffed his empty notepad into his suitcoat, watched the dutiful miners drift off, and saw de Cordoba hasten to the part of town he understood better. He stood a long while, waiting for the sweating undertaker's assistant to finish. He stood even when Parnassus, who nodded idly to him, mounted the seat of his ebony dray, along with the sweating subordinate, and hawed the black horse toward town. They grew smaller and smaller and finally vanished among the buildings.

The sun pierced his suitcoat and lanced into his face and

neck. Flint knew he could not long endure the brutality of this summer day. But at last he stood alone beside the fresh graves in a Madigan corner of the cemetery. He needed to find meaning in it but couldn't.

He had expected to fill his notepad; he had expected the burial to unleash a flood of feeling that he would translate into a beautiful eulogy. Instead, he had nothing but an empty pad, an unused pencil, and a sense of hollowness. Libby and Maureen lay half forgotten under clods of clay, and his inspired eulogy had withered aborning. Most of Oro Blanco knew Libby, all right, but who had been her friend? Her death had been sad, even cruel, but she was gone, and the town had turned back to its worldly pursuits. A month hence few people would remember her name. The thought desolated Flint. Libby deserved something immortal, carved in granite.

Flint had a paper to fill, two obituaries to write, a funeral story to compose, the story of the resignations of the entire constabulary to create, and more. But all he could think was that the hurried, furtive event had been hastened because of heat. Maybe that was how it should be. The world was for the living, not the dead. But the thought didn't please him.

He needed to write something beautiful. He hadn't much to give Libby, but he had his skill with words and his sensitivities. He had planned to give her this final gift—an account of her funeral and an obituary that made sense of her life and celebrated her brief incandescence among mortals. But the desultory affair in the white men's cemetery, at the opposite end of Oro Blanco from the greaser boneyard, had gutted his gift.

He entered the coolness of his adobe shop, grateful at once for the release from the heat. Adobe had that quality. Its thick mass seemed to extract heat from the air, making a room cool and pleasant even in an inferno.

He hung his scratchy suitcoat on an antler rack, donned his printer's smock, and willed himself to work. He would have to make something of nothing, fashion an obituary out of a brief life with few major events in it, and another from a longer life plagued by disease. He hardly knew where to begin.

He stood before his mended case boxes, his type stick in hand and a galley tray ready, and tried to say something kind and meaningful about a little girl who braved the worst that life had to offer and succumbed before she had reached womanhood.

"Not very many people came to Libby Madigan's funeral," he began. "Even at nine in the morning the heat was intolerable. And Theo Parnassas was in a hurry before corruption set in. Town Marshal Treat corralled a few miners into bearing Libby and her mother, Maureen, to their common grave. The undertaker's man had chopped it the previous night, mostly by lantern light, with a pick and shovel. So Libby's funeral and farewell were as hurried and desperate as her brief life. Somehow it seemed fitting to this observer."

Flint wasn't exactly pleased with that. He wanted something grand for Libby, something that glowed. But all he got for his efforts was a dreary account of a town's indifference.

All that morning he wrote, and the more he wrote the less satisfied he was. He wanted to do a grand elegy, but Libby's life hadn't been grand. So he wrote of her bare feet, her ferocious will, her desperation, and her amazing sense of good and evil.

Then he wrote about a church bell, a polluted creek, a town with only one bridge, Saturday market days, the glittering lure of gold, greed, and a lot more.

It wasn't very good, but it did Libby honor. He could say that much. Flint sighed, rubbed ink over the type with his chamois ink ball, and proofed it. The column didn't seem to be enough, but he had had only a blank notepad to write from.

53

A few days later, Sam Flint pulled the last of three hundred copies of *The Nugget* from his new flatbed press, but he didn't put in on the stack with the others. He set it aside to read. He knew it was the most memorable edition of a newspaper he had ever created. He wiped his press of ink, doffed his smock, and scrubbed his purpled fingers, a ritual that never removed the ink stain.

Then he lit a sooty coal-oil lamp over his composing table and laid his new edition under the buttery glow that somehow pierced through its neglected chimney. The new fonts looked crisp on the pages. Advertising bulged from this issue, and he had run two extra pages to give himself enough of a news hole. In this one issue he had enough profit to pay his debts and stow some change in Amelia Lowell's revived savings bank. Even Bulldog Malone had purchased a two-column-by-twelve-inch ad proclaiming the virtues of The Stamp Mill Saloon.

He scarcely knew which of the dozens of stories was the most important. He ran an account of Libby's death at the hands of Crawford on the hellish hottest day of July, and a story of the subsequent resignation of the whole constabulary under pressure from Weed. He reported the near-banishment of Treat, de Cordoba, Amelia Lowell, and himself and their rescue, from the least-expected quarter. There was a story about Mountain Jack Treat's temporary service as town marshal and the prospects for a permanent new town marshal from Silver City. He ran his reminiscence—it was that, rather than an obituary—of Libby, and another of Maureen Madigan. They had finally satisfied him, but he wished he could be more eloquent. He wanted their stories to light up the night sky, but that was beyond his ability.

A little story about an anonymous donor who was giving the mission church of San Juan a bell from a foundry in Durango got front-page placement. Inside, he covered the latest and most successful of the Saturday markets in the plaza and a community effort led by the Golconda mine to span the creek dividing the Avenida de la Virgen with two more plank bridges. On Sunday, mining crews paid by the Golconda had dropped the logs in place, bolted the planks to them, and graded the approaches. Now three bridges connected the two halves of Oro Blanco.

He returned to the Escalante grant story with a followup piece: Attorney Catron, erstwhile opponent of Attorney Baca in the matter of the Escalante grant, had joined forces with Baca, petitioning the federal court to recognize existing Mexican freeholdings even though the grant never existed. This was being done at the behest of Baca's clients, a consortium led by Mason Weed. The attorneys were almost certain the judge would accede.

A story reported the closing of *The Progress* by its owner, Mason Weed, and the departure to parts unknown of its editor, Phineas Clegg, and staff. Flint chose that venue to crow a little: A genuine newspaper, he wrote, printed all the news. He hoped *The Nugget* would fill the bill.

He studied the edition in the mellow light, satisfied. It contained no great scoops, no flowery or poetic prose. He would never be a Horace Greeley. But it did contain a healing force.

He had no illusions about how much a mere newspaper could change the human heart, but sometimes it could alter social institutions. Those on one side of town who despised the greasers would continue to despise them, and the Mexicans who saw all the gringos as diablos would continue to do so. But a paper could lead and cajole, and if it wasn't too preachy or arrogant, it could spark civility, reform, and real progress.

There would be no Libby to hawk his paper for him tomorrow, but Mountain Jack Treat had solved that problem. Tomorrow morning, two large, feisty boys with squeaky tonsils—the sons of miners—would try their hand at it uptown and downtown. No one would harass or bully them. They would probably sell out. The rumors and gossip of the last few days had built into a feverish curiosity that burned in the citizens of Oro Blanco. They would pounce on this edition as they had no other and pass each copy along.

Flint felt a certain euphoria. When he had set up shop in Oro Blanco, he had encountered something sinister, a furtive greed that threatened to destroy the town's original inhabitants. Oro Blanco had been in the thrall of a cabal of politicians and officers. They had influenced the merchants and stolen his advertising. They had thrown an opposition paper at him and filled it with canards. They had hired thugs to prevent the circulation of his paper.

They had jailed him, beaten him, destroyed his equipment, starved him, threatened him, and even tried to banish him. But they lacked truth.

He had weathered it all and had emerged triumphant. It wasn't because of his might but because he had stuck to his principles through the hellfire. There he found that the great paradox of human existence was still at work: Right was stronger than might.

Sam Flint knew he would stay a while in Oro Blanco, but he knew it wouldn't be long. Libby's ghost haunted him, and her snuffed-out life cast a pall over the town. He would sense her restless ghost beside him as he set type, her unhappy spirit pacing beside his newsboys when they hiked to their corners in the mornings.

He would report the news, bringing the Mexicans to the attention of his English-speaking readers and the gringos to the attention of the Mexicans. He would play chess with the padre, consult with that strange and reformed man, Mason Weed, and trade yarns and prejudices with Amelia Lowell. And he would enjoy the comfort of Jack Treat's law enforcement.

But in a year or so, he'd be wandering the fields in search of Sherman and Grant, looking over his harness and examining the hubs of his wagon wheels. And one day, when the itch finally governed him, he'd sell out to some enterprising and honest editor and roll away alone, a man bristling with principles and maxims, a man a bit stuffy and opinionated who would bestow his enterprise upon another little place on the breast of the new world.